THE TRUMPETS OF DOOM

THE *SAGA OF THE SINGING SWORD BRIGADE* SERIES:

Book One: Inception of a Brigade

Book Two: Into the Gloom

Book Three: The Trumpets of Doom

AND COMING SOON:

Book Four: The Siege of Logon's Bridge

Book Five: Turit's Rise

Book Six: Tremendum

SAGA OF THE SINGING SWORD BRIGADE

THE TRUMPETS OF DOOM

J.M. MacLeod

Ambassador International
Greenville, South Carolina & Belfast, Northern Ireland

www.ambassador-international.com

The Trumpets of Doom

Saga of the Singing Sword Brigade, Book Three

ISBN: 978-1-64960-019-6
eISBN: 978-1-64960-020-2

Cover Design by Magpie Designs LTD
Interior typesetting by Dentelle Design
Edited by Daphne Self

AMBASSADOR INTERNATIONAL
Emerald House
411 University Ridge, Suite B14
Greenville, SC 29601, USA
www.ambassador-international.com

AMBASSADOR BOOKS
The Mount
2 Woodstock Link
Belfast, BT6 8DD, Northern Ireland, UK
www.ambassadormedia.co.uk

The colophon is a trademark of Ambassador, a Christian publishing company.

Whoever is wise, let him understand these things;
Whoever is discerning, let him know them.
For the ways of the Sovereign are right,
And the righteous will walk in them,
But transgressors will stumble . . .

~ Hosea Ben Beeri

CHAPTER ONE

JEDA NEARLY STUMBLED OVER A fallen branch yet again but regained her balance. Her shoulders ached; her hands were bound behind her back and had turned numb hours ago. She didn't know if it was day or night. The snug-fitting hood that had been jammed down over her head was suffocating. Her captors lifted it only as far as her upper lip for occasional food and water during rare rest intervals. Beyond her physical discomforts, Jeda was even more distressed at entangling Spoena and Artil in this web of catastrophes, but at the same time, felt encouraged that she wasn't facing this horrid misery alone.

Jeda's toe caught on a root sending her sprawling headfirst, smacking her cheek and forehead on a rock. "Oo-oh!"

"Stupid oaf!" A dronnet seized the nape of her hood and dragged her to her feet.

"Jeda, are you all right?" Spoena blurted out from somewhere behind.

Something warm and moist trickled down Jeda's nose to her lips. Before Jeda could reply she heard a thwack followed by Spoena's whimper.

"No talk."

Jeda plodded forward, head bowed, biting her lip to keep from making matters worse by anything she might say. A sharp rap to her shoulder indicated a turn to the right; apparently, she'd been veering off trail yet again. Dronnets seemed to delight in guiding them by sharp, stinging raps on their shoulders. They never warned of obstacles in the path. The blackguards either didn't see them or didn't care.

"I deserve this, Logon," Jeda pled silently. "I should have heeded the Advisor's admonition to not pierce Balatz." She rued the deed all the more because precious moments had been wasted, moments they might have used to elude capture. Now Spoena and Artil were Hod-ya's captives, too. And she had fallen back into her enemy's grasp. "I was warned but listened to others instead of heeding you. Oh, Logon, forgive me and let Spoena and Artil escape. I deserve whatever happens, but they don't." Her tears were absorbed into the thick, canvas cowl over her face making the hood even stuffier.

Hod-ya and Captain Mileer strode down an ancient forest trail at the head of this prisoner escort consisting of seven dronnets and three prisoners, all the while holding a running conversation that had occasional lulls when neither spoke. When they resumed their discourse, the conversation picked up where it had left off.

"So, I surmise," Hod-ya resumed the dangling thread of their conversation, "that Ugen and Flarg are in cahoots with Deparis. Ugen has evaded my spies, but Flarg awaits my pleasure in my sister's castle."

Jeda was somewhat alarmed that neither Hod-ya nor Mileer made any effort to conceal this obviously politically sensitive conversation.

"Are you confidant of your ability, er, since you know, now that Psa's been—you know?"

Mileer's voice had a note of caution.

"Fool! Did you think Psa was my only connection to power? I was Psa's slave, not he mine. I was naive when our collusion began; he forced me to do his bidding, supplying the manipulations and power to do what he demanded. But now I'm free from him, free to do whatever I like. I've learned to bargain with the Chimeree. In many ways Psa restrained me from attaining greatness. Besides, I often wondered if he wasn't tiring of me, desiring some new vessel to enslave, like that sniveling wannabe, Deparis."

"You think he might've abandoned you at the most crucial moment of 'Scrarth and Avangar', switching to support her contestant instead of yours?" Mileer asked.

"Hmph! Especially since my wench was, as I suspected, Ecclessite. He would have been enraged at my bringing a defiling presence into that sacred ceremony if I failed to get her to renounce loyalty to you-know-who. Pity, I had such long-range plans for success, too."

"But if you succeed in making her renounce her loyalties, won't she be even more useful."

"If I can. She's strong. Back at the cabin she actually made an attempt to pierce my heart! Only two others ever found the will to point their swords at me, and they were men—warrior-generals—in fact. The first kingsman that tried escaped, but the other was captured and provided a most entertaining evening for my dronnets."

"That's not quite the account I heard. The way I heard it, you were the one that barely escaped from that first general?"

"Shut up, fool! I don't know why I tolerate you."

"Because, in spite of your mystical contacts and powers, you need my armies. Your dronnets are strong but few in number, and they aren't sufficient to fulfill your ambitions. You need my flesh, bone, and blood battalions to reinforce your achievements, and you know it."

A long silence followed. Unable to locate the direction of their voices as she had been doing, Jeda tried to hone in on the footfalls of the mismatched pair up ahead lest she stray off course, or trip again, or receive a stinging tap. Those shoulder raps were increasingly painful; both shoulders ached from the constant abuse and were almost certainly bruised.

She heard muffled sobs from behind. Was that Artil?

Remorse stabbed Jeda's heart afresh. What horror she'd led that sweet, young girl into. Spoena bore some responsibility for their predicament when she ignored the call to return to camp causing them to run into the half men. That in turn led to being lost in the swamp. Artil was suffering solely from the disobedience of others. Jeda longed to embrace the younger girl and comfort her and tell her it would be all right, that she would awaken any moment and this terrible nightmare would fade away.

"Oh Logon, please free them; they don't deserve any of this; especially Artil. Please, comfort her. Let her know you'll rescue her."

The girls trudged on, heads hooded and bowed low, hands bound, and elbows wedged by a staff across the small of their backs, their legs trembled from weariness. It had been hours since their last rest, but they dared not complain or even beg for a swig of water; every utterance was greeted with a painful swat.

Mileer picked up the thread of the conversation again. "So, what do you expect to happen in Pitland? Deparis is probably even now preparing her contestants while you're chasing around Ra-Amawl gathering your entries. As it is, you only have one of them. Whatever happened to the other is beyond me. We lost all trace of her in the swamp."

Jeda's ears perked up at the mention of Glend. It was good to know she was still at large and not held somewhere in Hod-ya's custody.

"Well, they're not much to choose from, but I can pick the best out of the other two. I only need 'Avangar', the survivor. Deparis will have only her Avangar after her elimination bout is done, too. Whoever wins the final round is all that matters, you know that."

"Ah, but your Avangar is doubtful at best. How can you trust someone who's been under kingsmen influence?"

"That's why I must make her recant. Those who recant can never return and serve him again. She'll have no one to turn to but me. And she will turn to me, make no mistake about that."

A chill ran down Jeda's spine. Hod-ya sounded so confident. "Logon, please protect me." There was no response from the Advisor. Had he abandoned her, too? It was what she deserved.

Despair settled on her as she recalled how easily Hod-ya disarmed her at the cabin. There had been no surge of power from her sword nor boldness in her heart. Her thrust at Hod-ya had been out of loathing, fear, and self-defense, not concern for Hod-ya. "How deep I've sunk, my liege, in such a short time. What would Bonu think of me now? I'm not the kingly woman he is attracted to. I'm not even the kingly woman I thought I was. Ah, Logon! If I'd only known how things could so quickly get out of hand."

An iron-like hand gripped her bruised shoulder. Jeda winced and halted. A moment later she heard the approach of a galloping horse.

"Into the bushes," commanded Hod-ya, her voice barely a whisper. "Slit their throat if any one of them makes a sound."

Jeda was yanked clear off the ground by a sinewy arm around her neck and dragged through a thick shrub that scratched her arms and lower legs. She was then pressed to the ground and something cold and sharp prickled on her throat. A whispered threat of, "One sound, one wiggle of toe . . . "

Artil and Spoena were plopped down on either side of Jeda and from the sounds of it were likewise pinned to the ground by a dronnet. Terrified and at the mercy of the ruthless, Jeda was, nonetheless, grateful for the momentary break. Her heart pounded in her ears as if in rhythm to the hoofbeats drawing near.

Jeda heard a dronnet suddenly spring through the bush, followed by a thud, a gasp, then another, louder thud and the whinny of a frightened horse. The horse went crashing into surrounding jungle.

"One move, I snap neck."

By the sounds of it the blackguard had disarmed the horseman and rendered him defenseless in mere seconds.

More bushes rustled and Mileer barked, "Who are you? What are you doing on this trail this time of day?"

A young man's voice croaked, "Messenger, looking for Hod-ya."

From nearby, Hod-ya spoke up. "I'm Hod-ya. What's the message, and who sent it?"

A coughing spell erupted as the messenger was released.

"Speak up man. We haven't all day."

"I'm from the White Priestess, sent with a message for you, if you are indeed Hod-ya kar Psa. Show yourself so I may know."

Though choked with fright and anger, the voice sounded familiar.

Bushes rustled as Hod-ya rose and descended the bank to the road. "So, look on me, messenger from the White Priestess. How would you know whether it's me or a pretender? And how do I know you are what you purport?"

"M'lady, it is I who brought word of Ugen's betrayal to your servants Gragnold and Sevrid."

"Gragnold," Hod-ya called, "do you know him?"

The dronnet pinning Jeda to the ground released her and stood, hauling Jeda to her feet. He slid down a small embankment, mercilessly dragging Jeda behind. "Yes, that him."

"And who is your date, Gragnold? Is she so ugly that her face needs to be hidden?"

Hod-ya grinned wickedly. "I believe you have already had the pleasure of meeting the young lady. Jeda of Kway."

Jeda's hood was snatched away. Even in the forest gloom Jeda recognized Juued standing before her.

"Firedrakes of Pitland, what have you done to her?" Juued reached out to touch Jeda's cheek.

Jeda blinked in the dim light under Ra-Amawl's canopy.

Juued's shocked countenance reflected the results of Jeda being repeatedly spun from one dronnet to another and slapped by each for an interminable length of time until memory failed to record all the brutality involved in her recapture.

"Hello, Juued. It is nice to see you again." And she did mean it. A concerned human face was rare lately, even if he was Carnalian. Her lips were puffy, and her jaw ached as she spoke, but her words weren't slurred.

Hod-ya stepped between them, removing Juued's fingers from Jeda's cheek. "Okay, so it is you after all, Juued. I hardly dare trust anyone anymore, even Gragnold. But if the girl knows you, you must be who you say you are. What's the message?"

Juued reluctantly tore his eyes from Jeda and turned to Hod-ya. "The White Priestess wants you to know there's a column of prisoners nearing the border escorted by a battle-weary, hodge-podge of guards comprised of men who aren't much use on the front lines anymore. It's feared they won't be able to control the prisoners if there's an escape attempt. Your orders are to meet and join up with them on the edge of Pitland at Willow House."

Hod-ya scowled. "Orders? I'm not a common prison guard she can issue directives to. What does my sister think I am?"

"If I may be so bold m'lady, she stressed that these are not common prisoners. There's at least one suspected general in their midst, and several other high-ranking Ecclessite officers."

"Well, we're a bit battle-weary ourselves, Juued. Report back to your mistress that Mileer and seven dronnets are all that's left of the fourth regiment, at least that we can find. We're bringing some special prisoners of our own and have no time to delay. Besides, our strength isn't sufficient to control a train of prisoners. If they aren't there by the time we're ready—"

"I'll tell her, but—"

"But what?"

"But Bablo-ya was imperative. You have what, one, two, three, seven dronnets? One dronnet is worth twenty soldiers. Besides, escaped prisoners could do immense harm if they get loose behind our lines. These are officers, remember. Sharpointers and Fullblades and the like. She'll likely hold you to account if you don't render what assistance you can."

"Willow House, eh?" said Hod-ya after a minute's reflection. "How far is that, Gragnold?"

"Two, three hours out of the way," the blackguard said.

"Very well, I'll go to Willow House, off my path as it is, but if they aren't there, I'll delay only long enough for refreshment and then be on my way. If they're not on time they're on their own. I have to get these contestants ready."

Juued nodded, turned to the forest, gave a low whistle and was answered from the undergrowth by a whinny. "That then, is your reply. If you like, after I deliver my message, I'll gladly come back and be of assistance by joining myself to your command."

"That won't be necessary." Hod-ya looked aside as Juued's horse came back to the road.

"On the contrary," Mileer stepped forward as the other prisoners and dronnets emerged from the bushes. "I think we should avail ourselves of every man who is fit and willing to assist. It'll be no easy task transporting prisoners into Pitland once they see where they're headed. Juued, you're welcome to join us."

Juued grabbed the saddle horn and swung onto his mount without touching the stirrup. He looked straight at Jeda. "I'll meet you somewhere along the way, then, and render what assistance I may." He dug his heels into his mount's flanks, tearing up turf in his retreat.

"What do you make of him, Mileer?" asked Hod-ya.

"Smitten by the girl no doubt, but he can be of some use. I personally wouldn't have taken him on, but when you gave me a signal to contradict you, I followed your lead and played along. What have you in mind?"

"We'll see, he may or may not prove useful. But I want him available, just in case." With that, Hod-ya marched up the trail again.

Gragnold hissed. "Hood girl?"

Hod-ya paused, considered for a moment, then said, "No, and take the hoods off the others, too. They might as well see where they're going. It's not likely they'll find their way back to their brigade should the impossible happen and they get loose."

Spoena and Artil gasped and blinked back tears as they were gruffly de-hooded. Two days had passed since they'd seen any light, which was a campfire on the old logging road. Both Spoena's and Artil's faces were discolored and puffy with bruises; Spoena's upper lip was split but scabbed over; Artil had one severely swollen eye, so much so that only a slit of her eye showed. Tears coursed down Jeda's cheeks at seeing her two friends in such a condition. All three exhibited welts, scratches, and bruises on shoulders, arms, and legs. Their necks were black and blue from the blows dealt by the dronnets in the course of travel.

Spoena spoke first. "Oh Jeda, what have they done to you?" Then she saw Artil's eye and caught her breath.

"No time for talk. March." Gragnold, roughly shoved Jeda up the trail in Hod-ya's and Mileer's wake.

Jeda stumbled forward but caught her balance and meekly followed. Spoena and Artil needed no prodding. They all traveled in virtual silence, Hod-ya and Mileer leading side by side, saying nothing, followed by Jeda and Gragnold, Spoena and her guard, Artil and her guard, and the remaining dronnets bringing up the rear.

It was early morning and warm for this time of year, but it didn't feel like morning. Jeda glimpsed a patch of blue through a patchwork of entwined branches and leafy vines. The overhead canopy was thinning! Were they leaving Ra-Amawl? She cast sideways glances at the forest and saw that indeed, tree trunks were no longer tightly packed with vines and penetration-defying flora. It was almost like a normal forest. A ray of sunlight splashed the trail ahead; shadows played dodge and tag with each other. It was one of the most wonderful sights Jeda had ever seen. Her heart lifted and she silently thanked Logon. She tried to linger in whatever spots of sunlight she crossed but Gragnold hissed and shoved her forward, hating the light, not wanting to dwell in it longer than necessary.

How strange? Jeda had entered Ra-Amawl under Gragnold's supervision, and now was leaving the same way. Glend had come, too, under Sevrid's oversight, but was still free somewhere within Ra-Amawl's shadowy realm, gone to ground with a courageous band of Ecclessites. She wondered about Sevrid's whereabouts, for he didn't seem to be among the company of dronnets; she knew better than to ask, however.

An hour later the trail leveled out and the forest's density diminished significantly. But, the lighter the environment, the darker the mood and actions of the dronnets. Hod-ya and Mileer seemed oblivious to the changes.

Pretty flowers bloomed cheerily along the path in the now frequent swaths of sunlight, insects hummed; birds and tree-climbing animals skittered and chattered from overhead branches, curious about the people trekking through their domain.

Jeda passed the time meditating on runes she'd tolled and memorized, and as she did, was filled with the Advisor's joy. Understanding dawned; the Advisor hadn't deserted her, rather, her complaints had drowned out his voice. She'd been so taken up with her misery and guilt that she forgot to trust Logon. Even if she must reap the consequence of disobedience it didn't mean that Logon had forsaken her. How could he turn away at the moment of her deepest need? She was ashamed to even have thought that. He had forgiven her, though at times she didn't feel forgiven. Feelings were unreliable. Basking afresh in the joy of communing with Logon she darted a furtive glance behind to see how Artil and Spoena fared.

~

At the same moment Artil looked up and locked eyes with Jeda's in unspoken communication. The younger sister recognized the return of hope to Jeda's eyes and took heart. Gragnold cuffed Jeda's neck forcing her to turn front again, but she did so at peace, concealing a slight smile. Artil was wonder-struck that Jeda was so at peace. Then she, too, understood and silently communicated her regrets for accusing Logon of not helping when they needed him. Lightheartedness leapt from within as the Advisor responded with messages of forgiveness and hope. Artil covertly turned around toward the rear of the column to encourage her sister.

~

Spoena hadn't been faring well at all. She was overcome with remorse at not having obeyed when signaled to return to camp. But such a small disobedience to warrant this severe punishment? Logon was harsher than she'd realized. She internally uttered her regrets but felt no better for confession. She played the scene over and over in her mind, climbing the tree to get manu, failing to immediately respond to the squad leader's call. Again and again she berated herself. She was so ashamed that she wanted to die. She stared at her feet as the group trudged along, thinking death couldn't possibly be worse. She was responsible for this mess, and they'd all suffer intolerable torments now because of her. She raised her head for a split second and caught Artil sneaking a furtive, backward glance. Artil flashed a smile! Spoena's brow wrinkled, even as the dronnet rapped Artil's neck. But Logon's joy had been communicated. The dronnet smacked the young girl's neck again, making her turn front. Spoena forced a smile to her scabbed lip so Artil could turn around in peace.

Spoena silently asked, "Logon? You're speaking to Artil? You're speaking to Jeda?" A warmth spread through her. Then she realized that she'd been trying to prove her sorrow by ruing her fate and berating herself instead of simply accepting forgiveness. "Logon, you *are* with us!"

~

Jeda nearly collided into Hod-ya who had stopped abruptly, her hand upraised, her long fingernails glistening in the sunlight filtering through the treetops. "Hold up! I sense the enemy! Hood the girls, quickly, before we engage whoever might be lying in wait out there. They're in a state of despair, and I don't want that interrupted. If we encounter any kingsmen full of their *esprit d'corps,* these girls will take heart and prove all the more difficult to break."

Instantly the hoods came over the girl's heads, blinding their eyes but not their hearts' vision. They'd been delivered from sorrow, their liege was with them in their trial, sharing their suffering, encouraging them to face whatever lay ahead. They clumsily staggered ahead in stuffy blackness, occasionally tripping; but a light burned again in each one's inner being. Logon was with them, that was all that mattered.

Hod-ya spun around. "Gragnold, send two scouts out. I sense the enemy but can't discern the direction."

Gragnold growled something low and guttural. The footsteps of two dronnets fanned out to either side, combing the hedgerows ahead until they'd passed beyond earshot.

Inside the privacy of her hood Jeda smiled, knowing that no kingsmen were nearby other than the three Hod-ya had in tow. She had to suppress laughing aloud lest she incur swift reprisal; nevertheless, tears of joy welled in her eyes. Never was her liege so near as at that moment.

They traipsed on another hour until at last Hod-ya halted. "Remove their hoods."

Jeda's hood was removed and she beheld a broad field of wildflowers: yellow, blue, red, violet, pink, purple, white, and all delicately beautiful. At the far end of the field was a grove of willow trees, bending and swaying their long, graceful branches in the breeze. Downslope in the midst of the grove stood a stark, forbidding stone structure of spires and gables with every window curtained black. This ominous edifice stood in stark contrast to the natural beauty surrounding it, a man-made obscenity amidst natural splendor. A dust cloud in the distance marked the location of a road wending its way from a distant mountain range, past the house and on down the trail as far across the meadow as the eye could see.

A wagon train lumbered slowly up the pike, heading for the inn. The prisoner wagon-train. Hod-ya hadn't beaten them to the finish line and would now have to act as escort.

Hod-ya muttered under her breath. Evidently the White Priestess wielded as much, if not more authority than Hod-ya.

Hod-ya spoke in a low voice to Mileer, then turned to address her prisoners. "We'll have to accompany—" She stopped mid-sentence, her mouth agape.

Then she flew into a violent rage rushing at Gragnold, pummeling his facemask so hard he was driven backward. The dronnets guarding Artil and Spoena cowered, holding up their arms to fend off attacks on themselves. They still held the ropes that bound the girls, however.

"What have you done?" Hod-ya screamed at Gragnold. "You let an enemy creep in and do this? How could you let that happen?" Flecks of foam flew from her lips in fury. "They were beaten, depressed, despairing, and you let an enemy get near them. Was it a bright? I've taught you how to summon cusps to interfere with the work of brights! Why did you not summon them?"

While Hod-ya raged at her dronnets, Jeda dared to peek behind at Artil and Spoena. She gasped when she saw Artil's face in the sunlight, for her swollen eye was back to normal, and all discoloration and bruising gone. It looked as if she'd never been beaten. Then she saw that Spoena's split lip had completely healed without a scar—and all her bruises as well! Even the cuts and scratches on arms and legs were gone.

"Jeda," whispered Artil. "You—you're healed! Your face isn't swollen and bruised anymore, and your nose doesn't look broken either."

Hod-ya lifted her fists to clobber Gragnold afresh but Mileer intervened, seizing her wrists. "Easy now, easy. This will accomplish nothing. It wasn't their fault. I've seen this sort of thing before. It happens once in a while. There's no explanation, but fortunately, it never happens twice. It's some sort of charm the Magician puts on them is my best guess, but it wears off. After all, we still have them in custody, don't we? The power wasn't enough to free them. So what if they recovered from bruises? We can still do what we need to with them. In fact, it's probably better this way, rather than taking damaged contestants to the preliminaries."

"You're a fool! Look at their eyes." Hod-ya released Gragnold. "Sure, we have their bodies, but inside they're free. Just look at them. All my work, all my plans, destroyed!"

"Scrarth and Avangar will change that." Mileer calmly stepped back out of reach. "Once they go into that arena they'll look out for their own skin. That will dim the light in their eyes, you'll see."

Hod-ya regarded him coldly. "You'd better hope so, Mileer. Your ambitions are tied to my own, and I don't have to remind you what awaits those who lose their position due to the outcome of Scrarth and Avangar."

"Do I look worried? I knew way back when I was a lieutenant that you were the rising power in Carnalia, and whoever hitched to your ambitions would rise with you. Now I'm in command of twenty crack legions, almost half of Carnalia's armed forces. I don't back losers, Hod-ya."

"Yes, but now Psa's absence looms larger than I expected."

"That's a chance we'll have to take. Meanwhile, we'd better get along to the inn if we're going to get served before that crowd of guards and prisoners. Come on, you blackguards, get these girls moving."

CHAPTER TWO

HOD-YA'S PARTY ARRIVED MERE MINUTES before the prisoner column, to the immense surprise of the portly innkeeper who was expecting neither. He acted beside himself, having so many patrons descend at once. He scurried about, calling for and chiding lazy servants hiding in the hayloft or wine cellar. Upon catching one, a few yelps accompanied by loud threats preceded the procrastinator's dashing from the bright sunshine of the courtyard into the darker environs of the inn to prepare for the travelers.

As the innkeeper scurried in hot pursuit of another young lad and lass who should've been baking sweetmeats in the kitchen, he was arrested by Gragnold who latched securely to the man's collar. The man's feet shot straight out; his threat at the fleeing helpers died in his throat. "I'm gonna—gaookh!"

"Serve us first," hissed the dronnet to the dangling innkeeper with bulging eyes.

The blackguard lowered him to the ground.

The innkeeper stammered, "Y-y-y-yessir! Right away, sir!" He backed away carefully eyeing Gragnold and the tall woman standing aloof beside him. "Y-y-you're her, aintcha? I knowed you was in the woods, but I never s'pected you'd show up here. You go in an' make yourselves comfortable 'round the hearth. I'll have some wenches see to your needs straight away." He turned and bellowed. "Olionay! In the house, Olionay, we got special guests. Olionay!" He disappeared into the recesses of his inn shouting the serving girl's name.

Before Hod-ya and Mileer crossed the door's threshold a weary, dust covered lieutenant strode up and saluted. "Lieutenant Farber reporting, sir. You are Captain Mileer?"

Mileer returned the salute. "Well, Farber? Stand easy, man, and report. This isn't a military compound and we've both been through too much lately to stand on ceremony."

"Yessir, thank you, sir. I, uh, have twenty guards, mostly Erotons, wounded Erotons, some barely able to walk much less guard prisoners. We have, in bonds, a hundred nineteen soldiers in the foremost drays; a few women and children loosely fettered in the rear two wagons."

Mileer glanced at the caravan and commented, "Seven wagons? That's all?"

"Correct, sir. One for supplies. We only feed the women and children. Two wagons to transport families of the prisoners, and four wagons loaded to the shanks with enemy soldiers. We've been on the road five days now. My men are worn out."

"That must be thirty prisoners to a wagon. Have you checked to see if they're still alive, lieutenant? In this heat, with no provisions . . . "

"Oh, they're alive all right. Too tough to kill. They wouldn't die on the battlefield, and they're proving too hard to kill with starvation, thirst, and heat." For the first time, Lieutenant Farber took note of the bound girls behind their dronnet guards. He let out a low whistle. "They must be dangerous indeed to warrant a dronnet escort, eh?"

"Never you mind, lieutenant," intoned Hod-ya. "They're only dangerous to you if you pry into matters above your station. Come, Gragnold, lead these *dangerous* beauties inside. Mileer, don't take long."

Mileer shot a curious glance back at Hod-ya, then went off with the lieutenant to dutifully inspect and inspire the war-worn troops. Hod-ya led the girls into the inn.

Jeda ascended the steps first, then came Artil with Spoena following behind.

Once inside the blackguards roughly shoved the girls into chairs. When seated their bonds were removed. They found themselves occupying three of four chairs at a round table; the fourth seat remained empty. The dronnets withdrew to the bar where they requisitioned a bottle of spirits from the shelves without asking the barkeep's permission. He said nothing as he watched the blackguards down drink after drink of the hard liquor.

Hod-ya stood at the bottom of a staircase talking to the flustered innkeeper who seemed to be full of excuses and complaints, yet not too much lest he offend the lady of power. "But my inn is noted for leagues around as having a limited store of excellent cuisine reserved for—"

A wave of Hod-ya's hand silenced further objections. She bent over and whispered in his ear.

Jeda turned away, choosing instead to drink in the glow upon Artil and Spoena's faces. Her wrists tingled as her bonds were loosed and circulation returned. "I think we dare whisper."

"What's to happen to us?" Artil surveyed the large room, her eyes wide with wonder.

"I don't know for sure," Jeda answered. "I heard some talk between Hod-ya and Mileer, but I'm not sure what it meant." There was no point in unduly frightening the sisters with her suspicions. "This much I know, Logon is with us; he'll not abandon us now, even on Pitland's border."

"Pitland?" Spoena's eyes widened. "That's where they have Scrarth and Avangar isn't it?"

"But . . . but this can't be near Pitland," protested Artil. "Didn't you see those beautiful flowers and lush vegetation. I always heard that Pitland is a place of darkness and death, not beautiful life."

"I don't want to alarm you, but Mileer and Hod-ya talked with Juued, the messenger, about Willow House on the border of Pitland. This must be Willow House. Look around."

The girls scanned the room full of tables and chairs with hearths on opposite walls and a wide staircase leading upstairs to couching chambers. There were windows, but each was draped in coarse, black cloth that suffered very little natural light to enter. Luxuriant, golden drapes however, adorned each inside window sash, and window seats made a charming addition to the elegant, grand dining room. The room itself had strategically placed lamps providing an even, soft, golden glow throughout.

"This hardly looks like the entry to Pitland, from what I've heard," remarked Spoena. "This is beautiful. Maybe the tales we heard aren't true?"

"I don't know." Jeda, coming from a wealthy background, recognized the furnishings as quality. "Opulence doesn't necessarily mean life and health."

"I know, but . . . " Artil stared wide-eyed all around, "this is hardly what I'd expect on the edge of Pitland. Just look at the sparkles and bright colors, and rubies, or whatever they are over there on those posts and—"

"Rubies, emeralds, pearls, diamonds, whatever your heart desires, little one." Hod-ya claimed the fourth chair. "There's hope for you, after all."

"What are you going to do with us, Hod-ya?" Jeda's audacity surprised even herself.

Hod-ya leveled her eyes at Jeda for several seconds. "You dare make demands? You betray me, flee from me, injure Glend's heart and make her slave to my enemy, and all because I offered to raise you out of your low estate as serving girl to become a lady of power with wealth and servants at your beck and call. Why have you repaid me evil for good, Jeda of Kway?"

Caught off balance by Hod-ya's challenge, Jeda fell speechless for a moment. The field of skulls flashed across her mind. "You chose Glend and me for Scrarth and Avangar but never told us what that is. I've learned, however, that it's a fight to the death. Is that not true?"

"Now where did you hear such a foolish thing? Living among those misguided Ecclessites, I suppose? For your information, Scrarth and Avangar is the culmination of a time of preparation in learning how to reign. It's a graduation from serfdom to ruler-ship. Avangar is the highest, and Scrarth is the second highest. The contest is to determine who's fit to bear rule. Much expense, time, and effort are invested in promising young women such as yourself. The death of even one contestant would be self-defeating. How foolish to believe silly superstitions!" Hod-ya rapped her pointed fingernails on the tabletop waiting for Jeda's reaction.

"Now, I must tell you about the White Priestess. The three of you are to be presented to her, so it's just as well your bruises have healed. I warn you; I'll tolerate no departure from protocol. Gragnold will instruct you in the details. No departure; it won't go well with me if you offend in the slightest matter. I leave to your imagination what will be your fate if it goes ill with me.

"After the presentation, you'll begin the training. I wonder which of you two sisters she'll approve. The greatest of wealth and treasures, along with high authority will be entrusted to those who finish, but alas, only two are allowed in the final competition, and there are three of you. I had thought that you, Spoena, being the elder sister, would most likely give a good account. But I see that Artil has an appreciation for the finer things life has to offer, so perhaps she's better suited to the contest. Jeda, I sense, and am surprised, that you still resist. Why?"

"I've seen your cutthroats at work, Hod-ya, and I know you're in league with Psa, one of the dreads. And you ask why I don't trust you?"

"In league with a dread? Psa? I assure you I'm not in league with him. Oh, in the past, I had occasion to resort to his powers, but now I no longer need him. Look into my eyes and tell me if you sense Psa." She leaned close, forcing eye contact.

Jeda flinched, but then stared boldly back. The veil over the witch-woman's eyes was still there, like a thin veil covering a cave, but Jeda sensed nothing of Psa's presence lurking within.

"You're satisfied?" Then Hod-ya's voice turned syrupy as she displayed an assortment of precious gems across the tabletop. "Now, all I need for your introduction to the White Priestess is for you to renounce all loyalties except to Lurcan. Nothing more difficult than that, and you can do that even now for me, as we sit at this table, with me being the only witness." With a greedy smile Hod-ya studied the girls who were eyeing the gems. "These, and many more like them, are promised to the contenders at the beginning of their training, to entice your best efforts. And this is just the beginning. You'll be given servants, men and women who will cater to your every whim. You'll receive fragrances, delicate fabrics of every hue, baths of perfumes, oils and spices, everything a young, beautiful woman could desire. You two, Spoena and Artil, have never tasted Carnalia's pleasures, hiding all your lives in that accursed forest as you did. Jeda here, has had a taste of wealth, prestige, and power, and knows what it's like; but you two will experience a whole new world of wonders."

"Enough!" Jeda's outburst drew the attention of the dronnets at the bar. "Don't listen Spoena, Artil. She's weaving a web of deception to ensnare your heart away from Logon! There, I said his name."

"Yes, you did." Hod-ya unfolded a napkin on the table and began placing the jewels in the center of it. "Is there some reason you shouldn't say the name of Logon? After all, his soldiers say the name of Lurcan, and tremble. Is there some reason I should fear to say aloud the name of an executed criminal? He is also known as Alfomega, is he not? I fear not him, nor his father, King Elyon, a toothless, doddering old regent, unable to command respect from his own armies anymore. I spit on their names. There, now if they had any power at all, would they tolerate my profaning them?"

Spoena and Artil regarded Hod-ya with eyebrows raised and lips parted.

"Oh, my sweet, young girls, so naive, so quick to believe what your kingsmen parents foisted upon you. I defy Elyon and Logon to strike me right now, if they have any power!" Hod-ya's arms were uplifted as her face tilted to the ceiling. "Alas, so much for their power." She lowered her face to the girls again. "Now, who do you trust? Me, who challenges them with impunity, or they, who, if they even exist, have no power to answer my defiance?"

"But . . . but we know him." Artil's face had drained of color.

"You know yourself, tulip bud. When you cry yourself to sleep because of your poverty, or because someone has taken advantage of you, and that voice comes to comfort you, your parents told you that's his voice, but it's really your own inner voice. I have just demonstrated, here and now in your presence, if your Logon and King Elyon are anything, they are feckless. Weak, fearful people too afraid to take charge of their own destinies have duped you. I offer you the chance to break free from that self-defeatist lifestyle; join me in power and pleasure."

So enthralled were the girls by Hod-ya's performance that they didn't notice Eroton guards seating some prisoner kingsmen officers at a nearby table.

"Here is power, girls," Hod-ya's fingers stirred the gems in the napkin so that they sparkled. Her tone had an effect, even on Jeda. But it wasn't enough.

Jeda read the obscure expression on Hod-ya's face as an indication the three of them were stronger than Hod-ya expected; nevertheless, there was some wavering even in Jeda's thoughts. "Just renounce all loyalties except to Lurcan. He's the only power in all the universe. Tell me now, Jeda, to whom do you pledge loyalty?"

Jeda blinked back tears. She'd expected Logon to strike Hod-ya down for speaking so defiantly against him. Her trust in him was undermined when nothing happened.

"Jeda, we're waiting. Show yourself wise; choose the obvious."

"Ahem! Ecclessites walk by faith, not by sight," intruded a masculine voice.

Hod-ya reeled back as if she'd been slapped; her chair's front feet lifted off the floor nearly toppling her over backwards.

The enticing charm on the girls was broken.

"Who are you?" Hod-ya angrily demanded of the blond-haired soldier in the blood-caked tunic who'd disrupted her spell.

"I'm Tren, soldier of Logon Xychirion."

"Well, Tren, your Logon doesn't seem to take very good care of you. Is your being held captive what you call walking by faith and not by sight? If it is, maybe you should use your eyes. I'm sure these young ladies have enough wisdom to perceive the folly of that course." She turned back to them. "Here's an excellent case in point. This soldier has been wounded about the head, stabbed in the arm, captured by his enemy, is on his way to Pitland to be, er, persuaded to return his fealty to Lurcan, yet he foolishly clings to the belief that Logon has his best interests at heart."

Then she turned and faced Tren. "If your Logon has such great power, why does he not strike me dead when I challenge him? I'll tell you why, because, if he exists at all, he lacks the power. Thus, I prove him powerless!" Hod-ya finished triumphantly, a smug smile upon her lips as if there could be no reply.

Tren turned and looked Hod-ya squarely in the face, then averted his eyes to study the girls for a moment, resting his eyes longest on Jeda.

Hod-ya verbally sparred again. "Well, what other reason could there be for your king not taking up my challenge other than he's powerless?"

"His refusal to bring swift retribution upon you is proof of his overwhelming love for even you, Hod-ya."

Hod-ya shrieked. "His what?"

Several dronnets at the bar instinctively went for their scimitars.

Tren lowered his eyes to his own tabletop as he replied. "His love for you. He doesn't respond to childish taunts: 'I dare you to do such and such.' Especially when the consequences are so final and devastating."

The other Ecclessite officers nodded in silent agreement. The Eroton guards stood ready but not interfering, but nonetheless listening.

Hod-ya's fingernails rapped in succession on the polished tabletop as she coldly replied. "Yes, well, you'll say anything now, won't you? Tren is your name? I'll see to your *repatriation* personally."

Captain Mileer and Lieutenant Farber entered the dim, coolness of the dining room talking in hushed tones and sat at a table close by.

Hod-ya demanded, "Farber, why are these kingsmen treated like royalty? Why are they not kept with the other prisoners?"

Farber looked up from his discussion with Mileer. "They're officers. Hitherto they've always been treated with deference, even if they are from the other side."

"Get them out of here. They're interfering with my girls."

Farber rose to his feet. "Right away." He strode to the door and summoned an orderly and gave instructions before returning to his seat. "It'll take a few minutes to make arrangements, m'lady. We have to keep them segregated from the other prisoners. It's hard to break morale with officers in their midst. These seven are real officers. Many kingsmen who bear rank are actually no more than run-of-the-mill soldiers with paper bona fides and delusions of grandeur. But these are quite dangerous, especially the tall, fair-haired one there. He sports no rank or insignia, but his bearing is unmistakably that of a captain, maybe higher."

"Hmmm," intoned Hod-ya. Saying nothing more, she rose and beckoned for Mileer to come aside and speak quietly with her at another table.

Jeda studied the Ecclessite officers at the next table, longing to talk with them, to learn from them. These warriors showed no sign of intimidation even though they were on the verge of disappearing into the dark regions of Pitland.

Tren gazed back at Jeda. "Have we met? You look so familiar."

"I'm certain we have not. I'd have remembered you. I've been an Ecclessite only a short while and have had limited prior dealings with kingsmen."

He smiled. "Funny, I feel like I should know you; even your mannerisms, speech, and facial expressions seem so familiar."

Hod-ya returned, preventing further conversation. Within minutes the orderly reported back to Lieutenant Farber who then relayed the orders moving the Ecclessite officers back outside.

Hod-ya watched them go with evident satisfaction. "Now then, as I was saying," she seated herself again at the girl's table, "I place before you a choice of life or death, girls. I'm being blunt, please forgive me, but I—er, you, have not much time." A cold gleam came to her eye. "I assure you, I do have persuasive measures at my disposal should the need arise, and you would finally agree to do whatever I wish, so, you can spare yourself needless suff—that is, hardship."

Jeda stared at her own folded hands on the table. Spoena did likewise, but Artil, seemed snared in the web of Hod-ya's gems. She reached out and touched the half-dozen sparkling jewels on the napkin.

"Ahh, wisest, though youngest," gloated Hod-ya. "Todar," she summoned one of the dronnets from the bar, "take this one on ahead. She'll give you very little trouble, I think. Tell Bablo-ya, my sister, that she is one of my potential contestants. I'll bring the others with me when I come. Oh, and these belong to her. Withhold nothing that she desires." Hod-ya folded the gems into the napkin, placed it in a pouch, and handed them to the blackguard. "Go with Todar, tulip bud. Your sister and friend will be along shortly. And Todar, take some refreshment for her." Then lowly in Todar's ear, but loud enough for Jeda to hear, "Don't turn aside till you reach the White Priestess' Castle, understand?"

"I understand," hissed the lanky, half-masked dronnet. He took Artil's hand to guide her away from her seat.

"No, you can't—" Spoena stood and protested.

Hod-ya's hand landed softly on Spoena's cheek. "Don't ever tell me what I can and can't do." The pointed fingernail lingered making an indentation at the top of Spoena's cheekbone. "Remember," Hod-ya reverted to the singsong tone, "I give the orders because I know what is best. Go now, Todar."

The dronnet tugged, and Artil reluctantly followed.

Alarm welled up within Jeda. It was useless to resist. She feared for Artil, herself, and Spoena, and for Bonu who, if he had survived, surely would come looking for her; also, for Glend, for Vawella and Captain Varter and the whole brigade, and for Tren, who'd dared to defy Hod-ya. The joy in Logon that she had so recently shared with the sisters now seemed remote. Fear mixed with anger registered on Spoena's face. Did her own face mirror the same?

Plates of hot food and a tankard which smelled of alcohol arrived. The girls were famished but trusted nothing Hod-ya offered.

"Eat," Hod-ya ordered, having lost her syrupy tone. "I'll not have you arrive in Pitland near starved. Eat." Her fist pounded the table making the silverware jump.

With her fork, Jeda reluctantly turned over a piece of brownish-gray meat lying alongside a helping of boiled potatoes. At least it was thoroughly cooked. She brought a morsel to her lips and tasted. Though saltier than she liked, it seemed all right, so she ate. Spoena followed her example and soon both hungrily devoured the meal before them. Thirst then beset them, and the only beverage was the brew sitting within arm's reach that smelled strongly of fermented hops.

"Is there no water?" Jeda asked.

"You have drink before you," Hod-ya replied indifferently.

"But this is strong ale. Hardly fitting for girls to drink."

"I'll determine what's fitting. That's all you'll have here, drink it or go thirsty; and may I inform you, it is a long, dusty trail from here to the castle." Hod-ya smiled. She herself neither drank nor ate.

The girls glanced briefly at each other and gave in to their need, draining the tankards as they gulped the bitters down, trying not to taste the beverage. It did assuage her thirst, though she immediately felt bloated after drinking so much so fast.

"Farber, are your troops ready? I'll not dawdle all day for the sake of a ragtag bunch of guards and prisoners."

The lieutenant looked up, surprised that his much-needed rest was already over. "Yes, m'lady. We await your pleasure."

"Get them moving. My party will occupy the last wagon."

"But the women and children?"

"Let them walk. Oh, and tell your prisoners that any escape attempts will answer to my dronnets."

Farber's face blanched. "Surely you don't mean women and children?"

"That's precisely who I mean. Now, get them moving. We'll be ready in about twenty minutes."

"On my way."

Hod-ya turned to Jeda and Spoena, saying, "Might as well take a little time to freshen up over there." She pointed to a ladies' powder room beneath a grandiose staircase. Jeda and Spoena wordlessly went to the washroom.

As they went, Jeda paused just around a corner and overheard Mileer say as he joined Hod-ya, "You've contacted Laroc? Good, very good. To enter Scrarth and Avangar without a dread as sponsor would be disastrous, especially in light of the challenger."

"What do you know of the matter? Besides, Laroc hasn't determined he will accept my conditions yet. I've decided to not give up all my rights like I did for Psa."

"You play a dangerous game Hod-ya. The dreads aren't known for being reasonable."

"Neither am I. If he wants my services and contacts—and he might as well since it would take years to train another to my level; he'll have to meet my terms."

Jeda heard no more and scurried to the privacy of the powder room. They took care of their needs and tidied up using the wall mirror.

Then Spoena, losing her brave front, tearfully sighed, "Jeda, I'm so frightened. What's going to happen to Artil? What's to become of us?"

Jeda hugged the teenager, drawing as much comfort as she gave. "I wish I knew. Hod-ya is going through some sort of transition, switching from one dread to another, or so it would seem. Why? I haven't the faintest idea. But remember, Logon bestowed joy upon us as we emerged from the forest. He knows where we are and what we face. He knows about Artil, too. He hasn't abandoned us. Remember the resolute looks on the officer's faces; they aren't afraid."

"No fear that showed, anyway." Spoena pushed one of her tresses behind her ear.

"Right. Whatever we face is no worse than what they face. We must show courage and not give in to fear. What can Hod-ya do besides kill our bodies? But if we deny Logon . . . "

Spoena closed her eyes, remembering, "There's a rune that says,

'Fear not those who threaten harm,
But lack the pow'r to control,
Rather fear the one whose arm,
Holds fate of spirit, body, soul.'

"Logon personally taught that rune to his original generals."

"I wish we had our Children of the Stars."

"Me, too," agreed Spoena. "All we have is what we can remember. I wish I'd spent more time studying and memorizing runes. They'd be such a comfort now."

"At least the Advisor will recall what we've faithfully studied. I wish I'd applied more diligence, so he'd have more material to draw from."

"It's time." Hod-ya's voice cut through the door. "Your wagon awaits."

CHAPTER THREE

"Shh!" Bonu cautioned. "Stay put 'til I signal all clear." He scurried beneath low hanging limbs and out of sight with barely a rustle.

Scung looked nervously at the wounded ex-Nutherway leader and his wife, smiling in an attempt to reassure them.

Earlier, Bonu and Scung had arrived back at the cabin following their encounter with the carnivorous plant, Voronon, to find Thorma reunited with Thoru, her husband, preparing to go in search of Carnalian forces rumored to still be in the woods. Balatz felt somewhat recovered in spite of his chest wound and decided to trek to Logon's Rock. Bletza had misgivings, but at the same time was determined to accompany her husband. The parting of the four former friends was stiff, uncomfortable.

Their journey's outset under Bonu's guidance toward the Ecclessite brigade was uneventful. As a precaution Bonu led roundabout detours to avoid Carnalian patrols. Even so, there were telltale footprints that might have been made by deserters, which meant dangerous, renegade Carnalians, or else scouting patrols. Bonu used extreme caution, consuming time and wandering further afield than he intended.

After a day and a half of meandering, Bonu, Scung, Bletza, and Balatz arrived on the outskirts of Captain Varter's new camp. Bonu signaled to alert the camp to their presence with grunts like wild peccaries; there was no reply. Leaving Scung temporarily in charge, Bonu headed into the undergrowth to investigate.

Half an hour later, hearing a slight rustle behind, Scung turned to discover Bonu crawling through dense shrubbery, his visage grim.

"Whutcha find?"

Bonu sighed, checked behind on either side then crawled through and sat beside the Eroton. His eyes were red and swollen.

"Bonu," Balatz was first to ask, "What is it?"

"They . . . they were raided. Sometime yesterday. It must've been an awful battle. Many died on both sides. Tophets ate well." He hung his head and sighed.

"Be's they all . . . ?"

Bonu composed himself. "Several escaped, some appear wounded. It was a massacre. Women, children, the elderly, the infirm—slaughtered mercilessly. And there were possible signs of another dread."

Bletza shuddered.

Balatz put an arm around his wife. "Is it near us?"

Bonu shook his head. "We're the only living beings within two or three leagues. I think Captain Varter managed to escape with a small contingent, but the tracks are so trampled I can't be sure."

"What do we do now?" Balatz's brow bore worrisome furrows. "It may be an awful time to ask, but what of our trip to Logon's Rock? I can't wander around much longer with this chest wound."

"No, of course you can't," Bonu agreed. "Besides, there's nothing we can do here. I think we should pursue Captain Varter's remnant since he seems to have fled in the direction of Logon's Rock."

Bletza took hold of her husband's hand. "Won't they be harried by Carnalian forces?"

"That's a chance we'll have to take. There's safety in numbers. However, if we don't find Captain Varter, I'll escort you to Logon's Rock myself."

"Not wi'out my help," Scung said. "Mebbe I hain't gots much ter offer, but whut I gots is at yer disposal, lieutenant."

Bonu gripped the Eroton's brawny biceps. "I know that, Scung. But it would be better for you to be properly trained in a brigade." He stood. "So, we'd best get a move on."

"Lieutenant," said Bletza, "can't we rest a while longer? I'm exhausted."

Bonu regarded her solemnly. "I'm sorry, but we should be as far away from here as possible before nightfall. Tophets, you understand."

Bletza nodded and struggled to her feet. "I'll try."

"That's the spirit, Bletza. It's dangerous remaining too long in one place." Bonu led off into the underbrush, following animal trails and dried creek beds through the greenery, causing as little disruption as possible.

Bonu plotted a path parallel to Captain Varter's retreat, veering slightly to the left, hoping to encounter his captain along the way. Bonu demonstrated to the Nutherway couple how to step on logs, exposed roots and rocks where possible, anything to not leave footprints. They followed, stealthy as shadows, gliding beneath overhanging boughs. Mile after tortuous mile melted away in the sweltering humidity, as did the hours until afternoon turned to twilight and finally faded to complete darkness.

Bonu used the light of his sword sparingly to break trail. He checked on Scung from time to time who was dutifully bringing up the rear, keeping his keen Eroton ears and eyes vigilantly on their back trail. Though Scung's sword had not much light, when held near the ground it provided sufficient light to avoid roots, ground-trailing vines and various other stumbling blocks.

Thus, the foursome trekked until total darkness enveloped the woodlands landscape, feeling their way around tree boles, pushing through clumps of fern and broadleaf, clambering over fallen logs and deviating around dense briar thickets.

When Bonu finally signaled a halt Bletza and Balatz gratefully sank to their knees on a bed of moss beneath an ancient oak. Scung took it upon himself to scout the perimeter of their stop, making sure no predators lurked nearby. Satisfied that at least a furlong in any direction there was no imminent danger, he reported to Bonu, “Seems ter be clear ‘nuff hereabouts.”

“Thanks, Scung. First off, let me remind you that I’m still not sure we’re following Captain Varter’s trail. I do know that Vawella, the captain’s daughter, is with this group we follow, but more than that, I can’t say. There’s a strong warrior with them, but he’s clever enough to leave no distinct tracks; I can only surmise that it’s Captain Varter.”

“So, what difference would it make?” asked Bletza.

“The difference is that I would likely be the ranking officer if Captain Varter isn’t leading them, and as such, would have to assume command.”

“And?” Bletza persisted.

“And not be able to take us to Logon’s Rock,” explained her husband.

“Oh. Then that leaves us—”

“Exactly where you are now, completely in Logon’s care.” Bonu settled on the mossy bed. “He knows your true intentions, and what you need, and when you need it.”

“Yes, well, that’s easy for you to say, isn’t it?” Balatz’s tone was petulant.

Bonu stared intently but without sternness at Balatz in the glow of his sword. Quick as a fly his right hand reached out to Balatz's neck and snatched a wriggly bug between forefinger and thumb. "Check for irks, everybody. It seems this area abounds with them." He placed the irk on the ground and touched his sword to it. It sizzled and vanished in a puff of smoke.

Scung immediately rubbed the back of his neck to make sure none had eluded his detection. "I ain't got none!"

"Nor will you, if you keep your mind on Logon. It's you two I'm concerned about."

"But irks were never more than a minor annoyance to us."

"They'll be more than that now since you've decided to seek Logon. As enemies of the king they'll do their utmost to return you to Lurcan's control, in which case, your final condition would be tragic."

Balatz and Bletza obligingly checked each other for the annoying parasites. Then Balatz said, "Now we have to watch out for irks. It seems like everything has gone from bad to worse since I decided to seek Logon. You'd think he'd make it easier to come to him."

"You're the ones who chose to live so far from Ecclessa's borders, so don't blame Logon if it's a long journey to his rock. You must endure these trials, and if you endure, you'll discover that these tribulations are preparation for even stronger opposition as you continue to follow him. On the other hand, if you don't fight through these hardships, well, it can only be concluded you didn't really want Logon, but merely relief from your troubles."

"That's rather severe, isn't it?" Bletza squeezed her husband's hand in hers. "I mean, after all, one can hardly be blamed for not serving Logon if they've never heard of him."

"Yeah, whut 'bout thet?" Scung joined in. "I been meanin' ter ask 'bout thet."

Bonu leaned back against a tree, withdrew his toller and rested his Child of the Stars across his lap. "It's time for a little rune study, eh? And I believe I know just the rune." His toller touched a raised marking midway down the blade. "Come on, Scung, do what I do. You two watch and learn."

The top part of the rune glowed as Bonu chanted softly, his voice joyful, his eyes shining:

"Advisor search, and know my thought,
My hopes to Logon send,
Of the battles I have fought,
Or threatening ills portend?

Is it in vain I cry aloud, do you know my pain?
Are all things in your control, do they show your way?
Or are my feet on slippery paths, my seeking for you vain?
Will you assist and not mock? 'Well done' I pray you'll say.

His own he knew, before they were,
He calls and guides, to show,
But to his will they must defer,
Then his voice they'll know.

And hear him speak, "For you 'tis all,
For you to work and blend,
For known you are, and yours the call,
Conformed to joyous end.

To be so chosen, to be thus nudged,
To find life's pure delight,
To be tried and yet not judged,
Born low, yet borne to height.

Though irks oppose, and cusps belie,
And tophets gorge, and dreads o'erwhelm,
Though life does fail and bodies die,
Logon rules a joy-filled realm."

Even as Scung continued sawing away at his blade, Bonu was finished; the entire rune on his sword gleamed brightly. Bonu laid his toller aside. "Do you understand?"

Bletza wept, her tears glistening in the sword's blue light. "I abandoned him. Will he take me back?"

Bonu looked steadily into her tear-rimmed eyes. "I honestly don't know."

"But you're certain he'll receive me, an enemy who counterfeited his sword? Why would he accept me and not her?" Balatz grimaced and clasped his chest as he spoke.

"Be's yer awright?" Scung reached out to comfort him.

"I, I need to know." Balatz gasped. "Because if she isn't received—ahhh!"

"Logon won't wrestle with you. Whatever you allow between yourself and him will keep him at bay. No irks, cusps, tophets or dreads, not even Lurcan himself can intervene if you truly want Logon. But if you allow a false sense of duty, another allegiance, or an earthly love to separate you from Logon, you separate yourself from his help."

"Is that what I've done?" asked Bletza.

"Perhaps. What does your heart tell you?"

"I hear nothing from my heart."

"Then tell me this, if it comes to serving Logon again, or following Balatz, which would you choose?"

"Can't I do both?"

"That's not the question. Indeed, if you do choose Logon, his command would be loyalty to your husband. But the question I put to you is—given the choice of 'either,' 'or,' which do you choose?"

Bletza bowed her head for a moment. "If he would receive me back, I would follow Logon." Bletza turned and solemnly gazed at her husband.

He remained expressionless.

"And you, Balatz. Where is your loyalty? To Logon, or your wife?"

"But I don't have to choose, as long as Logon receives her back, I can have both."

"I doubt Logon will be satisfied with that answer. Mada, ancestor of us all, had a similar choice. Ivi, his mate, fell under Lurcan's spell and disobeyed King Elyon's command. Mada, however, knew he was disobeying, but chose to stay with his errant wife rather than King Elyon. Thus, all Psychanon fell under Lurcan's dominion who then was able to enslave all humanity with one, subversive lie. But Elyon, and Logon his son, loved us so much that they provided a way—the only way—to return to his good graces. We must confess and forsake our disobedience and acknowledge there is nothing we can do to undo our crime and accept Logon's sacrifice on our behalf."

"Hain't thet be's whut I done?" The bright glow of his sword's point shone in Scung's eyes.

"That's exactly what you did, Scung, though you may not have understood all the ramifications."

"But, but how can he hold us responsible for what Mada did? After all, I wouldn't have done what he did?" protested Balatz.

"You think not? Consider your attitude when you thought Logon might not receive Bletza. What if your parents or siblings refuse to follow Logon? Are you ready because of another's stubbornness to forget the whole journey?"

Balatz remained silent.

"Make your decision, Balatz. Your ancestors were in Mada's loins when he made his fatal choice, and so you, as one of his descendants, have inherited the same weakness. But you can rectify that decision. Will you?"

"Choice? This wound in my chest won't give me any rest 'til I get it healed."

"If I were to tell you that the wound would eventually close without a trace, and you could resume a more or less normal life, would you pursue this course?"

"I . . . I'm not sure."

"And that's why you must make this difficult journey. At some point, you'll be forced into a clear-cut decision to either continue seeking Logon or return to your former ways. Logon will allow opposition to come at you, and you must deal with it until you're firm in your pursuit of him."

"But whut 'bout them thet never heered 'bout Logon?" Scung intruded. "Be's it fair o' Logon ter let 'em be destroyed fer not knowin' they oughta been a-seekin' him?"

Bonu quoted the still glowing rune:

"His own he knows, before they were,
He calls and guides, to show,
But to his will they must defer,
Then his voice they'll know.

And hear him speak, "For you 'tis all,
For you to work and blend,
For known you are, and yours the call,
Conformed to joyous end."

"That means Logon knows who will and who won't follow him. He makes sure those who would seek him have every opportunity.

But he has no obligation to extend the same opportunity to those he knows will never follow. Sometimes he does reveal his offer to them, however, if only to show them what they could have had; and what a tragedy for them when they find themselves before King Elyon after the Tremendum when Logon reveals that they rejected his amnesty." Bonu pensively leaned back against the oak trunk.

Balatz leaned forward. "And that could be me?"

"It's your choice. Will you follow Logon, or your own desires?"

Balatz reclined beside his wife, turning away from Bonu and the lit sword in the lieutenant's hand. "I'm here, aren't I?"

Bonu's lips parted and his eyes looked down as he tucked his sword away.

Scung followed suit, putting his own glowing tip under the corner of his cloak as he lay his head on the mossy turf and closed his eyes in preparation of sleep.

~

It was light when Scung awoke. He sat up and rubbed the sleep from his eyes. Then, looking around, realized he was alone. There were slight depressions in the moss bed where others had lain; he'd not been alone long. He stood to full height and peered through the foliage, cupping his hand to his ear and listening for any rustle that might indicate his companions' whereabouts. Only the buzzing of insects and the bustle of small creatures greeted his ears.

"Now whut?" He sank to his knees again on the soft turf, pondering his options.

Bushes parted and Bonu emerged with a swish of back-swinging branches, his face flushed, perspiration brimming his brow. "They're gone; both of them."

Scung nodded. "Whereabouts?"

Bonu shook his head. "They left little to no trail that I can follow. Funny, I really thought Bletza was serious. I more or less expected Balatz to turn back, but not her. There seemed to be a genuine hunger in her heart for truth." He squatted down on his haunches and shook his head. "Well, that simplifies our duty."

"Yer been obedient, agin yer own desires. Thet's gotta count fer summat."

Bonu looked at his friend and smiled. "Yeah, that's 'gotta count fer summat'."

Both men laughed then Bonu asked, "Ready?"

"Yep."

"Remember, step on rocks, or exposed roots as much as possible." With that admonition he led into the undergrowth following a barely discernible trail, yet quite certain of his course.

Through the heat of the day they pushed on, parallel to the kingsman trail Bonu had scouted. Rarely did Bonu check tracks anymore, keeping his tack twenty feet to the side of Varter's trail. Once they stumbled onto a nest of ground hornets, stirring up a vicious, stinging swarm that left them with numerous welts.

"This be's a nasty place," said Scung. Bonu merely nodded and bent back to his task.

Near dusk, Bonu hunkered down to the ground reading some new tracks. He stood; his eyes narrowed. "Carnalian patrol. Five men."

"Any dronnets?"

"I don't think so. Seems like five men struggling to survive. They accidentally came across Varter's trail and are tracking him, probably thinking of an easy kill. We must overtake them, for what I can read of Varter's trail indicates only two or three kingsmen are capable of bearing arms. We'll stay on their trail now, for the sake of speed." He set off at a trot with Scung following.

Not until it was almost completely dark did Bonu withdraw his sword.

"Won't thet attract enemies?" challenged Scung. The greater bulk of his person was exhausted by the heat and humidity more than Bonu.

"It doesn't matter anymore. We must catch up before these Carnalians fall upon the survivors. I hope we do draw attention."

They plodded through the dark by the light of Bonu's sword, following the trail left by the renegade Carnalians.

"Kingsmen! Save me!" a woman's voice cried out from the thick forest.

Both Bonu and Scung whirled about, their swords ready. "Help! I'm lost. I seek Logon Xychirion. Bonu, Scung, is that you?" Bletza, besmeared, exhausted and with the hem of her garment tattered, emerged from behind a tree trunk.

"Bletza! How did you, where—"

She collapsed at their feet sobbing. "I thought I was going to die alone. Carnalian's nearly caught me. I was so frightened. I guess you're wondering . . . "

Bonu knelt beside her and offered a sip from his waterskin. "Yes, I did wonder. But that can wait. I need to know how long ago did this Carnalian patrol pass?"

"Half an hour, maybe less. There were five of them, and they knew I was in the bushes. Their leader threatened they'd come back for me after they finished their 'other business'. They knew I wouldn't get far on my own."

Bonu rubbed his chin. "They left you because they knew you had no food. Scung, I place her in your charge. Stay and guard her 'til I get back. Uh, it'd probably be best if you went off trail and kept your sword covered. I'll be back when I can." He vanished leaving only fleeting glimpses of blue light flashing in the undergrowth.

~

Except for the light of Scung's sword tip all was dark.

Bletza shuddered and huddled close to Scung for warmth.

"C'mon, Missy. We'd best be doin' as Bonu says and git off'n this here trail." He lifted her by the elbow and lighting the way with his sword, led into the dense foliage. Well away from the trail, Scung found the kind of tree he was looking for with low branches. He hoisted Bletza to the attainable limbs. "Climb as high as yer kin. I be's stayin' below ter guard agin varmints, human or otherwise."

"You . . . you won't abandon me?" Her tone was frail, fearful.

"Nah! I be's goin' nowheres. I be's gonna sit myself down here an' stay hid. I recommends yer git yerself settled atwixt summat branches, so if'n yer falls asleep yer don't come a-tumblin' down."

"All right, but I don't think I'll get much sleep."

Scung settled back against the tree listening to the nighttime forest, identifying various sounds. He once thought he heard shouting and ringing of metal on metal in the distance, but the greenery muted sound so much he couldn't be sure.

Additionally, he had to guard against his imagination getting the better of him. He was responsible for Bletza, and with Logon's help, he'd keep her safe. "Logon, look after Bonu. Keep him safe. An' don't fergit me an' Bletza, neither."

"Did you say something?" Bletza called down from her lofty branches.

"Eh? Oh, no, jest talkin' ter Logon. Does yer hear anythin' unusual from up there?"

"Now that you mention it, I think I heard voices, but I'm not sure."

"Anythin' else?"

Bletza turned her ear to the windward. "No, only sounds that vaguely resemble voices. But it's probably just forest noises. I've been hearing such noises all day."

"Well, yer keep alert fer anythin' whut seems the least bit unusual, an' tell me, awright?"

"All right." Bletza yawned. "I just might fall asleep after all. I didn't realize how exhausted I am. Will that be safe?"

"Sure, sure. By the way, I hopes yer don't mind me askin', but I'd like ter ken why yers left Bonu an' me last night?"

"I thought you might ask. Well, I left because Balatz did. He woke me after you and Bonu fell asleep. He told me he was leaving, that it was a mistake to think Logon would receive either one of us. I was bewildered but didn't see any choice but to stay with my husband, so I followed."

Scung grunted. "Whereabouts be's he now?"

Bletza choked back a sob, then replied. "I don't know. I lost track of him when we dodged some gorrils. He went under some brush and I lost sight of him. I was petrified, afraid to move, and so, just waited, hoping the gorrils wouldn't find me. When they finally did pass, I heard him calling from a distance, saying he'd found a little clearing about the size of a tent where he thought we could safely spend the rest of the afternoon. That was the last I heard from him. He just disappeared. I thrashed about the undergrowth looking for him, but found no clearing, nor any sign of him. I finally decided to find you two again. Thank Logon I did! Maybe Bonu, with his expert tracking skills, can find Balatz."

Scung rested his chin on his chest, deciding not to mention the encounter with Voronon. "Yer'd best try an' git some sleep."

The night wore on through the wee hours, though Ra-Amawl's pre-dawn wasn't much different than midnight. Scung manfully resisted sleep, staying alert to guard Bletza who dozed a light, fitful sleep in her tree-crotch cradle. Scung stretched his legs out, pulling his toes upwards, stifling a yawn. All around was still, and for that he was thankful. But he couldn't help worrying about Bonu. He longed to toll his sword, but in this stillness, such activity would most certainly attract unwanted attention. In lieu of tolling he mused on the runes he could remember.

Had it only been a few days since he'd been in service to the emperor, hacking his way through the jungle in the company of a band of dronnets, watching them reactivate the empty shell of a dread? His understanding of life and loyalty were completely reversed now; he loved his new master and the daring lieutenant who'd taken it upon himself to instruct this crusty Eroton in the king's ways. "Ah, Logon, whut a wonderful realm yer be's abuildin'. Takin' riffraff an' castoffs the likes o' me ter turn inter warriors o' truth, removin' the hate an' fear and givin' me yer Advisor instead, ter teach love an' kindness."

"He is wonderful," came a voice out of the shrubbery behind him.

Scung was on his feet in a bound, sword held ready for a fight.

"Wha—what's happening?" Bletza's sleepy voice drifted down from above.

"Shhh! It's just me." Bonu stepped clear of the shrubbery. "I heard you communing with Logon, Scung. Sorry for disturbing you. I assume everything's quiet here?"

“Yer like ter scairt me outta me whiskers!” gasped Scung, lowering his weapon. “I be’s mighty pleased ter see yer, though. Whereat yer been all night?”

“I found Varter’s party; it is Captain Varter who’s leading them. And there are more warriors than I thought, though it’s still a pitifully small contingent. When daylight grows, I’ll lead you to them. They’ve found a remarkable location for a fort and are establishing a new base of operations.”

“Whut? Arter bein’ followed?”

“It’s quite safe, Logon has given definite word. It’s an invulnerable spot, really. You’ll understand when you see it.”

“Is it safe to come down?” called Bletza. “I’m stiff and sore from being up here all night. Ooh, my legs have gone asleep.”

“You kept her up there?” Bonu laughed quietly. “That’s imaginative. Yes, come on down, Bletza. We need to talk.”

CHAPTER FOUR

THE WAGON PITCHED OVER A deeply rutted road causing Jeda, Hod-ya, Captain Mileer, Gragnold, and Spoena to brace their feet against the floor and grasp the side rails just to stay seated. The canvas sides were raised allowing a warm but welcome breeze as well as a view of the countryside. Rays of sunlight mixed with shadows of puffy clouds flitting across the tall, swaying grasses mottled the meadows. Pitland was rumored to be a place of death, horror, stink, filth, fear, and despair, so it was with some surprise that Jeda found the approach to Pitland quite the opposite. Instead, lush wildflowers carpeted the meadows replete with swooping birds, scurrying rabbits and squirrels chiding from treetops. All in all, this could have been a rather pleasant outing were it not for the girls' grim companions and their ultimate destination.

"This isn't at all what I'd heard," whispered Spoena.

"Nor I." Jeda nodded.

Hod-ya's enigmatic expression disdained their naiveté, but she said nothing. She instead turned her attention to Captain Mileer who mumbled on and on about some battle or political ploy in which he'd played a significant role.

Gragnold, inscrutable as ever, riveted his attention to the road ahead, much as he had during the journey from Cosmopolis to Ra-Amawl.

"Gragnold," Jeda interrupted during a pause in Mileer's rambling monologue, drawing the immediate attention of all. "Whatever happened to Sevrid?"

Gragnold uttered a low growl and looked away out over the fields.

"Please, I'd like to know."

"Go ahead, Gragnold," said Hod-ya in a low monotone. "You may tell her. She'll find out sometime or sooner anyway."

Gragnold bent his head forward as if avoiding Hod-ya's penetrating stare. At long last, his voice merely a whisper. "Sevrid beneath Psa when explode, gone." There was the faintest glint of light as if a tear reflected from his eye-slit.

Jeda gasped, amazed that there might still lurk some humanity in Gragnold. Never before had she seen even a trace of eyes through the eye slits that masked his upper face, and though it was merely a brief reflection, Jeda pitied him.

"I know how you feel, Jeda. How horrible," said Spoena.

Jeda realized that the others supposed she gasped at realizing Psa had been undone, or at Sevrid's horrible fate.

Gragnold growled again and turned his head away.

"For a moment there, Gragnold," Hod-ya observed, "I thought I perceived a twinge of pity for Sevrid. You know how dangerous allowing such feelings are to your order. You'd have to undergo conditioning all over again should you weaken, understand?"

~

Gragnold hissed angrily; he sensed Jeda's pity and it touched him; he didn't know how to cope with that. But Hod-ya must not know. Hod-ya was less powerful than he'd ever seen her. Prior to Psa's explosion, Hod-ya always knew what he, or any dronnet in her presence, was thinking. Now she seemed at a loss; like when the Ecclessite prisoner bested her at Willow House. That had never happened in all his fifteen years of service to her. Nevertheless, Hod-ya was still a force to be reckoned with, and certainly not one to be underestimated. She still wielded the title, Mistress of Lurcan's Palace, and had many influential friends in high places. And then there were rumors that she was already courting another dread, and if successful would quickly regain any lost momentum.

Gragnold also had heard rumors that the war was going well, and that for the last two months Logon's Bridge was under heavy siege and would soon fall. This wouldn't be a good time to need reconditioning. Victory over Ecclessa was all but assured within the next year or two. Lurcan was mustering forces from other nations and minor baronies scattered around the edge of the empire as well as from the *kyllorn* realm, to sally forth with all his powers, girding his armies for battle against the inferior forces of the king. Ultimate and complete victory was imminent; nothing less would suffice.

Gragnold glanced at the two girls. Though these foolish girls meant well, they'd chosen their side poorly, and must bear their doom. There would be no giving or receiving mercy! Their survival depended upon forsaking any and all loyalty to Ecclessa. Gragnold was clear about his loyalties.

~

Jeda, not fully comprehending Psa's demise and the vacuum it left, resumed watching the scenery, taking some comfort from the bright sunlight highlighting the meadows, especially after the monotonous, ubiquitous green of Ra-Amawl. Maybe things weren't going to be so bad after all.

Up ahead storm clouds lingered like a shelf in the sky, dominating the horizon, a sharp contrast to the sunlit foreground. Perhaps there'd be thunder and lightning, that always was exciting. As they traveled along, she kept occasional watch on the storm front; but the clouds seemed stationary, roiling over and over in turbulence upon themselves but not advancing across the plains. Yet, windy gusts obviously blew south to north instead of the usual west to east pattern.

By late afternoon the rays of the lowering sun reflected on the underside of the storm making the charcoal gray clouds take on a crimson hue. After the sun sank below the rim of the mountains and the bloody hue disappeared, the sky became ominously dark without stars or moon.

Gragnold stirred from his morose reverie as the gloom increased, he seemed revitalized, enjoying the dark. "Ssssss, Pitland border," he pointed a gloved finger as he inhaled. "Ssssmell."

"Yuck, rotten eggs!" Spoena covered her nose. Jeda crinkled her nose at the noisome odor.

Hod-ya's lips curled upward in a rare smile and Gragnold hissed in pleasure.

Mileer corrected Spoena. "Not eggs, my dear, powders. Yellow powders used in the smelting of black iron ingots that are delivered to forges throughout the empire. These yellow powders are what give our black swords their strength. You'll get used to the smell of brimstone; it's the smell of Pitland. See those smoky billows? The smelters of Pitland are hard at work. Most of the prisoners we're escorting will find themselves slaving away what's left of their lives in those mills. Those billows rolling into the atmosphere demonstrate the empire's strength."

"Those aren't storm clouds?" Jeda stared at the undersides of the roiling clouds.

"Most who come this way mistakenly think so at first, but look again, we should be close to the descent, ah yes. Look up ahead. See where the land falls away? That's Land's End Cliff. There's a narrow trail carved out of the cliff face, a mere track-way, leading down to Pitland. This is where Carnalia ends and Pitland begins. Pitland is a sunken land below the level of Carnalia, Craniantium, Eroton, or any of the other minor duchies and fiefdoms comprising the empire. The only Carnalian access, which is guarded by the White Priestess' Castle, is this narrow cornice-road carved out of the rock face."

Jeda stared longingly back toward the meadow in the nearly lightless trail behind; they were, indeed, on the verge of a sheer cliff that would take them away from that cheerful grassland. And worse, what she'd thought to be refreshing rain clouds were actually billows of dense, sulfurous smoke.

The preceding wagon suddenly dipped sharply downward and out of sight. Before she knew it, she pitched forward as their wagon's front axle crested the descent. Jeda braced both hands against the side-rails as she peered out over the wagon's sides at the shadowed lands below with spots of flame scattered about. She was suddenly sick to her stomach. They were perhaps a thousand or more dizzying feet above Pitland on the narrowest of trails—without any guardrail. The stench intensified so that she had to release one hand from the rail in order to cover her mouth with the hem of her skirt. Spoena did likewise.

Gragnold and Hod-ya, however, gulped in the horrible stench, savoring the taste and smell. Mileer seemed neither to despise nor enjoy the pungent atmosphere. The further the dray descended the smokier it became, burning Jeda's eyes and obscuring Pitland's detail except for the fires which Jeda guessed to be furnaces.

Mileer chuckled. "Don't worry, girls, the smell diminishes down at the bottom."

"Before I'm done, you'll savor the atmospheric odors of this place," stated Hod-ya. "Look over there, beyond the smelting fires. See the White Castle lit by torches? That's the domain of my sister, Bablo-ya, the White Priestess of Pitland."

"Your sister?" Spoena gasped, learning what Jeda already knew. "The White Priestess is your sister?"

Hod-ya made no reply as Jeda and Spoena steadily gazed at the distant, torch-lit towers reflecting the illusion of being afire. There were bastions on each of the six corners, with a glint of light from each tower's main window. Mid-way between the towers was a breastwork overarching the gates.

"Bablo-ya, you know it should've been mine," Hod-ya muttered barely loud enough for Jeda to hear.

The brakes on the dray screeched, then chattered, then squealed. The horses whinnied as the wagon entered upon the steep decline rolling inexorably downward, running in the ruts formed by centuries of traffic. The driver plied all his skills to prevent the vehicle from careening out of control and ramming the wagons in front.

The dray jolted endlessly, unnervingly over rough bumps that threatened to disassemble the wagon. Jeda peered over the railing from time to time hoping to see how much more of this they had to endure until reaching the bottom, but she could only identify dim, flickering torches through the murk. Leaning out over the sideboard she stared straight down at the wheels and was startled to see the spoked rims were mere inches from the edge; she gripped the hand-rails so hard her knuckles turned white. Jeda finally sat back in her seat and observed Spoena, illumined in the wagon's sole torch, sitting rigid, eyes closed, lips quivering. Taking the younger girl's cue, Jeda closed her eyes but still clenched the rails.

At long last, after an eternity of squealing brakes and endless jarring, Jeda again dared open her eyes and peek cautiously over the edge. This time she discerned human forms scurrying about. "We're nearly down, Spoena."

Gragnold and Hod-ya relished what remained of the fading stench, which had, as Mileer predicted, diminished as they descended into Pitland proper. The wagon suddenly lurched to one side, then evened out with a clunk.

They were in Pitland. Dark shadows hindered them from seeing much except inky waves of murkiness rolling like mists across the roadway, torches on lampstands and overseers with whips driving sweat-glistened bodies of slaves passing close beside their dray.

Spoena snuggled close to Jeda, wringing her hands. "This is far worse than we'd heard, Jeda."

Jeda whispered so Hod-ya wouldn't hear. "He's with us."

Hod-ya sat meditating; when she eventually broke her silence, her voice seemed more masculine, perhaps due to the denser atmosphere. "We'll soon arrive at the castle. When in the presence of the White Priestess, you are only to speak when spoken to. And call her 'Majestic Madam', or she'll feed you to her pet water-dragons, understand? I haven't decided which of the two sisters to train for Scrarth, so your survival depends on currying my favor, which includes being respectful to my sister. Your usefulness to the empire will be determined over the next several days. This much I tell you now; of the three of you that I brought for Scrarth and Avangar, it's probable only one will survive. She will be the Avangar. The Scrarth sometimes receives a lesser title and reward; and other times is a tragic victim. That is the role I cast for your younger sister. Too bad! Someone has to win; someone has to lose. She's a loser. I could see that as soon as she was mesmerized by the fool's wealth I splayed on the table at the inn."

Hod-ya started to turn away, but quickly turned back around and came nose to nose with Jeda. "It would've been so much simpler if you and that other wench, Grend, or whatever her name, were my contestants. Did you not understand what I offered you? She was weak. You had only to defeat her. Now you may not even qualify to enter the arena. Foolish, foolish girl!" She turned away and stared at the castle towering over them.

Mileer studied Jeda as if to see what effect, if any, Hod-ya's rebuke had had. A smirk crossed his lips and an evil glint rose in his eyes. He merely sat, legs crossed, arms folded, leering wordlessly.

Jeda dropped her eyes, unwilling to guess what thoughts his twisted mind harbored.

Spoena leaned close. "Oh, Jeda, I'm so scared!" Her trembling hand gripped Jeda's.

The revelation that she was expected to kill Spoena was inherent in Hod-ya's scolding, deeply unnerving Jeda. What kind of training did Hod-ya have in mind that made her so confident? What kind of sinister power turned friends into vicious combatants anxious for each other's blood? That all three contestants were Ecclessite did nothing to dim Hod-ya's expectations. Was Logon able to deliver them even here, in the halls of such deep, corrosive evil and despair? Did Logon's reach extend this far into enemy territory?

The rest of the prisoner caravan veered left onto another road that led toward the dungeon.

The wagon with Hod-ya and her contestants stayed to the right track and soon drew up to an immense, torch-lit stairway ascending to a towering wall with battlements on either side of the ornate gateway balustrade. A pathway led through the gate and upward to an elevated courtyard and the palace beyond.

The Imperial castle itself stood as an awesome declaration of power, wealth, pomp, and pride. Jeda quailed at the sight of the intricate carvings decorating the ramparts along the top of the walls. She'd never seen the King's Gate Fortresses, but doubted they matched this grandeur. Each section of wall was constructed of three layers of huge, white-stone blocks, each thirty feet square, topped by armaments, crenellations and towers, all bathed in and colored by flickering torchlight.

The driver announced, "This is as near as I go. You are to disembark here."

Wordlessly Hod-ya rose, opened the rear tailgate before the attendants could arrive to open it, making their rush to assist a waste of time and effort. She stepped down out of the wagon stretching her lanky frame. Mileer followed, then Gragnold, who motioned for the girls to follow. Jeda and then Spoena stepped down to the crunchy turf and immediately felt warmth rising through the soles of their shoes. The stifling air after the long, uncomfortable ride overwhelmed their equilibrium.

"Steady there, steady." Captain Mileer took hold of Jeda's elbow. "Here, lean on me. It's cooler in the castle. There's a subterranean heat source around the palace perimeter, but eventually, in a couple of days, you'll get acclimated."

Jeda felt like she was going to vomit but took several deep breaths and controlled the impulse.

Spoena, however, bent over, convulsed and voided the contents of her stomach. Steam rose from the moist matter, adding a new befoulment to the air.

"Come on," said Mileer, leading Jeda and Spoena by their arms from the sizzling vomit. "Best not linger." Then to the abashed attendants standing idly by he ordered, "Clean that up."

Hod-ya ascended the elongated, white marble steps two at a time and upon reaching the top rapped her knuckles on the huge double doors, demanding, "Open up. I'm here."

Guards looked out through a peep hole and upon recognizing her, unbarred the stays, opened the latches and threw open the doors to scurry out and obsequiously bow with the utmost courtesy and deference to her. Then they swung the wood-and-wrought-iron inner gates open. From just inside the inner gateway a trumpeter sounded a fanfare announcing their arrival.

Hod-ya assumed her role with all the solemnity and circumstance of her station, neither enjoying nor despising the effusive attention, but merely filling the role of a "Grand Lady of the Empire."

Mileer attended the girls as they climbed the steps leading up to the castle doorway. "Things aren't what they look like here. It might help if you knew this: the White Priestess' Castle is merely the regional seat of government presiding over Pitland, and as such, no matter how grandiose things may appear inside, the White Priestess is accounted as less important than Hod-ya in the greater scheme of things. Lurcan bestowed upon Hod-ya a lesser title of 'Mistress of Lurcan's Palace' rather than Priestess, for he is lord and master over his own house when in residence, making Hod-ya appear as not much more than a glorified housekeeper, whereas her sister is known as mistress over her own house. Pitland borders Carnalia on the south, and as such, represents the ultimate achievement of Lurcan's intentions for mankind. Thus, Hod-ya's sister, Bablo-ya the White Priestess, has sole regency over her own domain. But in the empire as a whole, Hod-ya wields the scepter and whip."

Jeda and Spoena patiently heeded Mileer's explanation as they were hustled to walled-off chambers just outside the grand reception hall. Jeda overheard a page inform Mileer that a proper ceremony befitting Hod-ya's rank and authority was being arranged.

"M'ladies, please be seated until all is ready to greet you formally. It won't be but a few minutes," said an attendant. Without waiting to be dismissed he scurried away.

"Oh, do we have to go through all this rigmarole?" Mileer paced with both hands clenched behind his back. "Can't we just go in, say hello, get our rooms assigned, and eat a dinner without all this pomp? We've been in the wilds for weeks, endured days and nights of deprivation; not to mention that horrendous wagon ride. You'd think we could just get billeted without all this folderol."

Hod-ya eyed him for full minute. "It's necessary, Mileer. We happen to have arrived on one of the most important events of the year—the recognition and initiation of Scrarth and Avangar. To not to indulge the masses in their expectation of all this pageantry would cause agitation at the least and might possibly cause a major disruption to the government. You'll just have to suffer it. I know you like to be informal with your soldiers, ignoring protocol and living loose, but that doesn't go here and now, understand?"

Mileer rolled his eyes. The matter was settled.

Jeda inspected the bottoms of her shoes and to her surprise found that they hadn't been singed despite the heat she felt come through the soles. "How do people stand the heat out there?"

"A few days here, and you'll feel chilly whenever you leave," Mileer stated. "Besides, this castle sits atop one of the warmest spots in Pitland; elsewhere in this low-lying land, though warm in the extreme by ordinary standards, is somewhat cooler. Erotons never do adjust, however, being born in a much colder climate. They usually expire within a few months. Can't stand the heat. But you," he turned and stared at Spoena, "should do quite nicely, having been raised in the southern marches and jungles of Ra-Amawl."

Spoena sidled close to Jeda, whose arm instinctively went around the younger girl's shoulders.

Hod-ya swooped between them, wrenching them apart. "None of that! You're supposed to be potential Avangars and are not to enter her Majestic Madam's presence clinging to each other like frightened lambs."

Spoena whimpered as Hod-ya's fingernails pressed into the skin of her wrist. "Mileer, you escort this one; I'll take Jeda." Then turning to Gragnold, she said, "You're not necessary for these formalities. The celebrated captain and I are required for protocol. Go snoop around and see what you can find out about Deparis and her contestants, and oh yes, see if you can discover where that traitor, Ugen, is hiding."

Gragnold spun smartly on his heel and departed down the vast hallway, closing the chamber door behind so quietly, that if Jeda hadn't watched him leave she wouldn't have known he was gone. At the other end of the room a full-length mirror hung on the wall beside a gueridon replete with boxes of powder, jars of ointment, and various other cosmetics; Hod-ya took each girl by the chin and examined their features, clucked her tongue, shook her head and muttered, "Pitifully wretched looking, the pair of you; go over there and do what you can to pretty yourselves."

Jeda and Spoena apprehensively approached the floor-length looking glass by the small round table. But they had no need to fear their appearance. The meal and beverage Hod-ya had forced upon them had had a most lustrous effect, producing blushing cheeks and brightening their eyes. Their hair needed more attention than they could give considering the brevity of the moment, but was nevertheless, combed out till it hung straight, attractively framing their faces.

Mileer stepped close behind Jeda as she was nearly finished brushing her tresses. "You needn't attend to such things for yourself much longer. After your victory, servants will be assigned to you to perform your every whim."

Jeda, still currying out the remaining tangles, stared back at the high-ranking warrior's image in the mirror. "Is that what you think I want? To be pampered and spoiled while so many live in misery?"

"You will, you will," he said in a singsong tone as he sauntered to the other side of the room, "after your conditioning."

Jeda shuddered and took one last look at herself in the mirror.

Spoena's wide-eyed glance revealed her fear of Hod-ya's conditioning, too. "I can't fight my sister," she confided quietly to Jeda. "Nor can I fight you. But after they do who-knows-what to us . . . "

Jeda silently mouthed, "Logon." It was the right thing to say, but her own confidence had also been eroded. Was Logon in control here in this wretched land? Why did he seem so remote?

The door opened and a guard entered, announcing, "All things are in readiness, M'lady. If you'd be so kind as to follow."

"Come on," Hod-ya hissed.

Both girls nervously drew near Hod-ya. Mileer took Spoena's arm while Hod-ya seized Jeda's elbow in an iron grip as if she was afraid the girl might break and run. There was a brief trumpet fanfare and the procession began strolling down the middle of the grand ballroom; the attendants led, then following them came the two Cosmopolisian notables all but dragging their hapless contestants to their grand introduction amid the bemused smiles of onlookers.

Dignitaries of elite social classes, as well as political moguls appareled in the finery denoting their office lined the center of the ballroom, bowing slightly as Hod-ya and her entourage passed through the crowd toward the dais that supported an opulent throne against the rear wall of the hall. Hundreds had eagerly gathered and crammed the room for this spectacle to evaluate the contestants for the Scrarth and Avangar duels. On her way inside the grand ballroom Jeda glanced at a wall poster declaring that this year's contest boasted an upgrade from the usual program with the advent of challengers. The Lady Deparis' entries, who were also vying for the coveted title of "Undisputed Avangar of the Realm," would also be exhibited during the initiation rites so the crowd could size up the contestants for themselves.

Lest she faint dead away or else shake uncontrollably, Jeda forced herself to concentrate on placing each foot precisely in front of the other as she had been taught by her mother so long ago. Even so, her queasiness felt like it might still erupt in an embarrassing disaster. She also held her breath without realizing it. The room blurred, then tilted, but she inhaled deeply and regained composure, managing to appear graceful despite being lugged towards the far end of the hall. As the entourage drew closer to the dais Jeda glanced up and paused. There, enthroned upon an ivory dais, sat a dazzlingly beautiful woman clothed in shimmering white robes with a bejeweled crown upon her golden tresses.

Jeda lost all sense of her predicament, so taken was she by this woman's regal presence and bearing; Bablo-ya, so noble-looking, so proud and important, so terrible and fierce, yet grand and glorious.

Hod-ya jabbed Jeda's ribs to get her moving again. Suddenly, before she knew it, she stood at the base of the dais.

"Down, fool, bow down," Hod-ya hissed, interrupting Jeda's wonderment at the vision of ethereal beauty personified.

Jeda recollected her senses and curtsied but couldn't tear her eyes from this magnificent priestess-queen.

A herald below the dais announced, "The Lady Hod-ya kar—, er, of the emperor's own castle in Cosmopolis, capitol of all the realm of Carnalia. And her escort, Captain Mileer, conqueror of the Apos Fields, defeater of the Profetta Corps, destroyer of Evangg, Victor and Savager of—"

"Enough of me already," quipped Captain Mileer striding forward with his hand raised, then bowing to the White Priestess. "Why look at a chubby, gnarled old warrior when such beauty is present? Get to the young ladies. After all, that's what everyone is here for. They've all seen too much of me before."

Titters of polite laughter greeted the self-deprecating captain's comments; the court seemed to be well aware of the captain's disdain for formality.

"Let us do as the captain suggests." The White Priestess clapped her hands and as she did Jeda noted that when she smiled, her Majestic

Madam's front teeth, like Hod-ya's, had been filed to sharp points. The stately woman's glance flitted only once upon Spoena, as if needing no more than a mere glance to take the young girl's measure. Jeda trembled as the priestess turned and kept her visual inspection on her for several long seconds.

"The young ladies, contestants for the esteemed privilege of participating in Scrarth and Avangar," continued the herald, "the young Lady Spoena, of . . . parts unknown. And her rival, Lady Jeda of the house of Kway."

The priestess' eyes riveted on Jeda again. "Kway, as in Lord Kekinor Kway, of Cosmopolis?"

"Yes, M'lady." Jeda was all too conscious of the gawking crowd.

"Your father works in the Ministry of Re-education, does he not?"

"Yes, M'lady."

With a disdainful look the White Priestess demanded, "Hod-ya, as my sister and peer, Mistress of Lurcan's house in Carnalia, you may take certain liberties, even here in my court. However, I must insist that you instruct your contestants to revere and address me properly!"

"They have been duly instructed, dear sister. Methinks they forget themselves due to your overwhelming, inspiring presence."

"Oh?" Bablo-ya's lips curled slightly upward at the corners. "Well, in that case I can find it in me to overlook this breach of protocol; but I insist they follow proper procedure henceforth. Now, what do you know of other matters?"

"A challenger has arisen this year; and also, that infidelity plagues my ranking officers."

The White Priestess lips spread into a wider, wicked smile. She playfully ran her tongue over her pointed teeth. "So, are these your contestants? You are willing to place your reputation, prestige, and position in the hands of these girls?"

"I am prepared to—"

"Hold your answer, dear sister, lest you speak brashly and overcommit yourself. You ought to at least meet your opponent and have a long, hard, evaluating look at her contestants before obligating yourself. Future privileges and positions depend on the outcome of this contest, as you well know. You ought not enter unadvisedly if I am any judge of the contestants you bring, knowing the consequences should your Avangar fail." She raised her gaze to and nodded at the door-tender at the far end of the hall. "Summon the Lady Deparis and her Scrarth and Avangar combatants."

The doorman pulled the massive ballroom door open, disappeared into the vestibule, closing the door behind with a solid *clunk* that resounded throughout the hall. Jeda watched the White Priestess's fingernail trace a numeral "6" on the arm of her throne as she further studied Hod-ya's contestants. Dazzling all onlookers, each finger and thumb on both the White Priestess' hands bore a cumbersome ring fitted with an oversized, diversely colored stone that sparkled brilliantly in the candelabra lighting—with one exception. The ring that didn't sparkle was on the forefinger of her right hand, the digit that repetitively traced numeral sixes in the felt covering.

"Perhaps while we wait, you can enlighten me on another matter, dear sister."

~

Hod-ya drew a deep breath knowing what was coming. "As you desire." Though she resented being treated like a naughty schoolgirl, here in this place, and at this time, she was forced to acquiesce to her sister's petty games. She noticed the numeral that her sister subtly traced corresponded to the stone that no longer sparkled.

"Yes, well, something has, indeed, happened," the White Priestess arose and glided to the front edge of her platform, "about two-and-a-half weeks ago. Do you recall anything significant happening within that time frame?"

"Yes," Hod-ya despised her sister's cat and mouse tactics.

The hushed crowd attuned their ears lest they miss an acid-dripping syllable of this conversation.

"Hmmm, perhaps the subject is too painful. Were you involved in, shall we say, intrigues?"

"Intrigues?"

Fiery glances flew between the sisters. Then Bablo-ya purred, "Let me come to the point. You have, no doubt, noticed that my ruby ring has lost its shimmer, have you not?"

"Indeed, has it now?" Hod-ya feigned noticing the ring for the first time. She could play games, too. If it were the White Priestess visiting Cosmopolis, her sister would be the one ogled by dolts while Hod-ya played denigrating word games. "Are you growing careless, dear sister, in your responsibilities?"

One corner of Bablo-ya's lip curled in a snarl at Hod-ya; then she pressed her inquisition. "Let us concern ourselves with the ring connected with your association," she waved the ring aloft for all in the room to see, "the stone that once reflected Psa's fire seems to have been extinguished. Ten fingers, ten rings, ten dreads. But now only nine rings glow." Bablo-ya advanced another step and hovered over her sister, glaring down at her. "Can you explain why the dread that you contracted to enhance your powers no longer has a representative spark among my rings, dear sister?"

Hod-ya met her sister's gaze. "Can mortals account for immortals?"

"Don't bandy words with me, sister. You know that as the White Priestess, I am charged with safe-guarding and revering the shrines of the dreads, and that I'm responsible that nothing untoward interfere with their homage. It's in my power to ascribe their attentions upon deserving petitioners, such as yourself. But were I to suspect one of the dreads has met an ill fate due to that servant's carelessness, or selfish pursuits . . . "

"The Lady Deparis, and entourage," announced the doorman from the other side of the ballroom returning with three devastatingly beautiful women in tow.

"We'll talk more of this later, sister," whispered Bablo-ya.

CHAPTER FIVE

Jeda eyes turned to where the intricately decorated, double wooden doors yawed open revealing three stunning women as they stepped up to and paused at the threshold of the ballroom; they were garbed in gray, floor-length capes trimmed in luxurious, black fur. Elegance seemed to waft from the three demiurges; the adoring crowd hushed.

The foremost, the Lady Deparis, Jeda surmised because she appeared slightly older, wiser and more experienced than the girls off to either side, was sponsor of the other two. Her beauty was frightening to behold; disdainful arrogance crowned her devastating features. Her oval face with large, expertly-lined eyes and crescent-shaped brows above a delicately curved nose was completed by crimson lips, full and luscious. She was, if possible, more beautiful than the White Priestess. She carried herself with a regal mien, aware of her effect on the stupefied masses. Her svelte form moved effortlessly through the midst of the adoring assemblage with a combination of fluidity and grace of high breeding. Not a hair of her shiny-black tresses that draped down to her waistline was out of place. Her smirk revealed even, polished-white teeth. The Lady Deparis was a vision of ageless, feminine beauty, but such beauty couldn't mask the sinister darkness hidden behind her eyes.

"The Lady Deparis, hostess of the house of m'lord Angra, regent of Craniantium, center of the Intelligentsia Institute."

Polite applause rippled from the swell of the crowd greeting her formal introduction.

Neither of the younger ladies waiting just inside the doorway as much as twitched while Deparis made her grand entrance, not even when she floated past Hod-ya and her dowdy contestants without acknowledging their presence, arriving at the edge of the dais where Bablo-ya waited. Deparis tilted her head forward in symbolic submission and kissed one of the rings on the White Priestess' proffered hand, then stood back and nodded at the herald standing in the back of the ballroom where her contestants waited.

"Contestant from the noble land of Craniantium, vying for the coveted title 'Undisputed Avangar', the Lady Stullo of the house of Demium, daughter of the Grantor of Privilege."

Stullo, with auburn, shimmering, shoulder-length tresses, entered the grand hall exuding the majesty and demeanor of a queen, gracefully moving down the carpeted runway to the dais, her gray cape flowing freely in her wake, hinting at the lithe form beneath her garments. Her green eyes were clear and purposeful, her countenance every bit as beauteous and arrogant as her predecessor. She sauntered past Hod-ya, Jeda and Spoena as if they were shadows. In a low, sweeping motion Stullo extended her hands to either side as her head nearly touched her knee curtseying to Bablo-ya. In a strong, clear voice she intoned, "Majestic Madam."

Bablo-ya grinned in a momentary lapse of self-indulgent glory, casting a disdainful glance at Hod-ya, who bit her lip.

The Lady Stullo withdrew to Deparis' side.

Again, the herald announced, "Contestant from the noble land of Craniantium, vying for the coveted title of 'Undisputed Avangar', the Lady Dalicusi, of the house of Detend, daughter of m'lord high secretary Rep-Orobat."

The final, and from the adoration evident on the faces many, the loveliest vision of feminine beauty entered, pausing with each mincing step, purposely prolonging her entrance, drinking in the admiration of the masses. Her shoulder-length blonde hair swished sensuously with each step, her lissome form strong and confident, her features the envy of every woman in the room, including The White Priestess. Nobility, breeding, intelligence, and shrewdness were met in this terrible young woman's countenance. Only she, of the ladies from Craniantium, deigned to cast a momentary glance in the direction of Hod-ya's bedraggled contestants as she passed. Her bright blue eyes locked with Jeda's for several seconds. She smiled ever so subtly, as if having taken Jeda's measure and was assured of victory. She then made obeisance to the White Priestess, entreating, "Majestic Madam."

The Scrarth and Avangar contestants from Craniantium stood side by side, observing their adorers, gloating in the worship. Deparis, meanwhile, finally studied Hod-ya's entrants, sneering in undisguised disdain.

"And these," Deparis addressed Hod-ya, "are your qualifiers?" She stifled a laugh with her fist and winked at her own contestants. They, in turn, smiled condescendingly at their counterparts. Deparis declared, "Really, Hod-ya, I'd have thought you could've selected better contestants than these." She again suppressed a haughty laugh.

Hod-ya's lips narrowed to a thin line and her eyes became hostile slits. "Obviously, Deparis, my sister has kept some information from you. These are not my only contestants. I've not quite decided which of my challengers are to enter Scrarth and Avangar. Bablo-ya, why haven't you informed my distinguished opponent of my other entry?"

Doubt crossed the Lady Deparis' brow even as the expressions of her contestants changed perceptibly. "Other?" Deparis' eyebrows arched .

"Yes, sister, what 'other' are you talking about?" demanded the White Priestess.

"Oh, come now, don't tell me you're unaware of my first entry? I sent her on ahead so she'd get acclimated. One of my dronnets escorted her."

Bablo-ya pursed her lips and touched her chin with thumb and forefinger as she regarded her sister. "You're serious, aren't you? I've not been informed that anyone has come either yesterday or today with a dronnet, and certainly not a Scrarth and Avangar contestant."

"Are you sure?" Hod-ya's hands trembled. Her bluff was collapsing.

Jeda knew that Artil wasn't even considered by Hod-ya as a contender, but, if anything was expected of her, it was to defer. Jeda raised her eyes to Hod-ya's face and instantly discerned the witchy woman's ploy was to have Artil's mysterious existence unsettle Deparis and her challengers by keeping them guessing whether this unknown contestant was so beautiful, strong, and shrewd that Hod-ya chose to keep her under wraps?

Deparis stepped forward, shoving Hod-ya aside. "I demand to meet this unknown contestant. The protocols declare—"

"There's nothing in the rules about exhibiting one's contestants before the event. It isn't necessary, after all, to reveal one's skills and strengths to her opponents," Hod-ya retorted. Hod-ya pushed Deparis away and reacquired her position before the dais. "Bablo-ya, what do you mean my other contestant hasn't arrived? She must have! I sent her with an escort before the wagon train from Willow House departed, the wagon train of prisoners you insisted I escort, dear sister. I knew I shouldn't have conceded to accompany that prisoner train. Now one of my potential contestants has been delayed. I insist the duels be postponed so I can find out what's become of her."

"Majestic Madam," entreated Deparis, turning to Bablo-ya. "This is just a delaying tactic. Now that she's seen my candidates, she realizes how poorly she's chosen and wants to commission her dronnets to fetch another, more suitable combatant. I insist the terms of engagement be followed; let the activities proceed. The final two weeks of training and rituals yet remain to be accomplished. That ought to provide Hod-ya sufficient time for search parties to find the errant contestant, if she's wandered afield or been delayed by some pursuit of pleasure—if such a candidate even exists."

"She makes a strong case, Hod-ya," Bablo-ya conceded, concealing a smirk.

"It was due to compliance with your request that my contestant was misplaced," Hod-ya growled, approaching the dais, nudging Deparis aside again. "You know that Mileer can keep no secrets from you. Ask him."

"Mileer, my fabled warrior," cooed Bablo-ya. "Come, look into my eyes, tell me, is what my sister says true?"

Mileer was drawn to the dais gazing adoringly at the woman who would never be his and yet held sway over him. Chills ran down Jeda's spine as she beheld the power the White Priestess held over Mileer.

"It's true, Majestic Madam. Every word." Mileer couldn't help but blurt out. "Another lass was sent ahead of us from Willow House Inn. But she was hardly—"

"Enough said," Hod-ya intruded. "You heard, Bablo-ya. It would be revealing my strategy to say more, and that is breaking the rules. I quote: 'No sponsor shall be required to reveal any secrets in advance which may affect the outcome of Scrarth and Avangar.'"

Bablo-ya returned to her throne and sat, considering the appeals before her. "Hod-ya, you have two extra days to find your lost contestant. Forty-eight hours, no longer, for the season of Walloweven must begin at the next high moon. The dreads themselves will be present to observe this year's consummation, for the war against Carnalia's enemies is escalating and should soon be over and done. And this year's Avangar will be consecrated with the blood of captured foes."

A murmur of approval rumbled through the crowd.

Dalicusi approached the dais and curtsied so low that her silky-blonde hair nearly touched the floor.

She maintained her humble pose until Bablo-ya intoned, "Speak, Lady Dalicusi, you have ought to say?"

Dalicusi rose, squared her shoulders, arched her back. "If it please, Majestic Madam, may I put forth a question?"

"Now, here are courtly manners, Hod-ya. See to it that your contestants learn some of this." Then to the petitioner, "Ask what you will, Lady Dalicusi."

"I mean no disrespect," Dalicusi turned to face the assembly, "and I only wish to honor the will of your ladyship, and my sponsor, but how is it that these sacred ceremonies of devotion to Lurcan are allowed to be sullied by the inclusion of an Ecclessite?"

Hod-ya growled lowly.

Deparis whispered, "You go too far, Dalicusi!"

Ignoring her mentor, Dalicusi kept her eyes on the White Priestess, waiting an answer.

"No, let her speak, Deparis. I'd like to know of what she speaks. Go on, child. Speak your mind."

"Begging your dreadful madam's pardon, but I know, by the arts I've mastered and the cusps that contact me, that this golden-haired slip of a girl here," she pointed accusingly at Jeda, "has a spirit indwelling her that's not of this empire. She is an Ecclessite!"

A collective gasp rippled through the hall.

Jeda felt frumpy enough already, arriving in this august ceremony in her traveling duds without the added accusation of being a detested enemy. She and Spoena were clad in what was left of their outer skirts and blouses of the Runer brigade. The skirt hems were tattered and muddy, smudges mottled their blouses and their shoes were likewise soiled and scuffed. Their faces, though clean, weren't highlighted with feature enhancing eyeliners, lipsticks, cosmetics and powders; they appeared plain and dull compared to the startling beauty of the Craniantiumites.

Dalicusi continued. "Whether Mistress Hod-ya actually has another contestant lost somewhere out in the wilds, I don't know. But as I entered, I took the liberty to evaluate the one I assume will be my opponent in the ultimate combat. As our eyes locked, my guides alerted me to the entity within her. It is a spirit hostile to all the freedoms and privileges the empire holds dear." She curtsied briefly and backed away.

Bablo-ya rose, her formerly crimson lips a pale pink line, her eyes were as if she were trying to bore holes through Jeda's eye sockets.

Jeda fixed her eyes on the floor, not daring to look up.

"Logon," Jeda whispered, "I come to you."

"Look at me, girl," demanded the White Priestess, restrained outrage seething with every syllable.

Jeda slowly raised her eyes, feeling glowering hatred from every corner of the great hall. The White Priestess stepped down off the dais and approached. Hod-ya's original scrutiny when Jeda had been inducted into service in the emperor's palace paled in comparison to what she now faced.

Bablo-ya stood menacingly before Jeda, her foul breath filling Jeda with abhorrence. "You dare bring that presence here? Look at me, girl!"

With a courage not her own, Jeda lifted her head and stared unblinkingly into those beautiful but savage eyes.

Jeda never saw the hand coming that raked her cheek. The White Priestess' splayed fingernails were flecked with fresh blood. Crimson trickled down Jeda's cheek, but she never blinked.

Bablo-ya turned away and commanded a nearby guard. "Bring the iron implement that reveals. We'll test her here and now."

Within minutes two guards hustled forward and presented a pillow with a coverlet overtop it to the White Priestess. Beneath the coverlet bulged an object. Bablo-ya ordered, "Secure her hands behind."

Bablo-ya's guards wrenched Jeda's arms painfully back in a vise-like grip.

The White Priestess turned her back; Jeda couldn't see what she was uncovering. The coverlet fell to the floor; Bablo-ya waved her hands over the implement, chanting:

"Dreadful hosts, invoked by name,
Come protect this whitened flame,
Allow no sorcery of this tool,
To infect with mind of fool,
Vanquish all your cursed foes,
Come blind and bind and now expose."

Bablo-ya turned around with both hands raised overhead; the hidden implement, suspended in her hands dangled down behind Bablo-ya's back.

Jeda, unable to bear the suspense, shut her eyes. She whispered, "Logon, whatever happens, I'll not deny you."

Something cold, sharp and hard briefly touched Jeda's neck. There was a collective gasp from the crowd and the iron implement was lifted.

Jeda opened her eyes a slit. Bablo-ya's arms were again raised high overhead, the iron object still dangled behind the White Priestess' back, as if she were about to split a piece of firewood with an axe.

Jeda went numb; her head was the chunk of firewood; it seemed Bablo-ya was intent upon dividing her in half! She shut her eyes tight, not wanting to see the descending blow.

Time slowed; Jeda heard several people inhale sharply, the White Priestess' garments rustled with the motion of swinging the implement, steel whistled through the air . . . Jeda braced herself, expecting Logon to welcome her to his father's house in another instant.

~

Bonu stepped into the creek bed, his Child of the Stars at the ready. He peered through the dense underbrush. "All clear."

Bushes parted and Scung slid down the embankment to stand beside his mentor. Then Bletza, slightly out of control, slid down, squealing at her rapid descent.

Scung caught her. "She be's awright."

Bonu listened to the forest for a full minute before replying. "You really must stop unnecessary noises. We're not safe yet, if we ever will be again."

"I'm sorry, I . . . I just didn't expect to slide so fast."

Bonu nodded then turned and headed upstream. Bletza followed with Scung bringing up the rear. They trod on wide, smooth stones both above and sometimes below the water's surface, leaving no discernible trail. The gurgling stream tumbling over rocks covered any splashing sounds they couldn't avoid making.

Bonu found a deeper pool, and after a few minutes study, took advantage of two trout lolling under an overhanging bank, deftly flipping them out of the water with swift sword strokes. The scent of fish frying was too risky, so, after cleaning the innards and deboning the fish, they chewed the meat raw. Bonu briefly considered touching their swords together to cook the fish, but since there were only two swords, and Scung's didn't have much light, dismissed the idea. It was their first meal in two days. The trout were bland but gave their bellies something on which to gnaw.

The stream meandered, making their trek longer than if they had simply gone overland, but Bonu was determined to leave as few tracks as possible. Bletza, unskilled at broken-ground travel, might inadvertently leave traces of their passing which any skilled tracker could read.

Bonu had, on his visit during the night to Captain Varter, related his exploits, including the dread attack and his foolish intentions of rescuing Jeda. Varter was intensely interested in the description of Voronon, for, he explained, strange things had happened to many of their pursuers. There'd been a host of enemy soldiers hot on their trail as they fled, but after a few miles only a few straggling pursuers remained, and those were crazed with fear. Varter also related that they'd taken in three disoriented Carnalians, pierced their hearts, and sent them immediately to Logon's Rock.

"How much longer?" Bletza pleaded. Alternately wading through foot-sucking mud flats and waist deep currents had depleted her strength.

Every now and then Bonu turned to examine Bletza: clumps of hair strewn across her face, cheeks smudged and flushed, gasping for every breath, soaked garments weighing her down. She wouldn't be able to keep to the pace much longer even though the day was fresh. He wiped his brow and took a careful fix on their location. "Scung," he said at long last, "do you think you can carry her without leaving tracks?"

"Over the land?"

Bonu nodded.

"Well, fer a while, anyways."

"It'll be another two, maybe three hours or more if we stay in this streambed. If we go overland through the jungle, we can be there in little more than half an hour."

"I kin handle thet."

"Are you sure?"

"Yep."

"Hey, nobody asked me if I wanted to cling to his back for half an hour." Bletza bent over gasping for air.

Bonu shrugged. "It's your only option, Bletza. Personally, I don't care whether we slosh all afternoon through this stream or not. But I don't want to spend another night in the wilds without provision and protection. Ra-Amawl has been tolerant so far, but I don't want to push our luck. Besides, there's bound to be Carnalian patrols. And don't forget, there might be another dread on the prowl. The sooner we get to brigade the better. So, what's your pleasure? Follow the stream, or let Scung carry you?"

Bletza slapped a mosquito, sized Scung up again and shrugged her shoulders. "Oh, I might as well."

"Hmph! Do me no favors. I only watched over yer all night, keepin' yer safe so's yer needn't be afeered."

"Yes, you're right, please forgive me. It's just that, oh, I don't know what's the matter with me. I am grateful."

"Look, if'n yer don't trust me—"

"No, it's not that."

"Then what's the objection?" Bonu stared into Bletza's eyes.

"It's just that he's . . . that I was raised . . . that Erotons are, you know."

Scung's face flushed.

"This is about his being Eroton?"

"Oh dear, this is so awkward. Can you explain it, Scung?"

Without turning around Scung said in a low voice, "Yer prob'ly don't ken, Bonu, bein' raised up in one o' Logon's brigades most o' yer life, an' taught ter accept people fer who they was. But they's summat o' people whut taught their children ter hate a man jest cause o' his breedin'. I seen this afore, though I hoped it might be different wi' Logon's brigades."

Bonu faced Bletza squarely. "Is that it? Because he's Eroton? Splendora, woman! If we accept or reject people based on what they were before they met Logon, why, the whole unity of Ecclessa, precarious as it is, would dissolve. Have you forgotten when you first went to Logon's Rock, how you touched the rock and died? Whatever is left over of your old likes and dislikes should have been discarded at the base of that cliff. Logon put his life in you and he'd never dislike anyone, especially not based on what they were in Carnalia."

"I know. I guess I just forgot." Bletza hung her head

"Well, what's it going to be? Wade or ride?"

"Now I ain't so sure I wants ter be carryin' someone whut's prejudiced."

"Now don't you start."

"I means it, Bonu."

"Then you're just like her."

"Like her!"

"Like me! I think not!"

So caught up in their discussion, Bonu failed to pay due attention to a shadow creeping through the undergrowth toward them.

"Yes, that's exactly the way of it. You, Bletza, think of Scung as below yourself because he was born Eroton; while you, Scung, raise yourself above Bletza's biased upbringing, condemning her. Can't you see? You're both judging each other based on external things and not respecting each other. You've become judges with lurcanish motives, both of you! Logon will have none of it. Nothing you were in the past should ever count in Logon's kingdom, only what you're becoming. I'm ashamed of the both of you."

Scung's head drooped, but Bletza stared Bonu eyeball to eyeball. "Aren't you judging us?"

"Yeah whut about thet?"

"Yeah, Bonu, what about that?" came a voice from behind a hedgerow.

Scung and Bonu whirled around, while Bletza, startled at the intruding voice, slipped on a stone and nearly fell headlong into the shallow creek trying to run away and hide.

"Vawella! What, are you doing here?"

Vawella smirked. "Anyone could've come up on the three of you, arguing and accusing each other. Just be thankful I've probed the bushes for refugees and happen to know the area. I haven't seen my father in three days, but I assume you've come across him and know where you're heading?"

"I caught up with him last night. Uh, let me introduce Bletza, lately of a Nutherway brigade, but she'd been to Logon's Rock in the past."

Bletza nodded as she climbed up out of the creek bed.

"Indeed? Have you been to Logon recently? Or was it before you became a Nutherway brigader?"

"Before."

"Bonu, I don't know if this is well advised."

"I told your father all about it. He'll make a final disposition. And this is Scung, formerly of Captain Mileer's regiment, now freshly from Logon's Rock. A most dependable and honorable fellow."

"Pleased to meet you, Scung." Vawella vigorously took his wrist and gave it a pump. "In case you didn't catch it, my name is Vawella."

"Captain Varter's daughter," Bonu added.

"And I don't mean to snub you, Bletza; it's just that I've never heard of anyone who once knew Logon, then joined a false brigade like the Nutherway and then came back to Logon. I was under the impression it was impossible to—"

"Your father will decide," Bonu broke in. "Meanwhile, perhaps you can explain why you're parading around out here like a warrior, doing a man's job. I seem to remember, even when we were children you always competed with me, boasting of your accomplishments. Up to your old tricks, eh?" Then to his companions, "Our friendly rivalry goes back to childhood."

"Maybe," Vawella answered. "Or maybe it's just that our ranks have been so ravaged that those who can do a job, provided it's not proscribed by the runes, are the only ones left to do it. At any rate, I'm adept at scouting and other woodland skills, so here I am. The two seasoned warriors my father has with him are needed to defend the brigade in the event of attack. Besides, I'd be willing to bet I finally managed to best you in something."

"We're not in a competition, Vawella. I know you're accomplished at hunting, tracking, dueling and such. You don't have to prove anything."

Vawella smiled teasingly. "Afraid I might finally have outdone you in something, Bonu? Just for old time's sake, I'd be willing to put my best feat alongside yours and let Scung and Bletza judge if I haven't bested you."

"This is foolishness. Let's just head to camp, all right?"

"Ah-hah! You're afraid I finally beat you at something." She lightheartedly baited Bonu.

"Okay, suppose we compare our so-called greatest feats, then can we go to camp? You lead the way, since you obviously know these parts."

"Agreed. Are you ready for this? I slew a Craniantium lion! Can you believe that? Of course, it was already wounded. I just happened to be there at the right time. All I did was split its skull after it was already helpless. Still, I bet that beats your best." She smiled brightly, adding, "Still think I shouldn't do a man's job?"

"Vawella, really? You killed a Craniantium Lion? I'm impressed. You win. Let's press on to the encampment now, okay?"

"First, you've got to tell your greatest victory, just so I can gloat. Craniantium lions rate a little higher than tophets in some circles, you know."

"Very well, if you insist on this silly game . . . I guess I'd have to say my greatest conquest was, hmmm . . . a dread. Can we please go now?"

"Come on, Bonu, I'm serious. I finally manage to beat you in something, and you shrug it off, making jokes."

"It be's no joke, Vawella. I been there an' seen it. In fact, I rescued him from certain death jest the second arter he done it."

Vawella blinked and opened then closed her mouth several times, eyed Bonu suspiciously, then smiled. "A dread? Really? Which one, do you know? You fulfilled the prophecy then? Bonu, I don't know what to say."

"Say 'this way to camp'."

CHAPTER SIX

"You never did answer our question, Bonu," said Bletza, pushing through the dense greenery behind the lieutenant. Scung hadn't needed to carry Bletza after all, for Vawella revealed a stone-littered pathway that left little to no sign of their passing.

"What question is that?"

"Weren't you judging us for being judgmental? Weren't you, as you put it, 'become a judge with lurcanish motives,' too?"

"I been athinkin' 'bout thet an gots summat ter say." Scung brought up the rear swishing a broken-off pine bough behind him to remove any inadvertent tracks.

Bonu sighed. "Go ahead, Scung. You might as well voice your opinion."

"Well, me an' Bletza was usin' whut we seen in each other ter hurt one another; an' thet be's judgin'. But Bonu seen we was harmin' each other, an' thet we was defendin' ourselves. So he intervened by showin' usn's our true motives. He whar tryin' ter help us'ns, whiles we was tryin' ter hurt each other, so as I sees it, he warn't judgin'."

"That's it exactly, Scung," said Bonu. "Logon doesn't want us to shame or cause harm or elevate ourselves at another's expense. On the same rune that says 'criticize not lest you be criticized' however, he does urge that we use discernment. Apple trees produce apples; that's how we know they're apple trees."

"But how can you be sure when it comes to people?" Bletza held a limb from back-swishing on Scung. "It's such a fine line."

"I'd like to hear the answer to that one," ventured Vawella, glancing around to check the patrol's progress.

"Simple. When I'm not really concerned about another's well-being, only my own, I'm judging. When I'm concerned for others well-being regardless of my own status, risking my own safety, reputation or even my relationship with them, I'm being discerning. Criticism exalts self; discernment seeks to lift up others. Discernment is a special ability Logon gives to those who prove reliable in such matters."

"Makes sense to me," said Vawella. "Now, pay close attention, we're almost there. Once through this hedgerow you'll see the cliffs." She parted some densely-leaved branches and broke through the foliage barricade revealing the cliff caves.

They broke through and gawked at the towering, vertical rock. Pockmarks, crevices, and niches were etched onto its sheer wall as it rose some two hundred feet above the forest floor like a sentinel standing watch over the marshy bog.

"Home," Vawella announced, then cupped a hand over her lips and *chirred* like a squirrel.

A warrior appeared in the opening of an upper cave, waved his sword, then withdrew back into the recess behind him. A moment later Captain Varter appeared in the same entry leaning on a crude, tree-limb crutch. He waved, clearly glad to see his daughter and also that Bonu was with her. Two or three other kingsmen emerged from the dark cavern and stood alongside him.

"Amazing, isn't it?" said Vawella. "And the best part is how we get up there. Follow me."

"It looks so impregnable." Bonu was astounded by the cliff's sheer defense. "A frontal assault by an enemy up the wall certainly would render the attackers vulnerable to heart thrusts as they attain the ramparts. Amazing!"

"Kin yer scale it?" Scung studied the perpendicular rock.

"We haven't found a way yet," said Vawella with a hint of secrecy. "But I discovered a labyrinth inside the wall when I dodged a squad of Carnalians. I ducked into a hole in the base of the cliff and found myself in a virtual, honeycombed maze of tunnels behind the cliff face."

"You've become an accomplished scout, Vawella. I'm impressed."

"The cliff is full of caverns, some going up, some going down, though most lead downward to water. Many caves are dead ends, but I happened to run into the only one that leads to a greater complex of tunnels that heads upward and behind the vast stone front.

"My pursuers were baffled at my disappearance and soon left off the chase, so I took the liberty of exploring passage after passage, realizing it would make an excellent base of operations. Come, let me show you."

She disappeared behind a screening thorn bush that covered the entrance. Her voice teased from inside the entry. "Oh, come on, don't be afraid; the thorns don't hurt much, you big, strong men."

Bonu followed first, then Bletza, and finally Scung, mumbling, "I doesn't cotton ter this, no-how! It be's unnatural ter live in holes like critters. I doesn't trust this no-how!"

As they entered, light from their swords reflected off shiny mica deposits on the stone walls and floor of a small grotto. Vawella confidently led to one turnoff after another. Several minutes later after bypassing a dozen side-tunnels the pitch of the cavern floor inclined slightly upward.

“Vawella, have these passages been thoroughly scouted?” Bonu stared down the tunnel into one while passing its yawning entryway.

“I would assume so. I haven’t searched it all myself; I’ve been busy out in the jungle rounding up stragglers. But I’m sure my father had it reconnoitered before finally establishing it as our brigade site.”

“Yes, I’m sure he would. It just seems so, I don’t know, I can’t put it into words.”

“I kin, it be’s downright spooky!”

“Come now, Scung,” Vawella chided. “Your sword will put any spooks to flight. Nothing of that sort can hurt you.”

“Spooks hain’t whut I means. I means summat o’ Lurcan been here, though it been a long time ago.”

Vawella paused, turned, and held her sword close to Scung’s face. “Now how would you know that?”

Scung craned his neck studying the surrounding walls and ceiling. “I don’t rightly ken how, but I kens.”

“Dreadmoot!” Bonu said softly.

“Dreadmoot?” Vawella said. “That was long ago, if it ever really happened. Most brigade captains assume that rune is mythological.”

“So did I, once. But lately I’ve encountered many things once thought mythical. Like Jeda said—”

“Uh, Bonu, I’d better tell you something about Jeda. She disappeared the day before we were attacked. We think she and two other girls were captured, possibly tortured to reveal our brigade’s former location, which, we assume, is how the enemy found us.”

“Jeda didn’t fall into Carnalian hands until three days ago. I accidentally stumbled across her trail while scouting. I’ll tell you about it later.”

Vawella studied Bonu curiously. "Okay. At the nightly council fire we'll hear each other's exploits. By the way, I hope you've been paying attention to the turns we've been taking, you'll need to come and go without guidance."

"Oh dear, I haven't," moaned Bletza. "I've been occupied just trying to keep up."

"Well, I'll instruct you later. Have you two been paying attention?"

"I have," said Bonu, "but I'm still a bit confused."

"Me, too," agreed Scung. "Mebbe yer could mark each passage so's them thet doesn't learn too quick kin find their way."

"Too dangerous, Scung, Lurcan's agents are capable of discovering the subtlest signs. Our best defense is in the multiplicity of choices confronting invaders. We're so limited in number that we'd be overwhelmed if they attack *en masse*, no matter how valiantly we fight. Their confusion in these tunnels is our ally."

"Can't we rest? The climb is so steep," begged Bletza.

"No need. We're there." Vawella turned a corner, drew aside an animal hide that served as room divider and entered.

Cries of welcome echoed through to outer chambers. Bonu followed Vawella, trailed by Scung and Bletza. The soft light of many swords lit the inner chamber. Captain Varter and two other warriors rose to their feet. Only the captain leaning on his makeshift crutch and suspending his left foot bore any sign of injury. His knee was wrapped in a bloodstained cloth.

The chieftain greeted his lieutenant with a one-armed embrace, then stood back to examine him. "Well, you seem none the worse for the wear, Bonu. Who are your companions?"

"This is Bletza; as I mentioned, once a follower of Logon seeking to renew her relationship. And this," Bonu smiled, "is Scung, the man who saved my life."

"Bletza, we'll do what we can for you. But I'm not sure how much that will be. Nevertheless, we'll try. Scung, it's a pleasure to meet you. You saved the life of a very dear friend, not to mention a valued and trusted servant of Logon. You alone out of all that company received Logon's amnesty, eh?"

"'T'would seem so, sir."

"That's a tragedy. So many perished, so many. What a grief! Come, come, have some food, I'm sure you're hungry."

"Indeed." Vawella stood silhouetted in the doorway of a larger, daylight-lit room that exited to the outside world. Many animal skins lay scattered on the floor and a pile of firewood garnished a corner in preparation for a nighttime council fire. As the newcomers settled in one of the men went to the opening off the main room, calling softly, "Come meet our new brother and sister."

Children filed into the room, seven in all, ranging in age from three to eleven.

"This is all that's left?" Bonu asked, aghast.

"Oh no," said Varter. "Their parents and a few others are bivouacked in other rooms of the cave complex, or else out foraging. But as you can see, our numbers are depleted."

Strips of dried venison were handed to each new arrival along with a cool, refreshing cup of water. Bonu tore off a morsel of meat with his teeth as he listened to Vawella's report.

She'd scouted the immediate area, finding only Bonu and his party this last time out.

When Vawella finished, Captain Varter told them that most of the caves had been explored, finding dozens of niches and hollowed out rooms suitable for habitation. Plans were underway to camouflage those caverns. If Carnalians ever did find the main entry, it would still take hours, even days, to discover all the Ecclessite hiding places.

Bonu eyed the kindling and small logs in the corner. "Is it safe for a fire?"

Varter smiled. "Apparently. Smoke drafts backward into tunnels too small to crawl into. We discovered that just last night when we lit a fire so the children would be comforted. The smoke was drawn down into that crevice." He pointed at a crack in the rear of the cavern. "Put your hand there; you'll feel the draw. So, we lit a bigger fire for warmth and cooking. We're too high for anyone on the jungle floor to see its light if we keep it back far enough from the opening."

Bonu nodded. "But you haven't searched all the caves yet?"

"Not yet. We can't spare anyone from foraging yet, but Kyleah reported that Logon gave her a word that we should settle here. So, even though we haven't investigated the place properly, we're assured this is as safe a place as any. Perhaps you'd like to perform that detail for us, Bonu? You and Scung—"

Bonu waved his hand. "I must go after Jeda, with your leave, sir."

"But surely if what you've told me is true, she's beyond your help. I don't mean to be insensitive, Lieutenant, but, well, we've all been through upheaval and loss lately. You've got to know when to let go. If, as you say, Hod-ya and several of her dronnets have taken Jeda to Pitland, no good can come of throwing your life away in a lost cause. You're needed here, man, not off on some hopeless venture. There's no way Jeda can survive Pitland's Scrarth and Avangar duel. Either she'll refuse to participate—and suffer the consequences or will forfeit Logon by becoming one of them. I'm sorry to speak so bluntly, but you must face the facts."

"I can't accept that those are the only alternatives. Logon must have something else in mind. Before I left to go scouting on my own, Jeda told me that she felt Logon was going to use her to accomplish something that no army of warriors could accomplish. That only the unsuspected frailty of an innocent, young woman could slip beneath Lurcan's defenses to do Logon's work in the most infernal of places, the White Priestess' domain of Pitland."

A man and a woman entered the main room and caught the gist of Bonu's conversation. The woman interrupted, "If I may speak, captain?"

"Kyleah! Throll! You're back. Anything to report?"

"A roamer appeared while I was gathering berries."

"Yes?"

The eyes of all turned to the woman and her husband as they seated themselves.

Kyleah spoke. "I was talking to Logon about Throll's missing daughters, Artil and Spoena, while foraging. Suddenly a picture filled my mind. I saw square, white stones upon stones, all very large, white stones arranged like the seating of an arena. Suddenly a crack split the arena floor open; flames and lava spewed forth. Riding on the crest of the magma flow I saw five people on a raft that neither sank nor burned. Something huge and angry pursued them." Kyleah finished. "That's all."

Several moments of silence followed.

Captain Varter sighed and finally broke the quiet. "What do you suppose that means?"

Kyleah shrugged, looking to her new husband.

"There's only one arena in all the empire fitting that description; the Scrarth and Avangar arena," said Throll. "We think Spoena and Artil were taken to Pitland, and that Logon is somehow going to deliver them."

"Artil and Spoena, as well as my own beloved Jeda, are indeed captives. They've been taken to Pitland. We were just now talking about a rescue attempt." Bonu shifted his gaze to Captain Varter who was deep in thought.

Throll looked up, face flushed with indignation. "My daughters are in Pitland? They're just children. Logon couldn't possibly want them there, mission or no mission!" He rose from his seat and stalked to the entrance overlooking the bog. "Why would Logon require that of mere children?"

Captain Varter stretched out his wounded knee and checked the bandage. "Throll, it's not only rebellious but dangerous to criticize Logon's ways. Besides, your wife saw five escapees. Kyleah, did you happen to see who those five were? Were your step-daughters among the escapees?"

"I couldn't even tell if they were men or women, children or adults."

Throll leaned with one arm against the wall, still looking out over the jungle.

"I take Kyleah's vision as a hopeful word, a confirmation, captain. Let me go," Bonu begged.

Throll spun around. "You're going to try to rescue Jeda? Let me come. Two of us will have a better fighting chance—"

"We have no sure confirmation of what Kyleah's vision means," said Captain Varter. "And it's out of the question, Throll. I need both of you here. I'm sure many from our brigade have survived and are still wandering aimlessly about, lost in Ra-Amawl. If they're not rounded-up and brought here soon they'll perish. I'm unable to do more than direct operations from here, due to my injury, else I'd be out day and night 'til all possible survivors were secured."

Bonu pleaded. "Captain, I beg you. Jeda will survive. I believe Kyleah has seen the beginning of Pitland's destruction, which, may I remind you, is prophesied in the runes. I survived a duel with a dread; so, who's to say Jeda won't survive Scrarth and Avangar, bringing down the White Priestess with all her abominations in the process? I beg of you, let me go."

"And me," Throll added, stepping fully back into the room.

"No, Throll, you'd be too concerned for your daughters. You'd be a liability," Bonu objected.

"And you wouldn't be too concerned about your sweetheart?"

"Throll, what would your remaining daughters and I do if something happened to you?" Kyleah implored. "Captain Varter needs you here. You're a seasoned warrior, well acquainted with helping those in need and defending those in danger. I need you. Your remaining daughters need you."

"Heed your wife's cause, Throll," advised Varter. "Entrust Artil and Spoena to Logon's keeping. Bonu, I don't quite know what to say."

"Say yes, Captain. It's Logon's will. I'll be able to lead them back here when their mission is done, otherwise, they won't know where to find us."

"When their mission is done—if that's even the meaning of Kyleah's vision. According to the runes, the final battles begin only when Logon's bridge falls into Carnalian hands. That's when King Elyon will unleash powerful roamers bringing his fury. There will be little need to bring survivors here or anywhere. The end of all things will rapidly follow."

"I doubt Logon would show me such a thing," Kyleah intruded, "unless he intended those survivors to have somewhere to go. And even though the Tremendum, as the ancient seers called it, the end of all things might be starting, that doesn't mean the world will suddenly dissolve. Perhaps there will be respites between judgments, giving many a final opportunity to accept Logon's amnesty. I think, since I was specifically beseeching King Elyon on behalf of Artil and Spoena, that Throll's, that is, our daughters are among those five survivors. I admit, there are many prisoners in Pitland, and possibly it's some of them that I saw escaping. I don't know. But I think, I believe Bonu should go."

"Your opinion is highly regarded, Kyleah. Nevertheless, these are difficult times. We need every able-bodied person here. I wish I could release you, Bonu, but . . . "

Those seated around the circle heard Bonu's teeth grit.

"Honor me in this, Lieutenant," Varter urged, pulling rank as an appeal to Bonu's sense of duty. "If Logon reveals anything different to me, you'll be the first to know."

Bonu caught Scung glancing at him.

Captain Varter struggled to his feet, leaned heavily on his crutch. "Right, then. Bonu, you and Scung gather some more firewood to see us through the night. Throll, you and Kyleah tend these children while I get some sleep. I've been awake since this time yesterday and need to rest."

Bonu and Scung stood and made their way to the entrance. Emerging from the cliff tunnels Scung and Bonu scavenged dead wood for well over an hour from around the edge of the bog. The two of them lugged several bundles of branches and stored them just inside the main entry.

After dumping his load in a corner Scung grabbed Bonu's shoulder. "If'n yer wants ter take off, I'll cover fer yer."

A smile crossed Bonu's lips. "No, Scung. I'll follow orders. Logon wouldn't have me disobey the chain of command. If I'm to attempt a rescue, Logon will make a way. If I were to go off on my own . . . I'd never have the confidence of Logon's help; when an attack came, I'd be full of doubts, not trust. Voronon taught me a valuable lesson and I intend to profit from it."

Scung shrugged and broke some long branches into shorter pieces across his knee.

Scung and Bonu went back out and gathered two more bundles of sticks, and by tying sturdy leather thongs to secure the bundles and mounting them on Scung's broad back they bore their burden up through the tunnel maze where it divided between family groups. Older children carried the wood to their respective family rooms while Bonu and Scung ventured out to gather yet one more load. By dinnertime enough wood had been stored to supply each family and individual for several nights of burning.

Outside near a thicket Bonu took one last look around before retiring to the cliff when he spied a sleek hart stepping from cover not twenty yards away nonchalantly munching cat-o'-nine-tails. Bonu silently un-slung a borrowed crossbow from his shoulder and in one swift, fluid motion cocked, notched a dart, aimed and fired, providing several days' worth of meat.

Bonu and Scung entered the caves bearing a stout branch from which the stag was suspended. Women immediately set to skinning the carcass while the men honed their knives preparing to divide the meat into strips to be smoke-cured. Bonu and Scung washed the gore from their hands as Vawella started a fire of hickory wood and wild apple for smoking the meat.

"Don't it need ter be brined first?" queried Scung. "I hain't never seen meat be smoked thet warn't first brined."

"We have very little salt, Scung," Vawella explained, "but we'll braze the meat with our swords before we smoke it. It'll be preserved and will taste just as good."

"Hmph, not to a Eroton!"

Bonu stretched out by the fireside, his fingers interlocked behind his head. Anguished though he was, he resolved to let Logon settle the matter of Jeda's rescue; he'd not pester Captain Varter. He laid his head wearily on a folded deerskin and closed his eyes.

Sometime later, a gentle touch to his forearm roused him from his late afternoon nap. Captain Varter's bearded visage beamed down.

"Go find your Jeda, Bonu. Logon spoke to me as I slept. It's his will that you find her, if you can. But understand this—there are no guarantees. You might not succeed; or if you do, there's no certainty that she'll still be, that is, that they won't have corrupted her, or even that either of you will return. He also told me that the final battles for mankind will soon begin; your unmaking the dread was one of the initial fulfillments in a chain of prophetic events. If you and Jeda survive, you'll face even tougher battles in days to come, tougher than facing the dread and more sinister than Scrarth and Avangar."

Bonu sat up and stared into Varter's eyes. Then without a word, began jamming belongings into his rucksack.

"Don't leave now, Bonu. Morning light will come soon enough."

"I don't want to waste a moment."

"I understand, but you'll waste more than a night if you leave in your present exhausted condition. You need a full night's rest. Besides, you may find tonight's rune study interesting. It has to do with you rescuing Jeda, I believe."

"Me and Jeda?"

"Your duel with the dread was mentioned in the runes, though we didn't understand until after the fact. Why should you think it strange that Scrarth and Avangar might also be subtly mentioned?"

"Well, I mean, the runes were established from of old, and we're living, well now."

"The final runes will be revealed to be reality at some point in time. Ought not those who have a part in the fulfillment recognize their roles?"

"But—"

"I'll explain later. For now, rest. You'll need greater skill and stamina than ever. And you'll need to be especially sensitive to the Advisor's slightest suggestion. We'll soon eat the evening meal, roast venison, thanks to you. Then we'll have rune study before retiring to our quarters. You'll sleep in mine tonight."

Scung plopped down beside Bonu. "I be's goin', too!"

"Now just a minute—" Varter objected.

"I'd like to have him along, captain. I know he's a novice in the ways of the runes, but he's a fast learner and a loyal friend."

Captain Varter watched sparks spiral to the back of the cave as they burst from the burning, green, fruit-wood branches. At last he said, "All right. Not that I wouldn't like to have you here, Scung, for your strength would be of immeasurable help as we make this dwelling secure. Nevertheless, though Logon said nothing specifically about you,

I believe you're called to his service, in fact, as I say this my heart wells up; you will have great cause to rejoice before all things have drawn to an end. Go with my blessing and serve under Lieutenant Bonu; he's a wise and capable teacher."

Scung grinned, then turned to Bonu. "Kin we take other weapons, or jest the swords?"

"We'll likely encounter varieties of beasts, so we'd best be prepared. Too much weaponry will slow us down though, and speed is of the essence."

"Right. I'll make yer yer own cross-bow an' darts."

"You can make them overnight?"

"Didn't I never tell yer? I be's the best crossbow maker outta twenty divisions. Me an' me brother was good at makin' things wi' our hands. Jest give us an idee, an' we'd find a way ter git it done. It'll be ready come mornin'."

"Make sure you get enough sleep, too, Scung. Bonu will need you."

"I'll git 'nuff sleep whiles soakin' the wood ter bend inter shape."

Bonu lay back down and watched his unlikely protégé depart back outside to find just the right saplings. Then he drifted off to a light sleep, dreaming fitfully of fending off cusps, tophets, and dreads. Hours later a cool hand touching his brow woke him.

Kyleah announced, "Mealtime, Bonu."

Bonu sat up; all around sat the remnant of the Runer Brigade eager to partake of the meal. The venison was delicious, served with wild leeks, mushrooms, and various mashed nuts. But Scung was absent; a dish had been set aside for him. After the others had eaten, the first filling meal Bonu had eaten in over a week, Captain Varter withdrew his sword. Most of the captain's blade was now aglow, with only a few dull spots left. The sword glowed brightly in some places, though other portions were barely lit, but the increased, luminous effect of the sword in the darkened cavern was notable.

"Let clean-up go until after rune study," said Captain Varter. "I want to get right to it; some of you are weary and I want to make sure everyone learns this rune. Look to the runes that tell the tale of Vadiv."

"Vadiv, wasn't he the first overlord of Supplan's armies?" Throll gripped his toller and held it just over the sword.

"Actually, no! Vadiv replaced Lusa, the first kingly ruler of Elyon's people. And it is that precise rune which I want to discuss tonight. Look to the raised rune that says:

'First in the call, first to the fall,
Out from the law, chased to the wall . . .

"Do you all have the place?"

They nodded.

Bonu was familiar with the story and wondered if maybe he shouldn't retire so he and Scung could get an early start. But Captain Varter had said this study would be of particular interest to him and his mission to rescue Jeda, so he'd wait and see.

"Now," Varter commenced, assured that all were listening, "follow along on your own swords as I toll:

'To grant the fighter's heart's desire,
Elyon searched for souls afire,
Lusa the tall, magnificent, grand,
Provided emblem for Elyonites stand,
And gifted was he to lead the fight,
Against all foes midst Lurcan's night.
But Lurcan the crafty, seduced Lusa low,
Tricked him to pride spawned from below,
He acted as if great Elyon cared not,
For established laws he dared to blot,

The seer voided Elyon's gift,
Kingship now to another would shift.
To the house of Ben Sejje seer was sent,
To call forth a man with bent to repent,
The youngest of seven, Vadiv by name,
Anointed, appointed to win Elyon fame,
Lusa discovered and chased Vadiv out,
A rival put Lusa's heirs in doubt.
Two Elyonite armies fought 'gainst themselves,
While Lurcan's grim servants dug deeper delves,
Rejected king Lusa, jealous, outraged,
Lusted for blood, thus mortal war waged,
Fled Vadiv the valiant, though not from fear,
But loathing to fight the king he held dear.
Through mountains and pastures, o'er meadow and dell,
'Crost rivers and swamps, and jungles where dwell,
Fierce creatures violent and spellsters of spite,
Fled Vadiv the promised, the conqueror of night,
To cliffs of great depth without escape plan,
Verging on dry, hot, blistered land.
Cornered was Vadiv, with all his brave men,
Lusa closed in to slay ten of ten,
Then Vadiv stood up and buried his swords,
Daring king Lusa, "Do as your words,
I'll not raise hand 'gainst Elyon's own king,
I'll not be guilty of so foul a thing!"
Thus Lusa was shamed and turned from his will,
Vadiv was chosen, to succeed him, not kill,
He left off following Vadiv that day,
But forfeited his throne as Elyon did say,
Buried swords of Vadiv, remain as an oath,
A reminder to all to not break a troth.'"

CHAPTER SEVEN

"THET BE'S IT? I DON'T hardly git no special meanin' outta thet!" Scung dumped a handful of shafts and flint arrowheads on the stone floor. He had slipped in shortly after Captain Varter began reading the rune tale.

"Ah, yes, well," said Captain Varter, "you have to know the story of Lusa and Vadiv for the full impact."

Bonu tugged his beard to cover a yawn. "Yes, but captain, I know the story well, yet I don't see any particular importance either."

"Since you know the story so well you ought to have some clue as to the locality where Vadiv was caught and surrounded."

"I never thought about it. I just figured it was only necessary to know the lesson, not the actual location where those events took place."

"In most cases you'd be right. But this rune makes a diversion from the norm that I myself wouldn't have seen had not Logon revealed it to me. As it turns out, this rune has quite a bit to do with the predicted end of the age, although, it isn't meant in a predictive sense, but rather, in a provisional way. Vadiv and his men buried their swords," he paused for effect, "at the bottom of a sheer cliff."

"Yes, declining to fight against Elyon's anointed overlord. So?"

"Those swords have never been unearthed so, they're still buried, wherever that was."

"As a reminder to not to break a troth. So?"

Captain Varter smiled and turned to Throll, asking, "You, a former scout, know these lands as well as anyone in our brigade. If you had to guess, where would you say these swords are buried?"

"Well, if Lusa chased Vadiv through Ra-Amawl as the rune says, or some nearby vicinity, which seems to be what you're hinting at, and since the rune indicates a cliff, it could be where we now are. Are the swords buried out in that bog?"

Varter threw his hands up in frustration. "No! Does that bog look hot, dry, and blistered? Think, man, think. Where else are there high cliffs?"

Throll's face went blank for minute, then lit up. "The only other cliffs of any notable size are on the edges around Pitland."

"Exactly! And where are multitudes of Ecclessites held captive, defenseless, stripped of their swords?"

"Pitland!" exclaimed Bonu and Throll together.

Captain Varter sat back, folding his arms, smiling broadly.

"So, if I understand you, Scung and I, are to go to Pitland's bordering cliff and dig up the swords Vadiv and his men buried, and then what?"

Captain Varter leaned forward. "Then it'll be up to Logon to show you, Lieutenant. I suppose it might have something to do with arming whatever captives you liberate and organize into an irregular brigade; then set out to rescue Jeda before she's taken into the arena. Something like that, only let Logon show you. Don't presume to know how he wants it done. Mind you, this is all speculation on my part, not certainty. But I believe Logon revealed that Vadiv buried those swords somewhere along the base of a cliff in Pitland. Not ever having been to Pitland, I don't know the topography of the land except that it's below sea level and excessively hot and dry. But now you at least have some idea of your objective. Had you not waited . . . " Captain Varter shrugged. "Who knows what time you'd waste slogging about?"

Bonu stretched his arms overhead and yawned. "Unless you have any more revelations, I'm off to bed." With that, he rose and withdrew back behind the animal skin covering of Captain Varter's chambers, spread out his bedroll and lay quietly, envisioning the mission before him.

Bonu could both see and hear those who remained by the fire through the gap underneath the hanging skin. The murmur of soft voices in the main chamber gradually abated as various individuals retired to their own sleeping quarters leaving Scung and Captain Varter alone.

Scung had shaped enough shafts for twenty crossbow darts as Captain Varter explained the rune; a pile of shavings lay scattered about Scung's feet.

Captain Varter seemed fascinated watching Scung finish shaving the branches, smooth, balance, refine and fit them with tips and fletching in such a short time.

"You're a fine craftsman, Scung."

Scung looked up briefly. "I outfitted most o' me comrades, gettin' 'em ter pay me so's they didn't hafta make their own. Thet's how I got mosta me scrip fer ale." He paused to stare blankly into the fire. Then shook his head. "Well, them days be's gone fer ever!"

"Well said." Varter patted him on the back. "Don't dwell on those days; such reminiscing can become a snare."

"How could I ever go back? I loves Logon too much." Firelight reflected the moisture in Scung's eyes. He picked up another shaft. "'Twas likely my arrows an' darts whut kilt summat o' yer friends an' kin." He looked up briefly then down at his work.

"Does that bother you?"

"Summat."

Varter rubbed his injured knee for several moments, then in a hoarse voice said, "I forgive you."

The Eroton dabbed at his cheeks as if chasing away a bug as he squinted to see what his fingers were doing.

Captain Varter slowly rose, patted Scung's shoulder again and hobbled toward his quarters. "Goodnight, Scung."

Scung's lips trembled; his hands were stilled, his massive shoulders quaked as he hunched over his handiwork. He buried his head in his hands. He didn't see the twinkling column drift in through the cave opening and hover over him as he wept. He dabbed at his eyes again and carefully laid the shafts to cure on a makeshift rack over low, glowing coals. "Please Logon, keep these darts from harming any people." He stood and made his way to Captain Varter's quarters where a rolled-up animal skin awaited his weary bulk.

Bonu smiled, rolled over, and closed his eyes.

~

Bonu awoke refreshed and anxious to get underway. He went through the previous night's council room to the opening on the cliff and peered out at the bog. Glowing vapors of a violet hue that sometimes occurred around swamps and during thunderstorms had collected on reeds and cattails poking up out of the water. The sky had turned cobalt blue; sunrise was yet an hour off. Stars from various constellations blinked, as if winking at the nocturnal doings of Ra-Amawl's night denizens. Bonu stared at the stars, breathing petitions to Logon and inhaling the morning air. His thoughts dwelt on Jeda for several moments, then other concerns occupied his petitions, not only for his and Scung's journey, but for the brigade, for kingsmen who were lost, killed or injured, for Artil and Spoena, for those orphaned, and the bereaved. Last of all he fervently appealed for Logon himself to return and make all things new.

A movement in the reeds along the shoreline across the bog caught his attention. He unsheathed his sword and lifted the handle to his chin so the tip pointed outward. He gazed across the blade's azure haze and was able to identify human shapes hidden behind dense undergrowth across the bog. He cautiously lowered and re-sheathed his weapon.

"Whut be's yer seein'?"

Bonu flinched. "Scung! You nearly startled me into jumping off the cliff! Don't sneak up on me like that!"

"Sorry. Whut be's yer lookin' at?"

"I think there's a war party across the bog, or a troop of gorrils. Can't be sure, too foggy, too much undergrowth to get a good look, but something's afoot."

"Should we wake the cap'n?"

"Hmmm, I think not, at least not until we know if this bodes danger for the brigade. Let's investigate."

"Whutever yer says."

"What's all the commotion?" Vawella, her sword drawn, appeared at the inner doorway.

"Nothing. Scung just startled me, that's all."

"I think yer'd best be takin' a look at this, Vawella. They be's a war party or summat out acrost the bog."

Vawella peered through the opening. "A war party? Where? I see nothing."

"We don't know for sure."

“Look, Bonu, don’t hide anything from me. We’re in too much peril to worry about needless alarms. Is the brigade in danger or isn’t it?”

“I don’t know. We were just going to investigate.”

“I’ll come along.”

“Out of the question.”

“Uh, Bonu, I thinks mebbe she oughtta come. If’n it be’s nobbut ter be worryin’ ‘bout, it be’s no problem an’ we kin keep goin’, but if’n it be’s summat dangerous, she kin return and inform the cap’n. Either way it’ll be good ter have a extra sword.”

“I don’t know . . . ”

“Let me put it this way, Bonu,” intruded Vawella, “you can’t very well stop me. I’m a civilian, even if I am the captain’s daughter, so I’m not expressly under your chain of command, and I do have my father’s permission to scout around as much as I wish.”

Bonu considered for a moment. “Well, it’s on your own head, Vawella.”

“There are dangers out there . . . Would you like me to lead, Bonu? I know a path across the middle of the bog, unless you and your side-kick want to chance wading through who knows what all, not to mention creating a racket?”

“Lead on,” Bonu’s frown relaxed. “Just, when we get close to the other side, I’ll take the lead.”

“We’ll see, lieutenant. There are things you don’t yet know about this marsh.”

Scung lifted the cured darts off the drying rack. “Yer cross-bow be’s by the entrance, still dryin’. It’ll be two, mebbe three days afore yer kin use it.”

“It’s done already?”

The Eroton nodded.

"Sheath your swords so we can sneak out without revealing the entry," Vawella cautioned as she led down the corridor. "Two hundred paces or so to the left there's a stone pathway across the swamp. It meanders some, so pay attention or you may end up in the drink. By the way, when we get near the far side don't stare into the water."

"Why?"

"I don't know much about it myself, except that a sentry roamer warned me that if I ever crossed the stones at night, I should ignore any apparitions manifesting beneath the water's surface."

"Roamer, whut roamer?" Scung's eyes widened. "Yer means a bright doncher?" He came to a standstill.

"Brights, roamers, what's the difference? Hey, Scung! Come on! They're on our side, y'know," Vawella chided.

"Vawella's right, Scung. You have nothing to fear from brights, or roamers as Ecclessites call them. Roamers are what tophets and cusps were before the latter rebelliously disgraced themselves and followed Lurcan. Now, Vawella, what sentry roamer?"

"The one that taught me the path across the bog. Come on, Scung, you've nothing to fear."

"That's an order," Bonu said. "I hate to pull rank, but it's for your own good. Besides, it's not likely we'll even meet this roamer, is it Vawella?"

"Well, he guards the deeper pools on the other side that I spoke of, making sure his charges don't escape. So, we might encounter him."

"I hain't a-goin'!" The giant dug his heels in again.

"All right then, if that's what you want, stay here." Bonu turned Vawella around by her shoulder whispering, "Lead on."

"Hey! Where be's yers a-goin'? Don't leave wi'out me, Bonu?"

"Vawella and I are crossing over, Scung. If you're coming, get a move on. If not, head back."

"Oh, Logon, have mercy! Please don't let the bright be out there!" The Eroton grudgingly followed, his knees quivering like pudding, his breath shallow gasps. "Oh me! Whut be's I gettin' inter?"

They left the tunnels and pushed their way through the camouflage thicket. Scung kept muttering to himself, even as he stooped over to pick up the crossbow he'd deposited. "Please, please, please don't let the bright be there. I don't care if'n they be's on yer side, Logon, I jest ain't got no hankerin' ter be seein' one. Some other time, mebbe, but not today!"

Bonu chuckled. This champion who intimidated so many by his size and fierce countenance, who feared neither lions, dronnets nor dreads, nor being outnumbered dozens to one, was terrified of meeting a friendly entity from a higher plane of existence. Of course, such encounters weren't everyday occurrences, even for Ecclessites. And, roamers weren't to be trifled with. In his many battles with cusps and tophets, Bonu learned that although disgraced and banished, they still possessed the powers of illusion and deception, and so, he respected their potential and former position, though certainly not their choices. How many tophets had Logon given him victory over? Thirty? Forty? He'd lost count, yet he never took an encounter for granted. He'd seen their potential to wreak havoc all too clearly when unprepared or over-confidant kingsmen dueled them. Carnalians were right to be terrified of brights, so it was no wonder that Scung was loath to meet one.

"How long did you say 'til my cross-bow is dry, Scung?" Bonu attempted to distract his friend.

"Er, a day or two. It be's a little damp yet, but a coupla days oughtta cure thet. Then we kin string it an' try it proper. I got yer darts all but done, too."

"Yes, I noticed."

"Shh, quiet now," Vawella advised, veering left along the cliff base.

"Phee-yuu!" Bonu put his hand over his nose. "That could gag a rat. Smells like a tophet!"

"Swamp gas. That's why tophets smell the way they do, I guess, being formed in the mother of all swamps. I guess Carnalians smelled that and thought tophets were nearby and avoided this area."

"Phee-yuu! I'll say!"

Vawella compressed her lips and made a buzzing sound to mock her companions.

The three pressed on, guided by rays of light streaking above in the growing morning sky and the fading glow of faraway stars. Vawella located the trailhead easily, seemingly stepping out on top of the brackish water. Bonu and Scung stood astonished as she launched out step by step atop the waters. "Well, come on," she turned about and chided. "Don't you see the stones?"

"Stones?" Bonu asked. "Uh, no, I don't, do you Scung?"

"Nuh-uh!"

"Oh, for Splendora's sake! Shift over to the left a little more, where I stepped off the bank then you'll see the dark spot in the watery reflection. Step out then you'll see the next one."

"Yer means I hain't able ter see the next step 'til I takes the first one?"

"Exactly."

"Me thinks not!"

"Come on, Scung," urged the captain's daughter.

"Bonu, I hain't a goin' out leap-froggin' one unseen stone ter another. Brights be's one thing, but fallin' in swamp water, thet be's another thing entirely."

"I have to agree with Scung, Vawella. This is riskier than we bargained for."

"Fine. I guess I'll have to scout out the mysterious movement in the undergrowth myself. See you back at the caves." She headed across the swamp hopping rock to rock.

Before Bonu knew it Scung brushed past him and jumped to the first rock. "Hain't no woman gonna show up the 'Scourge o' the Southland', even if'n I be's retired."

Vawella's chuckle echoed back.

Not to be outdone by his recruit, Bonu apprehensively stepped on the dark spot in the watery reflection, following the Eroton's example. He immediately saw the next rock silhouetted against the shimmering reflection near a clump of saw grass. Upon attaining that, he saw the next. "How would you ever do this on a cloudy night?" he called softly to Vawella.

"With your sword tip close to the water. Believe me, having a glimmer of light from the sky is easier." In the middle of the wetlands she waited atop a large flat rock. "From this point on," she instructed as they drew near, "don't doubt me, please. I know what I'm doing. Just follow my instructions."

In single file they leapt stone to stone, one after the other, crossing the marshy expanse in a zigzag course. Ten minutes later the three of them stood side by side on a sizable, flat rock sticking out a few inches above the water, but still a hundred paces from the shore.

"I ain't jumped so much since me trainin' days," panted Scung, stretching his back then leaning his hands on his knees.

Vawella drew a deep breath then explained, “That was the easy part. From here on the stones are harder to locate; some are even just below the surface, oh, and turtles often rise for air in this part of the marsh, so don’t accidentally step on a turtle shell. Falling into these waters would prove disastrous. There’s also quicksand, flesh-eating fish, venomous snakes, underwater weeds that’ll entangle and pull you down—I’m not frightening you, am I?”

“Oh, no!” said Bonu.

“Course not!” Scung’s eyes were wide, furtively staring at the surrounding dark waters.

“Good, because that’s not the worst hazard. Closer to shore waterwights are the most treacherous things here; in this last stretch to shore is where they’ve been imprisoned since before Mada and Ivi walked the world. The good thing is that turtles don’t go among them, so there’s no chance of mistakenly stepping on one and falling in.”

“Waterwights?” Bonu regripped his sword handle.

“I don’t know exactly what they are; sometimes they look like one thing; other times they appear altogether different. The roamer told me that they’ll be released at the end of the age, but until then his assignment is to make sure none escape from their prison beneath this bog ahead of time. They’ll do anything to draw your attention hoping you’ll lose concentration and slip and fall in the water so they can devour you. The first time I saw them they looked like ancient monsters from another age speeding upward with jaws agape, as if to leap right out of the water at me. The roamer told me not to look at them. I almost lost my balance and, had I fallen in, would have been devoured.”

“I know of nothing in the runes about waterwights,” Bonu said.

"The roamer said they have something to do with the mystery runes."

Bonu shook his head. "I don't know, Vawella, there's so many events happening from the mystery runes . . . I believe the destruction of Carnalia is coming very soon."

"Lookit! Whut be's thet out yonder?" Scung pointed through the mists to a diaphanous light gliding across the bog toward them.

"That, my friend, is a roamer," said Bonu.

The column of twinkly lights veered straight for them passing through clumps of saw grass and overtop stagnant pools.

"He's the sentry," said Vawella. "Don't fear him, but don't offend him either. And remember, Scung, he's on our side."

The encroaching daylight in the sky muted the roamer's twinkling presence making it somewhat transparent as their surroundings grew lighter. A sudden rattling noise alarmed Bonu—until he discovered it was Scung's teeth.

"Scung, be still," said the lieutenant. "You'll alert every living thing within a league."

Scung clamped his hand to his chin.

The column of lights stopped within an arm's length. "Why do you tread this dangerous course?"

Vawella answered, "Movement was spotted on that side of the bog."

"You understand that I cannot lend assistance nor stray from the jurisdiction of my assignment should you have need. My sole duty lies here; I can in no wise leave this post. Should my watchfulness lapse for even a moment these rogue *kyllorn* in my keeping would escape before their time, wreaking great havoc."

"Then if you can't assist, can you at least tell us what's over there?" asked Bonu.

"My full attention is ever on the foul *kyllorn* beneath this water barrier. I know of the movement you mention, but that identity hasn't been revealed to me." The roamer paused as it rotated a few degrees and faced Scung. "You have misgivings about me."

Scung's teeth chattered again.

"He's a new recruit freshly won, with much to learn," Bonu explained.

That seemed to satisfy the roamer, for he turned back, paying Scung no more mind. "Vawella, the hour of ending my duty here draws near. How soon, I cannot tell, but it is near. Come not this path again if you see a great fiery glow rising in the midst of the swamp. An enemy *kyllorn* will soon fall from the realms above to wrestle with me and liberate his minions, releasing a scourge upon mankind such as has never been, nor ever will be again."

"When?" Vawella pressed.

The roamer ignored Vawella's question and turned to Bonu. "Your motives lieutenant are mixed; but despite your weakness attracting peril, Logon allows your mission to proceed. Even so, you must seek the Advisor's assistance to set aside personal desires lest they cloud your judgment. Then, and only then, will you find cause to rejoice. Otherwise, great woe will befall you. Now I must return to my duties. The defiled denizens below are aware of your approach and have planned special greetings for each of you. Ignore them. Whatever you see will be lies."

The column of lights drifted a few feet, then hovered near Vawella. "I have enjoyed our conversations in recent days; though I still do not comprehend why he is so devoted to you humans so as to become one of you and die for you. None of my order understand that." It then disappeared.

"I seen it, but I doesn't believe it." Scung marveled. A smile crossed his features. "I seen a roamer, an' he be's good, an' gentle, an', an' wise! Why hain't yer never told me how good they be's?"

Bonu nodded vacantly at Scung but was too busy trying to decipher the roamer's personal comments to him to answer.

But the Eroton didn't seem to mind; he had encountered a roamer and survived.

"We'd better get going if we intend to use what remains of the pre-dawn to cover our scouting," urged Bonu. "Lead on, Vawella."

Without another word Vawella sprang to a rock that had small ripples lapping onto it. She sprang to the next; Scung followed, and finally, Bonu. Mandatory silence was understood. The stones weren't inconveniently placed; however, they were smaller in size than on the first leg of the crossing.

Vawella paused, holding one foot aloft as she balanced the other on a rounded stone.

"What is it, Valwella?" Bonu's whisper carried across the watery surface.

"They're coming; I see a luminous disturbance rising from the bottom. Don't be frightened Scung if you see creatures with hideous grins and bulbous eyes glaring up at you."

The smooth, watery surface all around Vawella rippled then turned into a roiling turbulence that threatened to rise up and wash over the rock she balanced upon. Vawella fixed her gaze on the next stone in line and leapt, calling back over her shoulder, "Best not to linger; don't let them transfix you," as she lightly landed and proceeded to the next.

Scung became distracted. He saw beautiful colors blending and flowing into each other, creating hues beyond description. Then, when the patterns had his undivided attention the colors changed into objects, gradually taking on familiar faces of people he'd known. He was startled when he saw himself, then suddenly realized he was looking at his twin brother. Events that no one else knew unfolded before his startled eyes. He couldn't tear his eyes away from the scene of his brother's death at the hands of an enraged kingsmen mob. How did these *kyllorn* know? How could they re-create every detail of that awful day when he'd fled in terror as his brother called for help? How did they know how much he wished he'd gone to his brother's aid, and was even now tempted to jump in and rescue him from the mob? The over-attention to detail reminded Scung that this was a vision and not the actual events. He had almost been drawn in but found the will to pull his eyes away before the temptation overcame him.

A column of twinkling lights hovered just above him.

~

Bonu squinted, searching intently for the next steppingstone, deliberately keeping his eyes off the watery surface. He noted when Scung momentarily slowed his pace, then resumed. There appeared nothing unusual in the waters beside the recruit and Bonu thought perhaps the waterwights weren't going to test him. For the briefest of moments, he glanced down but saw nothing in the water. Looking ahead, he saw Vawella taking a final leap to the swamp's bank. Scung trailed a few paces behind. Bonu still had some twenty or so stones to go until he reached solid land. He mentally marked the next stone; in that momentary lapse he accidentally glanced down to make sure his foot would land on the rock; but his glance also encompassed the water around the rock. That was his mistake, for there waterwights had been lurking, hoping to whet his curiosity. The bait they used to lure him was the most cunning of all.

Bonu saw Jeda beneath the ripples, all alone, chained hand and foot to a wall. In his mind he heard her pitiful cries, "Help me, I'm in such pain. Help me."

Bonu froze. He saw clawed fingers crawling toward her as if to rip away at her flesh. She screamed in terror . . .

"It's a lie, Bonu, pay it no mind." The roamer hovered beside Bonu.

Bonu broke free of the trance and looked up. The last thing he saw as he tore his eyes away from the vision were angry, writhing serpents with human faces, sneering at the roamer who was already drifting away. Bonu rubbed his eyes and took one last bearing on the stones and leapt non-stop from one to the next until he stood beside Vawella and Scung.

Scung and Bonu glanced briefly at each other, sharing the embarrassment that their most intimate thoughts had been exposed. Vawella, who'd glimpsed but ignored the waterwights had no such discomfiture and was ready to get on with the mission.

"Bonu, take the lead."

"Uh, oh yes, well, let's get on with it. Hmmm, it's getting lighter. We'd best slip into the cover of the thickets."

Down on hands and knees Scung followed Bonu into the shrubbery, trying to avoid back-swinging branches. Vawella, on a parallel path, was more adept at maneuvering through the jungle's flora and ably kept a watchful eye to the rear.

Sunrise broke over the plateau's rim. Bonu located and focused on attaining the intruder's camp, belly-crawling to the perimeter from where he paused and observed the peaceful setting. Slumbering people lay scattered about near a campfire. Were they lost? Were they hunting Ecclessites? Did they know about the cliff and its hidden passages just across the swamp?

Not far away Scung had chosen his own trail and now nestled into cover, also with an overview of the encampment. Vawella remained several paces away from the camp's perimeter in case it became necessary to beat a hasty retreat and alert her father.

The fog was lifting off the surrounding environs; the spies' vision became clearer by the moment; the still air above in the trees kept the branches motionless. Bonu silently parted the bushes and pondered the calm weather as he watched the sleeping forms snug beneath blankets and pelts. They weren't all bedded down in the same large clearing making it impossible to tell how many were littered about beyond this fern bed, or that bush, or behind those trees. Concerning him more was the absence of pickets, for it wasn't protocol for any brigade—Carnalian or Ecclessite—to not post a watch.

One of the sleepers threw a blanket back, sat up, and extended his arms as he gave a raspy yawn. Eroton by the look of him, and rather large, though the lifting mist under Ra-Amawl's canopy still diffused the light, making it difficult to discern more detail. The man sat quietly for a moment, smacking his lips, a sound that carried as far as Vawella on her remote outpost. The man stiffly rose to his feet and prodded other sleepers nearby with his foot. "Get up sleepy-eyes, day be's a-wastin'. We gots summat unfinished business ter attend ter this mornin'."

From every direction stragglers awoke and wandered into the campsite to partake of a common breakfast. They came groaning, scratching, stretching and yawning—men, women, and children, quite unusual for an empire brigade, even an Eroton brigade.

Scung tossed an acorn at Bonu to get his attention, then shrugged, as if asking, "What's this?"

Bonu raised his eyebrows in answer and returned to studying the assembly. Some younger women kindled a fire while older ones rattled up cooking utensils preparing to cook a meal large enough to feed the entire group. A few men retired to one side, talking in subdued tones too far away for Bonu to hear. There were nearly twenty-five fighting-age men, again as many women, and a dozen or so children. One of the men with brawny arms and broad chest stood out among the circle of men. He leisurely extracted a splotchy Child of the Stars and began tolling, verbally encouraging the others to do likewise. Most of those seated around him on the ground barely had their sword tips alight, though a few had runes aglow in various places along the blade.

CHAPTER EIGHT

A COOL, METALLIC OBJECT AGAIN touched Jeda's scalp. Upon opening her eyes, she beheld Bablo-ya's gloved, double-fisted grip holding a Child of the Stars replicating the glow she'd invested in her own sword. The touch to her person called the blade and runes she'd tolled to life.

Bablo-ya stepped back, snarling. "Hold her tight. Don't let go."

The vise-like grip on Jeda's arms tightened. Jeda winced.

Bablo-ya spun around on her heel and glared. "Hod-ya, what's the meaning of this?" The Ecclessite sword was again a dull, unsharpened gray, having lost the momentary glow.

"Now, sister, before you jump to conclusions—"

"Jump to conclusions? Jump to conclusions!" Bablo-ya's eyes bulged so wide that Jeda wondered that they didn't pop from their sockets. "You bring an Ecclessite, and not just a Tipster, an Ecclessite who has spent time with . . . him? And you tell me not to jump to conclusions?" Bablo-ya paced to her throne, then stormed back pointing her bony finger with the dull ring at Hod-ya. "You may conduct experiments within the realm of Carnalia, dear sister, but here you are in my realm. Need I remind you that this is Pitland? I am priestess! You may court danger as much as you like in your own land, but not here. Flirting with danger by putting Ecclessites on your staff! The idea! I touched her with the cursed thing. I put all my strength into splitting the wench in half down through the middle—and it protects her, changing my strongest strike into a mere tap. Have you lost your mind? Or are you committing suicide? How dare you perform sacrilege against our hallowed ceremonies?"

Hod-ya strolled coolly to the base of the dais and stood unflinching before her crimson-faced sister. Then she turned and stared at the surrounding mob of angry faces. But there was something else, there was a sense of intrigue in their eyes almost as strong as their outrage. "None of the foregoing, Majestic Sister. It's my plan . . . "

Bablo-ya's eyeballs swiveled left to right without turning her head; her sister had piqued the crowd's curiosity. Bablo-ya changed her demeanor. "Explain." She retreated and sat on her throne, once again calm and collected, though her cheeks still exhibited tinges of purple.

"Well, this ought to be good," Deparis remarked snidely, arousing a ripple of titters from the crowd.

Watching these women of power parry and thrust at each other with insinuation and innuendo, Jeda's mind reeled as she realized this, too, was a life and death struggle. Suddenly given insight, Jeda briefly sensed Deparis' vulnerability of being disadvantaged; the cruel sisters possessed recognized titles, which she lacked outside of her own limited realm. But Jeda also was made aware that Deparis was no slouch when it came to vying for domination, especially in this opening ceremony in the grand ballroom of Pitland's palace.

Hod-ya ignored Deparis and addressed the White Priestess. "Any fool can bring a girl skilled in selfishness and ambition to Scrarth and Avangar, but I have come to demonstrate my ability to break an Ecclessite's loyalty and instead, conform her to my will."

Deparis, her words caustic, twirled around and commented aside to her contestants but loud enough to echo off the walls, "I hope the 'lost contestant', isn't as big a disappointment as this Ecclessite." Then she turned back to face the sisters.

Bablo-ya leaned forward, glowering. "Hmmm, have you any more surprises, Hod-ya?"

"Indeed, I have, Majestic Madam. Touch the other girl with that cursed sword too, and it will reveal her loyalty to our enemy as well."

A gasp went up around the room.

"And not only this one, but the missing one, this girl's sister, is Ecclessite as well."

"Hod-ya!" Deparis gasped and put the fingers of her left hand to her lips in mock amazement. "You out-do yourself. You tread a fine line this side of suicide!"

Bablo-ya sat back silently observing the great hall. The preliminary verbal jousts of Scrarth and Avangar had begun with this duel of wits, and she wasn't even aware. The two sponsoring ladies of power had embarked upon their tactics so subtly that it appeared to Jeda that Bablo-ya had completely failed to notice.

"Hardly, my dear child," Hod-ya's icy, condescending tone seemed to touch a nerve in the fell Lady of Craniantium evoking an uncontrolled flash of anger from her bewitching eyes. "I shall do what no one has ever dared—make two Ecclessites use the very skills learned from our enemy's runes to destroy their foes, quite the opposite of the Ecclessite claim that their swords are incapable of harm. You, Deparis, had better have prepared your nymphs against the wiles of Ecclessa rather than the sorcery of Carnalia."

Hod-ya turned on her heel and strode to Jeda's side, whispering, "Did you think I didn't know what I was about from the start? Fool! Before you left Cosmopolis, I knew. That's why I didn't travel with you. I instructed Gragnold not to interfere, but to let you be, for there is deep power in Ecclessite ways, power I could find useful under the right circumstances, and so will you, if you follow my instructions. Otherwise, you'll suffer a most disagreeable, prolonged death."

Jeda tried to focus her eyes straight ahead. She dared glance into Hod-ya's cold eyes pondering whether this powerful woman was capable of doing what she claimed. Oh, why had Logon sent her here, didn't he know she wasn't strong enough for this? Hod-ya seemed so smug, so confident of her methods. Jeda's knees went weak.

A cloud of doubt now shrouded Deparis' eyes as well; she unconsciously chewed her lower lip. Her contestants' demeanors also appeared momentarily shaken.

Dalicusi recovered first, stepping forward, proclaiming, "I welcome the opportunity to not only defeat Carnalia's ablest gladiatrix, but Ecclessa's as well. Then all the world will know that Craniantium is most suited to be the governmental seat of the empire, and as such, will bring a speedy end to this interminable and costly war with Ecclessa."

Instead of cheers, silence greeted Dalicusi's boast. She sauntered over to Jeda and sneered, "If you dare meet me on the arena floor, you'd better be skilled in Craniantium wiles." She spun so smartly on her heel that her train flew up and brushed Jeda's scratched cheek.

Applause rippled among the onlookers and gained momentum and turned into cheers praising Dalicusi's effrontery. The svelte blonde slowly ambled back to her place alongside Deparis, who nodded appreciatively at the adoring crowd. So, it was to be a contest between a power-hungry Craniantiumite, and a dubious Ecclessite! No matter who won, Hod-ya or Deparis, the emperor would be proclaimed as uncontested master over all mankind. Ecclessites would hear the results of this duel and despair, for now they, too, like it or not, were represented in this year's Scrarth and Avangar.

Bablo-ya raised a hand for silence. She dismounted her throne with majestic pomp and extended both hands to the audience that filled the great ballroom and announced, "So, let it begin. I accept your contestants, Lady Deparis of Craniantium. School your myrmidons in their final lessons so you can present them as accomplished champions in the arena two weeks hence.

"Hod-ya, I also accept your contestants, unorthodox as your challenge is. Should you succeed you will have accomplished a deed equal to Claygall's. Your name will be immortal. But I hasten to add, should you lose, your name will be the laughingstock of all the empire. And I have no doubt the council of ten, er, nine, will devise an exquisite reception especially for you. A most ingenious concept, I must admit, to re-condition Ecclessites into deliberately using their powers to harm. You may well have touched on the very strategy that will bring Ecclessa to its knees—if you succeed.

"Attendants," she called as she clapped her hands, "lead these ladies of power and their contestants to their assigned quarters. Oh, and assemble the scribes of notable events to publish news of this unique challenge to the farthest borders of the empire. I want it known throughout the realm, especially on the borders of Ecclessa. This year's contest will prove most entertaining, if not exceedingly unusual."

A guard approached, bowed then turned and escorted Hod-ya, Jeda, and Spoena through the large double doors and out of the grand ballroom. Some bystanders spat, bit their thumbs or made crude gestures at them saying, "Phah! I smell an Ecclessite," while others stood back silently observing.

The jeering and derision jolted Jeda out of her daze. But it was Hod-ya's confidence—and Logon's absence—that disturbed Jeda the most. Spoena was of no encouragement. She kept her eyes lowered to the polished marble floor as they paraded out through the midst of the raucous crowd.

Gragnold slipped into the procession beside his mistress as soon as they departed from under the arch of the doorway, quietly hissing, "Now?"

Hod-ya scanned the immense hallway, alcoves and portals on either side that was still crowded with exiting people. "Wait. We'll be shed of this rabble soon, as well as . . . " she nodded towards Deparis' entourage emerging to the applause and roaring cheers of the crowd traipsing about within the grand ballroom, "Tell me later."

"Your quarters are on the southern side of the castle, m'lady," advised a palace guard after ushering Deparis and her contestants to an opposite wing of the castle.

"I'm quite familiar with the location of my quarters, having been here betimes," Hod-ya icily retorted. "You may go."

"I'm to make certain the contestants' accommodations are suitable—"

"I said, you may go!"

The hostility in Hod-ya's voice, coupled with Gragnold's sneer and imposing presence persuaded the attendant to bow politely. "Uh, of course, if you're quite sure of your way," he mumbled, eyes wide and staring at Gragnold's hand that rested on his scimitar's handle. "I can always attend to other matters." He trotted up the corridor, giving a disdainful backward glance at Hod-ya and her Ecclessites.

When his clicking bootheels no longer echoed back through the halls Hod-ya demanded of her dronnet, "Tell me. Leave nothing out."

"Them?" Gragnold seemed reluctant to speak in the girls' presence.

Hod-ya turned and regarded Jeda and Spoena coldly for several seconds. "I especially want them to know. They can do no harm from this point on and will learn to do whatever I tell them, especially after their conditioning. You remember what that's like, don't you?"

Gragnold ignored her last comment. "Deparis, mistress of dungeons, tortures prisoners with sleeplessness, reshaping their thinking; mocks Ecclessite ideals and replaces with Carnalian philosophies. Recently rumored to contact dread, Abmum, who uses vain beauty to deceive and lure victims to toxic desires. Gained prominence by undermining several Ecclessite brigade commanders in major battles."

"Which brigades?"

Did Jeda detect a note of Hod-ya's urgency?

"Unknown."

"Hmmm, go on. Tell me about Stullo, the obvious Scrarth."

"Cusps have ruled her since childhood. She desires pleasures, servants, opulence, power. Has no affection except for self. Knows she's not as strong as Dalicusi, she'll abdicate in the opening arena ceremonies."

"Yes, of course. As I thought, she came for recognition, not conquest. It's an honor to even have achieved the notoriety of training for the contest and, as a matter of course, certain positions will be offered to her, of which she no doubt, has already made her choice."

"Lady of perfumes and toiletries."

"Indeed? I'd have thought she'd prefer something more sensate, lusty, and opportune, such as lady of stable hands." A smirk at her own joke momentarily turned Hod-ya's usually plain visage into a hideous, laughing hag's face. "Tell me of Dalicusi."

"A force to be reckoned with. Rumors say she might be in league with dread. Which one is unknown."

"So young!" Hod-ya marveled, her face returned to its normal expression. "Either she's remarkable in her abilities even beyond Deparis, or more likely she's being targeted for colossal treachery, an object of derision to the dread flirting with her. The *kyllorn* derive perverse pleasure by betraying those they beguile. But will they abandon her in the contest? If not . . . " Hod-ya set her calculating eyes first on Spoena, then Jeda. "I must make you willing to draw upon your Ecclessite powers, and then set them aside at the right moment. And believe me, you will set them aside. You'll have no choice."

"Logon won't let his power be used that way," protested Spoena.

"What do you know about it, stupid girl? I'll make you use Elyon's runic enchantments to defeat your opponent's cusps. Then you will turn those powers off and receive my power to defeat the girl, banishing her forever to the Hadel-fire pits. Whichever of you wins will enjoy rewards galore. But if you fail me, you'll face inconceivably horrid consequences."

Hod-ya spun about on her heel and stalked down the long, darkened hallway with the girls trotting to keep up, turning into certain side-tunnels, bypassing other doorways, until, at last, she pushed a thick, wooden door wide open. Jeda took note that the only latch was on the door's exterior.

The chamber inside was a complete black-out. Gragnold gave Jeda a shove and she was inside, stumbling across an unseen floor into the unknown. The door slammed shut and she found herself in total darkness.

Hod-ya's voice filtered through the door's thick planks. "Learn your lessons well, dearie."

Then there was silence.

Jeda extended her hands, cautiously searching out the confines of the room—or was it a cell? A sudden rush of air crossed her face causing her to halt. Exploring with her foot she discovered she stood at the edge of a precipice. A breeze flowed upward, carrying the faint, fetid smell of a decaying carcass.

"Oh Logon, why did you send me to Pitland?"

She turned back and with hands extended groped for the doorway. Not finding it where she supposed it might be, she became disoriented. She resisted an urge to cry out for Hod-ya to come back and get her. She'd yield to whatever Hod-ya wanted . . . But no, that was the very result Hod-ya wanted. Was she so easily demoralized, stripped of her dependence on Logon? Jeda knelt to all fours and crawled around, feeling the floor with her hands until she bumped into a stone that was large enough to sit upon. When settled, she recalled one of the runesongs she'd learned:

Deep flows the river, crimson red,
Those bathed in love's purest flow,
Fear not the tophet, cusp or dread,
No matter where they chance to go.

Shades of dark, their powers fail,
Threats subside, Short their reign,
For rescue comes midst their assail,
The salvage work, the king will gain.

Fulfill the call, rise to your part,
Cleansing comes at his command,
Waste not the day, but guard your heart,
Great power supports the king's demand.

Jeda smiled. "Oh Logon, that's the first runesong I ever heard, way back when, with Dancel, Jorna, Flan, and the Sharpointers in

Cosmopolis. Oh, my liege, please watch over them." Joy filled Jeda's heart as she communed with her master remembering other runes, recalling conversations with her brother Artka, as well as Tressa, Filke, and Glend, how she rejoiced that Glend wasn't mixed up in this, and she remembered Vawella, Captain Varter, and of course, Bonu. At the thought of Bonu, regrets again overwhelmed Jeda. "Ah, if only we'd met some other time, some other place . . . We had the potential to really love each other. Ah, Logon, this is perhaps hardest of all. All the others I love and will miss, but knowing that Bonu and I could've been more to each other . . . But I'd rather obey you. That runesong helped. I wouldn't change a day of my adventures, even though I'm now in this desperate estate. I have no idea how this tournament will end. I fear that Hod-ya is capable of anything and might cause me to say and do things I don't want to do, but please, please keep me from denying you in word or deed. Give me strength to endure whatever awaits. If you don't . . . "

Jeda shook her head; she mustn't dwell on that track of thought. "Watch over Bonu, and please let him know I love him and wished—and wished . . . " She fell silent. Several moments later she resumed, "And Spoena and Artil, what will become of them? Oh, I beg of you, help them stand firm. They're so young, so innocent. Oh, why didn't we listen when the call came to return to the brigade?"

Her peace ebbed, and she cried out. "Please, Advisor, don't be silent. How have I offended? Oh, I see. Well, if that's the way of it, I gladly accept all that's happened, from the day my father delivered me to the emperor's palace to this very moment in this, this dungeon or, or whatever. I'm to demonstrate your power by not denying you, even to the death. Will my willingness to die for your name's sake demonstrate your victory over Lurcan, indeed, over all the empire? Very well, I accept my fate, only, I'm so frightened. Please, don't desert me."

Joy welled up within her so that she thought she must burst; to honor her liege in such a way. Such glorious deaths were reserved for great-hearted warriors of renown. Well, wasn't she in a desperate battle? Fought on a different battlefield, granted, but a battle, nonetheless. Though she had no sword, she'd shout Logon's name as loud and long as she could draw breath. Let these Carnalians see how this Ecclessite sword-maiden was prepared to die for her liege.

She hugged her knees to her chest and rocked, comforting herself by reciting favorite runes, singing runesongs, trying to recall past lessons, and mentioning various people to Logon. Thoughts of Artka often flitted across her mind, and whenever they did, she felt strangely comforted. "Does he already know you? Or, will he soon? Please don't let news of my fate discourage him."

She awoke. She had no way of knowing how long she'd slept, or been in this dark cell, but it seemed hours. Her stomach growled, and her mouth was parched. In her discomfort other thoughts came to mind. *Forgive Hod-ya and Gragnold. Forgive Dalicusi; her ways will destroy her if she doesn't seek forgiveness, as well as Stullo and Lady Deparis. None who draw breath have gone beyond possibility of rescue.*

"Even Captain Mileer?" Jeda wondered aloud.

"Even Captain Mileer. And Bletza, Balatz, Thorma and Thoru. It's good that you beseech me for others; it advances my kingdom more than you know when you include those who have misunderstood, mistreated, and abused you."

"Oh Logon, I don't know—"

"To what ends are you willing to love me?"

"To the death."

"Then put to death now those defensive feelings which arise from within you. That's how you identify with me in my death."

"Is that necessary?"

"It is the true calling and end of those who follow me, though not all are granted the privilege of suffering in the body for me."

"Help me, Logon, I want to, it's just that I don't know if I'll be able to forgive and love all of them."

"Trust me. I can forgive them. I can love them; as you live in me, my love will grow in you and will eventually flow through you, and you will be delightfully surprised at the conclusion of these trials."

CHAPTER NINE

JEDA WOKE WITH A START. She hadn't intended to fall asleep, but the oppressive, silent darkness, added to the emotional drain of the initiation ceremonies and then being locked in this sensory-deprivation cell overwhelmed her.

What had awakened her? A noise? But, if so, what was the noise she heard? And since when had her hearing ever been this acute? Maybe it was intensifying because her sense of sight was inhibited by the ubiquitous dark? If so, were her other senses also taking up the slack?

Even as she pondered her increased sense of hearing, she became aware that she was able to differentiate various odors. Her nose twitched at the fragrances wafting past her. There was mustiness, to be sure, and the disgusting odor of a dead creature rotting, and a smell of water, but there also was a tantalizing aroma of something savory to eat? Was it . . . ? Yes, it definitely was roast beef. And potatoes, with green beans all smothered in gravy, and bread, complete with a dollop of butter. And wine! A fruity, red wine.

How did she know all this? She sniffed again and was certain not only of the food's presence, but that the meal had only recently been placed in her chamber. Perhaps that's what had awakened her. Jeda's stomach rumbled; it seemed such a long time since she'd eaten.

"Wait, wait a minute. It's a trap!" she warned herself aloud as she at the same time congratulated herself on being clever. "They expect me to stumble around in this pitch-black cell searching for their bait food 'til I plunge over the precipice to my doom. No, that can't be it. Not if Hod-ya wants me in Scrarth and Avangar. Well then, what's their game?" Once again, hugging her knees to her chest, she gently rocked, pondering.

Visions of dinnertimes past with her family floated across her mind: Artka sitting beside her regaling them all with yarns of daring-do while mother apportioned steaming slices of roast beef and vegetables, sweet meats, breads, puddings . . . Drool slid out the corner of Jeda's lips.

Her teeth unconsciously clamped down on . . . nothing. The vision had been so real that she momentarily forgot her surroundings. A petulant growl rising from her stomach reminded her that real food was nearby.

"Well, if they want me to eat, how do they expect me to find it? I'm not going to stumble around in the dark groping for my dinner. I'll most certainly plunge off the edge of that, that, whatever it is."

She turned her head to one side and the aroma increased, tantalizing her. She turned her head away and the intensity lessened. Was she now able to discern by smell the direction of things unseen? "Wait a minute, I'm not a dog that I should sniff about for my dinner. If they want me to eat, they'll have to present it to me proper; I won't descend to a bestial level." And so saying, she crossed her arms and rocked rapidly, angrily back and forth, trying to ignore her empty stomach.

Gradually her rocking slowed when she discovered she could identify minute sounds: bubbles popping as they erupted from a watery surface, air currents circulating overhead, insects crawling, not buzzing or chirping, but merely crawling on the walls of her prison. And soon other odors were presented to her nose, smells that she'd never before experienced. Her senses: smell, hearing, taste, and touch were more active and responsive in this blind environment than she'd thought possible. In fact, all her bodily sensations, even her skin's sensitivity to hair follicles and even her internal organs communicated by sending messages to her mind, making their presence known.

But dominant over all was hunger; her olfactory function transformed savory smells into temptation. Lavish meals she'd enjoyed in the past came to mind; her stomach rumbled again as drool dribbled down her chin.

Without willing it, she found herself crawling on all fours and sniffing, feeling her way with her hands so as not to blunder over the drop off. She was pleased at how adept she'd become at smell interpretation, isolating and following the scent of food and not being thrown off by other odors. Within moments her probing hand brushed the edge of a small platter. She let out an unintentional squeal of delight. With both hands she seized and lifted it to her nose, inhaling deeply. The meal had cooled, but still emitted a delicious aroma. She stuffed the entire contents of the plate into her mouth and swallowed, barely chewing, for there was no need. The entire meal was but a morsel of meat, a spoonful of potato and two or three beans with a crust of bread topped with a smidgen of butter and a drip of gravy, all of which fit into the palm of her hand. Hardly satisfying.

Then she experienced another unexpected perception; she smelled the wine, but she also saw the goblet! Not with her eyes, but in her mind's eye she conceived a goblet with red, effervescent wine sitting a mere foot away from the plate. As confidently as she'd followed her nose, she now obeyed the mental, non-visual instinct and stretched out her hand. Her fingers closed around the stem finding it exactly where expected. She hoisted it to her lips, pausing just a moment, wondering whether she ought to drink or not, though she conceived of no logical reason why not. She was still hungry, and thirsty, very, very thirsty—in fact, parched. Her throat and tongue felt as if a sere wind had blown through her mouth while she slept, evaporating every last drop of moisture.

Jeda shook her head. The deluge of messages temporarily halted. "What am I doing? Just a minute ago I was salivating so profusely I had to swallow to keep from slobbering all over myself. Now I'm so thirsty? Perhaps something in the food? Yes, that must be it. Well, just a sip to quench the burning thirst won't hurt. But that's all, just a sip," she sternly cautioned. "After all, I don't know what potions Hod-ya might have mixed in it."

Her lips and tongue touched the red wine and her taste buds exploded in delirious delight at subtleties of flavor she'd never known. Unable to restrain herself she drained the goblet and then licked the inside with her tongue, savoring every drop. The warmth of the alcohol passed immediately to her bloodstream, bringing a not-unpleasant, dizzy sensation.

Again, her mind was flooded with messages about her chamber. For instance, she suddenly knew exactly where the wall of her enclosure was, about a foot and a half in front of her. It was only a shadowy perception, just a vague shape in her mind, but she felt so certain of its location that she felt she must confirm its presence by reaching out.

Down, deep inside there was a vague hint of warning at the sudden appearance of these increased capabilities; but if these extra-sensory perceptions helped in her plight, how could using them be wrong? Still, there was an uneasiness; and yet, what else was she supposed to do?

Compulsion to find out if the wall really was where she anticipated forced all other thoughts aside.

On impulse she thrust her hand to within a fraction of an inch from the wall, then tentatively tapped it with a fingernail. The solid wall was there! She felt exhilaration at having such a precise ability to locate things despite being engulfed in absolute darkness. The stone wall was cool and rough, made of the same stone as the fortress—the ubiquitous, white granite that seemed to be the underlayment of Pitland.

How did she know that?

She slowly turned around and as she did the entire room came into focus, as if in a mist, starting at her feet and slowly expanding to encompass the entire chamber. In the center of the room, what she'd thought was a dangerous precipice she now recognized as the edge of a warm-water pool, replete with gently sloping tiles that provided a lounging area. Across the bubbling pool was a large, four-poster, canopied bed with pillows, sheets and covers turned down as if expecting her arrival. A beautiful mahogany wardrobe over six feet high with stacked drawers sat on one side of the bed, while two closet doors were on the other side, behind which were gowns more elegant than any she'd ever seen.

How could she know these things? What prompted the sudden release of these powers in her?

Regardless, these dazzling new abilities were very useful in this pitch-black chamber. Had Logon perhaps given them, since she had been deprived of her sword?

Her skin suddenly felt dry, itchy; she craved a dip in the replenishing waters of the pool. She did feel crusty, for she hadn't properly bathed since leaving the brigade two and a half weeks ago;

her hair was oily and tangled, her muscles stiff and sore from sleeping on the stone floor. She was surprised to find herself absent-mindedly scurrying across the floor, gaily stripping off outer garments in preparation for a plunge into the warm, swirling eddies. Her tattered brigade garments lay strewn behind as she poised on the edge, sensing the dimensions and depth of the pool, her toes hanging over the ledge. The gently lapping waters of the thermal pool beckoned, promising to soothe tired aches.

Only one thing hindered her leap into the bath—her Logon dress. It was odd, she could sense every other piece of her discarded wardrobe strewn behind without even turning to look; but as she made ready to plunge into the water she had to touch her Logon dress to make sure she hadn't accidentally taken that off as well. She couldn't sense its presence! In fact, she felt naked, which was why she grabbed at it to make sure it was still there. Why couldn't she sense it?

A strong urge to strip it off came over her. It suddenly felt old, scratchy, worn, and threadbare; a vile and disgusting garment that restrained her freedom . . .

What? Where did that thought come from? She loved her Logon dress, and would not part with it for any reason, except . . . she was instantly aware of sheer, shimmering, soft lingerie waiting in the drawers of the mahogany wardrobe. Undergarments of exotic materials, lush and comfortable, petticoats of satin and delicate frills, gowns of luxurious material; all waited for her to be bathed so she could be fresh and clean for the desirable garments. She had only to strip off this plain, simple Logon dress and bathe to her heart's content in the refreshing waters before emerging on the opposite side to don the finery.

"No, I won't!" Jeda declared aloud and jumped into the warm waters before further argument daunted her determination. She disappeared beneath a rippling splash. Every inch of skin tingled with delight, every hair follicle prickled, and her muscles released tension in the swirling warmth as she descended, once again luxuriating in her newly acquired abilities. But her dress dragged in the water, holding her back from swimming freely. It really was a nuisance. Why didn't she just shuck it off for a little while? Her head broke the surface and she drew a fresh lung-full of air. She was completely aware of her environs, her senses as acute as ever. Treading water, she grasped the neckline of her Logon dress and started to tug it over her head.

"Would you spurn all the preparation I made especially for you?"

Jeda immediately spun around, treading water, searching for the intruder. "Who said that?" She sensed no one else in the chamber. "I demand that you reveal yourself." Jeda whirled about in the water, searching vainly.

"I'm right here, Jeda, in front of you. Open your eyes."

Jeda hadn't realized her eyes were closed. "Oh." She opened them to a blinding stab of pure, bright, white light. She gasped and shut her eyes against the unwelcome glare. "Are you trying to blind me? Who are you?"

"There was a time you yearned to be bathed in my light."

"Logon? Is that you?" She opened her eyes again, shielding them with her hand. "Why are you shining that bright light into my eyes?"

"Why do you want to remove the dress I wove and fashioned just for you?"

"It drags in the waters, preventing me from moving freely. It isn't much help to me here."

"You mean, it hinders free enjoyment of those Carnalian baubles stored over there?" There was a hint of sadness in his tone.

"Well, that's not exactly—"

"Jeda, don't deceive yourself. If you can't bear to look at me, look at what's become of the dress I gave you."

Jeda dropped her gaze and saw revealed in the stark white light of Logon's presence several ugly splotches covering her dress. "How, how did this happen?"

"You weren't even aware, were you? You didn't pursue the answer to why you could sense everything around you except something of mine. I cannot be perceived by Pitland's sorcery, Jeda."

"But what am I supposed to do, stumble around in the dark?"

"Do you remember how you and Glend mocked the dronnets because of their eyes? Your eyes are becoming like theirs. Is that what you want?"

Jeda was shocked. What had become of her in such a short time? She was unquestioningly obeying every urge of her body, and as she did, every sensation become heightened, every perception deepened, such knowledge was heady, difficult to resist. But, become like a dronnet?

"Did you suppose you could engage Lurcan's tools without becoming lurcanish?"

"I thought you abandoned me; I was unarmed, alone."

"I sent you here; and though you were unaware of all that this mission entailed, you agreed to go. You trusted me that much. Has that changed?"

"You seemed so remote and powerless this far inside enemy territory," Jeda lamented. "I thought I was left to my own wits."

"I'll never send you where I can't keep you, Jeda. Even here, I exercise all authority, though only a few in this land besides you and Spoena know it."

"Spoena! How is she?"

"She petitions me hourly on your behalf."

"Logon, I, I beg forgiveness. Please, restore me."

"You have more to overcome now that you've tasted the enemy's wares. Your aroused *Mada* nature will resist you, longing for Lurcan's dominion again, but I've foreseen even that, and that conflict will be useful to you. You must remember that I put your Mada nature to death when I died, and it was accounted as your death when you touched my rock."

Logon's presence faded, leaving Jeda again in pitch darkness, but his voice rang in the air with one last admonition, "Remember what happened to you at my rock; reckon your old-self dead in my death."

"Logon, what do you mean? How can I reckon as dead what is obviously still so alive?"

There was no answer.

Jeda felt totally alone again. But she was aware once more of her Logon dress; and for that, she was grateful. But she also was aware of her surroundings every time she closed her eyes. With her eyes open she lost sight of her surroundings; with them closed awareness of her surroundings filled her consciousness and she lost all perception of her Logon dress. It was a struggle to keep her eyes open for any length of time, for she could see nothing and her eyes strained searching for some ray of light in her lightless environment.

After a while she decided to take another dip in the pool. She slipped into the water, cautiously holding to the side until she was sure of her bearings. As she bobbed in the water, the odor of some dead, rotting thing bubbled up through the waters. She'd smelled the fetidness previously, but only now did she know the source of the stink was this very pool. Was there some dead thing on the pool's bottom? If she was to bathe in it and drink from it, she must know; just this once she'd use her *orphic* abilities to find out if something dead was in the pool.

She closed her eyes. Immediately the pool came into focus. She swam toward the bottom, sensing that it had an irregular shape, much like a natural hot spring. There were artificial vents added which sent fresh water in and let old water out. The incoming water was hot, almost too hot to bear, whereas the water at the outgoing vent on the other side was cooler, though still warm by most standards. Though she tried to extend her second-sighted ability, she could perceive nothing beyond the confines of her chamber. She couldn't tell if the water was from a natural source or was piped in. It little mattered. She resurfaced for a breath and again smelled the odor of death wafting out of the breaking bubbles.

"Yes," she reminded herself, "I must locate the source of that smell." Again, she dove, and this time discovered a small niche tucked away in the bottom's far corner. A long, fleshy piece of something lay there. She extended her hand, grasped it, and headed for the surface.

Torchlight illuminated the room as she broke the surface. On the edge of the pool stood Gragnold and another dronnet, both flanking Hod-ya.

"Well, I see you've begun to grasp the finer things of life," Hod-ya acidly observed.

CHAPTER TEN

"Come up out of there, girl. Don't you know that prolonged exposure to the salts in that pool will shrivel your skin?" Hod-ya impatiently tapped her foot. "That water is slightly alkaline and will crack your skin if you indulge too much. We want you gorgeous for the contest, not wrinkled and shriveled-up."

Jeda climbed out of the bath, self-conscious in her Logon dress, but very glad for it, nonetheless.

Hod-ya eyed Jeda as she stood shivering in the draft from the open door. "You haven't discarded that old rag yet?"

"What? My Logo—er, my under dress?"

"Exactly. That thing is so faded and splotched. Great Pitland, girl! What have you been doing to stain it so? Killing snakes?"

"Snakes?"

"What's that in your hand if not a dead snake?"

For the first time since surfacing Jeda beheld the object she'd brought from the pool's bottom. A three-foot-long snake dangled from her hand; even as she turned to look, a whitish, rotting hunk of flesh dropped off. The stench of decay assaulted her nostrils afresh. Jeda shrieked and flung it away, barely missing Gragnold. The other dronnet hissed in merriment.

Jeda's hand reeked. Slimy scales and fetid flesh stuck between her fingers. She stooped and vigorously swirled her hand in the pool to rid herself of the foulness, splashing water on Hod-ya's feet.

"I'll send the guards out while you take that horrid garment off."

Jeda's eyes narrowed. "If it offends you so, why not remove it yourself? Or have your blackguards do it. I'm sure they'd be willing."

"We can't, er, don't want to interfere with your choices, Jeda. You have to remove it yourself." Hod-ya paced back and forth a few steps then abruptly turned and stood. "You haven't asked why I've come."

"I assume you'll tell me." Jeda sniffed her hand. A faint trace of the rotted serpent remained, but its overpowering scent was gone. "Why have you come?"

"Brace yourself, child," said Hod-ya without emotion. "I have bad news."

Jeda stiffened. "What? Tell me, what happened?"

"Gruds, inform the captain that he may enter," Hod-ya commanded the dronnet behind.

The other blackguard retreated to the doorway where his dark form stood silhouetted against the tunnel's torch light. He mumbled in low tones to someone waiting in the outer hallway.

"Hod-ya, what's going on?" Jeda summoned the courage to demand. "Have your found Artil? Oh, no! What's happened to her?"

"Hush, child. What's that wench to you? I have news that strikes closer to home. I truly regret bringing such tidings, especially during the beginning of your preparation."

A uniformed man walked stiffly into the chamber followed by Gruds.

Hod-ya raised her hand and the soldier stopped just short of the torch's light in Hod-ya's hand.

Hod-ya laid her other hand on Jeda's shoulder, from most people a comforting gesture, but not here, not now, and not from her.

Jeda trembled. What woeful tidings portended? Bonu? Glend? The Runer brigade? Spoena?

"You have a brother, I believe, assigned to the Roaring Lion Brigade?" Hod-ya inquired, her eyes revealing that she already knew the answer.

Jeda covered her mouth. "Oh no! Not Artka! Please, Logon, not Artka!"

Hod-ya's hand recoiled off Jeda's shoulder as the witch-woman reeled backward as if slapped. It took several seconds for her to regain her voice; when she did, she rasped vehemently, "When are you going to quit saying that name? Don't you understand how useless it is here?"

"What about my brother?" Jeda demanded, stepping forward, grasping the front of Hod-ya's vestments.

Hod-ya yanked Jeda's hands off her clothing, her fingernails indenting Jeda's skin. For a moment their eyes locked and Jeda noted the kindling of a yellow flame in the recesses of Hod-ya's pupils. Jeda dropped her eyes and meekly stepped back.

"Aggression? Yes, you're coming along nicely," simpered Hod-ya, "and caution, too. That's good." She turned to the soldier standing in the shadow. "Tell her."

The soldier stepped forward with his helmet tucked jauntily into the crook of his elbow. "Lady Jeda of Kway, I swear, it's no pleasure, in fact, I rue the deed, but I must inform you of grim news."

Jeda recognized the gallant officer who'd saved her from Snetch's ugly temper when she'd been ejected from her home and taken to Cosmopolis. "Captain Fitcher?"

"The same. Hod-ya told me I must be the one to inform you, thinking you probably wouldn't trust her word alone. Believe me, Miss Jeda, I, I care for you, and would never, ever do anything to hurt you or bring you grief unless it was absolutely necessary. Your brother, Artka, is dead."

"Liar!" Jeda screamed. Her knees went weak; the room tilted. The next thing she knew, Captain Fitcher was carrying her toward the bed around the other side of the pool.

He gently placed her head on a pillow and sat stroking her hand. "Please, Jeda, don't hold the evil tidings I bear against me. If you were left unaware of his death until the day of the duels your adversary would certainly use that news to stun you, costing you the contest, and possibly your life. I couldn't bear that."

"You're mistaken. You must be." Jeda turned toward the wall biting her knuckles.

Fitcher persisted, grabbing her arm and turning her back to face him. "Jeda, there's no mistake. I knew Artka. He was in my regiment. I saw him die."

Jeda sobbed, not wanting to believe. "How, how did he die?"

"Are you sure you want to know?"

Jeda sat up, fighting back tears. She took a deep breath and calmed herself. "Tell me."

Hod-ya came over and stood by Fitcher's side as he related, "He died a hero, Jeda. He somehow got lost the first day of battle, and I thought him a casualty, you know, lost to the enemy, either by death or capture. But several weeks later he emerged again marching with a band of Eroton cutthroats. What a warrior he was to hold his own in that band! Anyway, they were hard-pressed by the enemy near the Windbreak Forest. My brigade was sent to bolster them. By the time we arrived almost all the Erotons had either fled, were killed, or turned traitor.

"I saw a horse rearing in the thickest part of the battle, and knew it belonged to the captain of the Eroton troops. The enemy closed in on Captain Sarcas and his lone armor bearer, the last holdout. That foot soldier was your brother. I recognized him instantly; his hair shone brightly in the sun and his noble face radiated the excitement of mortal combat. When his captain was felled, overwhelmed by dozens of Ecclessites eager to smear their blue-glowing blades in the blood of a fallen Carnalian champion, Artka sounded his battle cry, the roar of a Craniantium lion; the bloodthirsty kingsmen were temporarily driven back from his unhorsed captain. But the damage was already done; Sarcas lay on the ground soaked in his own blood. Artka, outraged with grief, hewed his way through Ecclessites like a woodcutter through saplings. Jeda, he was a champion. If only he'd been fighting toward our redoubt, he might have survived. He slew dozens before being overwhelmed . . . and, well, I think I should say no more."

"Tell her all of it," Hod-ya demanded. "She has to know."

Captain Fitcher dropped his gaze to his hand holding Jeda's. Tears welled up, and he paused to swallow the lump in his throat. His voice was husky as he finally blurted, "He was hacked to pieces, Jeda, hacked to shreds by those, those bright-possessed maniacs."

A cold hand gripped Jeda's heart; life itself seemed squeezed out of her. A black cloud of oblivion descended.

Before she swooned completely Hod-ya grabbed and yanked the hair atop Jeda's head. "No, you don't, my pretty. You're not allowed to sink into self-pity. You have work to do. You must avenge your brother's slaughter. That can only happen if you win Scrarth and Avangar. Devote yourself to all I can teach you. The tools are all here in this chamber, as you've begun to discover. I see it working in you. Learn your craft, Jeda. Need I remind you that the Avangar will decide the fate of all Ecclessite captives. Need I say more? Turn your grief into hatred, child. Let bitterness guide you to strength. If you fail in this quest, your brother's death will be a mockery, a song and a jest among the weak-minded followers of the king. Artka was a hero for all Carnalia. Don't let his death be for nothing. Make a mountain of the bones of those who slew your brother, a memorial for all Carnalia and Ecclessa to remember. Turn sorrow to bitterness; let your rage grow; let your power rise." Hod-ya's voice receded into echoes.

~

Several hours later Jeda awoke and found herself alone. Hod-ya's words echoed in her ears, " . . . let your power rise." She was powerless to filter the phrase out. And beyond that, hunger again gnawed the pit of her stomach and wouldn't be ignored, pre-empting all other thought, insisting that she satisfy that craving. There was something else . . . a very painful memory that she couldn't face, at least not until after taking some nourishment.

Jeda closed her eyes and explored the enclosure with heightened senses, searching for some morsel of food. She recalled the delicious morsels, tidbits really, of roast beef, potatoes, and beans with gravy that had previously been slipped into her chamber. Had it been a day or merely an hour ago?

Her stomach growled. There was no plate by the door, no savory odors, no tantalizing images, but her hunger intensified. Her skin felt stretched, her muscles crampy, and she had a slight headache, yet the insistent demands of her stomach were not to be ignored. She sniffed the air, capably interpreting various scents, searching for some sign of anything edible. But the smell dominating her chamber was the rotten snake she'd carried up from the pool's bottom. "Ugh!" she reacted as its stench assaulted her nostrils.

A petulant, compulsive thought bombarded her mind:

Eat the snake, eat the snake, eat the snake,
It's all a fake, it tastes like cake, your teeth won't break,
Eat the snake, eat the snake, eat the snake.

She was powerless to dismiss it. She put her fingers into her ears to block the chant. When that failed, she sang loudly, "La la la lalaaa la la la," to no avail. The incessant chant numbed her resistance. Her stomach rumbled louder, and though she was filled with loathing, she had the sensation of remotely watching as her feet slipped over the edge of the bed and carried her body in search of the rotted snake despite her mental protests; she was unable to stop. Jeda opened her eyes, hoping that if she didn't sense the snake, she could resist. It didn't help. She still sensed everything in the chamber, eyes open or closed. She located the putrid hunk of flesh where it had fallen as it barely missed Gragnold. Her feet took her closer, closer to the rotten carcass.

Eat the snake, eat the snake, eat the snake,
It's all a fake, it tastes like cake, your teeth won't break,
Eat the snake, eat the snake, eat the snake.

"What's happening to me?" Jeda wailed into the darkness as she stopped just short of the wretched carcass and extended her hand. "Help me, Logo—"

A vivid scene of Artka fighting, seized by hundreds of Ecclessite hands, hurled to the ground, slashed and hacked to a bloody pulp flashed before her eyes.

Somewhere echoing screams faded to a whimper. She was the screamer, collapsed to a sitting position, sobbing, shuddering. How could Logon let her brother be killed by a bloodthirsty mob of kingsmen? How could she now call on Logon who'd betrayed her? And wasn't he the one who had sent her to the arena to fight to the death before gawking spectators? Truth was found to be a lie. What hope was there? All those experiences, those joyous revelations of Logon's person and character, were they false? All those visitations during moments of need, were they all a hoax? How could Logon send her on such an expedition, promising her—? What indeed, had he promised? When it came down to it, he'd promised nothing! Not even success. What a dupe she'd been.

It tastes like cake, it tastes like cake, it tastes like cake,
It's not a fake, it's not a fake, it's not a fake,
Your teeth won't break, your teeth won't break, your teeth won't break.

Hunger like she'd never known welled up amidst her dark thoughts. "Here I sit with all manner of power within my grasp . . . Am I going to cling to some jaded, future hope of eternal bliss when I'm in such dire need right now, when for the mere asking, I can have whatever I desire?"

She deliberately lifted the rotten snake from the stone floor and brought it to her lips. It didn't smell quite so bad anymore . . . Her lips parted, her teeth sank into the yielding flesh, and tore off a hunk.

~

High above in the dark, vaulted ceiling, a tile soundlessly moved back into place. "That should do it," said Hod-ya to Captain Fitcher. They both stood on a narrow catwalk overtop the conditioning chambers. "The snake is embedded with hallucinatory herbs that will make her even more sensitive to the cusps swirling around her. Nice touch, that bit about 'caring for her' and then shedding a couple of tears. She fell for that, if nothing else. That's probably why she believed you."

"I'm off the hook now. I did what you wanted. I left a major campaign for this little errand. But anything is worth getting you off my back. I owe you nothing now."

"This 'little errand' as you put it, is going to do more for the empire than a thousand military campaigns, especially if her brother is under the tutelage of Saygus, as my spies reported. They may have gotten the brother, but we have his counterpart. And the female is always the more susceptible, and therefore, the more dangerous. Remember that, Fitcher, next time you desire a favor from me."

"You know of this Saygus?"

"A long time ago, in a high and hazardous mountain range, he and I matched wits. He was just a brigade leader then, but his concept of sharpening the entire sword threatened our methods of subverting Ecclessite brigades. He learned his weapon thoroughly and trained others to know it as well. Such training could have produced kingsmen that would've infected all Ecclessites with the desire to discover and utilize the powers inherent in their swords. That would've set us back to the beginning when Carnalia ceded city after city to Xychirion's armies. I was but a fledgling myself when Saygus and I tangled, just discovering how to contact dreads. But my counsel helped the Craniantiumites defeat his brigade. Some of those taken prisoner from that campaign are still in bonds here to this day. Saygus alone escaped, albeit broken and dispirited. Our double agents spread rumors about him so that no kingsmen would trust him ever again, forcing him to become a reclusive hermit.

"We thought his threat was over, that is, until some tophets tracking Jeda's brother, Artka, were undone by Saygus and sent screaming back to their swamp." Hod-ya gripped the railing. "I thought Saygus had been so discouraged he'd never come back. Evidently time has healed even his wounds. It's been reported that he's readying a new brigade to sally forth from his isolated mountain refuge. When he tries, I'll be waiting; he'll find me more powerful than he ever imagined. And young master Artka will receive quite a surprise to find his lovely sister on my right bower, dressed to the sixes in delicious wickedness."

Captain Fitcher silently considered Hod-ya's boast as they negotiated the narrow catwalk back down to ground level. Finally, he asked, "That rotten snake won't harm her, will it?"

"Why, Fitcher, I almost believe you're capable of caring. Of course not! That wasn't really a snake. While you were engaged carrying her over to the bed, Gragnold substituted a carefully blended mixture of cake dough which, with some cuspian assistance, she perceived as a snake."

Gragnold, walking behind the pair, hissed in the odd, dronnet style of laughing.

"It's a type of unbaked dough that feels like flesh. Very tasty, and quite nourishing, actually. And to her utter horror, she'll think she's become addicted to the taste of dead, rotten things, as well as other abominations her former liege considers hateful. Her inability to keep from indulging her needs and pleasures will further alienate her from her Ecclessite prince. Of course, it'll all be in her mind. She'll feel too defiled to even consider asking his pardon, thereby falling more and more under my influence. You've done your part well, Fitcher. I won't forget it."

"And the other girl, Spoena?"

"What's she to you? Don't pry into things that aren't your concern."

"I just wondered if she was a threat to Jeda's success, that's all."

"Make sure that that's all. Spoena is of no consequence. I won't allow a contest between them. She could prove to be Jeda's weak spot; I won't risk Jeda going to pieces in the arena. Spoena will be properly disposed of after she's fulfilled her role. Deparis's contestant, Dalicusi, is far more dangerous to Jeda, indeed, to me; but she woefully underestimated our Jeda during the initiation ceremonies. Dalicusi won't take her preparation seriously enough. When she meets the new, empowered Jeda, both Deparis and Dalicusi will be deeply shaken."

"Only you could come up with such a diabolical plan of entering Ecclessites in Scrarth and Avangar. I'm impressed."

"That's just the beginning, Fitcher. After I've dealt with that traitor, Ugen, I may find a prestigious position for a military commander who's proven useful."

"Mileer is of no further use to you?"

"Mileer is none of your concern. He has his place; you could have yours, if you do as you're told. Now, hadn't you better get back to your 'major campaign' before it falls apart without you?"

They reached the bottom stair. Fitcher respectfully clicked his heels, turned, and made his way outside to the castle bailey.

~

"Hold fast!" Bonu shouted, raising his sword aloft as he stepped out of the bushes.

Men leapt to their feet shouting; women screamed, grabbed their children and ran for the undergrowth.

"You're safe. We're friends!"

Scung joined Bonu in the outer edge of the campsite, causing even greater pandemonium.

Then a shrill whistle pierced the air, and everyone froze. The leader stood in the middle of the alarmed campers saying, "Calm down, everyone. They're not Carnalian." He waded through his people and stood before Bonu. "Who are you? If you're friends, as you say, why sneak up on us?"

Bonu saluted recognizing the rank of captain almost hidden beneath outer garments. "Lieutenant Bonu, of a Runer brigade under Captain Varter. This is Scung, lately of Eroton and Carnalian brigades, but now following Logon." Bonu turned and called into the undergrowth. "Vawella."

Vawella pushed through some bushes. The frightened campsite relaxed at the appearance of a woman. "It's her!" some children excitedly whispered to one another.

"Do you know me?" Vawella asked.

The captain took a few steps toward her. "You led us to a cache of foodstuffs, though you didn't know it. Some of my people watched you sneaking through the woods and followed you. When you departed, I'm afraid we raided your supply; we were nearly starved, having been on the run for three weeks, unable to forage or hunt. I'm Captain Porast. This is, or was, a Runer brigade that dwelt in the shadow of the Forbidden Mountains until several weeks ago when a Carnalian task force raided us." Porast turned, raised his hands and spoke quietly to his people. "It's all right. They're allies. Go about your business. We travel today, so make the necessary preparations."

Vawella walked up to the leader. "Captain Porast, I believe your traveling days are over, that is, if you're looking for a safe haven to bivouac. Our brigade is but a shout away."

"You're from that brigade rumored to thrive in Ra-Amawl despite Carnalians, cusps, and tophets? We'd heard tales about you time to time from passing kingsmen and tried to contact you, but you always avoided our emissaries."

"You forgot to mention dreads and Craniantium lions," chimed in Vawella. "My father is captain of that brigade. Just recently, we, too, were raided and lost many of our people. We've been living on the run, so to speak, for the last week or so, until we found a safe place just the other side of all this greenery and a swamp in yonder cliffs. The food reserves you found were left intentionally for wandering Ecclessites who would recognize the secret signs. That was our former campsite."

"I'm afraid we've depleted your stores. Our need was great. It was a real Logon-send. If another day had passed without provision, we'd have lost some children and elderly. What manner of brigade did you say you were?"

"Well," Bonu eyed their swords, "we were Runers, like yourselves, but lately discovered that those basic runes, important as they are, aren't sufficient for the intensified warfare we're encountering these days."

"At least you're not Tipsters or Sharpointers. I'd very much like to meet with your captain and discuss merging brigades." Then he espied Bonu's sword. "Say, you're not Wholebladers, are you. I've never met any, but I've heard horror stories about those zealots."

"Come, talk to my father. He was commissioned in a Runer brigade. You'll see you have nothing to worry about," encouraged Vawella.

"And you, lieutenant, aren't you coming? I have many recruits, some of whom were wandering around in the woods, recently chest-wounded, undoubtedly fruit of encounters with your brigade. Aren't you going to take a hand in their training? You can see that my hands are full as it is."

"I'd like to, Captain Porast, but I'm on a mission, and must not be delayed. Vawella is a capable guide, and warrioress. She'll lead you to safety."

"Well, I think I should speak with your captain before I decide. I don't want to lead my people into more danger. I'll just go myself."

"You're too cautious, captain. You have nothing to fear. Your people will be vulnerable if left out here on their own. Take your people to the comfort and protection of the caves. There's plenty of food and fresh water, and you can all rest comfortably. There's no telling what might come prowling around out here. If you should decide not to stay, no one will pressure you. You're free to go as you please. But I beg of you, don't leave your charges at the mercy of this forest."

"You make a strong case, lieutenant, but I'm afraid if some of these inexperienced recruits get too comfortable, and I decide this isn't where Logon wants us, they may want to stay. I couldn't allow that."

"Why, captain," Vawella blurted, "you act as if these people belonged to you instead of Logon. Don't they have a right to serve wherever they feel Logon leads?"

"Despite your impertinence, young lady, I'll reply to that challenge. Logon has brought them to me; I have to give account of them; therefore, I can allow nothing that doesn't agree with my own views."

Vawella crossed her arms. "Captain Porast, I meant no impertinence, and I ask your pardon if I seemed to be so, but isn't my point valid that they have the right to discern what Logon is telling them for themselves?"

Porast turned to Bonu. "Are the women in your brigade encouraged to challenge leaders so freely?"

"No one is prohibited from speaking their mind, if that's what you mean. I don't think she's out of line, sir, and she makes a good point. But this isn't the time or place to debate the issue. Scung and I must depart to our mission. If you decide to join Captain Varter, you'll find capable help in training your recruits. If not, well, you seem to have been doing a fine job. Your vulnerability that I see at this point is safety, and that's what we offer. Take or leave it, but I must go.

"Vawella, if Captain Porast remains hesitant, perhaps you can have your father send someone to him to discuss the issues. Unfortunately, sir, Captain Varter is wounded in the leg, and thus, can't come himself.

King's road to you. Vawella, thank-you for showing us the stone path across the marsh."

Without a backward glance Bonu darted into the underbrush, followed by Scung. Vawella and the captain's voices faded. The last thing he heard Captain Porast say was, "Well, that young man speaks his mind, doesn't he?"

~

Bonu and Scung jogged, trying to make up for lost time whenever they came upon sparser jungle tracts. Perspiration trickled down Bonu's neck. He thought of the northern mountain climes that had probably turned cold and were snow-covered by this time, yet in these jungles the sweltering heat was relentless, despite the shady, overgrown canopy. Their effort, combined with the humidity, made prolonged, rapid travel exhausting. Bonu turned to check on Scung, whose tremendous size was an additional hazard for the Eroton. Indeed, the Eroton labored for breath, though he made no complaint. Bonu slackened his pace for Scung's sake despite his own urgent desire.

Where was Jeda now? What inhuman tortures were tasking her? What schemes had the witchy-woman concocted to make Jeda revert to a Carnalian state? What if Jeda resisted? What if she didn't? So preoccupied was he that Scung's arm clipping hard upon his shoulder took him by surprise, sending him sprawling to a moss bed.

"Why did you do that?"

Scung's beefy hand clamped over Bonu's mouth. The giant's hairy face snuggled close to Bonu's ear, whispering, "Summat be's a-comin'. Lots o' em. Lissen."

Bonu quit struggling and lay still. Sure enough, a large company, relatively quiet for such a sizable contingent, was passing a mere twenty yards away. Scung released Bonu's mouth, and the two of them inched forward on their bellies to peer through the foliage at the jack-booted feet tramping by.

Carnalians.

If Scung hadn't stopped him they would've blundered right into them.

Scung whispered, "Wanna go back an' warn Varter?"

For an agonizing moment Bonu wrestled with conflicted motives. Then, realizing Varter would be safe, and that he and Scung must continue their journey, shook his head. "They're headed away from the cliffs."

It took a quarter of an hour for the empire troops to pass. The kingsmen pair waited another quarter-hour after their passing to make sure there wasn't a second contingent or any stragglers. The brigade had posted no rear guard, which probably meant they were an advance company. Another, possibly larger, force would soon follow.

"I hope Porast took our advice," said Bonu, as he resumed their trek.

Scung grunted an affirmative and traipsed through the undergrowth after his mentor.

After an uninterrupted twenty minutes Bonu suddenly dodged behind a clump of sawgrass and froze. Scung landed beside him, breaking a branch.

"Who's there?" demanded a voice from nearby.

"I know that voice." Bonu stood to his feet and softly called, "Kraga, it's me, Bonu."

"Bonu? You're not dead? Glend, it's Bonu. Tell the others."

Glend's pert features, now smudged and scratched, appeared some several paces behind Kraga. "Bonu! Oh, thank, Logon! Is Jeda with you?"

CHAPTER ELEVEN

Two dozen survivors from Varter's scattered brigade surrounded Bonu pummeling him with questions about friends and relatives. Little by little Bonu surmised out how each had escaped capture. At the initial outset of the Carnalian attack some recognized the stampede of animals rushing past and took the cue to flee for safety. Others were caught unawares and at first put up a fight but were overwhelmed by Carnalians, cusps, tophets and, some thought, possibly a dread and retreated into the underbrush. After wandering through the bush for days avoiding predators, both human and bestial, many of the escapees eventually stumbled into each other.

Bonu raised his hands for quiet and introduced Scung, telling of his heroic rescue of Bonu lest they mistrust the gruff-looking Eroton standing there. He then informed them of the cliff brigade's whereabouts. The caves were shelter not only from the elements, but predators as well as Carnalian attacks. Kraga, who'd taken over the leadership of this small contingent, was greatly relieved to learn that his friend and captain survived, nonetheless he was concerned upon learning of Varter's wound.

"But what of Jeda?" asked Glend during a lull.

Bonu's voice became husky. "Speak often of her to Logon. Hod-ya has recaptured her and taken her to Pitland." He was too choked up to say more.

"Yer friend be's in a mighty hard place," said Scung. "I doesn't ken the lass, but I kens Bonu be's quite taken wi' her. In fact, we be's on our way ter Pitland ter see if'n we cain't do summat ter rescue her an' t'others."

"Others?" questioned Kraga. "What others?"

"Spoena and Artil." Bonu found his voice again. "We really must get back to our mission. There's no time to lose; let me direct you to the cliffs—"

"I'll not hear of it," interrupted Kraga. "If you go to Pitland, so do we! The two of you won't be able to do much by yourselves in such an evil place."

"No, Kraga. Your offer is honorable, but not expedient, nor is it of Logon. You're moved by a sense of honor, but it's not Logon's command. We were dispatched with Captain Varter's blessing. Were you to join us without a direct word from Logon, it might imperil the mission. Two might slip unnoticed into that infernal land; whereas a company, even a small company, would surely draw attention, be challenged, captured and summarily executed. As I see it, your duty is to get these stragglers to safety. Besides, from the looks of it, you are more in need of receiving assistance than capable of rendering it."

Several faces behind Kraga lit up in relief.

"Well," Kraga hedged, "If that's how you feel."

"It can be no other way. Besides, Varter needs you. Your abilities would be wasted in Pitland. I believe that another band of Ecclessites has already joined Varter's brigade today. We encountered them earlier this morning camping by the marsh alongside the cliffs. We told them how to contact Varter's brigade. What a joy now, to find you alive and safe. I have no doubt that you'll greatly relieve Captain Varter's mind. The dispersion and loss of so many weighs heavily on him."

"I suppose you're right, Bonu. All right, I'll take this contingent to the cliffs."

"You'll find only a remnant of our brigade residing there. Despite running into you, we met no one else from Varter's brigade; there must have been many casualties. How many? I don't know. The captain's own daughter, Vawella, has proven wise in the ways of the forest, spying and prowling about, leading stragglers back to the brigade; even so, she's only encountered a handful. There's not much hope; indeed, we'd all but abandoned hope of finding any others."

Bonu and Kraga knelt close to the ground and after brushing away leaves to make the earth bare where Bonu drew a crude map in the dirt with a stick, pointing out specific landmarks along the way. Kraga studied the drawing, nodded, then stood to set the order of march.

"One more thing, Kraga," Bonu said, "a Carnalian brigade or larger passed through little more than half an hour ago. I believe they're the vanguard of a larger force. I may be mistaken, but I fear that the forest will soon be swarming with Carnalians. Waste no time, but don't be foolhardy, either. Take every precaution."

Kraga nodded. "We'll do what we can. Any message I should convey to Captain Varter?"

"Only that you've met us, and that we're on course, if not on pace."

"Done."

Bonu hoisted his knapsack and scuffed away the impromptu map with his foot. "King's road to you."

"And to you." Kraga squeezed Bonu's shoulder; the two held each other's eyes for a long moment before Bonu gave a brief nod. Then he and Scung rapidly blended into the undergrowth.

The duo meandered and dodged through the dense jungle for another half-hour, scrupulously avoiding obvious trails and pathways, leaving little to no sign of their passing. It was arduous going, and Scung, though not complaining, was overtaxed, as evidenced by the perspiration soaking past under garments out to the giant's vest.

After another hour of slogging through the undergrowth the pair took a break and, breathing heavily, sat side by side sipping from their water skins. A nearby rustling in the bushes alerted them to someone's approach; they dropped down and squeezed beneath the log they'd been sitting on. Bonu inched forward under exposed roots that supported the bole of the fallen tree several inches off the ground, but Scung, squirm and wriggle as he might, couldn't slide his bulk under. He finally gave up and just lay still, barely drawing a breath.

The bushes parted and a woman's smudged face emerged; she had long, dark hair and had torn the hem of her skirt. Her startled eyes grew round at spying Scung's backside sticking up over the trunk of a fallen tree. Automatically lifting hands to her lips she stifled her cry as she turned to flee. Her retreat was impeded by several people following her.

Scung rose up to his knees, drawing his sword. "Who be's yers?"

Bonu scrambled out from beneath the other side of the log and stood alongside his friend, sword in hand.

"Hold fast, Beninda, they're Ecclessites!" exclaimed a masculine voice. A man stepped out from behind the woman, presenting a sword that glowed several inches from the tip. "Words of the word?"

"Words of the word, and well met." Bonu smiled broadly and lowered his sword.

The bearded man, tall and dark-haired, stepped out of the shrubbery into full view, extending a hand in greeting. "Oronet, lieutenant of a Sharpointer brigade. I assume by the portions of light on your swords that you're Runers?"

Bonu grasped the man's proffered hand. "Bonu, lieutenant of, as you suspect, a Runer brigade, or at least we were. Our captain has lately urged sharpening both sides of the entire blade; he's convinced that it's necessary to know all of Logon's counsel in these dark days. Whence do you hail, and how many follow with you?"

"This is my wife, actually, my bride, Beninda; we've been married but a few weeks. Following us, several paces apart are about fifty of our brigade. We hail from central Craniantium."

"Indeed, how came you to these distant regions?"

"That's a rather involved story."

"Tell me quickly, if you can. My companion and I can spare but a few moments, but I need to know if you can be trusted."

"Very well, I'll be brief. An event occurred during one of our brigade meetings that was so startling it sent us into these bewildering, fearsome haunts."

Bonu and Scung looked behind Oronet and observed more movement in the bushes.

"A bright suddenly appeared bringing a warning for us to flee. Our brigade, some five hundred strong, had several captains who immediately debated whether to believe the bright or not, most claiming it was a tophet masquerading as a bright. I was the only officer who believed the visitation was Logon's doing. The resulting decision was that all who trusted that the oracle was from Logon were permitted to follow their conscience. The kingsmen trailing behind me are the ones who left the city in obedience to the vision. I was chosen as their acting captain. It was a difficult decision. I was torn between two minds myself; hesitant to forsake the officers I had trusted and learned from for so long, not to mention leaving most of my family and friends who were convinced I was being deluded by the enemy."

"What convinced you the messenger was of Logon?"

"I'd been persuaded early in life that certain runes of bygone eras no longer applied in these days, in effect, I was encouraged to know about them but not act on them. But one day as I tolled my blade a voice spoke to me about those 'obsolete' runes. I looked up from my work and saw a bright. That bright was the very one that later appeared in our meeting speaking the very same message to the whole assembly. I was convinced it was true and said so, right in the meeting. That caused quite a stir, different leaders argued that Logon didn't do that kind of thing anymore. I tried to tell them of my visitation, and that I believed the so-called 'obsolete' runes were not only to be studied but applied. I was mocked; most rejected my counsel. I was warned that all those who followed me would suffer dire consequences. Beninda and I were immediately married 'cause it wouldn't be proper for us to journey into the wilds unless we were married." He turned to his bride and said, "Beninda, signal the others to come forward."

Beninda placed two fingers in the corners of her lips and chirred like a cricket.

"Isn't she talented?" beamed the lieutenant.

A cricket's chirp returned from the depths of the forest. Quiet, questioning voices were then heard from people pushing through the undergrowth.

"That cricket signal should only be used towards night," advised Bonu. "Had any enemies been about, that would've been a dead giveaway. But you haven't explained why you're in Ra-Amawl, of all places."

"Oh, didn't I make that clear? The roamer told us to seek safety in Ra-Amawl. That's what caused the division in the brigade because most of the brigade believed the message to be a deception. Our captain argued that Logon wouldn't send us to a dark place full of vile things."

"And you didn't believe him?" Bonu asked.

"I used to; that's what I'd always been taught. But the more I studied the runes, the less support for that understanding I found. Nevertheless, like everyone else, I never challenged the consensus, after all, there were many officers of higher rank better skilled in sword lore than myself. Who was I to contradict? That is, until the day my swordrunes lit up of their own accord revealing a catastrophic war would rage across the world before Logon rescues his own. Personally, I believe Logon's bridge will soon fall into Carnalian hands; then the darkest hours mankind has ever known will befall the world."

"Whoa! Yer don't say!" Scung was aghast, having not been taught the runes concerning the end of Carnalia. "Be's these things so, Bonu?"

"Yes, Scung, I'm afraid they are. And our mission may play a small part in those events, if I interpret Kyleah's seeing a-right."

"You have a seer in your brigade?" Oronet's eyes widened.

Bonu regarded this Sharpointer, aware that tip-honing brigades regarded such offices as general and seer obsolete, if not dangerous. "Yes, my friend," he finally answered, deciding that complete honesty was best. "We have a seer in our brigade. We've learned more secrets about the sword, too. Lately we've discovered that our rune knowledge has been woefully insufficient. The whole blade must be sharpened if we're going to stand our ground in the kind of war that's coming." Bonu braced for an argument but was pleasantly surprised when Oronet merely knelt to contemplate.

"Well, that explains a lot," he looked up. "Yes, since I've begun learning the runes instead of brigade protocols, I see the need to be open to whoever and whatever Logon sends my way, but not to be incautious, either. There's a rune that declares, 'He who is not against me is for me.' I never expected to align with Runers, though. I wonder what else I've been mis-taught?"

"I like your open-minded attitude; you'll do well. I must warn you, however, Ra-Amawl is a dangerous place, and lately even more so. Within the last couple of hours we've evaded a Carnalian company, probably the advance of a larger task force. If you decide to join our brigade, I'll direct you, but you'll need to exercise greater caution."

"I can see you're an experienced woodsmen and bow to your skills. As for joining your brigade, that's why, I suppose, the bright sent us here in the first place. He said a kingsman task force is gathering in Ra-Amawl which would become part of a larger Ecclessite advance. We'd like to join."

"I know nothing the size of a regiment or task force, but I can point out the way to our brigade's cliffs." Bonu, squatted down and drew a rough map in the dirt. "And keep in mind, the jungle is crawling with Carnalians."

"Lieutenant Bonu, thank you for your help. Are you sure you won't lead us? It'd be much easier with you leading the way."

"Sorry, but I have urgent business in Pitland that cannot wait."

"Pitland! You mean the border of Pitland?"

"I only wish I didn't."

"But, but kingsmen who enter Pitland never return."

"Be that as it may, I'm duty bound. I'm drawn by two loves that are greater than my own life. My love and obedience to Logon Xychirion and Jeda, my beloved, who awaits a hideous doom in the Scrarth and

Avangar duels unless I find a way to rescue her; or failing rescue, die with her."

"Scrarth and Avangar! Hod-ya's Ecclessite contestant is your Jeda? How can that be?"

"Yer talks as if'n yer kenned summat 'bout this," Scung intruded.

"Postings on every community pillar tell of a spectacular Scrarth and Avangar this year. It's a contest between a repatriated Ecclessite and the pride of Craniantium. So, it's true. Posters line the highways and byways to the border of Ecclessa, taunting kingsmen that one of our own has turned traitor and might well become the next Avangar Ultimate."

"When did you see this?" demanded Bonu.

"About two or three days ago as we crossed a road. The residents were so taken with the news that they failed to notice our pairs of cloaked brigaders walking right down the main street of their town. We couldn't help but overhear the gossip."

Bonu bit his lower lip.

"I'm sorry, I . . . I wasn't thinking," Oronet offered.

"No, I'm glad. I needed to know. Come on, Scung, that doesn't change anything."

The two men rose and wordlessly passed into the underbrush.

"King's road to you," Oronet called after them.

Bonu's vision blurred; he angrily forced his way through brambles, grief nearly overwhelming him. Operating solely on reflexes, he rushed past trees and hacked through tangled vines, no longer considerate of the giant slogging after him.

Scung managed as best he could, but Bonu's gait took a toll; the Eroton was sweating profusely, frequently pausing to sip from his water skin.

Three quarters of an hour later the pair came upon another Ecclessite band of fifteen men standing guard over wives and children. Bonu held his sword aloft proving he was no threat before revealing himself. After the initial shock, they gladly received directions to the cliffs. Scung took advantage of the respite to flop down on a bed of moss and catch his breath and refill his water skin from a small spring.

They hadn't gone ten more minutes into their journey when they bumped into yet another, larger company of nearly a hundred Ecclessites. Again, Bonu drew a hasty map and gave directions to the cliffs.

Peering over his shoulder as he and Scung crept back into the bush he mused aloud, "I've never encountered so many Ecclessites in my life as are in the woods today. What's going on?"

"Must be's thet regiment the feller tole usn's 'bout, doncher reckon?"

"I don't know, but if I send any more brigades to Captain Varter, he'll soon be a regimental leader. I hope the unexplored caves can accommodate all these refugees. I wish we could have taken time to hear each group's story, but our mission is more pressing."

"I be's wonderin' if'n mebbe our real mission, instead o' goin' ter Pitland, hain't sendin' all o' these reinforcements ter Varter."

Bonu stopped so short that Scung bumped into him. "I think you've hit on something, Scung. Not that we aren't supposed to go to Pitland, but that as we go, we'll find wandering kingsmen and send them to their objective, known or unknown to them. What a plan, Logon, what a plan. Who else could've arranged something the like? Little did we know when our brigade was attacked and split apart that it was all part of Elyon's strategy."

"Unmakin' the dread had summat ter do wi' all o' this, didn't it?"

"It may have been the long-awaited catalyst."

"Don't it make yer feel kinda special?"

Bonu spun around and checked his companion's neck.

"Whut?"

"Just looking for irks. They might try to get to me prideful again through you. Flattery is dangerous, Scung, especially on this mission. I take no credit for what happened, and you know it. I was boxed in, with no hope of escape. The Advisor led me; the idea wasn't mine, nor the courage. Logon gets all the glory for that episode. That goes for this mission, too, should we succeed. Now, let's keep our mind on what we're about lest we stumble into Carnalians." He lowered his head and charged into the next row of bushes.

A contrite Scung silently trailed.

They encountered twenty-three Ecclessite groups in all that day, and twenty-eight more the next. Some just a handful of refugees fearfully searching for shelter, other groups were larger and organized. Bonu patiently directed each group in the direction of the cliffs though it delayed his journey. It seemed like no sooner had they finished directing one group to the cliff caves before he and Scung barged through another hedgerow to meet another wandering group.

Only once, on the second day, were they forced to scurry under a tangle of vines upon encountering a Carnalian patrol that passed within arm's length of their meager hiding place.

On the third day they encountered ten more Ecclessite bands; they were large, each with upwards of a hundred souls. Bonu was concerned that such large companies couldn't travel undetected for long. Nevertheless, these brigades had found their way from the outlands to the relative safety of Ra-Amawl. A vast pogrom must be taking place in the empire for he and Scung to encounter so many refugees.

Dusk of the third day found Bonu and Scung overlooking a vast flowered meadow as they wearily plopped down behind a hedgerow. This last remnant of dense foliage marked the border of Ra-Amawl. Their trek had taken a toll; the elevated temperature and humidity especially affected Scung.

"Look, there's a Carnalian patrol camped right out in the open field, Scung. If we had more men we could overpower them and keep traveling through the night. As it is, we'll have to wait 'til they move on."

"Thanks be's ter Logon," muttered Scung flopping to his back.

Bonu turned and evaluated his companion. "I know this journey has been hard on you, Scung. It has on me, too, but for Jeda's sake, I intentionally spared no time. As it is, we have only days 'til the contest. That's not much time to cover the ground between here and the arena, let alone find and dig up the hidden swords to arm the kingsmen prisoners. I have no idea where to begin or even how to convey such a load of swords to the captives. Nevertheless, I truly regret that I wasn't more sensitive to your needs."

Scung nodded. "T'warn't nuthin' yer couldda helped. I kenned whut I be's gettin' inter afore I come along. I gots no complaints."

"You're a true Logon-man, Scung. You'll go far in the kingdom, if we survive."

"Hmmph! If'n we survives." Scung smiled. "I be's gonna git a good night's sleep, an' then we go."

"Let's sharpen our swords before we sleep. We may not get another chance for a while. Those watchmen aren't aware of and don't suspect an enemy presence; if we keep quiet, these bushes will cover the light."

"Sounds good ter me," said Scung withdrawing sword and toller.

Bonu stroked his blade; Scung imitated his every move, placing his toller on exactly the same spot on his own sword. For several minutes they filed in relative silence, then faintly at first, but gradually increasing in intensity, the light of a rune shone upon their faces. A subtle, almost inaudible, hum filled the air as their tollers vibrated in their hands.

Scung paused and watched in wonder as Bonu whispered the words coursing through both their minds:

"Logon triumphed o'er Lurcan and grave,
Rising on high in victorious shout,
With life and power; able to save,
Driving shadows from hiding place out,
Giving gifts to those proven brave,
A strong army sent leaders devout,
Generals with wisdom set battle wave,
Seers revealing more sure than scout,
Recruiters enlist those that truth crave,
Captains train and lead to the rout,
Lieutenants and sergeants free advice gave,
So grows the force, o'ercoming all doubt.

Diverse brigades lay down your feuds, 'tis unity's demand,
One king, one hope, one prince of all, one hearty, mighty band,
Will rise again rejoined at last for battle long-time planned,
Against the day of fierce, dark wrath o'er spreading all the land."

"I gits it, Bonu, I unnerstands whut it means! Thet's why we been runnin' inter all different brigades. The king be's done wi' allowin' things whut separates Ecclessites. He be's gonna put usn's all together ter learn ter git along, an' meet the enemy in one final, do or die battle."

"History shows that such confrontations shed much blood."

The two lay their swords down and contemplated the rune.

"I ain't afeered ter die, Bonu. I kens Logon now, an' ain't afeered o' death no more," Scung said softly, staring at dark, voluminous clouds scudding along the horizon.

Bonu, preoccupied with his own thoughts of Jeda didn't really listen, but grunted an affirmative anyway. "I think we'd better take what rest we can, Scung. Once inside Pitland I doubt we'll get much opportunity."

Bonu watched Scung cover himself with leaves and branches for both camouflage and warmth. Scung sighed, stretched his legs, and finished layering forest detritus overtop himself.

As Bonu drifted off to sleep he sent thoughts of Jeda to Logon. She undoubtedly faced unspeakable horrors; and all he could do was appeal to Logon on her behalf. He also mentioned Captain Varter, the various brigades they'd met, Kraga, Glend, and Scung—this valiant recruit who'd so immediately and completely reversed the course of his life, forsaking Eroton's pleasures for Ecclessa's struggles.

Within minutes the two kingsmen were asleep, yet semi-conscious of the forest around them.

Hours later Bonu stirred, rising in the dim glow of pre-dawn. He stretched, then nudged Scung with a foot. The pair brushed off the desiccated camouflage and rose. Within minutes both had taken care of their needs and made preparation to resume their journey.

"I see a low fire," intoned Bonu. "I assume they stood watch all night. That's not usual. I wonder what's up?"

"I dunno, but them watchmen looks ter be a sleepin now'. We kin sneak past."

"Sure be quicker than circling way out and around. Besides, we might run into other watch fires along the perimeter. Let's give it a try."

"Walk on me outterside, lieutenant. In this dim light, me Eroton leathers might make 'em think we be's jest a couple o' Erotons."

"Good idea, Scung."

The two boldly walked across the meadow leaving bent wildflower stalks in their wake. Copious dew splashed their boots and leggings as they pursued an oblique course a safe distance from the campfire. Bonu decided that passing close by the fire would raise less suspicions than wandering far afield. As they approached the guardpost they counted seven men laying prone and an eighth seated but leaning heavily on his spear, chin slumped onto his chest. Bonu and Scung scarce took a breath as they passed. The guard who was most likely to sound an alarm slept blissfully, unaware that his post was being compromised by an enemy slipping across the border into Pitland.

Every nerve taut, the duo picked up their pace after they passed the campsite. Half-a-mile later they broke into a jog until they found themselves peering down over the edge of sheer cliffs into the sunken lands of Pitland.

"Thus ends the easy part of our journey, Scung. Now we face the final descent to the sere, infernal realm of the White Priestess."

Daybreak on the edge of Pitland made little difference, for dense, roiling clouds obscured both the sun and blue of sky, producing a perpetual dusk as surely as the bowers of Ra-Amawl banished daylight under its verdant canopy.

"Lurcan's work to be sure, this darkness at mid-morning," Bonu wiped his nose.

"Aye. It be's the furnaces o' Pitland forgin' black-steel. Soon yer'll smell the brimstone. We be's close."

"You've been here before?"

"Naw, but I heered from them whut has. Lookit over yonder, hain't thet a inn or summat?"

"Looks like it."

"Thet must be the Woeful Willows Inn, as I heered it called. I don't ken what its right name be's—summat 'bout willow trees, I thinks. I do ken we be's on the road whut leads ter the descent. On the cliff o' Pitland there be's few descents down inter Pitland; and nary but this one fer leagues an' leagues either way—carved right outta the stone wall an' barely wide enuf fer nobbut a wagon. Thet be's the path we gots ter go."

"So I've heard. I expect Logon will show us where to dig for the swords of Vadiv once we get down there."

The pair trotted through the waist-high grass along the edge of the cliff marking the final leg of their journey. An hour later, breathing heavily and dripping with perspiration they peered again into Pitland's sunken territory, making note of the carved road Scung had mentioned—barely a wagon track on a steep decline with no guardrails. There were no vehicles on the narrow cornice-road, but they were so high and the air rising from the valley so murky that it was nigh impossible to distinguish anything below them.

"Once we start down, there'll be nowhere to run or hide if we're discovered."

"Let's git goin'."

CHAPTER TWELVE

Bonu and Scung needed to pause halfway down the narrow cornice. To relieve and stretch their fatigued calf muscles they turned and faced uphill.

"Arrgh!" muttered Scung. "An' ter think our escape be's up this selfsame trail. I dunno, Bonu, it be's a weariness ter me bones."

"We probably won't escape anyway, so what's the problem?" Bonu smiled grimly.

"Oh yeah, right! Thet makes me feel a whole lot better."

"Come on, let's not waste too much time. Say, is that a dray coming downhill toward us?"

Scung squinted at the distant object.

A vehicle occupying nearly the trail's width had just crested the top of the road and was indeed, headed downhill. "Yep! Looks ter be a two-trace wagon o' some sort. We'd best hurry ter keep ahead o' it."

"Right," said Bonu turning and trotting downhill. With each jarring step their leg muscles ached more. "Whoever constructed this road must have been in a hurry; the lower half is even steeper than the upper."

"Aye."

The balls of Bonu's feet slapped so hard his toes stung. He had the disconcerting thought that if he fell he would continue sliding downhill on his belly or spin out of control and fly off the ledge.

Bonu glanced over his shoulder at his friend. "I'm glad you're along, Scung, I wouldn't want to face what lies ahead on my lonesome."

"Uh huh," puffed Scung, focused on the path ahead.

Bonu doubted Scung even heard him, but was, nonetheless, glad he'd said it.

Ahead Bonu spotted two patrols assaying to come uphill, with about twenty men each, oblivious to the distant wagon rumbling downhill! The first patrol preceded the other by some fifty paces. "Uh-oh, here comes more trouble."

"Eh?" The giant raised his eyes from the path. "Nah, they's jest on their way up. I doubts they's gonna give usn's nary trouble. See their battle packs? They gots troubles enuf o' their own; headin' fer some battle zone, I be's guessin'."

"I hope you're right. I look like neither Carnalian nor Eroton in these garments, woodsy though they are. If they scrutinize me at all we could be in for a rough time."

"I'll distract 'em if'n they suspects yer. Or we kin make like yer be's me prisoner."

Urgent shouting behind them suddenly erupted. The driver of the dray heading down the cliff road was unsuccessfully trying to restrain the mule-team by pulling back on the reins with all his weight while at the same time the brakeman thrust his bulk against the brake handle.

"Scung, something is wrong. That wagon is coming too fast."

Sure enough, smoke swirled from overheated hubs, then a flickering flame jumped to the wagon's underbelly and spread to the grease on the front axle. Even as Bonu and Scung watched, the brakeman's handle snapped completely off. The freewheeling wagon bumped into the mules' backsides. The outer beast veered away toward the edge of the road to escape the cumbersome vehicle ramming it, drawing its yoke-mate directly into the path of the careering dray. Then the outer mule lost its footing and disappeared over the ledge still secured in the harness, hanging inverted, braying and kicking. The other mule's feet got tangled in the reins and fell under the wagon's foremost wheels. The wagon jolted to a stop. Both mules brayed in fear and pain; men angrily shouted, and the shrill scream of a girl was heard.

In the front of the wagon a young girl clad in a Logon dress appeared, trying to fend off a dronnet who was grasping at her from behind. An iron collar around the girl's neck was connected to a chain in the dronnet's fist. The dronnet appeared intent on dragging the girl out the back gate of the dray. He gave a fierce tug on the chain to pull the girl along with him as he leapt out the back of the burning wagon.

In the struggle, the driver was knocked off his perch and sent flying over the cliff's edge. The girl, however, became jammed between the driver's seat and the front foot brace where the chain snagged on a strut. Struggle as she did, the girl couldn't extricate herself.

"Artil!" Bonu exclaimed.

"Artil?" Scung echoed. "Mebbe Jeda an' Spoena be's in thet wagon, too!"

"Come on," Bonu unsheathed his Child of the Stars and churned uphill as fast as his legs would go.

"Bonu, they'll kens we be's Ecclessite!"

"Can't be helped; no time for being inconspicuous. You coming or not?"

Scung drew his own sword and charged uphill.

The backside covering canvas had caught fire, shredding sparks and pieces of flaming fabric onto the trail behind. The mule wedged beneath the wheel's double tree furiously kicked at the vehicle. Each smashing kick splintered the wagon's underside little by little until at last the double tree was dislodged. The dangling mule, no longer suspended by the harness, plummeted over the edge braying in terror.

The wagon, suddenly free of the blockage, lurched up and over the remaining mule and free-wheeled downhill. The dronnet got entangled in his chain and was dragged behind. Artil was yanked back and pinned against a brace, her face turned blue as her fingers desperately tugged at the collar around her neck. Artil struggled, gasping for each breath, but couldn't free herself of the chain as the dray picked up momentum.

The oncoming Carnalian troops heading uphill froze at the unfolding scene above them; they were in the wagon's path with nowhere to dodge and no niche to duck into to evade the vehicle. Even if they jammed themselves tight against the cliff wall, the dray was bound to scrape them off as it careered past if it didn't swerve over the ledge first but stayed in the ruts of the road.

Bonu outpaced Scung, charging uphill to Artil's rescue.

~

Spots floated before Artil's eyes followed by a growing darkness. She dimly saw the dronnet trying but unable to release the chain knotted around his wrist. The flapping canvas scattered pieces of flaming fabric in the wagon's wake and onto the dronnet. He hissed, sputtered, then howled as his clothing began to smolder. In his frantic flailing at the flames his mask was knocked askew, revealing pallid, haggard features.

The wagon lurched sharply into the rocky wall; for a moment Artil's throat constriction was relieved and she sucked in another breath.

~

Bonu feared the wagon would rebound and plummet over the edge, taking Artil and any other passengers with it. But suddenly the front wheel turned and ground into the wall sending a shower of sparks into the air, slowing the vehicle, keeping it on the path. Bonu saw his chance as the vehicle drew closer and leapt at the driver's perch, grasping the braces for balance. With one swipe of his sword he severed the chain choking Artil. Sputtering, she collapsed into the bed. In the roadway behind the dray lay the battered, smoldering dronnet still spinning around like a top, finally slowing to rest in the middle of the trail between the wagon ruts, growling and slapping at his clothing.

Bonu hacked away at the remaining canvas, slicing through ribs, tie-downs, and ropes with abandon to remove the threat of fire claiming the rest of vehicle. Then, bracing against a front-rib, he shouted at Scung who still labored uphill. "When you get close enough, jump up here, Scung, I'll grab you!"

By Scung's puzzled expression Bonu realized that the Eroton didn't comprehend his words, but hopefully could decipher Bonu's hand motions that he was to leap aboard the oncoming wagon.

"Be's yer daft? I'll break me legs!" Scung slowed his pace. He quickly checked downhill on the progress of the Carnalian troops and was startled to see they were charging full tilt uphill, howling to have at him! His own blue-tipped sword—insignificant alongside Bonu's—was nonetheless quite visible in Pitland's dim light.

"Scung, jump. It's your only chance," Bonu shouted. The wagon, still grinding into the wall, drew closer.

Artil, with a length of the severed chain dangling from her collar, rose and knelt beside Bonu, holding onto him more for comfort than balance. She hoarsely called, "Come on, Scung, come on, you can do it."

"Oh, Logon, whut be's I gonna do now? I'd rather fight them Carnalians than jump onter thet wagon. I be's nary good at jumpin'."

"Scung, I order you, jump!"

The wagon clattered closer, its iron-rimmed front wheel sparking against the stone wall, showering stone chips in a spray of dust and pebbles. Bonu clearly saw that Scung was sure to be run over unless he either turned downhill and ran into the attacking Carnalians or did as Bonu commanded.

"Jump!" Bonu shouted again.

Scung leapt, using the tongue as a springboard. His thighs slammed into and splintered the boards, catapulting him into the cargo space, knocking Bonu and Artil to the floor. The three lay there dazed.

Bonu mumbled, "Ugh! Get off me, Scung."

Scung moaned, but obediently rolled away. Bonu, sword drawn, took a defensive stance at the fore of the wagon, shouting to the onrushing Carnalians, "Let me pierce your hearts, for your own sake."

A hail of arrows clattered harmlessly around him. Bonu's sword swiftly swung about, knocking the better-aimed projectiles off their intended course. The wagon's front wheels suddenly lurched upward, accompanied by sickening thumps and shrill screams as the wagon cruised through the first band of Carnalians. Some lay crumpled in the path behind, others leapt or were bumped over the ledge and still others prostrated themselves flat in the middle of the roadway in the hopes that the vehicle's undercarriage would pass over them. Tears welled in Bonu's eyes as he beheld the carnage strewn behind.

Scung shook his head, sat up and massaged his bruised thighs, checking for fractures. Finding none he gritted his teeth and forced himself to stand beside Bonu as the free-wheeling wagon approached the second band of soldiers.

Artil clambered to her feet and braced herself against the upright ribs of the wagon as she wrestled the bung out of a water barrel. Water spurted from the bunghole onto the wooden planks, quenching any hungry flames in a hiss of steam.

"Hold your sword like this," Bonu instructed Scung, demonstrating a defensive position.

Scung imitated Bonu as best he could, then looked backwards over the wagon over. "Say, whut be's keepin' this here wagon from plungin' over the edge?"

"Don't you see the bright?"

The hairs on Scung's neck visibly rose. "Bright? Did you say bright?"

There was no time to answer; the second band of Carnalians, slashing their black swords, hurled themselves at the wagon. The Ecclessites' swords swung into action, deflecting the empire weapons, knocking attackers to either side and beneath the rolling wagon where most were harmlessly passed over. Three Carnalians attacked the wagon front at the same time, one jumping high and undershooting his mark, catching his foot in the spinning spokes of the front wheel. There was a loud snap as the man was separated from his leg at the hip. The dray plowed through the last of them who were making a final attempt to board the dray.

"Let me pierce your hearts!" pleaded Bonu, leaning over the front edge. "Before it's too late, let me pierce your hearts."

More arrows pelted down around them. Bonu, Scung, and Artil dodged back to the floorboards, unable to maintain their balance in the front any longer as the wagon yawed up first on one side, then the other. All at once the wagon came down hard on all four wheels and gained momentum in its headlong descent.

"We be's goin' o'er the edge," howled Scung.

"Look at the wagon's fork, Scung." Artil pointed a shaky finger. "Don't you see the roamer?"

Scung peered nervously at what looked to be sparks off the broken iron-clad steering tongue. A barely discernible column of lights hovered within the display of sparks.

"It's safer in the wagon than outside," Bonu said.

"But at what expense?" wondered Artil, looking backward at the broken and dazed bodies littered behind.

"Casualties are inevitable. We must never intentionally bring harm, but we also must go where we're sent, and do what we're commanded, leaving the results in his hands. The final harvest of souls is beginning; those who perish without pierced hearts wouldn't have come to Logon anyway. Logon loves them more than we do, yet knows they'll never respond to his amnesty.

"The runes make it clear that most Carnalians will scoff at Logon's offer. This is a one-way mission; there's little doubt how it will end for us."

"I thought I was being rescued," Artil glumly sank to her knees. "I'm so young, my whole life is before me."

"Maybe your whole life's purpose is to glorify your prince with a sacrifice of your future ambitions and hopes. To die in the king's service at the hands of infidels is a great honor, Artil, even to one so young. Not many attain that level of devotion, indeed, few are even called to it; not many see beyond the natural world. If you truly believe it's better to be with Logon than to have all that the empire offers, you qualify to receive the honor of risking your life in his service. There are great rewards in Splendora for such ones if they don't shrink back."

Artil nodded as she splashed more water on the smoldering floorboards.

"I wants thet. I kens I be's nobbut a novice myself in Logon's ways, but I wants thet. They be's naught in this here world I desires. I found Logon, an' he be's all I could ever want."

Bonu laid his hand on Scung's shoulder and gave it a squeeze. "How are your legs?"

"Mighty sore, but jest bruised, I reckons. Here, we be's gettin close ter the bottom. Hain't usn's better be layin' down an' hide?" advised Scung.

"Right," agreed Bonu, shifting his attention to the guard post at the bottom of the trail. "Artil, crawl under this blanket; Scung and I will take our chances lying close to the sides. Do you have enough room to stretch out, Scung?"

"Almost."

With swords hidden beneath them, the two assumed supine positions tight against the sides of the wagon. Scung bent his knees slightly to keep his feet from dangling out over the tailgate.

The wagon jounced unswervingly into Pitland, carrying the clandestine agents of an enemy nation. Had Bonu and Scung walked the entire length of their trail, it would have taken hours, yet the careering wagon covered the distance in less than three-quarters of an hour.

The wagon leveled off as it came off the grade and continued on beyond the men guarding the gateway. It maintained its speed, rumbling past curious onlookers and sentries at the checkpoint. Such a wagon rolling down the trail on its own would naturally draw a little curious attention of many people; however, the spectacle of two Carnalian squads getting demolished in the careering wagon's wake drew the attention of everyone in the vicinity of the lower gateway. A company of soldiers was hastily deployed across the road to stop the approaching wagon.

The wagon never slowed, but smashed through the crossing gate, rolling unhindered, scattering guards in all directions. It cruised over level ground kicking up a dust cloud, drawing even more attention. On an upgrade, where it seemed the wagon should have slowed, several soldiers rallied in an attempt to leap aboard, but the wagon increased velocity and the soldiers arrived too late with nothing to do but haplessly stand in the middle of the road and watch it depart for unknown destinations.

Only a few Ecclessite prisoners laboring under heavy burdens in chains along the road noted the twinkling column at the fore of the speeding wagon and took hope.

Shouting and clamor gradually faded to the trio sprawled in the bed of the jolting wagon as it traversed the highway through towns and hamlets and further out into unpopulated hinterlands.

Bonu finally dared to raise his head and peek over the sides. “We’re clear,” he said, “we’re coming to a desert; there’s nobody or nothing around except miles and miles of sand and sere brush.”

Scung’s head immediately popped up. He surveyed the horizon and wondered aloud, “We hain’t slowed up nary a bit?”

“The bright is still transporting us.”

Artil slowly peered over the edge, her eyes wide. “We’re not being chased by empire soldiers?”

“The bright is taking us to a safe place.”

“I hain’t never seen the likes. A wagon coasting in a straight line, even over knolls, at the same speed as when usn’s was rushin’ downhill! Wi’out horses, mules or nuthin’. Taint natural!”

Bonu smiled and got to his feet. "Of course, 'taint natural', Scung. Logon 'taint natural'. Neither are his roamers."

"Yeah, thet's right, roamers be's on our side. I gots ta remember thet." The shaggy Eroton shook his head and tugged his beard, staring wonderingly at the sparkles at the fore of the wagon.

A quarter of an hour later the wagon suddenly veered off the road to smash its way through a scrubby bush-barrens, leaving a trail, to Bonu's concern, that could easily be followed.

"Trackers are sure to come," Bonu mumbled.

The surrounding landscape was dry, cracked open and with shimmering heatwaves, and no hint of moisture anywhere. Bonu looked regretfully at the water barrel Artil opened to douse the fire; it was now nearly empty. Perhaps enough liquid still sloshed in the bottom for the three to share a warm but wet drink.

On and on the wagon rumbled through Pitland's interior, heading unerringly toward some destination known only to the bright.

Bonu propped himself in a corner. "Well, as long as we're being chauffeured, I should like to hear your story, Artil. What happened, and where are Jeda and Spoena?"

Scung settled into the opposite corner, massaging his thighs.

Artil hugged her knees to her chest.

Bonu added, "It might be useful for us to know the circumstances, painful as they may be to relive in the telling. Is it because you don't know Scung?"

Artil studied the Eroton, evidently fearful of the over-sized Eroton.

"He's been to Logon's Rock, Artil. I had the privilege of piercing his chest. You need not feel strange around him; trust me, he is a brother."

Artil sighed, "All right. You have a right to know, I suppose." Artil recounted events starting with Bonu setting forth on his scouting expedition to be alone with his broken heart. She related how the three girls got separated from the main group while foraging, encountered gorrils, were lost in Ra-Amawl and stumbled into the Nutherway brigade.

Bonu interrupted her. "Those scary men you saw on the cliff were Scung and me."

Artil's eyes went round with wonder as Bonu described his encounter with the dread and how he was rescued by Scung.

"You, you killed a dread?"

"Not killed, unmade. And I'm afraid I had very little to do with it. I desperately flung my sword and Logon somehow directed it to land where the monster, in his arrogance, would pierce himself, causing his own demise. Now before you finish your story, I'll tell you what happened with the Nutherway brigaders." He briefly told of chasing after the battlefield scavengers who turned out to be the Nutherway Brigade.

"You were that close? Why didn't you rescue us?"

"Logon's ways are not our ways. For whatever reasons, he prevented our rescuing you then, and even again after that. I, that is, Scung and I tracked you to the trail through the jungle and even watched your campfire one night. Logon restrained us from interfering. Here's what happened after that . . . "

Artil listened as the fate of each Nutherway member was related. "I'm glad Bletza was rescued and is with a proper brigade. I could tell she regretted betraying us to Hod-ya." Artil then resumed her narrative, recounting the journey through Ra-Amawl past the flowery meadow and their arrival at Willow House. "That's where I got separated from Spoena and Jeda. Hod-ya thought she'd deceived me with her precious gems, that I'd been subverted by desire for riches. She didn't know that one of the captured kingsmen at the table next to ours, Tren was his name, whispered to me that Logon was going to set me free, and in order to accomplish this, I should pretend to desire wealth and power. I was sent toward Pitland ahead of Spoena and Jeda with only one dronnet as my escort. Before we reached the road going down the cliff, a lion, huge as a house and black as midnight, sprang out of the high grasses. The dronnet dropped my chain to defend himself. I'd never seen a man fight a Craniantium lion by himself."

"That's the test they must pass to become dronnets," commented Bonu, "by individually killing a lion."

"I was so engrossed in watching the fight that I forgot to run; I almost missed my chance. I dashed off into the high grass, but then got scared there might be more lions. So I turned back to the road but got lost and wandered for hours. Finally, I stumbled back into the woods where we had paused with Hod-ya just before she took us to Willow House. I found a small satchel of food, it must have accidentally been dropped, along with a water bag. I went deeper into the woods, hoping to find my way back to Captain Varter's brigade. I slept in trees at night for fear of prowling animals. During the day I wandered, not sure of my direction; clouds blotted out the sun, and the trees were unfamiliar, I wasn't able to tell north from south. I guess I got turned around and wandered back toward Pitland. After a couple more days, I'm not sure how many, I wandered into the campsite of the men who were searching for me, including the dronnet who killed the lion. They recaptured me, and well, here I am. I was loaded into the first supply wagon that happened by. The dronnet wanted to get me to Pitland as fast as possible. Suddenly a fight broke out between two guards in the wagon. When others tried to intervene, things got out of control. They threw supplies at each other, most of it went out the tailgate or over the cliff; I'm not sure what happened next until you broke the chain that kept me prisoner."

Bonu rose to his knees and looked ahead. "We're slowing down. Hey! It's gone!"

"Who?" demanded Scung. "Not the bright?"

"Yes, the bright; he's gone! Without so much as a fare-thee-well."

"Bonu," Artil pleaded, "Why am I in Pitland? Why are you here? Why didn't Logon keep us out of this awful place?"

"Because," Bonu expressed with more optimism than he felt, "we have work to do. King Vadiv buried swords somewhere along these cliffs bordering Pitland; we've been sent to recover them and arm captured Ecclessites in order to raise a revolt against the powers that rule Pitland."

"What?" Artil put her hands n her hips. "Bonu, have cusps taken over your mind? No one can invade Pitland. Especially just two men."

"That's the beauty of Logon's plan. He's already invaded Pitland with thousands of soldiers, only they're here as prisoners, unarmed, beaten-down and discouraged. Most, if not all, expect they'll spend the rest of their miserable lives as prisoners here. But Logon sent us to restore their confidence, rally their hope, and re-arm them with the swords of Vadiv. The day of Pitland's fall has come!"

Artil turned to face Scung. "Did he hit his head or get irk bit?"

"Nay, lassie, we be's here ter ignite the overthrow."

"You're both mad."

"No, Artil, not mad, wrathful! We're agents of Logon's wrath sent against Lurcan, which will commence shortly after we find those swords. See, he's even provided a wagon for us to cart them—remember how concerned I was about that detail, Scung? Behold Logon's provision."

"Aye."

"But Bonu?"

"What?"

"Aren't you forgetting that we're to love, not hate; restore, not revenge."

"Yes, dear, sweet Artil, I know that; we don't seek revenge, but grieve even for those who, without a second thought, would've killed us today. But I also recognize that Elyon's wrath is coming and most Carnalians have made their choice; there's nothing more we can do except present them with one last chance to seek Logon's amnesty. That's the ultimate act of love. Don't forget, our swords can't harm. Even wounds from these swords bring life. Nevertheless, those who resist will face severe consequences. That can't be helped; indeed, we oppose Logon's will if we try any other tactic than what he's chosen."

"I guess you're right. It's just that I don't know why I'm here. I'm not a warrior; I'm not even grown up yet. I'm only twelve years old. Why would Logon bring me here?"

"You're here, so it must be his will. That's all you need to know."

Artil resigned herself. "Okay, so tell me, how can I help?"

"Yer kin keep a lookout whiles me an' Bonu digs up the swords. Where does we start, Bonu?"

Bonu stood up in the wagon bed and scanned over the tops of the dried shrubbery cluttering the plain. "I'm not sure. I thought the roamer might give us some instructions before he left, but he didn't."

"Mebbe we oughtta toll our blades an' see if'n Logon don't light up a rune."

"Good idea, Scung. You're learning fast."

They sat on the sideboards, their swords across their thighs, plying their tollers. "I thinks I gots a rune beginnin' ter glow."

"Really? Let me see." Bonu inspected his recruit's sword. "No, I don't think so, Scung. But keep trying."

The two continued several more minutes, laboring diligently tolling by various spots along the blade, Artil anxiously watching over their shoulders. No fresh glow came to any rune, no humming arose from their blades and no sense came of what to do next. Finally, Bonu sighed. "Well, I guess we should expect Logon to guide us another way; let's start digging."

"Where?" Scung shrugged and looked around in a circle.

Bonu pointed left. "Let's try over there, at the base of those white stone cliffs. Fighting our way through this brush isn't going to be easy. Artil, maybe you'd better stay with the wagon."

"Nuh-uh! I was set free once, only to be captured again, so I'm not about to let you get away. Wherever you go, I go!"

"These are dense pricker bushes with thorns this long," Bonu demonstrated holding his thumb and forefinger apart, "and who knows what manner of bugs or venomous reptiles are here."

"You're not leaving me. Suppose they send trackers while you two are off digging up swords? What then?"

"She be's right, Bonu. It hain't hardly right ter be leavin' her behind. Arter all, usn's don't perzactly kens whut usn's be's gettin' inter, ourselves. She might prove useful."

Bonu reconsidered. “Well,” he leveled a finger under her nose, “I want no complaints about how hard the going gets. You’ll be bruised and scratched, at the very least. Are you ready for that?”

“Anything is better than being left alone.”

“All right, but I don’t want to hear one word of complaint!”

“You won’t.”

CHAPTER THIRTEEN

Branches snagged Artil's hair and spines pricked her palms and knees as she crawled in Bonu's wake through the thorny bushes littering the barrens. "Ouch!" she inadvertently blurted but recovered quickly before Bonu could chastise her.

Bonu, preoccupied with trail blazing, barely noticed Artil's whimper. Dense undergrowth hindered his sense of direction. And more than that, when and if they found the swords, just how were the three of them to transport a wagonload of weapons to Ecclessite prisoners?

Bonu cleared a swath through the tangled growth with his Child of the Stars keeping a watchful eye out for venomous reptiles, spiders, and stinging insects. A trail of chopped vegetation mixed with little bloody dots littered the ground, but compared with weightier matters, these stings and stabs were trifling annoyances.

~

Scung did what he could to render thorns, spines, and nuisance branches harmless for Artil's sake. His own knees and shins were somewhat protected by his leggings and leather battle gear, but his hands that bore the brunt of the prickly pathway were studded with tiny thorns. He winced every time Artil whimpered, blaming himself for not thoroughly removing harmful objects from Artil's path. Formerly he would've expected anyone following him to fend for themselves while he avoided the painful thorns. He'd have even mocked their difficulty; but Logon had thoroughly changed his heart; now he actually cared for his . . . dare he think of Artil and Bonu as family? In his heart he loved them as if, perhaps even more than, family. Was that proper? How could these people he'd known such a short time have gotten inside his heart's defenses?

He twisted around to see how Artil fared, feeling protective; she was his little sister doggedly following in his wake.

"What's the matter; why are you looking at me? Did I do something wrong?" Artil challenged.

"I hain't never had a little sister afore, an' wants ter make sure yer be's okay."

"Ouch!" she uttered as a thorn nicked her ankle. "Well, if you want to be my big brother, tell Bonu to find a softer path. This one is full of briars, sticks, and, and, I don't know what all." Catching Bonu's disapproving glance she quickly added, "But that's the way I like it."

Artil's quick-wit amused the men.

"Take a break while I get my bearings." Bonu stood up and attacked the interlaced branches overhead, showering the trio in twigs and dried leaves. Debris rained down on Artil and Scung, clinging in their hair and on their shoulders. Bonu made enough of a hole to rise to full height and thrust his sword further into the tangled overhead network. "Bah! It's still tightly interlocked up there. Scung, I need to sit on your shoulders so I can break through."

"Awright." Scung crawled over to Bonu. "Stand on me back an' have at it."

Bonu climbed aboard Scung's broad back and thrust his sword upward, pelting more vegetation down. "I'm through," he finally said, widening the hole with his sword. "Stand on your feet and let me perch on your shoulders so I can get a fix on the cliffs."

"I do hope this is where the swords are buried." Artil wistfully surveyed the dense thicket surrounding them.

"Artil, how can you doubt it? Why else would the roamer leave us here alongside these cliffs?"

"Well, there have been times something seemed to be Logon's will but, look at the mess we three girls got ourselves into."

"Yes, and now you're safe with us, aren't you?"

"Hardly whut I be's callin' safe." Scung winked at Artil.

"Thanks for that comforting word, Scung. Hold still, will you."

"It's jest thet I feels funny 'bout findin' them swords hereabouts. I hain't got knowledge o' the runes like yer, but I doesn't feel we be's anywhars near them swords."

"You sense it, too?" Artil looked up hopefully. "I've been feeling that we ought to head toward the amphitheater instead of digging for swords here."

"The swords are the key to the revolt," Bonu patiently explained.

"Kyleah's 'seein' showed nobbut five people escapin' Pitland, not a army, accordin' ter the capt'n."

"Kyleah, my stepmother, had a vision?" Artil got upright on her knees.

Scung nodded.

"Hey! Hold still. Okay, steady now, I'm up. Uh-oh."

"Whut?"

"There's some kind of activity at the cliff base."

"Whut be's it?" Scung's tone was hushed.

"Can't tell for sure. It might be slaves—no wait, they're prisoners of war."

"Be's it Carnalians lookin' fer us?"

"No, I don't think so. It looks more like a work crew of some kind—or, oh no!"

"Whut? Tell me, Bonu. Don't be keepin' me in suspense."

"It's an execution squad. They're binding kingsmen to posts."

"Execution!" exclaimed Scung and Artil together.

"Let me down. We've got to get over there."

"But won't they hear us coming?"

"I can't stand idly by and watch an execution. I hope they do hear us and think we're a battalion of kingsmen charging through the canebrake."

"Thet actually might work, Bonu. Let usn's split up an' start hollerin' as if'n we be's three brigades. We kin thrash about an' make all the noise we wants. How close be's the cliffs?"

"A hundred paces or so, but the bushes thin out nearer the cliffs. Artil, you stay here in the middle and make no noise until my signal, here, take my hunting knife and do what you can to get through the thicket. I'm sorry, but it's all I have besides my sword. Scung, you sneak about fifty paces to Artil's left while I outflank them the same distance on the right"

"On me way."

"Signal when you're ready. Can you imitate a desert thrush?"

Scung grunted an affirmative, already pushing through the bushes.

"I hope thrushes are common to Pitland. When you hear my reply, make as much commotion as you can, thrashing branches, shouting war commands, try to sound like a large attack force."

~

Minutes later Artil heard Scung's thrush imitation. She almost didn't recognize it for it blended perfectly with other natural sounds. In another minute Bonu's response came from the opposite direction, followed by a loud shout, "Kingsmen, form up, ready on the left!"

"Form up, ready on the right! CHARGE! LIVES FOR THE KING!"

From Artil's left Scung's unmistakable, gravelly voice bellowed, echoing Bonu's commands, ending with Ecclessa's battle cry, "LIVES FOR THE KING!"

A ruckus simultaneously erupted from both sides; shaking bushes, loud shouts, battle commands. Artil suddenly remembered that she had a part to play in this attack, so, joining in with bush-whacking and high-pitched screams, hoots and shouts, sounding more like a brigade of banshees than kingsmen she added to the overall chaos. Armed only with Bonu's foot-long hunting dirk, Artil made little progress through the undergrowth.

"Captain, send a hundred men to the flank," Bonu shouted.

"Aye," answered Scung. "An' I'll add another corps."

"No prisoners!" Bonu ordered.

"Gottem surrounded, sir!" returned Scung. "No prisoners it be's!"

"No prisoners!" shrieked Artil, her soprano voice blending in the confusion.

A covey of quail exploded from cover with booming thunder in their wings right in front of Artil, scaring the wits out of her, but adding to the cacophony like the melee of a large attack force.

Confusion broke out among the Carnalians. Orders were shouted, then countermanded:

"Hold your line men, it's a bluff."

"Form up, draw your line."

"Belay that order. Come back here and hold your ground."

"Retreat! Send for reinforcements."

"We don't have enough to hold out against a regiment, I say retreat."

"I'll put an arrow through the first man who retreats."

"Here's an arrow for you, then."

"He shot the sergeant!"

"Retreat!"

"Hold the line."

From Artil's right Bonu's voice commanded, "We've got them on the run! Now up to the chase."

"That's it. I'm getting out," cried Scung, sounding very Carnalian and close by Artil.

"Me, too."

"Wait up."

Weapons thudded as they hit the hard, baked ground. The pounding of retreating feet faded to the left, and so did the commanding and countermanding of orders.

"Artil, where are you?" Bonu called.

"I'm . . . here, arrgh, in this tangle—"

A blue flash arced in front of her eyes and Bonu's blood-flecked face peered through an opening. "Are you wounded?" she asked.

"Huh? Oh, no, just scratched by briars. Are you all right?"

"I'm fine, just tired from hacking at branches with this knife."

"You did fine. That was brilliant scaring those birds into the air."

"It's not as if I meant to. They were just nesting—"

"Scung, are you all right? The executioners must have fled right over top of you."

"Aye, an' I near ter stabbed one o' 'em!" The huge Eroton stood, scratched and blood-speckled on his outer gear but smiling ear to ear. Both men's outer garments were even more tattered about the sleeves and shoulders than previously. Bloody splotches showed through wherever their Logon tunics didn't cover, but neither kingsman minded. "How be's the executees?"

"I forgot to check. I haven't heard a word from them. You don't suppose—"

"Let's find out. Mebbe yer oughtta stay back, missy; we gots ter see how the prisoners be's."

"Oh, Logon, let them be safe," begged Artil, ignoring Scung's suggestion and stumbling along behind Bonu and Scung. As Bonu had said, the vegetation thinned-out considerably nearer the cliffs. "Bonu, are they—" she called.

"They're, yes, they're all okay."

Artil entered the clearing and saw seven gagged and blindfolded men still bound to upright poles. Bonu and Scung attended the first two; Artil went to the third, cutting his bonds. When he untied his gag and removed his blindfold Artil gasped at the familiar face. A shock of unkempt, hair and clear, blue eyes were unmistakable, though he was quite bruised about his forehead, nose, and cheeks.

"Don't I know you?" Artil asked.

Bonu and Scung released two more as the first two went to release their remaining comrades.

The man Artil released rubbed his wrists and observed Artil closely. "Weren't you with the Scrarth and Avangar contestants at the inn?"

"Yes, I was there. You were one of the generals at the other table. What happened to the man named Tren?"

"I'm right here, miss."

Artil turned and looked up into Tren's battered, swollen face. "Oh, you're alive! But what happened to you?"

"They had some entertainment at our expense. I see I was right about you being set free."

"Yes, yes you certainly were. Though for a time I thought I was going to be returned to Hod-ya."

Tren shifted his eyes to the sky, then turned his gaze on Bonu. "Lieutenant, I think it best not to tarry. We should head southwest."

"Well, sir, er—you're an officer?"

"I am. But these two belong to your expedition. We are officers, though captured and disarmed. Logon sent you to effect our rescue, though I'm not sure how rescued we'll be, in the final analysis. At any rate, lead on."

"Well, sir—"

"Tren, call me Tren."

~

Bonu suddenly felt awkward in the bearing of this officer who'd been humiliated, abused and nearly executed, yet maintained confidence and dignity in the face of severe cruelty. Aware of this man's relationship to Logon, Bonu asked, "Tren, would you hold my sword for a moment."

Tren solemnly took the offered handle; blue light instantly sprang from tip to haft, illuminating runes on both sides up and down the blade. "Satisfied, lieutenant?"

"I never knew anyone who had this much light on his sword. You keep it, sir, and lead us."

"It's not my mission, lieutenant. It's yours. My comrades and I will, however, seek instructions from the Advisor as to what we do now."

"You hear the Advisor without tolling?" Bonu asked incredulously.

"Yes. Here, take it back. I haven't had a sword in my hand for months—ever since I was betrayed into enemy hands, but as you can see, Logon's light is still alive in me. I've memorized runes and meditated on them often as I was moved prison to prison."

The sword's light reduced to a lesser glory as Bonu received it back. Bonu explained, "I, uh, that is, the Runer brigade I belong to, has recently begun sharpening the whole blade ever since a young woman, Jeda of the house of Kway, came into our midst."

"No explanation is necessary, Lieut—did you say Jeda of Kway?"

"Aye, he did, she be's his sweetheart!" said Scung coming up from behind with a bright grin, tucking his own, barely-glowing sword behind his leg.

Tren started at seeing the Eroton, then rested a hand on the giant's shoulder. For a long moment he stared into the giant's eyes. "Well met, brother of Scang."

Scung's jaw dropped.

"Not only have I met your brother, dear Eroton, but Lieutenant, I also know your beloved's brother."

"Jeda's brother? Yer kens him?"

"I had the honor of piercing his heart. He and I traveled a difficult trail, and now he's begun to walk in King Elyon's ways with the help of his devoted friend, Scang. They're a formidable pair."

Scung seized Tren's collar, nearly lifting him off the ground. "Scang? Yer seen Scang alive? But two years ago me own eyes seen him git killed."

Tren shrugged. "All I know is that several months ago at the King's Gate Fortress, Jeda's brother, Artka, became fast friends with your brother, Scang. How he got there, or when, I don't know. Now, hopefully, they're with a band of trainees in Ecclessa under the tutelage of one Saygus in the Prophecy Mountains. No doubt they're as good for him as he is for them." The twinkle in Tren's eyes revealed a deep and peaceful joy. "I knew that girl at Willow House reminded me of someone. I was trying to remember a woman, but she strongly favors her brother, Artka, which explains why I didn't make the connection. Jeda of Kway, imagine that! Artka mentioned her often. And to think that her beloved's friend is her brother's friend's brother. Bonu, you have no idea how this meeting encourages me."

"We must talk, Tren," said Bonu, "part of my mission is to dig up the swords of Vadiv in order to rearm Ecclessite prisoners and start an uprising throughout Pitland. But I have no idea what to do now, except search for those swords, which, are presumably buried nearby. You can help us dig and rearm prisoners, then lead the fight."

"The swords of Vadiv?" Tren stroked his chin. "Here in Pitland?" Then he turned, remarking, "Of course! That makes perfect sense. As to whether our mission includes assisting you, I have no such leading. Do any of you?" He looked to the other released prisoners.

One of the other officers replied, "No, Tren, we don't believe that's our course, at least not for the moment. We ought to keep to what Alfomega instructed us. He's kept this much of his promise; he'll do the rest."

Tren explained, "A roamer visited our cell a couple of days ago, telling us not to fear, though we'd been sentenced to death, we'd be delivered from execution. You are Logon's agents of deliverance, proving his promise. The rest of his instructions must be followed. I'd like to help you search for the swords of Vadiv; I was unaware that they're part of the unfolding of the mystery runes until the moment you declared it. But now I begin to grasp more of Logon's plan. Amazing!"

"Yer ain't gonna help usn's dig?" Scung couldn't believe his ears. "Seems ter me thet's why Logon had usn's rescue yers."

"There are many things that might seem to be Logon's plan, but upon careful examination, would work contrary to his purposes. I trust you understand, Bonu?"

"Yes sir, but—"

"We're deep in enemy territory, Lieutenant, and can spare no time for personal objectives. Now's the time to obey his will without seeking to understand. We have our task; you have yours. But before we take our leave, I'll say this: I don't believe the swords you seek are here."

A shadow crossed Bonu's face. "Not here? But why would the roamer stop our wagon here?"

"To rescue us."

"Well, if the swords aren't here, where should we search?"

"I wish I knew. The Advisor is silent, else I'd tell you what I surmise."

"You won't even help search? What gratitude is that? We saved you from being target practice, and yet you won't help?"

"I understand your frustration, Lieutenant, but remember who it is that saved us, not you; though you have our gratitude, you have no claim on us. Were I to speak my own mind without Logon's prompting I could do incalculable harm to your mission and all parties concerned. It may merely be a matter of timing, but even so, if that gets offset, who can say what harm will come? Besides, you were unwitting agents of our deliverance, I'd wager. You were heading toward the cliffs in pursuit of the swords when you stumbled upon our situation, were you not?"

Bonu was silent a moment, then sighed. "You're right. Forgive me, it's just that Jeda's life depends on—"

"Logon. Her life, and yours, and mine, depends on Logon."

"You don't know for certain that the swords aren't here, do you?"

"No, not for certain."

"Then I have to do as I feel led and dig up the base of this cliff. I'm certain they're along the base of Pitland's border cliffs."

"Read the runes again. They're at the base of *a* cliff, but not necessarily this cliff."

Bonu traced the rune with his forefinger.

To cliffs of great depth without escape plan,
Verging on a hot, dry, blistered land.

"If that doesn't mean these cliffs, I don't know where else . . . It must mean these cliffs. 'On the verge of a hot, dry, blistered land, where else fits that description. Even Kyleah, the seer thought it meant the cliffs bordering Pitland."

"Seers are gifted by Logon, and their abilities are unique; however, they don't always comprehend the entire message of what Logon shows them. A wise seer reports only their oracle and adds nothing unless the Advisor gives them fuller understanding. To speculate is dangerous. There may be more borders and cliffs in Pitland than you or I know."

"Well, what are we to do, go traipsing around Pitland in search of more cliffs?"

One of the rescued officers tugged Tren's sleeve. "They're coming."

"Yes, Ollo, I'm aware, and you're right; we mustn't prolong this. Bonu, if you insist on staying to search for those swords my comrades and I will draw the pursuers away; you hide in the bush until the Carnalians pass. We'll lead them on a merry chase far enough away that you can discover whether the swords are here or not."

"That doesn't sound safe; after all, they'll be searching for signs of a regiment's passing; the thicket will be the first place they'll look."

"I think not," Tren responded. The increasing crescendo of the approaching Pitlanders could be heard. "They'll be here in minutes. Make up your mind; either come with us, or burrow into the underbrush, trusting Logon to hide you."

Ollo called over his shoulder as he and the others were already headed toward the thicket. "We'll be just around the bend, Tren. Come as soon as you can. We'll lay three false trails before branching off. The real trail will veer hard right." Ollo trotted off after his departing comrades.

"Right. I'll catch up," he returned. "Bonu, make up your mind."

"We'll stay. I believe the swords are here, and Logon will help me find them."

"So be it." Tren placed his hands on Bonu's head, catching the young lieutenant off guard. "Logon, I seek your protection on Bonu and his friends, cover them; let their enemy be blind to their presence. And in due season, reveal what Bonu needs to know." Tren removed his hands and smiled. "We'll meet again, soon." With that, he took off after his companions.

"Peculiar!" muttered Scung, watching Tren depart.

"Come on," said Bonu, "peculiar or not, he's right about that Pitland war party bearing down. Look!"

Saplings bobbed and branches snapped deep in the thicket off to the left as great beasts of burden the like of which none of them had ever seen trampled the brushy barrens. Armed men rode atop these massive, slow-moving animals, directing them with prods applied to tender areas around the mammals' gigantic, flapping ears. The beasts were covered top to bottom with coarse, brown hair; each leg was the size of a tree trunk. In the front of each beast where there ought to have been a nose, dangled a serpentine appendage, occasionally grasping and tossing branches or small trees out of its way. On either side of this dangling appendage grew two great tusks with which it tore up chunks of ground and uprooted stubborn thickets. A dozen of these monsters rumbled through the thicket. Close on their heels was a phalanx of Carnalian guards, walking easily in the crushed pathways left in the wake of the beasts.

"Gore an' blood! Whut be's them?"

"Quick, into the bush before they see us." Bonu urged. They flopped into a small ditch and covered themselves with branches and leaves.

"I hopes them beasties doesn't come tramplin' usn's."

Artil whimpered.

"Scung!" Bonu chided.

"Sorry, Bonu, I warn't thinkin', but I hopes they doesn't."

There was no more time for chatter; already the ponderous feet shook the ground; riders called to each other, directing their mounts this way or that.

"I'm telling you, there was no regiment! That wagon is the same one that coasted down the cliff road crashing through the checkpoints and causing havoc along the way. There can't be more than five or six. Turn, you dumb thick-skin." The beast trumpeted through its nasal appendage as the rider poked a tender spot.

"Five or six? Are you kidding me? All the noise we heard couldn't have been less than a hundred well-armed men."

"Where are the tracks? Such a force would leave a trail. Where is it?"

"It's here . . . somewhere, just keep looking."

"Spread out; we're too bunched up."

A shadow crossed overtop the ditch where Bonu, Scung, and Artil lay. But the animal stepped over them safely. The men following the beasts either jumped the ditch or fanned out wider, blindly passing the hidden trio.

"Wait till Bablo-ya hears that you're the one who was in charge of the execution squad and let those generals escape. You'll roast for sure."

"Shut up and keep looking. What's that over there? It looks like a trail."

"Yessir, but there's only evidence of two, or at most, three men passing through. It leads straight to the cliffs, away from the runaway wagon."

"I told you it was a small party. How did they know we were going to execute those officers?"

"And when and where?" echoed another. "How do Ecclessites know anything? It's a mystery to me."

"Yeah! And now we've got ten or more dangerous enemy warriors on the loose, possibly armed with their cursed, glowing weapons; all because you let three warriors make a lot of noise and run you off. And with Scrarth and Avangar tomorrow, I wouldn't be in your boots for all the ale in Eroton."

"Shut up, will you, just shut up."

A voice floated back. "Up here, we found a trail. Looks like they all went this way."

With prods and curses the beasts obediently turned and carried their riders away from the thicket. A commander of the foot troops barked an order and the soldiers trotted behind the huge beasts, ignoring the thickets and ditch where the intrepid Ecclessites hid.

CHAPTER FOURTEEN

Dawn's dim, gray light stole softly under the roiling clouds hanging above the cliffs on Pitland's border.

Artil yawned and stretched her arms overhead. Her back ached, her legs were restless, and her hair matted and hanging in her begrimed face. They'd searched all the previous afternoon, into the night and on through the wee hours of the morning, poking the two Children of the Stars into the soil but with no sign of the swords of Vadiv. Much of the time Artil used Scung's sword since it had more light in her hands than his. Though fatigued, she plunged the blade into the rocky earth once more, then, leaving the sword sticking in the ground, she paused and pressed her hands in the small of her back and arched her shoulders.

Their quest for the elusive swords of Vadiv covered a swath fifty yards wide by a quarter mile long outward from the very base of the cliff. Now dawn was breaking; the day of Scrarth and Avangar was at hand and they were still without armaments to foment a prisoner uprising.

"Scung," Artil called, "here, take your sword back and try again."

Scung, some twenty yards away, lumbered through the brume to simply stand beside her, his shoulders hunched, head bowed. His whole demeanor expressed futility. He sighed, looked into Artil's eyes, and took up his weapon again.

A short distance away Bonu pressed his sword into the dirt yet again, leaning all his weight on it until the hilt-guard touched ground. Then stooping over, he extracted it, counted off several paces and repeated the process; he'd been at it all night, barely resting, and now began to exhibit signs of exhaustion.

Scung reluctantly paced off twenty steps by Bonu's measure lest his long legs over-carry the search grid. He resignedly inserted his sword into the ground. Bonu had told him to expect some sort of a tingle or vibration if the sword came within fifteen or so feet of a buried kingsman sword. Scung plucked the sword up and repeated the procedure several more times as Artil plopped down, playfully sifted loose dirt through her fingers and surveyed their surroundings, then she drooped her chin on her chest.

Suddenly as Scung inserted his sword into a new hole it *thunked* on something underground. "Bonu, I thinks I gots summat."

Artil raised her head.

Bonu plucked his own sword out of its slot and trotted several yards to Scung's side. "Let me have it." He elbowed Scung out of the way. With both hands firmly gripping the handle he rocked the weapon back and forth.

A hard, scraping sound emitted from the hole.

"Yes, something's down there, Scung, but," Bonu plied the sword back and forth creating more grinding noises, "it's not sounding like what I expected."

"Well, dig it up, man, let's have a looksee."

"Artil, you hold the sword. Your greater light will bring quicker results than Scung's strength. Oh Logon, please let it be . . . "

Artil loosened the soil around the hole while Scung dropped to his knees and scooped loose soil away by handfuls. Bonu probed the hole with his own sword. After several frantic moments the curved edge of a large, round, off-white object lay exposed.

"What's that?" Artil asked.

"Whatever it is," Bonu got on his knees, "I'm sure it contains the swords of Vadiv." He vigorously applied his blade around the object's perimeter revealing it as a huge clay pot. "This is why it didn't feel right," exulted Bonu, all sign of fatigue gone from his smudged brow. "The swords must be in this jar, and are therefore, insensitive to the presence of our swords."

"But Bonu," Artil, rose to her feet and checked their surroundings for intruders, "Vadiv buried hundreds of swords; they wouldn't all fit in this jar, would they?"

"Huh? Oh, I guess you're right. There must be several jars buried hereabouts." He jumped into the widened hole and groped the vessel's exterior for an opening. "I'll bet this holds at least twenty, maybe thirty."

"How many swords be's buried?"

"Well, I believe if Artil is right, Vadiv had several hundred men with him, so I figure there must be dozens of jars to unearth. We'd better get busy. We'll step off every two or three paces from this spot."

"That's just great." Scung rolled his eyes skyward.

"I can't . . . seem . . . to find an opening. It appears to be completely sealed. What do you think, Scung?"

"Artil, hand over me sword." Scung took his weapon and raised it overhead. "Yer best git outta me way."

Bonu protested holding up both hands, "No Scung, don't, you'll—"

The clay vessel shattered.

"—break it to pieces." Bonu leaned back scowling at Scung. "That might have been preserved. It's a relic from a bygone era, you know."

"I was thinkin' o' savin' summat o' this era. If'n we gots dozens o' these things ter find we cain't be bothered 'bout savin' relics."

"Yes, of course, you're right. I'm so tired I'm not thinking straight."

Artil was already down in the hole carefully poking around the shattered, jagged shards, examining the jar's contents. "Hey! These aren't swords."

"Whut?"

"Not swords? What are they?" Both Bonu and Scung jumped into the hole and collided with Artil, knocking all three backwards to sit on the edge of the crater they'd made, looking stupidly at each other.

"They look like musical instruments," Artil said finally.

"Musical instru—?" Bonu plunged his hand inside the jar's opening, extracting a tarnished, brass horn. "A trumpet?" His other hand brought out another sullied trumpet. "There's more."

Scung straddled the broken vase's base and braced it between his legs as he stuck his hand into the orifice and extracted another horn. "Whut be's? I thot we was gettin' swords, not trumpets?"

"May I see?" Artil leaned forward.

Scung handed her the horn and stuck his massive fist in again, pulling up two more. With his other hand he extracted two more. "Thet be's all. Seven horns. The jar be's empty now."

Bonu put his hands over his face and sobbed. "No, it can't be, they must be here, they must."

Scung and Artil climbed out of the hole, still holding the horns, too disappointed to say anything. Scung finally ventured, "Come on, Bonu, we ain't doin' no good hereabouts. Let's get ter the arena afore it be's too late."

"This can't be, it just can't be. They must be here. Keep probing." He stood to his feet, a fanatic gleam in his eye. "We're not leaving until we find them!"

Scung and Artil exchanged glances, then Scung slipped around slightly behind Bonu and brought the meaty part of his fist down on the top of the lieutenant's head.

Bonu dropped, senseless.

Artil's eyes went wide. "Oh, Scung, you shouldn't have done that!"

Scung hefted Bonu's limp form atop his shoulder. "Had ter. He'd a had usn's here all day diggin' fer swords thet hain't here. We be's needed at Scrarth an' Avangar. We'd best git movin' along; we wasted 'nuff time hereabouts."

"What about the trumpets?"

"Leave 'em—no . . . bring 'em along. They might come in handy."

Artil embraced all seven trumpets in her arms and traipsed after Scung who toted Bonu on his shoulders like a deer taken in the hunt. "Scung, wait for me, I dropped a couple."

Scung watched Artil re-gather the fallen trumpets and sighed as three more slipped from her grasp as she bent over to retrieve the first two.

"Oh bother! Can't I just leave them? They're such a nuisance."

Scung shifted Bonu to his other shoulder. "No, I be's thinkin' usn's can use 'em. Yer ever played on a trumpet afore?"

"No, never."

"I'll show yer later. Here, lemme have Bonu's sword afore yer loses it an' we be's left wi' only one sword atween usn's."

Artil handed Bonu's sword to the giant, and then discovered that by slipping her fingers through various rings and tubes, she could manage to hold all seven trumpets.

"How's thet?"

"Better, much better."

"They ain't too heavy fer yer?"

"Nuh-uh. They're not heavy at all. How about you? Isn't he too heavy to carry all the way to the arena?"

"I ain't carryin' him ter the arena. I'm gonna dump him in the wagon and pull yer an' him both."

"But I told you, they destroyed the wagon. Knocked it on its side and broke whatever wasn't ruined in our wild ride."

"Now Missy Artil, yer jest let ol' Scung have a looksee afore yer goes havin' a funeral fer our ride, awright?"

"Suit yourself." She studied the trumpets as she trailed after the Eroton beelining toward the wagon. "Hey, Scung?"

"Whut?"

"Did you look closely at these horns?"

"Horns be's horns. Music and me never did git along, anyhow. I learnt how ter make 'em sound but wouldn't ken a note from a squawk if'n I tried me durndest. Why?"

"Well, it may be nothing, but—"

"C'mon, out wi' it girl."

"They're numbered."

"Numbered eh? Probly some way ter ken which note be's which."

"No, I don't think so. They're numbered in sequence from one to seven."

"Mebbe it tells which player when ter give a toot."

"Maybe. I hope Bonu can explain it when he wakes up. How hard did you hit him?"

"Jest hard 'nuff ter put him ter sleep fer a while. He needed ter sleep, anyways."

At the thickest part of the barrens Scung was forced to lower Bonu to the ground and drag him through the briar tunnel they'd previously made. Artil's trumpets presented a problem in those confines as well, which she solved by stringing the horns together and dragging them behind on a ripped strand from the hem of her outer dress.

The three emerged at the overturned wagon to find two of its wheels lying nearby on the ground.

"Ah, I sees whut yer means, Artil." Scung propped Bonu against a rock. "I guess I conked him purty good. Well, let him sleep. I'll see whut I kin do fer the wagon." Scung picked up the wheels one at a time, inspected them, and placed each one on an axle end, pushing down with his full weight to seat them. Then he hunkered under the wagon and lifted, grunting with the effort; the wagon bounced over onto all four wheels. "There, now it don't seem so bad, eh? I kin fix whut be's wrong in good order, doncher worry none, Missy. Jest dump yer trumpets in the cargo space."

Artil complied, gratefully loading the brass instruments into the wagon.

Scung gently rolled Bonu into the wagon, then examined some loose boards, paying special attention to repairing the steering fork and front axle. He peered over Artil's shoulder as she arranged the horns and started polishing them, causing him to remark, "Kinda purty, ain't they?"

Artil examined the one numbered with an archaic "5" on the bell. She rubbed it with a scrap of her torn, outer skirt until even under Pitland's glowering sky it shone with a golden luster.

Scung emitted a low whistle. "Here, lemme have a looksee." He took the horn in his callused palms and rubbed another portion clean. "Hey, there be's writin'!"

"What does it say?"

"I dunno, cain't hardly read it, the printin' be's so tiny. Summat 'bout a roamer an' wights o' the pit an' a fallen *kyllorn*. Kin yer make anythin' o' thet?"

"I can't say that I do, though I remember hearing my father and Captain Varter talking about horrid flying creatures that sting people. I think they were called wights, but I'm not sure. Let me see if I can read the script."

She squinted trying to make out the indistinct characters. "They are tiny aren't they? I can make out 'roamers' all right, but I don't see 'wights'."

"Mebbe t'other horns gots summat written." He lifted another trumpet embossed with a number "2," cleaned it, and discovered writing in the same esoteric script. "I dunno, Artil, it seems ter be sayin' summat 'bout a mountain fallin' inter the sea."

"What? That can't be right. Let me see." She wiped it again then studied it for several moments. "Yes, that's what it says all right."

"Ooh, what happened?" Bonu groaned and rolled over.

"I be's sorry, lieutenant. Yer wouldda kept usn's diggin' all day, and we'd a missed the contest if'n I hadn't put out yer lights."

"Scrarth and Avangar . . . yes, of course. I suppose I should thank you, but my head doesn't want to, at least not yet."

"But yer heart does, I kens it."

"Yes, my heart does. What are these doing here?" he referred to the trumpets beside him.

"I thot usn's might as well bring 'em. They might prove useful. Besides, they's all usn's gots ter show fer a day an' night o' diggin'."

"Bonu," said Artil, "have a look. They're numbered in sequence from one to seven, and there's writing. It seems to be written in some language that's not quite Ecclessite, but almost."

Bonu sat up and held his head in both hands, his eyes tightly closed. "Ooh! My head."

"Thet'll wear off in a hour or so. I done it lots ter me ol' comrades ter keep 'em from bein' a nuisance. I gots jest the right touch."

"Says you!" Bonu picked up a horn. "Hmmm, I see what you mean. This looks like the script of the original generals. I studied it once long ago. Let's see if I can remember, yes, I can make out most of it. But if I interpret these writings, we'll lose precious travel time."

"Yer sit in the wagon an' study on them horns, whiles I gits it turned around and back ter the main road. All I has ter do is follow the path it made which opened considerable when them Carnalians an' their thick-skin pachys was searchin' fer usn's. Should be easy. Yer an' the missy sit back an' let me do whut I come along fer."

As Scung pulled the battered-but-serviceable wagon through trampled thickets, Artil busily removed grime and tarnish from the trumpets while Bonu attempted to read the ancient, runic writing. Then he lightly slapped his forehead.

"What am I doing?" In another second he took his sword and laid the tip against the trumpet's inscription. The blue haze magnified the letters, enabling him to read without difficulty. After Artil finished cleaning them off he placed them in ascending numerical order on the bed of the wagon. Bonu compared the messages, going from one to another, then back again.

"How be's it?" asked Scung calling over his shoulder. He effortlessly pulled the wagon clear of the bramble patch onto a rutted, albeit deserted road, making good time on the slight downgrade; he had only to elevate the steering tines to keep the vehicle on the trail while the wagon gathered momentum.

"Where are we going?" Bonu looked up, distracted from studying the trumpets. "You can't possibly know the right direction. What if the arena is the other way?"

"Don't yer worry 'bout where ol' Scung be's takin' yers. I gots a sense 'bout these things."

"Scung, you can't trust the senses you used in Lurcan's service. You'll lead us into a trap."

"Yer jest decipher the writin' on them there horns and let the direction findin' ter me. I kens whut I be's doin'."

"Scung," protested Bonu, rising from his seat.

"Relax, lieutenant. I seen a road sign a bit back whut tole me I be's headin' the right way."

"Well, why didn't you say so?"

Artil giggled.

Scung, jogging steadily, turned and grinned impishly. Bonu resettled himself and placed the number "1" trumpet on his lap.

"I be's sorry. I jest couldn't resist."

"Listen to me both of you; we're in dangerous territory. This is no place for pranks. We must keep our minds on what we're about. Here, I'll read to you what these say."

"Awright, sounds good ter me." Scung winked at Artil.

Bonu raised his sword and scrutinized the first trumpet, reading aloud:

"Hail and fire and mixture of blood,
On all grass and a third of trees,
The first roamer sounds announcing this flood,
Who escapes though he runs and flees?"

"Whuzzat mean?" Scung called back.

"I wish I knew. Listen to the second trumpet's message:

"A great mountain burning, cast into the sea,
Bubbling and boiling a third of its beasts,
Roamer the second blows unhindered, free,
As ships and crews become death's feasts."

"Bonu, this is scaring me." Artil stared at the floorboards.

"It scares me, too, though probably not for the same reason. What have we uncovered? It sounds like we've dug up the end of the world as we know it."

"Whut be's yer sayin'?"

"I know it sounds incredible, but, if these trumpets are what I think they are, Pitland, indeed, all Carnalia, Eroton, and possibly Ecclessa are on the verge of destruction."

"Ecclessa?" Artil looked up.

"Ecclessa exists solely for the purpose of training and preparing soldiers to wage war against evil and rescue lives to Logon. When that purpose is accomplished and the last person that can be rescued is recruited, even Ecclessa's usefulness will be finished. Ecclessa is only in part. The whole will only come when the partial has run its course."

"And yer thinks that end be's soon accomplished?"

"I don't know. These same lines appear in the mystery runes telling of the time the world is to be destroyed."

"Bonu!" Artil shuddered.

"Say whut?" gasped Scung.

"For those who follow Logon, it means the final vindication and rising up into his presence to dwell with him forever. But those under judgment will be destroyed by calamity upon calamity."

"Then we be's safe? All we gots ter do is blow them there horns an commence the end o' the world?"

"Uh, not quite. From what I understand, no man possesses the power to sustain the sound of these horns, only roamers."

"Then if'n we find some roamers and deliver these horns ter 'em, they kin begin the tootin'?"

"I doubt it's that easy. Elyon has assigned special roamers to sound these trumpets, and they can only sound them at the proper time. Besides, where in Pitland are we going to find roamers? Here, let me read the next one:

"A great meteor from the sky, bright as a thousand lamps,
Fell churning and burning on rivers and streams,
Third roamer has sounded, polluting all damps,
Corrupter the worm-eaten brings death in its dreams."

"The next one says:

"Sun and moon and stars, all a third,
Part have they lost of what they once had,
Dim and short, day and night at this word,
Fades all hope, for Lurcan, 'tis bad.'"

"Then there's something written but not part of that rune, let me see . . . " He held his sword close to the lettering. "It says:

"Then rose up roamer, the sounder of fourth,
And flying discreetly o'er all the earth,
Cried a message of worse woes come forth,
Three judgments more cruel about to have birth."

The wagon slowed as the grade turned uphill; Scung leaned into the trace, huffing as he commented, "Thet there be's summat; thet sure be's summat."

"Are you tired, Scung?" Bonu observed the giant straining. "You've had no sleep and look about wore out. Should we get out and walk, or help you pull?" Bonu asked.

"Nah! I be's awright. Jest needs a minute ter ketch me breath, s'all. It be's downhill jest ahead over thet rise. Git on wi' yer readin'. It be's fascinatin' stuff. I never heered the like. Kin yer make sense o' any o' it?"

"Better strategists and tacticians than I have tried and failed to make much sense of it. But now that these trumpets have been discovered, they'll soon enough be understood. Want to hear more?"

"Absolutely," blurted Artil.

"Right. Let me see, which trumpet is next?"

"Fifth," chorused Artil and Scung at the same time.

"Ah, yes, the fifth trumpet." He placed it on his knees and again scoped it through the bright haze of his sword:

"At the fifth roamer's sound,
A power from great heights,
Fell toward the ground,
And released the fell wights,
From waters undrowned,
Rising darker than nights,
As smoke pours renowned,
And vapor takes sights,
Tormenting men found,
Without Logon's signet, whiter than brights."

"Dark omen, thet!"

"It's the first woe," commented Artil. "I sometimes heard my father and Captain Varter talking about those things around the nightly campfires. Captain Varter described winged lizards or scorpions flying out of a deep hole where they'd been imprisoned from the dawn of time, waiting for their appointed day to be unleashed."

"Yes, the first woe," observed Bonu, "The fifth roamer's sounding brings the first woe, like the old nursery rhyme says:

"Fifth is first,
Sixth is second,
And seventh the worst."

"How's thet?"

"Oh, it's part of a nursery rhyme. I never realized until now that it applied to the seven trumpets of the mystery runes. These seven trumpets! Artil, can you recall any more of those conversations between your father and Captain Varter?"

"Not nearly enough. I was only eight or nine then and didn't pay much attention. I wish I had. I remember them saying the pain of those bites is so severe that men would try to kill themselves but be unable to find death. What do you suppose that means?"

"I haven't a guess. Let me finish reading. There's only two more.

"Came forth a cry out from sky's dome,
'Dry up the river withholding invasion,
Cast down the bridge that spanned o'er foam,'
Despoiled appears, oft threatened nation,
Minions by millions, warriors come roam,
Spoiler is spoiled in desecration,
The vengeance he brought now come to his home.
Mankind a third in devastation,
Yet bitter and hard, still cursing fate's tome,
Those who remain fie supplication."

"Bonu, these are hard sayings," said Artil, "and painful to my heart, but if I understand correctly, Logon and King Elyon will offer amnesty, which will be refused?"

"That's about what I make of it, Artil."

The wagon surged forward as Scung, having caught his breath on the downhill, quickened the pace.

Bonu read the last inscription:

"Voices come shout,
Thunders come rout,
Lightnings come play,
Earthquakes come slay,
Deliverance at last,
Last trumpet fast."

"Thet's it? There be's no more?"

"That's it, Scung. Make of it what you will."

"Why would Logon drop something so awesome in our laps?" Artil shifted to get a better look at the passing countryside.

"Logon often shrouds things in mystery, so we don't get ourselves in trouble by trying to assist his plan. Many have wrenched his sayings out of context to their own embarrassment and sometimes, destruction. Another reason Logon keeps his intentions shrouded in mystery is to unbalance his adversary; the Advisor will correctly interpret these signs to his faithful servants at the proper time. That way Lurcan won't know exactly when or how Elyon will seize and drag him off to his punishment. Why have these landed in our laps?" Bonu shrugged. "Here, let's gather these horns in this sack. It'll be easier carrying them and keep them from prying eyes."

"Bonu, we be's there." Scung slowed the wagon to a stop on a gentle rise. Below them about a quarter of a mile was a convergence of several roads crowded with throngs of people merging into one main procession headed for an edifice towering above the distant plain. The three stared spellbound at the sinister amphitheater rising amid the shadows under Pitland's charcoal sky.

CHAPTER FIFTEEN

Pitland's amphitheater stood sentinel over a vast, broad plain on the sere eastern border of Pitland. It was the only man-made object visible in all the wasteland from Craniantium's border to the massive granite bluffs that served as the semi-circular arena's back wall. Fumes from the forges leagues away spewed dark, low-hanging clouds that obliterated from view the summit of the precipice which the arena utilized as its rear barrier.

Craniantium was known far and wide for its elite intelligentsia that provided Lurcan with many of his best policymakers. As a result, Craniantiumites were a nation of haughty people. Their small but influential nation was wedged among Ecclessa, Pitland, and Carnalia, and had at one time been independent of the empire, entertaining ambassadors from various other states. But Lurcan imposed his will on that nation, too, annexing it with promises of bounty and at the same time threatening to remove their government should they prove rebellious. In return for Craniantium's allegiance, he selected most of the empire's leadership from her erudite borders.

For the last thousand years only Ecclessa, loyal to King Elyon, remained free from Lurcan's dominion, thanks largely to the un-navigable Flaming Sword River. The nations under the shadow of the emperor soon lost any thought of resistance against Lurcan. Even so, Lurcan stripped the borderlands of both Craniantium and Pitland bare of trees and lush vegetation, leaving only stubborn, scrubby thickets and desert grasses. Invaders entering Pitland to free captives—as was prophesied on kingsmen swords—could not venture across those barrens undetected. In the same way any military force would be immediately spotted against the backdrop of these stark borderlands.

The road Bonu, Scung, and Artil traversed was one of those border patrol routes, hence the lack of commercial or passenger traffic. The mismatched trio and their wagon stood out conspicuously atop a knoll overlooking the busier conjoining of highways below. Nor could they help but stare in awe at the smooth-polished edifice prevailing over the landscape. The arena's primary building material was blocks of Pitland's prevalent off-white rock that had been chiseled to accommodate seating for a hundred thousand revelers. The main event, though not the only affair presented here every year, was the Scrarth and Avangar celebration. Other gladiatorial contests, various kinds of races and circuses were held at this venue from time to time, but none compared in gratuitous violence or grandiose ostentation as this wanton, bloodletting event. The crowds thronging the roads guaranteed that the stadium would be packed and overflowing with standees lining the rim of the battlefield or sitting upon the edge walls to view the spectacle. The amphitheater's semi-circular, sixty-foot-high, block walls enclosed nearly a square quarter mile in circumference. It would also make a formidable fortress if need arose, and perhaps, had been designed with that in mind.

The Ecclessite trio collectively felt a sinking in the pit of their stomachs. This vile theater with its grossly exaggerated carvings on the cliffs that formed the back wall of the battle floor was a mockery of Logon's Rock. Contrary to the norm, these bluffs towering above the plain, overshadowing all, were granite and not the ubiquitous white rock of Pitland.

"The Arena." Bonu's voice bespoke dismay. "This is a place of evil legend; here the powers of the empire tossed unarmed kingsmen to wild beasts for the entertainment of the masses. This arena is the execution site of those who reject Lurcan's dictates, being the empire's ultimate expression of rebellion against King Elyon. Here ethereal *kyllorn* mutineers take glee in reprisals against mankind by manipulating people to destroy their own kind, coercing them to forswear themselves of Elyon's amnesty. This stadium has been, since its inception, a pit of torture for Logon Xychirion's followers. Here Logon's followers have been mercilessly slaughtered, deceiving the blood-lusty spectators that the empire's credo—LIVE FOR THE MOMENT—is only a sensible, natural law.

"Our destination," mused Bonu, "true followers of Logon cannot find a nobler end. The runes say, *'and they loved Logon more than their own lives, even to their deaths.'* Before this day is done it's quite possible, we'll have a chance to prove those words."

"We best git off'n this here road, else we might live up ter them words right where we be's a standin'."

"Yes, you're right. Help me push the wagon into those bushes and cover it. Artil, get the sack with the trumpets."

Artil slung the sack over her shoulder and followed Bonu into a wadi alongside the road where they hunkered down out of sight until Scung finished covering the wagon with brush.

"Whut now?" asked the giant sidling in beside Artil.

Bonu took the measure of his squad. "Well, we need to mix in with that throng heading into the arena, but garbed like this, I don't know."

They were travel-ragged and grimy compared to the masses filing toward the arena dressed in festive attire. Artil peeked over the edge of the ditch. Passersby surged toward the amphitheater a few hundred feet away.

"Like sheep going to the slaughter," she murmured.

"Aye, an' they little kens that summat day they's gonna be the sheep gittin' slaughtered. They thinks it be's entertainment, ter watch people slayin' each other."

"Especially women fighting each other in the Scrarth and Avangar, and one of them is my Jeda. Well, we've got to join that throng but be inconspicuous about it. Any suggestions?"

"Even if we could clean up, our clothes are too tattered."

Scung studied the procession parading past. "Ere, lookit whut be's a comin' down the road."

Bonu and Artil turned to see.

"See 'em?"

"See what, Scung? I see crowds heading for the arena."

"Don't yer ken whut yer eyes be's seein'? Lookit there man: Erotons be's a'comin' down the road. They hain't never gussied up fer nuthin'. Tain't comfortable, an' we never does whut ain't comfortable 'less they be's summat o' profit in it. Them Erotons be's a comin' ter watch the festivities dressed as they please, which be's sloppy an' dirty—like usn's. We kin slip in alongside o' 'em. Make like we's jest comin' back from tendin' our necessities in the weeds."

"Do you think we can do that without getting spotted?"

"I kin. An' if'n yer kens how yer talks, yer kin pass fer Eroton, too."

Bonu considered, then said, "I wasn't aware there were this many Erotons in Pitland. I thought the heat bothered them."

"Well, they musta come from afar off fer the contest. Does yer wanna take this opportunity or no?"

"I don't think we're going to get a better one. Artil, are you up to it?"

"Ohh, I don't know, Bonu. I'm scared. What if I forget to talk Eroton?"

"Jest let me do most o' the talkin', both o' yers. I'll say thet yer both sorta slow-witted, an' don't like ter talk much."

"Oh great!" Bonu rose to his feet. "C'mon Artil, we's gots ter git a goin'."

"Uh, okay. I mean, awright, Bonu. Oh, I hope we's pull this off."

"Yer ain't a kiddin'." Scung rolled his eyes. "An' don't say 'we's', say 'usn's'. 'We's' ain't proper most o' the time."

Bonu glanced back at the Eroton. "Right. Proper. Usn's gots ter be's proper."

"Aye, thet's better."

"I'll never be able to keep it up. Suppose I pretend to be mute?" pleaded Artil.

"No, you'll lapse in an unguarded moment and give us away. Better do as we decided."

"Oh, all right, er, awright."

"Awright, here be's our story: yer Bonu, be's me war buddy; Artil, yer be's me little sister. Don't go spinnin' no yarns 'bout yer mam an' pap; yer'll find it too hard ter remember. Jest let me do whutever talkin' be's necessary."

The three climbed out of the ditch and self-consciously sauntered downhill toward the masses. As they neared the parade of revelers they received blank, even repugnant stares from the gaily-clad crowd. Ignoring the disdainful glances, they joined themselves to the undulating line progressing toward the gate. Carnalians didn't usually intermingle with Erotons.

The Erotons cavorted amongst themselves, occupying their own segment of the parade of partiers. A few Carnalians or Craniantiumites mixed in but also weren't welcome, nor were any Erotons invited to break rank and join the "more civilized" people of the empire. Occasionally jeers flew back and forth, but nothing serious came of it. The day was still early; boozing and revelry hadn't begun in earnest yet, so all were single-mindedly focused on the contest of Scrarth and Avangar.

It promised to be the most unique duel since the event's inception. Never had an Ecclessite entered the arena in defiance of her prince; Ecclessites weren't even considered a threat—until this one: Jeda of Kway—or "Jeda the Terrible," as she was billed.

Bonu, Scung, and Artil paused to read a wayside poster, waiting for the main Eroton contingent to finally catch up to them. *"Hod-ya's best pupil ever,"* stated the follow-up, *"combining the mysticism of the empire with the mysterious powers of Ecclessa; a duel with Dalicusi, the most-promising Craniantium contestant in a hundred years."* As they read the advertisement Bonu's heart caught in his throat and Scung whistled lowly.

"Bonu, what could they have done to force her to participate? How could they turn a true Ecclessite away from Logon?" Artil bit her lip.

"Shhh! Speak Eroton," warned Scung, tapping Artil's shoulder.

Bonu beheld Artil through his teary eyes. He opened his mouth but only a choking sound came out. He shook his head and turned away.

"Scung!" cried a gravelly voice. "Yer old tophet-bait! I thot sure yer'd a been kilt or summat. I hain't seen yer since . . . lemme think, since the day we went inter Ra-Amawl. Yep, thet be's it, since Ra-Amawl. Where at yer been?"

"Trunch, yer old scum-suckin' toad eater!" Scung affected a happy air, playing the part of a war chum finding a long-lost buddy. "Why, I guesses it must be's thet long since we seen each other!"

"Where'd yer git to, anyways?"

Trunch was Bonu's size, but rougher looking, even considering Bonu's ragged, unkempt condition. Trunch's beard tangled its way down over his chest, matting fiery red and gray whiskers together while his bushy eyebrows gave him a gnome-like appearance, especially with his bulbous nose and rheumy eyes. He was with a party of twenty or so comrades swaggering and boasting aloud about their exploits on and off the battlefield.

"Seems ter me yer went off wi' them dronnets. Say didya hear thet a dread got unmade? A bunch o' 'em yer was wi' got themselves kilt. But yer hain't kilt? How come?" The man's eyes narrowed.

Scung cupped his hand over Trunch's ear. "I be's on a secret mission. Yer kens how me *talents* be's appreciated in certain circles, doncher?"

"Eh? Secret missi—"

Scung clamped his hand over his acquaintance's mouth. "I still be's on it yer worm-wit. Nobody's asposed ter ken."

Trunch's eyes widened, then he winked. Scung released his grip and his friend coughed and drew a deep breath. "Well, why din't yer say summat. Up an' gone yer was, leavin' usn's ter think yer be's tophet fodder."

"Now if'n I'd a tole yer it wouldn't a been a secret no more, would it?"

Trunch stared at his pal, grinned and replied, "I guesses not! Yer kens how whatever comes inter me ears flies outta me mouth!" At that he guffawed loudly and slapped Scung on the back. "Well, I be's mighty glad ter see yer alive." Then Trunch pulled Scung's sleeve, drawing him aside. "Who be's them?"

"Part o' me mission. Best ter not say much 'bout it, right?"

"Gotcha!" Another wink and the gnome-faced man strode back to his cronies, shouting, "Hey! Lookit whut the buzzard dropped. Scung be's back!"

Scung groaned and looked apologetically at Bonu.

"It's all right, Scung. At least we fit in."

Trunch turned around and sized up Scung's companions. "Who be's the scrawny, little girl?"

Artil's eyes grew wide with offense and she was about to speak her mind when Bonu broke in without an accent. "She's my kid sister, coming along to see the contest for the first time. Uh, I'm, Bonu." He extended his hand.

Scung covered his face. Peering out from between his fingers, Scung looked amazed that Trunch cautiously took Bonu's proffered hand; Erotons never shook hands.

"Any friend o' Scung's be's a friend o' mine. Got yer seats yet?"

"Well, we're not sure where we're going to sit."

"Thet settles it, yers be gonna sit wi' me an' me chums. We gots seats right down front whar the blood splatters if'n we git lucky. Whut yer got in the bag, little missy?"

Artil hugged the trumpets to herself.

"Musical instruments," Bonu responded.

"Musical insterments. Whut fer?"

"Er, ter celebrate when our contestant wins," Scung ad-libbed, following Bonu's lead.

"Ah, an' who might yer choice be, as if'n I din't already ken?"

"Why, Jeda the Terrible."

"He never could resist cheerin' fer a purty blonde." Trunch winked at Bonu. "Me, too, though most Erotons favors t'other. Yer kens how Erotons always favors Craniantiumites. They be's summat thet thinks Craniantium once been part o' Eroton, usn's bein' so close in mental prowess an' all." Then Trunch pulled Scung aside again, cupping his hand over his friend's ear so none of his comrades could hear, "Whut fer be's yer goin' 'round wi' Carnalians, Scung? It hain't like yer."

"They be's lotsa things whut hain't like me no more, Trunch; it be's on account o' the secret mission. Today will bear the fruit o' all me secrecy. Yer kin count on thet."

"Yer gots summat ter do wi' the contest outcome? Scung, yer ol' rascal. Lemme in, will yer. I cut yer in on lotsa stuff afore. Who should I place me bets on?"

"I cain't say."

"Aww, c'mon, Scung. I done yer lots o' favors, remember?"

"Cain't do it, Trunch. But if'n yer keeps me mission quiet, yer'll git yer share."

"Yer wants I should guard yers or summat?"

"There may be's a time when I needs yer help, an' if'n yer helps, yer'll be right in the center o' the action. Be's yer willin'?"

"Yer bets! Count me in. But, does we hafta do it wi' the likes o' them? Cain't yer lose 'em now thet yer gots me? If'n yer needs a little girl ter help, we kin git a Eroton instead o' thet slip o' a thing."

"No, no, they're 'specially trained. They kens the plan better than me. I be's along ter help 'em, not them help me."

"Naw! Yer doesn't say? 'Scung, Scourge o' the Southland,' takin' orders from a Carnalian? Won't wonders never cease?"

"Wait'll yer see whut happens later."

"I kin hardly wait. If'n yer be's involved, it gotta be's amazin', o' thet I be's sure."

"Jest don't say nuthin' ter nobody, or you'll git left out."

"Thet be's harsh."

"Our secret mission has ter do wi' Hod-ya, an' I kens yer doesn't wanna be on the wrong side o' her, does yer?"

"The witchy woman herself? No! Say, be's yer makin' all o' this up?"

"Jest tag along an' watch, an' don't say nobbut ter nobody."

Trunch nodded, then fell out of step, rejoining his comrades a few paces behind, keeping a close eye on Scung, not joining in his friends' bawdy self-amusements.

"Trouble?" Bonu sidled close to Scung, watching the Erotons over his shoulder.

"I thinks not. Trunch be's a busybody, always pokin' his nose in ter other people's business. If'n I tried ter keep him outta our affairs he'd o' been a pest; so I enlisted him. Now he be's sworn ter secrecy."

"But we don't even know what we're going to do."

"He don't ken thet. Besides, he may come in useful. He has a powerful lot o' friends, an' kin git us a lot o' help on a moment's notice. I done awright, ain't I?"

"Well, it's done, for better or worse. I don't think any harm will come of it, but you never know."

Scung chuckled.

"What are you laughing at?"

"S'jest thet he be's wonderin' why I took a assignment thet gots me obeyin' Carnalians. I wouldda died afore I followed nobbut orders 'ceptin' o' Eroton officers. He doesn't ken yer be's a Ecclessite officer."

"Let's keep it that way."

The Eroton contingent neared the arena's yawning gates where revelers were admitted a score at a time, paying admission in various currencies. Bonu watched as a carnival atmosphere permeated the air with macabre overtones. Later, when liquor consumption reached massive quantities, fights, thefts, murders, and other abuses would break out, inhibitions, already rare in Pitland, would be nonexistent. The toll in human suffering resulting from this singular event would stagger the imagination, but multitudes still flocked to this debased ordeal pitting two beautiful, young women in a fight the death.

Bonu, Scung, and Artil passed beneath the yawning arches, glancing up at the overhead frieze depicting two women locked in mortal combat with two slain women beneath their feet. A gold-embossed motto below the frieze extolled the virtues of Scrarth and Avangar:

From such battles rise women who rule,
From such rulers rises a daring universe,
From such a universe rises a defiant breed,
From such a defiant breed rises a goddess.
Today a goddess goes to battle.

Beneath it, another motto in white paint on hastily nailed-together boards was somewhat less philosophic:

Support your favorite:
DALICUSI WEARS RED,
JEDA WEARS GREEN.

Vendors did a brisk business as large, dyed feathers of both colors were sold below this sign. Supporters passionately argued the strong points of their chosen contestant; here and there the taunting became so severe that insults threatened to overflow into punches.

"There's no mention of Spoena," said Artil. "You don't suppose—"

"No, Artil, set your mind at ease. In such vaunted contests, elimination rounds are usually dismissed lest the headlining contestants get too battered to give a good account in the main duel. For the sake of heightened anticipation, Scrarths will be put on display, possibly even in a staged combat prior to the main event. No doubt this was already determined days ago during the preliminaries. Dalicusi's Scrarth will have deferred to her, as Spoena must surely have done for Jeda; albeit, she likely loathed the entire proceedings, wanting no part of it."

"Will Spoena be made an example of?" Artil asked, tears brimming and running down her cheeks.

"Now, now, Artil, we aren't even sure Spoena has been found out," said Bonu.

"But what if she has?"

"If she's found out, she's no worse off than we'll be when our identity is discovered. Speaking of which, we'd better come up with some kind of plan, eh, Scung?"

"I dunno, Bonu, I jest sort o' spected summat idee wouldda come ter usn's by now. But we better do summat soon. F'rinstance, how be's usn's gonna pay fer tickets?"

"Bonu," said Artil in a hushed voice, "those dronnets over there are eyeing us."

Four half-hooded blackguards leaned against a wall beside a tunnel leading into the arena. All four blackguards stared unwaveringly at the three ragged revelers.

"Uh," Bonu muttered, "let's duck down the gangway and go to another entry."

Scung fell in behind Bonu, gripping Artil's arm lest she be swallowed up in the bustle of the crowd. The three made slow progress bucking against the current of human jetsam flooding the gangway.

Cries of:

"Hey, you didn't pay!"

"What do you think you're doing?"

"Lookout, yer goin' the wrong way."

And other angry insults flew at them, but they pushed headlong into the crowd to evade the dronnets.

"Scung, hey, Scung!" bellowed Trunch as he and his cronies were swept away by the crowd on the other side of the gangway. Within moments he and his cronies were out of sight.

"Did we lose the dronnets, Scung?" Bonu asked as he ducked an elbow aimed at his face.

Scung, head and shoulders above the crowd saw the dronnets still in their wake. "They be's follerin'! People be's clearin' outta their way. Ere, lemme lead, I'll make usn's a path." Bonu gratefully stepped aside and let the giant to take the lead.

"Outta me way yer maggots!" bellowed Scung, his thunderous voice resonating off the passageway walls. Startled Carnalians backed away from the bellicose, rampaging Eroton giant, choosing to face the jostling crowd behind rather than the fierce, oncoming Eroton. A path opened before the trio.

But it also remained clear for the pursuing dronnets.

"Outta me way!" Scung bellowed again, his massive fists intimidating any who dared to oppose him. Verbal abuse was hurled but none called the Eroton's bluff and dared to stand in his way. The trio scurried past, hoping to mingle inconspicuously among the crowd once inside the arena's concourse. Then Scung skidded to a halt so abruptly that Bonu and Artil bumped into him. "Dronnets dead ahead."

Bonu peered around Scung's massive shoulder and saw three more dronnets who had been leaning against a wall staring directly at them, now rousing themselves.

"It be's me, Bonu. I sticks out like a watermelon in a cucumber patch. Scatter, save yerselves. I'll hold 'em off long as I kin. Yer an' Artil do whut we come fer." Scung extracted and began swinging his Child of the Stars in an arc, its small-but-brilliant-tip glowing cheerily in the tunnel's gloom. Frightened screams and peals of laughter rose simultaneously from the surrounding throng as Scung sallied forth.

Bonu seized Artil's chin and whispered in her ear. "Go find Jeda, then pull out the trumpet with the number "1" engraved on it. If she's in a trance it might wake her up. Get away. Now!" He picked her up and tossed her into the midst of curious onlookers who were reacting as if Scung's antics were part of the pre-fight entertainments.

Artil, dazed by Bonu's brusque manner, stumbled blindly into the hooting, jeering swarm.

Bonu stood back to back with Scung and withdrew his own Child of the Stars. His sword crackled with electrifying blue light in the dark of the tunnel. The crowd suddenly realized this was no mock entertainment, but an assault by real Ecclessites.

"I couldn't leave you alone, Scung," he said over his shoulder.

Fury boiled over against the interloping kingsmen who dared wave their glowing swords here of all places and now of all times.

Artil was enveloped into the crowd.

The first of the dronnets reached the audacious Ecclessites, one of them announcing in a loud, clear voice. "All right everyone, move on. We'll handle this, move on and no one will get hurt. Go on about your business. We'll have these two in hand in just a moment. Move along to your seating; the festivities are about to begin. Go along now." His stern voice overpowered the throng's mumbling hubbub, causing them to reluctantly disperse.

Another dronnet joined the first one and proclaimed, "We'll bring them to the arena after the Avangar has been determined; she'll choose their fate. First, we must question them to see if they have any fellow conspirators about. Now move along as you were told."

By this time seven dronnets surrounded Bonu and Scung, encircling the duo, preventing any possibility of escape. The crowd sensed impending doom for the two Ecclessites who'd foolishly tried to disrupt their games. They had no chance of survival, much less accomplishing their mission.

"Come on wi' yers; I'll teach yers whut Ecclessite steel feels like," threatened Scung, bringing gales of laughter from dronnets and onlookers alike.

"You're frightening us with all that light on your sword, Eroton." More gales of laughter. The two kingsmen appeared to be in for the most desperate fight of their lives.

"Maybe you'd like to test my blade first," defied Bonu, undaunted, rising to the challenge. He cast a sidelong glance making sure Artil had escaped. She was nowhere to be seen.

"Hey, where's the girl?" one of the dronnets suddenly asked, catching Bonu's searching glance. "We must get the girl, too."

"See if you can take me as easily as you think, blackguard," dared Bonu, drawing their attention to himself.

"Easily done," bragged the foremost dronnet as he advanced on Bonu well within range of the kingsman's sword.

Needing no further invitation, Bonu lunged, his sword level as he'd done dozens of times with positive results. But this time was different, very different. But then he'd never battled a dronnet face to face before. His straight-forward thrust was seized in mid-air inches from its target. Bonu's eyes widened with surprise: the dronnet suffered no ill effects. That dronnet's hand should have, at the least, been burned or stung as a warning! Instead, Bonu's sword flashed bright blue from tip to haft. The dronnet then shoved it aside and snared Bonu about the neck, pinioning his arms behind. Meanwhile, the sword returned to its original glow before clattering to the floor. Another of the dronnets carefully scooped up the offending weapon in a towel, careful to let his hands touch neither blade nor handle. Another dronnet jumped Bonu and the three spilled to the floor. Bonu was trussed hand and foot within seconds. Scung fared little better, for though he was still on his feet, three dronnets hung on him, rendering him immobile.

"My sword never failed me before," Bonu muttered as he was dragged away. A loud thud drew his attention. Looking behind he saw Scung, finally toppled by the addition of a fourth dronnet. Then Scung was disarmed and bound as Bonu had been.

"That's all there is to it, folks, keep moving; go to your seats so you don't miss the opening exercises. You'll see these two later as additional entertainment. Now, move along."

Bonu's head was kept forcibly bent downward, and so was Scung's as the two were dragged down the hallway. Four dronnets gripped Scung and two had Bonu; one was unaccounted for. Where was he? Chasing Artil? If they caught her, the whole effort would collapse. Artil was their last and only chance of preventing the savage duel. As long as Artil remained free, Jeda had a chance of regaining her proper state of heart and mind.

Hasty footsteps drew alongside Bonu, reporting to the dronnet in charge. "I can't find her anywhere. She's slipped away."

Bonu wanted to shout the glad news to Scung but restrained himself lest it give their adversaries added impetus to search for Artil, especially if they had any inkling of the contents of her haversack.

CHAPTER SIXTEEN

THE SIX DRONNETS FORCED BONU and Scung through a doorway. The defeated lieutenant peered into the gloomy interior of the room lit by a solitary candle on a tabletop. A heap of unwashed laundry lay on the floor beside the table. Other than that, there was nothing of note in the room, in fact, the chamber was void even of essentials, such as chairs. Bonu surmised it was a detention room for dealing with unruly spectators. As his eyes adjusted to the darkness he glanced over at his partner. Scung's eyes were dark and angry, his jaw muscles worked; he seemed sorely tempted to revert to Eroton problem-solving methods.

One of the dronnets stood close to Scung, his hood almost reaching the Eroton's beard. "You're doing a fine job of inhibiting those old passions. Your liege will be pleased with you."

Another dronnet untied Bonu's bonds, commenting, "You, too, lieutenant. You are doing remarkably well yourself reining in those fighting impulses."

"Who are you?" Bonu challenged, neck hairs bristling.

"Come now, did you really think it would take four dronnets to subdue an Eroton, even one as large as a house? And, furthermore, when was the last time you saw a dronnet's eyes? And, don't you know dronnets rarely use their voices, and when they do, it's little better than a scratchy whisper? Carnalians don't pay much attention to those characteristics, but Ecclessites," the speaker removed his half-hood and

Tren's familiar visage grinned at him, "Ecclessite lives may hang in the balance by observing such details." The other dronnets stripped off their hoods and stood revealed as the other nearly-executed kingsmen officers. "We were beginning to wonder whether you were going to arrive on time."

Astonished, Bonu looked from one to another, embracing Tren at long last, scarcely daring to believe it. "You, you're safe!"

A groan came from the pile of dirty laundry.

Bonu was further amazed to discover that the pile wasn't grubby laundry after all, but a heap of unconscious, scrawny, sallow-skinned men clad in long underwear. "Dronnets?"

"We needed their outfits," Tren explained with a shrug.

"Yer conked them there dronnets cold?" Scung whispered incredulously. "An' wi'out swords?"

One of the other officers shook his head and explained, "Oh no! Not us, him." He pointed to the candle, or rather, to the roamer hovering just behind the candle, disguising himself as it were, in the candle's soft glow. "That bright prepared our way. They were already unconscious when we found them. All we did was don their clothing, after which we went out to the arena's entries to await your arrival. There's no question that Logon is very much guiding this rescue! We need only be willing and brave enough to follow through."

"Then usn's will survive an' return ter the regiment formin' in the cliffs of Ra-Amawl?"

Tren lifted his head. "I didn't say that. Our lives are not our own, remember. Wait . . . did you say that a regiment is forming?"

"In the cliffs whence Scung and I came, back in Carnalia's deep forest of Ra-Amawl."

"Is that brigade in a cliff, by any chance?"

"Yes. Why?"

"Describe those cliffs."

"Well, I don't know much," Bonu grimaced trying to recall what the cliffs looked like. "I'd just returned from the waterfall and didn't have much chance to explore. Vawella, the Captain's daughter, told me that she explored it somewhat and found caverns possibly meandering for miles behind the cliff face as well as delving below ground; there were some that opened into rooms complete with fresh running water and they even found some cave-dwelling creatures fit for food. Why are you so interested in these cliffs? Wait—don't tell me . . . those are the cliffs where the swords of Vadiv are hidden!"

"No, I don't think so. But if they're the cliffs I think they are, they have as much significance, if not more, than your sought-after escarpment. Lurcan's forces will be seriously challenged by a large kingsmen contingent setting out from cliffs deep in Ra-Amawl. The prophecies are lining up." Tren's finger tapped one of the mystery runes on Bonu's sword.

One of the other generals overlaid his hand on Tren's forearm. "We're not all agreed on that concept, Tren, remember. Some of us," he nodded to his companions, "hold to other interpretations."

"That may be, Leton, and I will hold to our agreement as long as we're still together or until it becomes clear whether your school of thought, or mine is right. Though it looks more and more as if the things I expected are coming to pass, does it not?"

"Well, yes, but that doesn't mean we're to base our actions on your supposed dialogues with Logon."

"Like I said, I hold to our agreement. Logon's plan won't be thwarted as long as we whole-heartedly desire to obey him and don't stubbornly cling to erroneous notions." Then turning back to the lieutenant, Tren said, "Bonu, are you ready for some action?"

"I'm at your disposal, but do I understand that there's a disagreement among you officers? How are we ever going to effect Jeda's rescue if there's division?"

"Tut, tut!" chided Leton. "Lieutenant, we didn't waste a day and a night looking for swords that weren't there."

"Leton is right, Bonu. It's not for you to criticize senior officers; nevertheless, Leton, Bonu is right, too. We must be united; especially now. I'd hoped I was wrong about those swords, Bonu. Those weapons would surely come in handy. I didn't know for sure, but I had a strong hunch you were way off in your guess of their location. How disappointed you must be to have nothing to show for your labor."

"Well, it's not as if we came away with nothing, is it Scung?"

"Eh? Oh, yer means them other things?"

Tren's brow knitted. "Other things?"

"Right. We may not have found what we were looking for, but we did find something of note, I think."

Tren's lips parted and his eyes widened. "Of note? I catch your joke, lieutenant. If you found what I think you did. Where are they?"

"Artil has them in her sack."

"All seven?"

Bonu nodded. "You know, then?"

Leton interposed "What are you talking about? What did you find?"

"Tell him, Bonu."

"Trumpets, sir." Bonu smiled. "Just before we left off searching for the swords Scung stumbled on an earthen pot containing seven ancient trumpets."

"Do you need further proof?" Tren stared unblinkingly at Leton.

The older man stroked his stubbly chin. "It doesn't necessarily mean anything. Could be any trumpets." Two of the other officers standing alongside him nodded. "Tell me," Leton challenged Bonu, "Was there anything, shall we say, peculiar about these horns?"

Scung took it on himself to reply. "Only thet they had summat o' writin' on 'em. Bonu read 'em ter usn's as we was a comin' along the trail. Whut was it yer was readin', Bonu?"

"They were trumpets of unusual design, first of all," Bonu began. "With inscriptions in archaic writing on each bell, oh yes, and each trumpet had a number from one to seven."

"Still think it could be any trumpets?" Tren's palms were face up and held at waist level toward the three reluctant officers.

Then one of the men flanking Leton said, "That's good enough for me."

"Yeah, me, too," agreed the other. "We're with you, Tren. Logon has indeed shown you how this will go today. What do you want us to do?"

"Leton?" Tren asked.

Leton shrugged. "I don't know. I suppose it all fits just like you said, Tren. But it goes against everything I've ever been taught."

"Look, I don't understand what's going on here," Bonu protested, "but Jeda is going into the arena any moment now, with a howling mob calling for her blood. If you've got a plan, hadn't we better figure out how to disrupt the proceedings?"

"Patience, Bonu. All in good time, but first, it's better we all be in one accord. Leton, you still seem unconvinced."

"I can't help it, Tren. I don't want to be a hindrance, but I can't ignore everything I've learned from when I was a child, either."

"All right. Let me run it by you one more time. Just as Logon told me: first, we would not be executed, but set free, as you yourself heard from the roamer. Second, disguises would be waiting for us which we're now wearing. Third, our number would grow to ten. Counting these two, we are nine. We lack but one to fulfill that prediction."

"Well, we're closer, but it still isn't ten. And you did say ten *men*, so the little girl can't be counted, right?"

"I only counts eight!" Scung interrupted.

"One of us is out there looking for your Artil. Had we known what her sack carried we wouldn't have sent Ollo after her. She'll perform her duty best if left alone. Now, where was I? Oh yes, the confirmation, the trumpeted cavalcade would be our signal to run to the midst of the battle floor and do the obvious."

"How do we know the trumpet cavalcade isn't the fanfare announcing the opening of the contest, like you originally thought?" Leton posed.

"Perhaps, but we now know there are superior trumpets on hand, trumpets of Logon's design. Ecclessites follow Logon's trumpets, not Lurcan's. But, either way, we'll know when the time comes."

The door opened and Ollo, dressed as a dronnet head-to-foot, entered. Firmly closing the door behind and tugging off his hood, he confessed, "I lost her. She slipped into the crowd and disappeared. I tried to find her, but some real dronnets arrived with the contestants in their respective carriages. I retreated lest I be discovered; they likely would have spotted me right off as an imposter."

"You did the right thing. Artil has the trumpets."

"Trumpets?"

"*The* trumpets, you know."

Understanding dawned in Ollo's widened eyes. "Oh, you mean *the* trumpets. Well then, it's a good thing I didn't catch her, eh?"

"Exactly. You say the contestants have arrived?"

"I didn't actually see them, only their carriages and accompanying dronnets and Hadel guards. But the girls were in the coaches. I felt the chill of the phantoms sponsoring this event descend, too. Scuffles and arguments broke out all over the stadium. Immediately following the contestant's carriages came the great ladies themselves in festively decorated broughams. Bablo-ya, followed by her wretched sister with a brigade of her henchmen; and then Deparis, cold and lethal, escorted by her own Craniantium bodyguard. The players are all here, gentlemen."

"Let's strip off these repugnant clothes and find more suitable garb so we can mingle amidst the crowd as we await our cue," suggested Tren, looking to Leton for endorsement.

"Oh, all right. I'm not totally convinced, mind you, but since you all seem so sure, I'll go along."

"That's good enough for now, Leton. But I warn you, once we receive the signal you must act in concert with us."

"You're waiting for one of the seven trumpets, not just any old trumpet, right? Well, in that case, since according to my beliefs I don't see anything in the runes about those trumpets sounding 'til after we're safe in Splendora with Logon Xychirion, I guess there's no harm. If I do hear one of *those* trumpets sounding, I'll believe you."

"Good enough!" agreed Tren.

"Ollo, you and Leton go back out there and get us some suitable clothing, and don't forget, there are nine of us now, and one will require extra-extra-large."

Scung looked up with a "Hmmph!"

Without another word the pair put their half masks back on and exited to the corridor.

Bonu watched them leave, then asked, "Tren, what about those dronnets in the corner? Are you just going to leave them?"

"They're safe enough under the watchful care of their warden," Tren chuckled.

"I mean, shouldn't we, you know, try to pierce their hearts or something?"

Tren spun on his heel and looked at the unconscious pile of blackguards. "Bonu, you're absolutely right! We didn't try it before because we had no weapons. But now, we have yours and Scung's. Give it a try."

Marn, one of the other generals, stepped over to Tren. "Isn't it dangerous; I mean for them. If a man's heart is too hard, he'll be tormented or even likely die because of his own resistance to Logon. And dronnets are notoriously hard-hearted."

Tren nodded. "Nevertheless, consider their plight should we leave them as they are, mindless dupes of Lurcan. Will they fare any better? I think not. We owe them this chance."

"And Ecclessite love," offered another general.

"Very well," Bonu sighed. "Uh, just how do I go about this? I've never pierced a man who wasn't awake and aware. Are you sure you wouldn't be better at this, having so much more light on the sword than I?"

"No, Bonu, it's your sword. And it was your idea. This is your call; it's for you and Scung to try their hearts."

"Me?" gasped Scung. "I hain't got nobbut light on me blade but jest a teensy weensy—"

"It's not you, nor even the amount of light on your sword, Scung. It's the Advisor who bears witness to the truth. If any of these wretched examples of Carnalia's elite have a latent desire for truth, the sword will enlighten their heart even as it pierces their flesh. You only need apply the light you have; the Advisor will do the rest."

Scung gulped, nodded and said nothing more as he wiped his hands on his breeches. Bonu smiled, so, Scung's palms were suddenly sweaty, too.

Tren, Bonu, and Scung stood over the hapless pile of dronnets subdued under the roamer's power. Scung looked apprehensively at the roamer for a moment, but remembering his previous encounters, relaxed, stood well back and watched Bonu tug one of the unconscious blackguards off the pile.

"Does yer want I should hold him fer yer?"

"I don't think that's necessary."

The roamer stretched forth a beam of twinkly lights and touched the insensible blackguard.

The man's eyes popped open and he stared first at the surrounding kingsmen, then at his slumbering comrades-at-arms beside him. If he saw the roamer, he gave no indication. His raspy voice demanded, "Who thinks you are? Now you suffer!" He tried to stand, but the roamer again touched the man's shoulders, pushing him back down to the floor. His eyes bulged. "How you do that? What kyllorn you know?"

Tren leaned over putting his own face an inch from the bewildered dronnet's visage. "We are under the authority of the most dread power in the universe, if you be against him."

The man's eyes widened; rising from his neck a purple rage contorted his visage. He spat out, "Ecclessites!" He struggled again to rise, but to no avail.

"Now's as good a time as any, Bonu," encouraged Tren.

Bonu nervously fingered the haft of his sword then slowly pointed the tip at the dronnet's chest.

The man's eyes fixed on the approaching, glowing blade. He struggled, but the roamer held him firm. The sword touched his chest and sizzled, sending a billow of smoke and the reek of burnt flesh, but the chest wall didn't open. He cried out in anguish before lapsing into unconsciousness.

Tren's hand stayed Bonu. "Enough, his heart is too hard."

"Scung, suppose you try the next one," suggested Tren.

"Awright." The Eroton gulped and gripped his sword so tight his knuckles turned white. The man awoke just as the bright sword tip frayed his shirt open. The dronnet jerked trying to pull away. Scung hesitated, the sword tip rested gently on his skin. "I kens yer!"

The dronnet blinked uncomprehendingly, unable to make any sense of what was happening.

"Scung? You know this dronnet? Are you sure? After all, you've never seen him without his hood," Tren posed quietly. "Where do you know him from? From your service in the southern marches?"

"Mebbe. But mostly I kens him from when me an' Bonu trailed this wretch o' a man an' his cronies, an' Hod-ya herself, with three helpless, captive girls, bringin' 'em ter Pitland. This'n be's Hod-ya's chief dronnet. Bonu, doncher ken him?"

Bonu leaned closer to inspect the pale, drawn face. "I, I can't tell, Scung. They all had their masks on. I see nothing that would make me think—"

"Lookit his chin. Doncher remember seein' thet scar on his chin line afore? Thet be's him, awright. He brung Jeda an' Spoena an' Artil here ter this awful place."

The dronnet stared at the men holding him captive with wonder. "You know girls? How?"

Tren placed his forefinger on the man's forehead. "We'll ask the questions here. Just who are you?"

Disdain and contempt overcame the man's features as he finally realized these men were kingsmen, and why they'd come. "So, you're who trailed us. Fools! What you expect accomplish. I not know so many of you. Only knew of two."

Tren, affecting great restraint, bent over and stared into the man's beady eyes. "Who are you?"

The dronnet reacted coolly, unperturbed at the kingsman's interrogation. Finally, deciding no harm would come of revealing his name, admitted, "Gragnold, chief of Hod-ya's bodyguard. And I know you, as well."

"Oh? And who might we be?" Tren played along.

"You're the ones I'm going to personally feed to Hod-ya's pet waterdragons piece by piece."

"All right, we've played around long enough. Stick him, Scung."

Gragnold's squinty eyes opened round. It apparently never crossed his mind that they might actually try to make an Ecclessite of him.

Scung pointed his sword at Gragnold's chest where it came to rest on the outer layer of skin.

"Wait!" Gragnold said as loud as he could. "I know arena rooms where they're kept before entering arena. I'll take you."

Bonu's hand stayed Scung's sword from penetrating any deeper. "Wait, that's what we want to know."

"No, Bonu," said Tren. "We have our plan. Don't play into their hands by stalling or changing Logon's instructions. Proceed Scung."

"No, no," begged Gragnold. "I can help you find her. She's your sweetheart?"

"Pierce him," commanded Tren.

"At least hear him out," demanded Bonu.

Tren turned to Bonu. "Do you remember when I said that personal passions must be left out? Lieutenant, I'm ordering you to stand down. Scung, to your duty."

Bonu reached overtop of Tren's arm grasping at Scung's sword hand.

Tren twisted Bonu's arm back, threatening to break it.

Scung looked back to Gragnold and applied pressure to Gragnold's chest. The sword passed through the skin; the dronnet slumped. Scung looked to Tren for explanation; this was a far different result from the first dronnet.

Tren's raised eyebrows showed he was just as surprised that the sword penetrated the blackguard's chest.

Gragnold, his eyes closed, muttered, "Hod-ya knew, somehow she knew. Said I needed reconditioning." He whimpered like a little child, then mumbled incoherently for several moments, yet, was obviously talking to someone.

Then he suddenly sat up and swiveled his head around as if viewing something high overhead, though his eyes remained closed. He spoke clearly in a strong voice, "You would indeed be justified. Ah, but that is the question. I don't remember giving permission, but, yes, I am glad. Even if I must forfeit my worthless life by touching this rock, at least I will no longer be in rebellion. I accept whatever my fate may be." His hand reached out as if touching something invisible to the kingsmen in the room.

Even Scung, the instrument of Gragnold's piercing, dabbed his eyes.

A white tunic formed over Gragnold's body; then a sword and toller appeared in his hands.

Tren whispered, "Who would have believed?"

Scung asked, "Whut does we do wi' him now?"

Tren laughed. "Why Scung, you of all people shouldn't have to ask that. He's one of us now and is to be accorded full fellowship and trust. Let's see if any of these others will switch sides."

One by one they tried each of the remaining dronnets, but no other chestwalls opened to receive the blade of truth. One of them, becoming aware of his predicament, pretended receptivity, but when the sword touched, the man's skin was scorched, causing him to faint dead away.

Tren remarked, "He would have feigned joining us only to betray us. Logon knew, and thus prevented us from being cruelly deceived in our greatest hour of need. We must be vigilant against those who claim to follow Logon but are really subversive agents in our midst. Behold, now we are ten."

Gragnold suddenly sat up and blinked several times. "Where'd he go?"

Scung suddenly gasped, exclaiming, "Logon," as he stared at an empty space. No one else saw anything. "He . . . he smiled at me then vanished." Scung looked from face to face. "Really, he was right there." Scung's forefinger pointed toward the doorway.

"It all truly h-h-happened?" Gragnold probed the healed scar on his chest.

Smiling faces all around confirmed the reality of the event. "Not a kingsman here hasn't gone through it, just like you," offered Marn.

"But surely none of you was as evil-bent, intent on pursuing wickedness as I?"

Tren extended his hand and helped Gragnold off the floor. "We all pursued the son of King Elyon to his death, rationalizing our actions, calling him and his ways unjust. There's no greater evil than accusing the purest and most righteous one of wickedness."

"And these?" Gragnold pointed at his former comrades laying scattered about on the floor.

"Too hard-hearted. They wouldn't admit their need for mercy. I'm afraid they do present a problem of what to do with them."

"Let the roamer keep them," offered Marn. "He's done all right so far, hasn't he? I see no reason to assume he'll quit his post."

"I suppose you're right." Tren turned around. "Now, what about you, Gragnold. How are we going to get you past your former comrades stationed around the arena? They'll sense something has changed."

Gragnold examined the sword in his hand, comparing it with Scung's, which had nearly an inch aglow. He looked back to Tren and said, "Perhaps, if I don't wear dronnet garments, I'll not be recognized or challenged."

"Not likely. Your pallid complexion is a dead giveaway. Only a dronnet would be that pale. No, we've got to do something creative. Any suggestions?"

The door to the hallway opened admitting Ollo and Leton bearing a bulging burlap sack. They quickly closed the door and emptied the contents onto the floor. There were colorful shirts and a few pair of mismatched breeches. Only then did Ollo and Leton behold the former dronnet awkwardly tolling a Child of the Stars.

Tren ignored their questioning looks. "So, how did you fare getting us disguises?"

"We did the best we could, under the circumstances," explained Ollo. "Even dronnets aren't above suspicion, it seems. There was a brigade of Carnalian regulars assigned to crowd control who kept looking us over as we went from bin to bin collecting what we have. I'm afraid there are only enough outfits for five. And, they're jester costumes."

"Jester outfits!" Tren massaged his forehead. "Whatever are we going to do with jester outfits?"

Gragnold looked up from his tolling. "Jesters play an important role in the ceremonies. Perhaps, perhaps, yes! I'll wear one of those harlequin outfits and set an example for you of what to do and how to act. Jesters are integral to the pre-battle entertainment leading up to the main event." He sifted through the pile of brightly colored clothing. "These are old outfits—discarded and replaced a couple of years ago." Gragnold turned and found the others watching him. "But they'll do in a pinch."

"Are you sure you're up to it? After all, you've only just become one of us."

"I'm ready to die for Logon, if need be. I touched that rock fully expecting death, so whatever life I have left belongs to him. Though I knew there was no future in serving Hod-ya, I was in bondage to her, nonetheless. Now I have a hope and a destiny and an opportunity to exercise my choice to follow him who bought my release. I'd be very disappointed if, having the intimate knowledge of this day's events as I do, I was relegated to some less-risky function. Please, let me share the danger. After all, I'm the one who brought Jeda here."

"He's makes a good point," said Marn, "if you think we dare trust him."

"You see the tunic, sword, and toller. Logon doesn't bestow them lightly. If Logon trusts him, blackguard though he was, we must accept him, too."

Bonu leaned over staring at Gragnold. The former dronnet sat, knees drawn to his chin, embracing his sword. "What's Jeda's condition?"

Gragnold lowered his eyes. "Not good. Hod-ya lied to her that her brother was killed, savagely hacked to pieces by you Ecclessites. Up until then she'd been able to put up some resistance to the cusps in the conditioning cell. But when Hod-ya delivered that bit of misinformation, Jeda yielded to bitterness, falling entirely under Hod-ya's spell. It was all a lie, and I participated. I bear the guilt for assisting her descent to villainy."

Bonu stepped back, struggling with the emotions tearing at his heart.

"Steady, Lieutenant," Tren warned, "remember, those same forces of hatred are able to find you even here and now if your heart invites them. Don't let them make you unfit for Logon's service."

"But he knowingly, willingly took part in turning Jeda away from Logon. How can I handle that? How can I receive him into our company as if he'd done nothing wrong? Tell me, how?"

"Rather, you should ask how can you not accept him?" Tren's tone was stern as he held Bonu's arm. "I don't know if Jeda has gone as far as denying her liege, but if she has, remember what Logon said: *'If anyone denies me, I must deny them!'* If she has denied Logon, and Gragnold here has embraced him, you must clarify your loyalties and make the appropriate adjustments. Else you, too, fall into danger of denying him."

Bonu pulled away from Tren's grasp. "I don't know. I need time to think."

"Time is what we don't have, Lieutenant. Your duty calls; will you put aside your personal feelings and obey, or not?"

Gragnold slowly rose to his feet and approached Bonu. His voice thready, but strengthening as he implored, "Please Bonu, Logon told me I needed to ask your forgiveness for my part during her captivity. Will you forgive?"

Bonu stared for a long minute at Gragnold, not blinking, as if trying to outstare the recent proselyte.

"Bonu," Scung whispered, leaning close, "does yer love Jeda more than yer loves Logon?"

Bonu spun around to face Scung, aware of the impression he was making on this tender, new recruit.

"What will you choose, Bonu, 'live for a moment' of revenge, or will you follow Logon no matter what demands are made on you?" Tren's eyes bored into Bonu's. "It's a choice, as you know full well."

"It's not that I want to harbor bitterness, but my feelings are so strong. I never expected it to be like this."

"You can be sure that anything remaining in you that endangers your love for Logon will be exposed by some situation in which you are brought to that choice. This is what it means to die to yourself, Bonu, and there's no other way to fully be Logon's servant."

Stomping feet resonating from overhead in the vast stadium seating reminded them that a mob eagerly demonstrated their passion for the blood-letting to begin.

"So, Bonu," Tren urged, "make your choice, and make it quick; we're out of time."

"Yes," said one of the generals rummaging through the pile of clothing on the floor, "as Gragnold says, we need to get in our positions out on the battle-floor."

"Bonu."

"All right, Gragnold, it won't be easy, but I'm willing to let Logon take my hurt." Bonu extended his hand. Gragnold took it, pumping it once.

"I'm satisfied," said Tren. "All right, Bonu, you and Gragnold and Scung don these jester outfits, as will Ollo and I. We have to keep you, Gragnold, away from your former comrades, else all is lost."

"I understand. Being a jester is such a comedown for me. Ooh, I feel so weak."

"That's because you now only have natural human strength. When you wholeheartedly came to Logon, the dark powers imbuing supernatural strength in you were driven out. You're no stronger than an ordinary man now, remember that. Logon must be your only source of strength. And keep your sword out of sight until the right moment. Here let me show you how to conceal it. See, it fits nicely without interfering with your stride, but is easily released when the need arises. How does that feel?"

"A little awkward, but I can manage. You have no swords?"

"We'll be okay; Logon will provide."

The selected five donned jester garb while the other five in plain clothes sneaked a peek at the outer corridor, waiting for the chance to inconspicuously slip out one at a time.

The harlequin full-face masks obliterated the features of the five jesters, so there was little danger of recognition. They knew each other; that was enough. Scung's outfit, though larger than all the other outfits, was ridiculously small, adding to the absurdity of his appearance.

"Just what are we supposed to do out there?" Bonu felt awkward in the garb of a Pitland harlequin.

Gragnold answered, "Jester is a highly coveted position, and those who win the right are ruthless in protecting their position. Us entering the arena, dressed as ragamuffin harlequins in these discarded outfits is a serious breach of protocol which could be perceived as an invitation to duel for the right to perform as jesters in the Scrarth and Avangar ceremonies. Other than that, once the Avangar duels begin, harlequins are needed to keep things lively if there's a slowdown in the action."

"Slowdown?" questioned Tren.

"You know, if one or even both contestants consistently back away, refusing to fight, it's the harlequins' job to physically nudge the adversaries back together so the fight continues."

Tren put an arm around Gragnold's shoulders. "Fill us in on details along the way. We must head out there now."

The five jesters exited the chamber leaving the remaining unconscious dronnets under the roamer's watchful eye. Along the passageway they collected the other five generals garbed in civilian clothing who had been feigning idleness by leaning against the wall as they waited. The ten, five in a clump of jesters, the other five strung loosely behind, hurried toward the opening at the far end of the stadium tunnel.

They emerged onto the arena's field under Pitland's lead clouded sky. Rowdy spectators packed the stands, even overflowing and ringing the field, greedy for blood. Bonu stopped just outside the exit and stared at the multitude in the stands while the five plain-clothed generals mixed in with the standing room only spectators ringing the field.

"Keep moving, Bonu, or you'll rouse suspicious," Gragnold whispered, nodding toward the official, smartly outfitted jesters waiting in the paddock across the way beside the next entry to the battleground. These harlequins eyed the *ad hoc* batch of jokers with surprise and not a little disdain. "They could present a problem. It's not likely they'll accept competitors sharing their responsibilities."

Even as Gragnold spoke, two of the genuine jesters broke off from their group and sauntered arrogantly toward the disguised Ecclessites.

The crowd had been enjoying the antics of the official jesters prancing and clowning around in the center of the arena. But when the second set of jesters appeared on the field the crowd became distracted, confused.

The two real harlequins picked up their pace as they jogged toward the five motley harlequins. The crowd restlessly watched, trying to figure out why a change had been made in the program, for there were only supposed to be a limited number of jesters, the six listed in the program. Cries of, "Who the inferno are they?" erupted from the throng, followed by various other derogatory shouts.

"Don't you mean 'what' the inferno are they?"

Laughter rippled through the assemblage.

More calls of, "Look at the huge one; his breeches don't hardly cover his knees!" Gales of laughter greeted this observation. The light-hearted taunting of the masses gradually turned more insulting with catcalls and hisses at the disguised kingsmen.

The two genuine jesters drew near the five imposters, but just before they arrived someone in the crowd called out, "They look like Erotons!"

Individual jeers turned into a unified chant: "Rotten Erotons, Rotten Erotons, Rotten Erotons!"

Ethnic derision was hurled at the group until several hundred Erotons in the stands rose to their feet and began hooting back, challenging anyone nearby to back up their taunts. The whole arena teetered on the verge of riot.

As if in response to the dangerous situation brewing in the stands, Bablo-ya's bodyguards, along with Hod-ya's dronnets, flooded from entryways onto the field.

Seeing elite warriors from the two competing nations take up threatening stances had an immediate calming effect. The crowd reseated themselves; no one, not even Erotons, wanted to bring *the laws* into the stands.

The two genuine jesters arrived beside the five disguised Ecclessites. The taller of the two demanded, "Who are you? What do you think you're doing?"

To the other kingsmen's surprise Scung stepped forward. "We be's here ter make sure they hain't no favoritism in how yer does yer duty."

"Who authorized this? No one notified us of any changes," challenged the other.

"Our ruler sent usn's," Scung said. The others behind him nodded in agreement.

"But, but the regent of Eroton has no challenger involved in Scrarth and Avangar, he's in the campaign besieging King's Gate Fortress last we heard. How could he order you to be here?"

"Our ruler hisself be's here today, an' since yers hain't recognized him, he be's mighty offended, an' he says he be's gonna settle things wi' the White Priestess fer the way she be's a treatin' his people."

Underneath his clownish makeup, the man's face manifested uncertainty, even fear at Scung's threats. The two Pitland jesters conferred and then backed off a step, unsure just what the giant Eroton meant.

The crowd, calmed by the imposing presence of dronnets and Hadel guards stationed on the stairway aisles and row ends, watched the interchange on the field with growing curiosity.

Most Erotons weren't as large as the one contending with the original harlequins, either. The two genuine jesters stepped back and whispered to each other.

Scung took advantage of their moment of doubt. With a ferocious roar he leapt forward at them with outspread arms as if intending to crush them in a bear-hug.

The two startled jesters jumped a foot high in the air, one of them dropping his scepter in the process.

The rowdy crowd roared in laughter, pointing fingers and clapping in delight.

Scung bent over, slapping his knees, guffawing heartily as the two retreated in embarrassment. The newcomers had made their mark and earned a place, even if they were Erotons.

"We're in," said Gragnold through compressed lips. "That's how jester positions are sometimes won by coming out during the prelude and challenging each other's bluff. Ordinarily two jesters, like dronnets, would have put a dozen ordinary men to flight, but your man there turned the tables on them. I've never seen the like."

"It wasn't Scung who put fear in their hearts, Gragnold." Tren scanned the amphitheater with his eyes. "Many forces, invisible forces, are at work, more intense than I've felt since slicing off Neask's tongue. Our liege is giving us boldness and dealing out fear to our enemies. Let's get in position."

The five joined hands and Ollo whispered, "Lives for the King!" To which they all responded, "Words of the Word!"

Scattered nearby amongst the standing room only crowd the five generals in plain dress heard and understood. Logon Xychirion indeed stood with them. How this would play out was still a mystery, but they all knew that something outrageous was in the offing.

Others in the audience, noting the unity of these newcomers, thought they heard a clap of thunder when the five dowdy harlequins lifted a shout.

And at a trumpeted blast from Bablo-ya's dais the anxious crowd knew the ceremonies were about to begin.

CHAPTER SEVENTEEN

HOD-YA PAUSED UPON DEPARTING THE brougham, then stiffened as she entered the main gateway of the Arena, then lowered her head and passed hurriedly through the tunnels beneath the filled-to-capacity rows of revelers come to bask vicariously in blood-sport. The roar of the crowd rose and fell in spirited crescendos at the antics of the jesters. But that wasn't what caused the chill to slide down Hod-ya's spine. She had expected and sensed powerful, unseen entities as her carriage drew near the arena, but there was something more, like a foreign tremor in the ether that she'd never before encountered during any Scrarth and Avangar. Was Deparis more powerful than Hod-ya anticipated? If so, this could turn out to be a combat of titanic proportions.

Neither Deparis nor her prodigy expected the tigress she'd evoked from Jeda. Hod-ya herself was mildly surprised at how quickly Jeda took to being cusp-led after she gave in to anger and despair. Jeda was now formidable. Her rage at injustice buttressed her wrath; she was now a sullen, cruel gladiatrix with a grievance. Jeda had become what Glend had longed to be back in the emperor's palace: a fell lady of renown, replete with power to wreak havoc upon all that crossed her path. And it was Hod-ya who had accomplished transforming the meek and mild Jeda into this work of wrath. Well, that would teach them to underestimate the Lady of Lurcan's castle. Not even her own sister, Bablo-ya, who ought to have had more respect for

Hod-ya's capabilities, anticipated the Jeda who was coming forth to battle today.

Hod-ya glanced aside at Bablo-ya and Deparis as the three paraded down the gangway behind their armed escorts toward their readiness rooms. Bablo-ya had allowed only her own Hadel Guards for this initial promenade through the arena tunnels lest friction between Deparis' rangers and Hod-ya's dronnets arise. Upon leaving the readiness rooms and entering the battlefield to ascend to their lofty seats high in the stands, each Majestic Madam would summon her own bodyguard. They were to leave their delegates on the battle-floor behind wooden *burladero*s in the care of nearby jesters until they were summoned to stand forth.

Earlier, Deparis' Craniantiumite Rangers had worn smug expressions, obviously expecting Jeda to be the same, naive weakling Hod-ya had presented two weeks prior. Dalicusi would have been, no doubt, a worthy opponent to any of Hod-ya's past contestants.

But when Jeda fell into Hod-ya's clutches, naive and innocent though she was, Hod-ya recognized the damsel's propensity to be governed by greater forces. Hod-ya's moment of doubt was when the fool girl somehow learned of Logon; all seemed lost. But then stubborn determination took over as Hod-ya's dark creativity whelmed with an ingenious scheme to lure this young, Ecclessite maid away from her prince.

And the contact with a new dread was paying off. Laroc was a smart, powerful ally with clever ideas. She wasn't used to his ways yet, not as she'd been with Psa, but that would come in time. Theirs would be a mutually beneficial relationship that would propel her to invincibility; and through her, Laroc would gain possession of all that had formerly been Psa's. The contract would be fulfilled when Jeda slew Dalicusi, then her Scrarth, then Jeda would storm into the stands and attack Deparis. Craniantium's Great Dame didn't really expect to return to her homeland after challenging the Lady of Carnalia, did she? If so, the more a fool she! Today's events were going to go beyond Scrarth and Avangar, with so much blood-shedding that even Bablo-ya would pale at the satiating of Hod-ya's rage.

"Here's my door," Hod-ya announced as she turned into Jeda's ready room, breaking off from the entourage.

Bablo-ya merely glanced over her shoulder, a gesture as enigmatic as it was impolite, she then crossed through the entry to the field and up the staircase leading to her dais high in the arena's seating to await the beginning ceremonies.

Hod-ya scorned her sister, and Deparis as well. They'd be repaid in full for their condescending attitudes. Bablo-ya would have to crawl even to keep her position. And as for Deparis, who was just turning aside to the ready room of her protégé . . . well, tophets would dine gourmet tonight.

Hod-ya entered Jeda's murky chamber recesses and observed the girl's lithe form bathed in orange glow as she stood between candle lit sconces against the far wall. The outcome of Hod-ya's future plans rested on this slip of a girl dressed in a flowing, light green gown that swept to the floor. Jeda's face was void of expression except that she was awake and aware. Jeda nodded, noting Hod-ya's presence, but saying nothing.

"Are you ready?" Hod-ya inquired.

Jeda stared steadily back, no longer fearful, yet respectful of Hod-ya's power. She lifted her right arm and displayed a dagger; her weapon of choice.

"How apropos; each of you chose a weapon corresponding with your nation. You chose the dagger to pierce hearts, Dalicusi selected a cudgel for shattering skulls, where the mind dwells," Hod-ya mused. "Now pay attention: there are several other weapons, deadlier, better weapons, buried in shallow holes all around the arena's floor; you are to find and use them at will. Your original weapon of choice must be used when you initiate battle and at the climax when you administer the coup-de-grace." Hod-ya stepped back and observed for a full minute. "Yes, you're ready. Devastatingly beautiful—thanks to our cosmetologists, and treacherously dangerous as strengthened by suppressed rage. Are you quite sure you are done with your allegiance to Ecclessa?"

Jeda's eyes flashed angrily and her lips parted for a moment, but no word escaped.

Silent though the response, Hod-ya was satisfied.

"Good. Now remember, when the fight is at the end, act like you're going to show mercy, then when she drops her guard, plunge your dagger straight into the sow's heart. Then rise and stand over your kill and proclaim your triumph. Slay her Scrarth with whatever weapon comes to hand, and after that make your way into the stands and strike that would-be Regina, Deparis. I'll make sure she stays near my sister and me on the dais. You'll be invincible once you taste slaughter, remember that. Gragnold will see to neutralizing her bodyguards, so you should have no trouble gaining access. Do you understand?"

~

Jeda nodded and turned away, returning her eyes to a spot on the wall she'd been meditating upon before Hod-ya intruded. Did Hod-ya really have no hint of her real plan? There would be no end to the bloodletting today, not until Jeda herself fell broken and spent upon the last of her vanquished enemies. She was resigned to death. What use was living anymore? If Logon really existed, and if he was as righteous as she'd once believed, he'd surely want nothing more to do with her after all the vile things she'd done during her conditioning. Well, she was determined to survive the duel, and then vent the remainder of her wrath on Deparis, Hod-ya, Bablo-ya, Gragnold, and any other fool that crossed her path. Jeda turned back around to observe Hod-ya. No, it was obvious she didn't suspect the full scope of Jeda's wrath. Jeda quickly turned back lest the cold gleam in her eye betray her.

Half an hour passed in silence between mentor and pupil; time Jeda used to steel herself.

~

Hod-ya paced, muttering, "Where is Gragnold? He should have been here by now. He better not bungle his mission. This is the most important detail of his life, if he bungles it—"

Several sharp raps rattled the door.

Hod-ya looked up. "It's about time. Where have you—" Hod-ya stopped short upon not seeing Gragnold but one of her sister's pages.

"You are summoned."

Hod-ya's filed teeth gritted.

The lad asked, "You are ready?"

Jeda pushed past Hod-ya. "Lead on."

Hod-ya's eyebrows bunched over narrowed eyes, but she quickly regained composure and followed.

Deparis and Dalicusi awaited them in the hallway eyeing Jeda as she emerged. Hod-ya bit the inside of her cheek to keep from smiling. It was obvious that neither of the Craniantiumites suspected the transformation that had taken place in Jeda. Hod-ya fell in beside Deparis; Jeda followed behind. The cortege somberly walked the long tunnel toward the light at the far end. Though it was approaching high noon, the atmosphere in the arena had become thicker and darker since they'd arrived. Indeed, the very torches lining the walls seemed to struggle against the murk.

Hod-ya breathed in deeply. "Delicious, isn't it?"

Deparis never batted an eyelash. "Yes, they all have come to observe this momentous occasion, haven't they?"

Hod-ya didn't miss the subtle taunt that the power-lords of Craniantium had come to watch the undoing of the Lady of Carnalia. "We shall see," she said as she hitched her skirt and haughtily preceded the entourage toward the battle floor. Except for the echoes of their shoes the remainder of the tunnel was walked in silence.

Both Avangars wore gowns of their own selection: Jeda's was a simple, floor-length gown that draped over her shoulders with a squared-off neckline. She also wore the obligatory green cape embossed with gold symbols of Carnalia and Hod-ya's authority. Dalicusi wore a red gown, ankle length, loose and flowing, offsetting her pale blue eyes, making her appearance startling and gorgeous. She'd artfully applied her own cosmetics, enhancing her beauty. Her bright crimson cloak was likewise embroidered in gold thread with the insignias of Craniantium and the house of Deparis. Thus, majestic and exquisite, the two primary contestants promenaded side by side in the wake of their sponsors toward the deadly melee that would leave one of them slaughtered, and the other a murderess.

~

An ache slowly throbbed in Jeda's heart: an unnamed qualm she'd been dreading. For hours she battled doubts about going through with her plan. Now, however, when she most needed resolve—not wanting to sort out right from wrong, truth from lie—she feared her conscience might undo her. She mentally braced herself, forcing her mind to dwell on techniques and spells she'd recently mastered.

~

Dalicusi sensed instability permeating the atmosphere around Jeda, misreading it as fear. She smiled, unable to conceal her delight; Abmum, the dread, had promised to replace Deparis with her at her victory. Jeda would just be the first in a string of grisly deaths that would propel Dalicusi to fame, wealth, and power. Dalicusi dared a sideways glance at Jeda, noting her stern concentration. This would be no great contest.

Even Deparis had underestimated Dalicusi's true potential. Her very own sponsor was unaware that Dalicusi had an alliance with a dread, and thus was, unbeknownst to all, an equal among the company of the great ladies. Dalicusi shifted her attention to the two majestic dames of the empire strutting before her, inwardly mocking, *Move over, "Majestic Ladies"; the new, the young, the strong is about to replace you."*

~

Halfway down the tunnel to the battle floor doors on opposite sides suddenly opened admitting the two Scrarths led forth by Hadel guards. They joined at the rear of the procession.

Jeda stole a look at Dalicusi, then behind her at Stullo, Craniantium's Scrarth.

Stullo stared back brazenly.

Jeda returned her focus to the fore. Only the shuffling of reluctant feet told Jeda that her own Scrarth, Spoena, had emerged from the other room and now trailed her. She dared not look or even think upon her.

The party ascended from the bowels of the stadium on an inclined ramp and neared the edge of the field. They halted just out of sight of the masses in the stands under a canopy.

A brass trumpet sounded out a martial fanfare signaling the commencement of the ceremony.

The crowd hushed.

The Hadel bodyguard left the two Scrarth and two Avangar combatants alone to take up positions behind the wooden *burladero*s wall with their shields, clubs, and spears that prevented over-zealous spectators caught up in the heat of the moment from leaping onto the battlefield. The only other persons within the ring of bristling weapons were the jesters, whose services were to play an essential role in the day's entertainment.

A voice cried out from a parapet. "Attend ye, attend ye! Hearken now unto this solemn event whereby the undisputed strength of the Carnalian Empire is demonstrated by its confederacy with the nations of the north, south, east, and west and all points therein: most notably Eroton, Pitland, and Craniantium. The sacred revelry of Scrarth and Avangar now commences."

Another trumpet fanfare followed. The audience, come hither to relieve the boredom of their lackluster lives, clapped and hooted for the morbid entertainment to begin.

The crier continued, "From the land of Craniantium, the Lady Deparis, mistress and hostess of the House of Lord Angra, bringing two superior-rated pupils to vie for the coveted title of Avangar of the

Realm." He waited for the crowd's noise to subside before continuing. "Presenting the Lady Stullo, of the House of Demium, daughter of the Grantor of Privilege."

Jeda took another brief glimpse of Stullo escorted by two rangers toward the center of the arena. As tradition dictated, each probable Scrarth was announced before her Avangar. Stullo tossed her head, scattering red highlights from her shimmering hair. The smug expression on her comely features bespoke long inbred class and disdain. She passed from Jeda's field of view, but the applause greeting her continued unabated as she sauntered to a white, chalk-lined, nine-foot diameter circle in the center of the arena.

"And from the House of Detend, daughter of the Lord High Secretary Rep-Orobat, the Lady Dalicusi."

Deparis, tight lipped and grim, turned, looked one last time at her protégé, and nodded. Dalicusi stepped away from her sponsor and paused upon entering the arena's precincts to acknowledge the rousing cheers, whistles, and screams of admiration, luxuriating in the homage the crowd lauded her beauty and prowess. When the crowd's excitement peaked, she proceeded forward with mincing steps, drawing attention to every movement, enticing the delirious crowd to admire her even more. Dalicusi smiled slightly, no doubt musing that this was more than mere fulfillment of vanity Jeda suspected; this calculated saunter to the middle of the arena had as its purpose to drain the crowd's energy so when the opposing realm's contestants were introduced the audience would be weary of cheering and want to get on with the action. An edge, no matter how slight, is still an edge. Dalicusi strolled toward the center of the arena where Stullo waited. Dalicusi's well-armed escorts impatiently kept to her indolent pace. When Dalicusi finally arrived at Stullo's side she took her fellow Craniantiumite's hand and lifted it as together they turned allowing the masses the privilege of gazing upon their beauty. Then, facing away from the granite cliff at the rear of the battlefield, they curtsied deeply from the waist.

The audience went wild.

"You certainly know how to play the crowd; I'll give you that, Deparis," begrudged Hod-ya from the shadowed entry.

"Hod-ya, in all fairness, I advise you to relinquish your seat and power now, spare yourself the degradation of losing. I'll be merciful and let you retain dominion over Carnalia—all that is, except Lurcan's own castle."

"Oh, would you be so kind?" Hod-ya sneered. "I'm surprised you'd let me live."

"I'll allow your survival if you surrender before the contest begins. Of course, that cheap imitation of an Avangar will have to be put to a slow, torturous death. We can't let this mob go without some pandering to their desire for blood."

"Save your breath and your merciful offers, Deparis. I am mistress of the realm and intend to stay that way. But may I give you this advice: Keep your hounds nearby, if you can."

The announcer's voice again rang out, proclaiming, "The Lady Deparis, hostess of the House of m'lord Angra, regent of the realm of Craniantium, Center of the Intelligentsia Institute, and sponsor of the two visions of lethal loveliness you now behold."

"Cryptic advice that, Hod-ya. I suppose by 'hounds' you mean my rangers. You are threatening me, then? I *urgently* hope so, I do." She licked her lips.

Hod-ya glared but said nothing.

~

Deparis marched into the arena to a trumpeted fanfare, rousing cheers from the stadium. Unlike her contestants, she didn't go to the center circle of the battlefield but was ushered to the stairway leading up to the dais from where Bablo-ya presided. She nodded from side to side at revelers as she ascended, staunchly confident that this day, so many years in planning, was to be her highest achievement. And she'd planted a seed of doubt as she left Hod-ya. How many dronnets had been subverted with Ugen's assistance? Deparis grinned and flicked her tongue out.

She neared the top where three thrones were set to oversee the duels. As custom dictated, Deparis nodded politely to Bablo-ya, but thinking to herself, *Don't look so smug, Majestic Madam, you weren't born to your position. A better than yourself is come to replace you.*

"Welcome, Lady Deparis," Bablo-ya intoned. The acoustically efficient amphitheater had been purposely constructed to amplify voices from this one, unique position, so that voices carried even to the towering granite walls lining the back of the battlefield, making it possible for every reveler to hear all but the most low-toned conversations from the dais. The crowd obligingly hushed as Bablo-ya continued, "I welcome you to Scrarth and Avangar. Have you brought worthy contestants for the entertainment of the masses of the empire this day?"

Deparis' arm swept outward toward the battle floor. "You behold them on the field before you. The Ladies Stullo and Dalicusi await your pleasure."

"And have you determined to let them vie between themselves for the coveted title of Avangar of Craniantium?"

"If it pleases your ladyship, since there is another sponsor with contestants vying for the title of Avangar of the Realm, a battle between my contestants would surely expend energy from the eventual victor. Should the other contestants decline the preliminary fray, her Avangar would be fresh and unscathed, putting my entrant at a serious disadvantage."

Catcalls and boos filtered through the crowd.

Deparis waited until the arena quieted, then continued, "For this cause, the Lady Stullo of the House of Demium, daughter of the Grantor of Privilege, has relinquished her right to duel the Lady Dalicusi of the House of Detend, daughter of the Lord High Secretary, Rep-Orobat. She accepts Dalicusi as her superior, standing by as her second to assist in non-combative ways as Dalicusi meets her match."

Down on the field Stullo knelt and kissed Dalicusi's proffered hand. Murmurs arose here and there in the throng, though most were content with the arrangement, understanding that this had been prearranged anyway.

Bablo-ya raised her hand for silence before uttering her decision. Nothing was settled until she publicly declared it so. The crowd again hushed in anticipation; would she allow the Scrarths to get off so easily, or would she contradict the sponsors as she occasionally did?
"My decision is . . . Dalicusi is awarded title of Avangar of Craniantium."

Cheering Craniantiumites leapt to their feet with thunderous applause. The Erotons were relieved that their champion, Dalicusi, would enter the fight against the Avangar of Carnalia unscathed. Mismatched as the Carnalian contestants were, Jeda would doubtless win hands down over her Scrarth; whereas the duel between

Craniantium's contestants, had it been held, could've resulted in a strength-sapping duel.

Two of the original jesters escorted Stullo to the edge of the battle-floor and placed her in a box seat on the edge of the arena. Here she would remain until needed. Dalicusi was led by another jester several paces from the center of the battle floor, allowing room for the new contestants, but still engendering admiration from the crowd, hoping to steal the show from Jeda's entrance.

"Bid the next pair of contestants, herald," ordered Bablo-ya.

The trumpets sounded again, and the herald announced, "The young Lady Spoena of," he shrugged, lacking anything else to say, "Ra-Amawl."

The girl was half-dragged onto the field by two of Hod-ya's dronnets.

Laughter greeted her reluctance.

Spoena nearly fell when one of the dronnets shoved her toward the center of the circle. Neither rangers nor dronnets were allowed to remain inside the barrier of Bablo-ya's Hadel troops, so after depositing their charge, the two retreated into the stands. Spoena gained her footing and stood with shoulders slumped, vulnerable and helpless, staring at the jeering throng.

Vicious catcalls and obscenities carried down to the entry where Jeda and Hod-ya waited. The crowd was turning rabid. Hod-ya peeked around a corner and caught her breath as for the first time that day she glimpsed Spoena. "That fool of a girl still has on her Logon dress. Gragnold was specifically instructed to make her remove it. Speaking of Gragnold—" Hod-ya searched nervously around the stadium.

Jeda, standing on tiptoe, peeked over a barrier and caught a glimpse of Spoena, shoulders hunched, standing in the center of the arena, hair neatly quaffed, face artfully made-up enhancing her natural beauty. But her only garment was her Logon dress, and though plain, bore neither tatters nor smudges. In her hand was a stick trailing behind in the dirt, presumably her weapon of choice. By the immaculate appearance of her Logon dress, Jeda knew that Spoena had overcome Hod-ya's conditioning.

A pang of guilt caused Jeda a moment's unsteadiness. Spoena had remained true, while she had withered, succumbed, fallen away. Well, be that as it may, Jeda was no longer part of that realm. Nor could she bear to claim any part of Pitland or Carnalia, having once tasted of Ecclessa.

Spoena bore the look of one who'd been beaten but not broken: her head bowed, hands hanging limp . . .

Jeers from the audience tortured Jeda more than they seemed to affect Spoena. Would Jeda be acclaimed a heroine and adored as a goddess? Possibly, though she knew she deserved no better than Spoena was receiving, and worse, for she'd forsaken all that she knew to be true.

"The Lady Jeda of the house of Kway, daughter of m'lord High Secretary of Re-Education," the herald disrupted Jeda's reverie. The stadium erupted afresh in cheers and applause.

The combat between Dalicusi and Jeda had been all the talk of Pitland and surrounding environs for a fortnight. At last, Hod-ya's mysterious, ex-Ecclessite would face the strongest and most dangerous warrioress Craniantium had to offer. No matter who won, Ecclessa would be exposed as inferior to the nations of the empire. If Jeda won, it would be said that Ecclessa had one of the great ones but couldn't keep her. If she lost, then she was the best Ecclessa could ever hope to offer, and what a failure she turned out to be. Win or lose, Hod-ya had pulled off the propaganda coup of all time: a fact that would not escape the notice of higher powers.

"Go on, girl," Hod-ya nudged from behind. "That's your cue. Get out there and dazzle your adoring worshippers. Do yourself proud today."

Despite all that Dalicusi had done to deplete the crowd's energy, Jeda stepped over the threshold and was greeted with a vigorous volley of applause and cheers. Green feathers waved throughout the crowd; their holders frantically waving them to catch the attention of their new idol. She forced herself to take a step, then another, and another, determination building as she went. Jeda gritted her teeth. She must cling to hatred or this would end in a fiasco with herself the prime victim. Hod-ya had managed to steal Logon and the joys of Ecclessa from her, but it would cost all of them dearly. If she faltered now she'd not only lose all she ever held dear, but her last-ditch attempt at revenge, too. At least she could damage them as she'd been damaged.

She suddenly remembered herself seated on a hay bale across from Tressa and Filke who were asking if the Great Avenger would avenge them.

She shut her eyes. No! She must not allow those thoughts to creep into her mind. She'd been naive then; now she realized how important revenge is when it's all you have. She lifted her head, squared her shoulders and marched toward Dalicusi instead of the circle where Spoena waited, disdaining the approval and rejection of the mindless, pleasure-maddened masses. She was intent on one thing: destroy them all. Her dagger slid down out of her sleeve as she gained momentum.

As Jeda approached nearer to Dalicusi a jester blocked her path and grabbed her by the arm, whispering, "No, not yet. You'll get your chance.

First you must be declared Avangar of Carnalia over that pathetic thing," he indicated Spoena who stood with eyes closed. Jeda yielded, allowing herself to be led alongside Spoena.

The crowd laughed at the sight: the gorgeous but dangerous gladiatrix versus the trembling, frumpy, woodland nymph from Ra-Amawl wearing a simple, Ecclessite dress.

"The Lady Hod-ya, of the emperor's own castle in Cosmopolis, capital of all the empire," called the crier.

Hod-ya emerged from the tunnel and with long strides proceeded past Jeda and Spoena to ascend the stairway, ignoring the crowd who both cheered and booed. Only once did she slow her pace upon noticing the extra cluster of jesters off to one side in their own tight-knit group. There was something familiar about one of them in particular, in fact, that they were even there at all was ominous. Bablo-ya had said that the usual harlequins would be performing their tasks. Something about this motley-looking crew, especially the lanky one, bothered her. But she couldn't be concerned with such trivial details now. Protocol demanded her full attention. She'd sort the mystery out later.

"Welcome, Lady Hod-ya," intoned Bablo-ya as Hod-ya gained the topmost step. "Have you brought worthy contestants to do battle this day for the coveted title Avangar of the Realm?"

Hod-ya looked down to the battle floor and saw the pitiful, trembling form of Spoena beside Jeda who stood tall, sullen, and resolute. "Majestic Madam," she began, "as you know, the contest today has been greatly touted as between Jeda of Kway, and Dalicusi of Detend, and it's unlikely that any of these worthy citizens have come to see a lamb butchered without putting up any defense. Therefore I—"

Bablo-ya silenced her sister with a wave of her hand. "I asked if you have brought opponents worthy of the honor of fighting to the death for the glory of the Carnalian Empire. Have you?" Then, under her breath she hissed, "Don't you dare change protocol now, sister. Follow the script."

Deparis' eyes flashed with glee at Hod-ya being rebuked.

For a split second Hod-ya seemed to consider a retort that she would, no doubt, later regret, so restraining herself, she replied, "You see what I've brought, standing and awaiting your disposition."

"Yes, I see, but I'm not convinced both are worthy."

Hod-ya glanced up keenly at her sister, whispering, "Don't you dare go back on your word."

"You should have kept yours, to bring two fit contestants," Bablo-ya whispered back. Then aloud to the stadium, "You told me you had a plan to turn Ecclessites back into Carnalians. One of them is obviously still Ecclessite. Has your plan failed?"

"What do your eyes tell you of the other, Majestic Madam?"

Bablo-ya rested her eyes on Jeda for a long moment. "Yes, you have done well with that one. But I wonder, is she totally ours? My decision therefore is: in order for Jeda of Kway to prove her commitment, she must duel her Scrarth."

Spoena lifted her eyes to the dais.

"What?" Jeda muttered staring at the ground.

"What?" shrieked Hod-ya simultaneously with Jeda's utterance.

All heads turned towards the dais.

Deparis covered her mouth and turned away, unable to suppress her delight.

"That is my decision, Hod-ya."

"But, but she won't fight."

"Who won't fight? Jeda?"

"No, the other."

"Good, that simplifies things, doesn't it? Your Avangar can get a taste for killing early on without expending any energy."

Hod-ya's pointed teeth gritted. She whispered, "You know that will undo all the effort I've put into her. I insist you declare Jeda as Avangar and get on with the real contest."

"You insist? Who do you think you are, coming to my realm, insisting I do this or that? I insist that you have your entrants engage in mortal combat, such as they are."

Down on the field Spoena whispered, "Jeda, have you forgotten how much he loves you?"

Jeda's eyes closed. "I can't, I won't harm you Spoena. If Logon loved me once, he can do so no longer. I've gone too far."

"He told me to tell you he loves you still."

Tears dripped from her closed eyelids, she couldn't face her friend. "No, stop it, you're just saying that."

"He also told me Bonu will come to your aid when you least expect."

"Stop it, Spoena; you're doing more harm than you know."

"You're not one of them. Why, you still have your Logon dress underneath. If you're one of them, why do you still wear it?"

"I, I couldn't bear to take it off. I especially chose this gown to cover it. How do you know—"

"The Advisor told me this morning while I waited alone in the ready room."

"Hod-ya, begin the contest; set the duel," demanded The White Priestess, impatiently.

The stadium had grown deathly quiet. The contest of wills between the vaunted sisters was an unexpected contest of mind and will, a bonus entertainment.

~

Hod-ya's mind raced. She'd vowed upon the dreads of the gate, at Jeda's insistence, that Jeda would not be forced to harm Spoena in any way. There was nothing she could do to force Jeda to slay her companion. How then was she going to qualify Jeda to fight Dalicusi?

"Well? Or do I declare Spoena the Avangar, put Jeda to death, and let Dalicusi do what your pathetic contestant won't?"

The crowd murmured angrily at Bablo-ya's suggestion. They paid to see a fight involving violent clashes, strategic maneuvering, and clever battle tactics, not boring executions.

Bablo-ya was forced to turn away from the recalcitrant sponsor and lift her hands demanding silence. Her Hadel guards surrounding the field slapped broadswords on their shields three times in unison at Bablo-ya's upraised arms.

The crowd quelled.

But the interruption had given Hod-ya an idea to gain the upper hand after all. "Citizens of the empire," Hod-ya appealed directly to the masses, overstepping her sister's authority. "Hear me. Do you want a tedious, public execution, a dreary shedding of blood with no strategy, no fight, no uncertainty, no prolonged suffering, just a quick slash of the knife and a dropped body?"

"No!" The crowd stood to their feet roaring.

Hod-ya lifted her hands and the blood-lusty mob quieted. Glancing slyly over at her sister she thought she detected a note of hesitation. "Or," Hod-ya continued, "do you want the excitement and thrill of the duel with attack and defense, the gradual weakening of one combatant, the pursuit, the hunt, then the slow, humiliating death by degrees?"

"Give us the duel!" the multitude resounded. A chant started near the Eroton contingent and grew till it encompassed the whole stadium: "We want the duel. We want the duel. We want the duel!"

Hod-ya stepped back, smugly folded her arms, and smiled maliciously. "There will be no duel if you insist that Jeda kills Spoena."

"We want the duel! We want the duel! We want the duel! We want the duel!"

Jeda was relieved as she stared up at the mob howling for her to fight Dalicusi.

Dalicusi remained unmoved; dueling Jeda was what she'd expected; this was why she'd come. She shifted her position to study Jeda and found Jeda was studying her.

"Jeda, please don't do this," Spoena whispered low. "Call out to Logon; he awaits your plea."

Jeda cringed.

Dalicusi didn't hear the conversation but her eyes lit up when she caught Jeda's momentary flash of uncertainty.

Jeda noted the flickering smile on Dalicusi's lips and steeled herself. She must not weaken!

"Jeda." Spoena pressed her case.

Jeda whirled around and with the back of her hand, lashed out, smiting Spoena across the mouth. "Don't do this. You'll kill me if you sap my resolve, don't you understand?"

Spoena staggered backward at the force of Jeda's blow, then bent over weeping, head bowed, hand to her lip; blood dripped through her fingers.

The crowd stopped chanting and cheered, focusing attention from the dais back to the field.

"See," Hod-ya snapped, "there's no love between them. Set the real duel, as your public demands." She threw a fierce, triumphant glance at Deparis.

Bablo-ya pursed her lips as if considering her options. Again the White priestess raised her hands and short, black swords slapped shields in unison, restoring order.

"I have decided," Bablo-ya lowered her hands, "to reverse my decision, yielding to the wishes of my people. Live for the moment . . . "

The arena again erupted in cheers; Bablo-ya bowed, magnanimously currying favor. A crowd expecting blood is an unstable mob, capable of anything. Hod-ya exploited that principle to the undoing of a White Priestess' decision—a major coup for the Lady of Carnalia. Bablo-ya's fingers twirled a wisp of her hair; she had underestimated her sister and paid the price.

Deparis tried to conceal a consuming lust for power evident in her eyes, too. No one was invulnerable, no one.

~

Hod-ya had defiantly manifested that same hunger. Very well, mused Bablo-ya, she'd slipped—just a little, but she was still the Majestic Madam of Pitland, with powers and *kyllorn* confederates beyond her opponents' ken. There had better be no more intrigues lest the rampant crowds get far more than they'd bargained for. She had the power to bring down the wrath of the dreads upon the arena and all in it. They'd better not take her lightly.

CHAPTER EIGHTEEN

"Retire the Carnalian Scrarth to her place on the opposite side of the *gladiatorium*," ordered Bablo-ya. "I trust this meets with your approval, Hod-ya?"

"Yes, that's fine." Hod-ya nodded, careful not to gloat. She must remain inscrutable in case Jeda made a poorer showing than anticipated.

"And should that pitiful thing be named as Jeda's second?" Deparis pushed the limits of Hod-ya's tolerance.

"Oh yes, I'd quite forgotten," Hod-ya replied, stifling a snicker. "How thoughtful of you to remind me."

Deparis' eyebrow raised as she settled into her seat, seemingly stymied at Hod-ya's lack of anger and suppressed mirth.

"And let the Scrarth of Carnalia be named as Jeda of Kway's second," Bablo-ya announced so all the stadium could hear. "Lady Dalicusi, display your weapon."

On the battle-floor Dalicusi took a step forward and opened her cloak revealing a full-length, red, ruby-studded gown. In her right hand she gripped a small, gold-gilt cudgel. She slowly turned and raised her hand displaying the object for all to see. Then in a loud, clear voice, she cried, "I hereby dedicate this cudgel to the destruction of Craniantium's enemies, starting with this Ecclessite wench who dares profane our hallowed ceremony with her corrosive influence!"

A rousing cheer from Dalicusi's supporters rumbled across the breadth of the arena.

Jeda was unmoved, in fact, she was barely aware of the commotion surrounding her. She was preoccupied with silencing one small, nagging fragment of her conscience that threatened to undo her.

"Lady Jeda, display your weapon of choice," commanded Bablo-ya from her high dais.

Jeda's inward reverie was interrupted. She incrementally raised her head and parted her cloak to reveal her floor-length, light green, emerald-studded gown, then stepped forward. She lifted her hand overhead automatically displaying her glittering dagger for all to see. Unlike Dalicusi, Jeda neither turned in a circle nor made any dedication.

~

"Hod-ya," whispered Bablo-ya after a few uncomfortable moments, "she says nothing?"

"Her actions will reveal her strength, not idle boasts." Hod-ya decided to allow Jeda that privilege; though Jeda's reasons were unknown to her, Hod-ya saw benefit in that it would irritate both Deparis and Dalicusi.

It apparently produced the desired effect, for the Craniantiumites exchanged quick glances between the battle-floor and dais. Hod-ya had now scored two prestige points; Deparis none.

~

A smile flitted ever so briefly across Bablo-ya's face. She also caught the fleeting glance between Deparis and Dalicusi and noted the briefest of smirks on Hod-ya's lips as well. It mattered little to her who scored petty points, or even who won Scrarth and Avangar, for that matter. All that mattered was that she retain her regency over Pitland. Scrarth and Avangar had been a large part of her success; thus, the more intriguing the contests, the more certain she was to remain in power. And this year's event promised to be a match of legend, with as much animosity on the dais as on the battle-floor.

The White Priestess continued in a clear voice for all the arena to hear, "According to the rules of Scrarth and Avangar, this duel is to the death, using whatever training methods you've mastered, whatever ethereal powers you're in league with, and whatever weapons come into your hands. The only laws you must follow are that the weapons you displayed must start and end the conflict; and the other is that you must stay within the confines of the arena, that is, between the cliffs of granite behind you and the semi-circle seats of the stadium surrounding you.

"Your seconds may assist only as you call them, and their assistance may only be to hand your chosen weapon to you at the *coup-de-grace*. After the initial clash those weapons will be entrusted to your second by a harlequin. Are you ready?"

"I am ready, Majestic Madam," Dalicusi curtsied.

"I am ready, Majestic Madam," echoed Jeda, unenthusiastically and without a curtsy.

"Your training has lessons in impudence as well, Hod-ya?" Deparis commented joining beside Bablo-ya and Hod-ya. Point for Deparis.

Two jesters commenced the ceremony by jogging toward the girls, doing flips and cartwheels to the amusement of the crowd on the way. Their job was to receive the combatants' cloaks and wait nearby for the weapons of choice to be turned over to the seconds waiting in their separate box-seats behind the *burladeros* on the battle-floor.

On the other side of the arena huddled the intruding jesters; the tall, lanky one prodded one of his comrades who then raced toward the contestants without acrobatics, thus arriving before the regular jesters. He performed a leaping dive that resolved into a forward roll, landing him squarely in front of Jeda. He bowed so low that he ended up looking backward between his legs as one of the original jesters drew near to Jeda. He stayed bent over to the onlookers' merriment, blocking the appointed harlequin from receiving Jeda's cloak. Meanwhile, the other genuine jester arrived and took Dalicusi's carmine mantle in custody.

The bent-over joker suddenly reached back between his legs and seized the jester's legs, toppling him backward. Then this harlequin stood upright and extended his arms to the crowd receiving applause from the laughing audience.

Jeda remained unruffled, turning her focus away from the buffoonery, that is, until this same jester pranced around behind her, unleashed the clasps of her cloak and whispered in her ear, "Jeda, it's me, Bonu."

Jeda's eyes widened and she gasped.

The toppled jester arose, livid at being cheated of his cape-bearing duty for the Avangar of Carnalia. He had won the honor by tossing *lucky-knuckle bones* with his cronies or some such game of chance, as Hod-ya had explained the order of events to Jeda, and now he wasn't about to be denied by some joker-come-lately. He sprang at the usurper but grabbed only empty air. The trespasser had anticipated the attack and dodged. The rightful jester chased the usurper, arms outstretched, fingers splayed intent on squeezing the very breath out of the imposter.

The crowd howled with glee at the brash antics of the ungainly-dressed harlequin, enjoying this unexpected addition to the ceremony. Bonu raced figure eights around the girls with the jester in hot pursuit. Dalicusi's cloak-bearer backed out of the way. Just as Bonu was about to be caught he fell to the ground and rolled up in a tight ball. The chasing jester, unable to avoid the sudden obstacle, tripped over him and sprawled face down in the dust.

Again, the masses roared, delighted at the escapades of the shabby jester.

Dalicusi, watched with mild interest, limbering her arms, testing the balance of the cudgel nestled snugly in the palm of her hand. She looked more than prepared to assail Jeda with a punishing rain of blows that would leave her opponent's arms shattered. The harlequins' delaying antics appeared to be little more than a temporary annoyance to her. Finally, having had enough of the harlequins cat and mouse game, she looked up to the dais and opened her mouth as if to demand that this foolishness stop, and the real contest commence . . . but she uttered not a word.

The three great ladies themselves were watching the erratic behavior of the jesters with surprise—especially the unexpected, uninvited ones.

~

A wrinkle of doubt appeared on Dalicusi's forehead upon seeing the three grand dames perplexed. None of the grand dames on the dais seemed to have foreseen this turn of events. Dalicusi slowly turned and observed Jeda.

Jeda stood in the spot where she'd been relieved of her cloak. Could Jeda be responsible for this, all by herself, apart from her sponsor's assistance? A tingle of fear coursed up Dalicusi's spine. Was Jeda even manipulating the bizarre antics of the jesters? For the first time Dalicusi wondered if she hadn't underestimated her rival.

~

Deparis, upon the dais, was at first merely irritated by the additional jesters, and somewhat more so when one of them interrupted the proceedings with his playful "catch-me" game. But these time-wasting pranks would sometime or sooner prove to be a distraction to her prodigy. Anxious to see her well-laid plans activated, Deparis' could do nothing but grit her teeth; her patience wearing thin. At the least she could complain about Hod-ya's interfering, unorthodox methods, but she swallowed the words before they passed her lips when she saw Hod-ya gnawing her bottom lip. Hod-ya hadn't expected this distraction either!

If Hod-ya wasn't the architect of this gambit, who was? A quick glance at Bablo-ya told her that the White Priestess was as baffled as the two sponsors. So, who was responsible for this confusing fiasco?

~

Down on the field, both sets of sidelined jesters charged into the center of the arena to assist their respective comrades.

Bonu winced when the jester caught him in a vise-like grip, thinking his neck was about to break.

Fortunately, Scung arrived none too soon, hurling his full weight like a runaway bull into the harlequin manhandling his beloved lieutenant. The bona fide jester released his grip on Bonu as he sailed through the air and crash landed with a resounding thump. By then the jesters of both parties had arrived, faced off and were about to have at each other.

Bonu and Scung, still equipped with their kingsmen swords, kept them hidden; an armed melee at this point would prove disastrous.

The White Priestess stepped to the fore of the dais and raised her hands.

Pitland's soldiers lining the rim of the field beat their shields again, sending a thunderous echo reverberating off the back wall, interrupting the harlequin donnybrook before blood was shed.

Bablo-ya cried out, "Stop it! Stop it, I say. This field is dedicated to Scrarth and Avangar today, not a fool's duel. If it's a blood feud you want, we'll be happy to give you satisfaction. But not now, not today. Today must determine the Avangar of the Realm, not the buffoons of the arena. Now desist from further folly or I'll have your heads removed."

~

Tren backed out of line, no longer facing the original harlequins, attempting to edge beside Jeda, but was unfortunately thwarted by three real jesters.

The settling crowd was restive, eager to relish in the bonus fray of the joker's argument. But would the jesters back off as the White Priestess demanded, or would the first blood to saturate the arena floor be harlequin?

The opposing sets of jesters warily eyed each other, waiting to see who would back down. Scung reached beneath his ill-fitting jerkin and nervously fingered his sword's haft.

Bonu slipped away from the two lines of jesters and tried to sidle beside Jeda but she saw him and turned away, avoiding him, refusing to even look at him.

~

This time Dalicusi didn't miss Jeda's trembling lips as a certain jester approached. Here then, was something Jeda of Kway didn't expect, something not anticipated; a weakness?

~

"This is my last warning," Bablo-ya's angry voice hung in the air. Then she called down to her guard, "Lepur, take those ill-favored jesters into custody."

Instantly thirty men clad similar to Hod-ya's dronnets, but without masks or hoods, trotted out surrounding the Avangar contestants and the eleven jesters. It was clear they meant business; it was well known that they were as tough a breed as Hod-ya's dronnets. Even the real jesters, recognizing their peril, relaxed their stance and stepped back from the confrontation.

Tren announced, "Right then, men, we've had our fun. Back to our station." At that, he turned and playfully skipped, sometimes clicking his heels back across the arena, followed by Scung and the others, laughing uproariously as if it had all been a joke. Last of all, Bonu reluctantly followed, somberly gazing over his shoulder at Jeda.

The real jesters also slowly retreated in bewilderment. They'd never ended up the brunt of a joke before; they'd always been the perpetrators of such pranks, but for now they had no choice but to play along.

"Hod-ya, any more of your subversive plots and I'll personally—"

"I had nothing to do with those jesters, Bablo-ya! I thought you appointed them."

"Deparis."

"Not mine! I thought . . . Then whose—"

Hod-ya laid her hand on her sister's forearm. "Bablo-ya, stop the ceremony. I sensed an unusually strong presence earlier today, and since none of us claims responsibility . . . Delay the ceremony just for a couple of days before we regret this day's activities."

"Stop the ceremony? Certainly not! I sense nothing more unusual than normal. Mayhap you sense the dreads come hither, having left their bodily forms somewhere safely in the desert so they might hover above the cliff in their *kyllorn* form, watching from on high to see who the Avangar will be, waiting to laud and use her to their purposes. There's no stopping the duel now, sister, lest we incur their wrath, in which case none of us would escape. Besides, the three of us ought to be able to handle whatever surprises arise. Don't tell me you've grown timid, sister?"

"I feel something greater than a pod of dreads has come among us," said Hod-ya surveying the arena, "and I believe that somehow those aberrant jesters are involved."

Bablo-ya flashed a wicked grin, but quickly recovered. "Yes, there's a great power here today, but not involved, I think, with those intruding harlequins."

"Perhaps we should summon those unknown jesters and question them before we allow the ceremony to continue," advised Deparis.

Bablo-ya turned and stared directly into Deparis' eyes. "But what dangers would a time-consuming interrogation unleash? Especially when it would mean not deferring to the desires of a blood-thirsty crowd already taxed beyond its patience and attention span. Do you accept the responsibility of making the masses endure another delay?"

"I say do even more, stop it altogether, Bablo-ya," Hod-ya hissed in her sister's ear. "Postpone 'til tomorrow and promise an added attraction of Ecclessite prisoners forced to fight wild beasts if you're so worried about this rabble's displeasure. I'm telling you, I sense danger. My chief of staff, Gragnold, was supposed to report to me over an hour ago, but he's disappeared, along with others of my most trusted dronnets. Something has gone way wrong. Stop the proceedings."

"Are you cusp-touched?" Bablo-ya pushed her sister back a step. "Look at those people; they're ready to climb the walls and come after us if we delay. I don't even know how safe it is to follow Deparis' suggestion of taking a few moments to interrogate those jesters, much less suspend activities for the day."

Hod-ya followed the White Priestess' finger circumscribing the semi-circle arena abutting the granite cliffs. Even the ground at the back walls overflowed with people who arrived too late to obtain stadium seating, milling restlessly around the edges of the battle floor, murmuring, looking up at the dais, wondering what the hold-up was, anxious to get on with it. Here and there arguments broke out; the entire mass of humanity threatened to become violent. Their appetite had been whetted for action and gore, but so far had been served only buffoonery. All right, Bablo-ya might be right; the masses would tolerate no delay. "I see your point. Nevertheless, if you insist on going through with it, don't be surprised if your domain comes crumbling down around your ears."

"Perhaps Hod-ya is really saying she doesn't think you have your subjects under control," Deparis exploited the opportunity. "My advice to examine the jesters will merely stretch what's been strained—and in my opinion can be stretched a bit more to satisfy our curiosity. Hod-ya's plan will push the rabble past their limit—not to mention, allowing her contestant another day of preparation, which is against the rules, as you well know."

"Don't lecture me on rules," snapped Bablo-ya. "I have no need to be instructed by either of you. As for your suggestions, I'll follow my own counsel." With a flick of her forefinger she summoned a page, hastily scribbled on a slip of paper and put it in his hand with the admonition, "Lepur's eyes only, understand? Only your captain is allowed to see this."

The lad left on the run, striding three stairs down at a time.

"What are you up to?" Deparis frowned.

"Aren't you the inquisitive one? Well, for your information, I've decided to continue without further delay, and to summon the leader of those mysterious jesters to an inquest here on the dais. That way the crowd will be focused on the field while we discover who's behind that ragtag squad of harlequins. That way, you see, their purpose which likely is no more than delaying our agenda for whatever reason, will be defeated. Our job will be to find out who and why. I'm certain you ladies are up to assisting me in wringing answers out of one of them, are you not?"

"Clever, I must admit." Deparis bowed her head. "You truly are among the shrewdest of women," she fawned.

Hod-ya rolled her eyes, but Bablo-ya lapped up the adulation, insincere as it was; hers was a world invested in and consisting of vapid superficiality.

Hod-ya remained unpersuaded. "Don't listen to her flattery. You know as well as I that she loathes both of us as much as we loathe each other. I'm telling you there's a real, palpable danger here today, to us personally. If you let the contest continue—"

"Hush! No more; I've decided." Bablo-ya stepped forward and clapped her hands, drawing the arena's attention.

Instant quiet descended.

Bablo-ya curled her upper lip and glanced at the women behind as if to say: "Now you see who is in control here." Turning back to the masses she raised an arm announcing, "Let the contest begin."

A rousing cheer erupted from the semi-circular seating. There would be no more delay. The mob's mood had indeed grown ugly when they observed the messenger rush from the dais to the captain of the guard with a message. Suspicions ran deep that they'd be cheated out of watching the most highly touted duel of the century. But now, their goddess, the White Priestess, had provided, titillating their senses, making them happy. Unrest evaporated. Let the fight begin!

"Avangar of the realm of Craniantium, Avangar of the realm of Carnalia, approach each other and proffer your weapons."

~

Jeda lifted her eyes off the ground. Now that the ceremony was underway, she felt her bitter hate rising. She approached Dalicusi to perform "The Kiss of Death."

Both girls approached each other step by measured step, stopping a full arm's length apart. Slowly and in unison Dalicusi and Jeda raised their weapons from waist level to within inches of each other's face. Jeda leveled her dagger at Dalicusi's throat; Dalicusi's cudgel hovered menacingly near Jeda's temple.

The crowd hushed.

Jeda mentally reviewed her plan.

Dalicusi silently summoned her *kyllorn* guides.

After long moments of absolute stillness, their weapons poised, Bablo-ya's voice rang out over the hewn-stone amphitheater:

"Kiss your bane,
Scoff blood's plain,

Shame your slain,
Do not complain,
Nor lift refrain,
Scorn the reign,
That bears your pain,
And die in vain."

A clap of thunder broke over the stadium.

The three women on the dais reflexively ducked, glancing fearfully upward, as did all the amphitheater—except Jeda and Dalicusi. Their eyes remained locked, fiercely wrestling with and probing each other for weakness. They tentatively leaned forward and touched their lips to each other's weapon. Neither blinked nor shifted their gaze until both weapons were lowered and they turned once more to face the dais.

"I'm telling you, Bablo-ya, there's something more going on here than we know," Hod-ya persisted.

"Perhaps your sister is right, Bablo-ya." Deparis kept her wide-eyed gaze skyward. "I'm told it never thunders this time of year."

"Afraid of a clap of thunder?" Bablo-ya countered. "I can evoke fireworks that will stand your hair on end. I've decreed that the contest will go on; go on it will! I care not what powers come to observe this day; I defy them all. My allegiances will override all subterfuge. Do either of you think I know nothing of your plots to overthrow me as well as each other? Fools! I will decide the day."

The timbre of Bablo-ya's voice suddenly changed, dropping several pitches as her face swelled and reddened and her eyes bulged. "I know who challenges me today, and as I defeated him long ago, so will I thwart him now. My time is not yet come!"

Hod-ya, keeper of the emperor's castle in Carnalia, recognized the visage superimposed upon her sister's countenance all too well. She backed away whispering, "Lurcan." So, her sister consorted with the most dreaded of dreads!

As quickly as Lurcan's face manifested, Bablo-ya features were reasserted, as if nothing out of the ordinary had happened.

But Deparis sprawled over backwards, half-hanging off her throne, her face ashen gray.

Hod-ya herself had to retreat a step and grasp her throne's arm for support, standing cautiously out of reach, thinking and muttering aloud, "So, not only the remaining dreads had come to this fracas, but the lord of the underworld, the emperor himself!" Was he perhaps seeking a flesh and blood residence in order to attain his ultimate goal of antagonizing his enemy? Did he expect to find a human host among today's contestants? If so, such a person would become the prophesied Kar-Sak, destined to rule all nations, Ecclessa included.

"Begin," the White Priestess ordered the Avangars, her voice normal again but with an added flavor of cruelty. "Let this contest reveal the victorious."

Upon Bablo-ya's command, Dalicusi and Jeda crossed weapons, then backed away from each other; Scrarth and Avangar was underway.

Flecks of dark matter, dense and unnatural, filtered out of the sky like a black snowfall, almost blotting out torchlight from the sconces placed strategically around the arena. Shadows darted at will between the two contestants who dodged and thrust their weapons at each other in feints and dodges. Dalicusi's cudgel swooshed through Jeda's tresses fractions of an inch from her chin.

Jeda dipped to the left just in time avoiding the blow that would have, at the least, broken her jaw.

In return, Jeda spun quickly on one heel and lunged, secretly shifting her dagger to her other hand in the hope that Dalicusi would mistakenly dodge into it instead of avoiding the danger. The ploy worked, but wasn't well executed, for though Dalicusi leapt to Jeda's left, Jeda's grip on her dagger wasn't firm, merely tearing a hole through the gown just deep enough to nick Dalicusi's skin by her ribcage. The dagger almost fell to the dirt.

The crowd roared its pleasure as the two women merged, grasping each other in earnest combat, yanking hair, scratching and wrestling for control over the other's weapon-hand. The pair was well-matched; worth the wait and expense. This day's Scrarth and Avangar had all the legendary components of being epic.

The required initial contact with their weapons of choice completed, they broke apart to search the arena floor where a variety of weapons had been buried under loose dirt piles for them.

Dalicusi momentarily stepped back and examined the slice in her gown and side, withdrawing her fingers smudged with blood. Jeda had drawn first blood, but the wound was merely a scratch. Dalicusi gritted her teeth. She seemed incredulous that Jeda's head wasn't where she'd aimed.

Two jesters trotted up behind the combatants and hovered nearby, waiting for the girls to drop their weapons so they could bear them safely from the fray to the seconds.

~

Dalicusi again held her blooded fingers before her face, astonished that Jeda had actually drawn blood. The slit in her gown was small and of no significance, but she had to admit that she was lucky Jeda's dagger only glanced off her ribcage. She was furious at herself for being so careless. She hadn't spent months studying technique and tactics only to be undone by this Ecclessite turncoat. She took another step back and scanned the arena for a loose pile of dirt that might conceal a buried weapon with a longer reach than her cudgel. She immediately spied some loose dirt not twenty feet away.

Jeda followed Dalicusi's eyes to the same dirt pile. Both girls raced toward the spot, still clinging to their chosen weapons in case they were unsuccessful in obtaining the hidden prize.

~

Around the arena other events unfolded which few noticed: a small band of Hadel Guards surrounded the grubby-looking jesters, separating one from among the rest despite his cronies scuffling with the guards to keep him. The leader, thus apprehended, was dragged across the near end of the field, then bodily carried against his will up the stairway toward the dais where Bablo-ya, Hod-ya, and Deparis sat overseeing events. The guards struggled to control the resisting harlequin at almost every step, stopping every few moments to clout him about the head with clubs to subdue him. The other intruding jokers were forced back into their dugout at sword point.

From the other end of the field and at the same time a file of manacled prisoners were led around the circumference of the battle-floor inside the ring of guards lining the field. These were some five hundred Ecclessite prisoners who'd been unbreakable in their devotion to king and country, refusing to produce the empire's black swords, and were, therefore, only useful as "entertainment." The guards forced these captives to lie down shoulder to shoulder, chained in pairs, until their prostrate bodies rimmed the entire back section of the battle floor.

~

Jeda and Dalicusi both delved one-handed into the loose dirt, jabbing and punching each other while assaying to dig up the concealed weapon.

Jeda's foot found her opponent's stomach. Dalicusi rolled away frantically sucking in air. Jeda dropped her dagger and plunged both hands into the loose soil, where her fingertips touched a metallic handle. She thrust her arm deeper and grasped the item. She rose to her knees and with both hands pulled upward with all her weight.

Dalicusi sucked in her breath, rolled to her stomach, rose, and leapt on Jeda's back, hammering shoulders and collarbones with the cudgel, but she couldn't get a clear strike at Jeda.

Unable to extricate the weapon from the hole and wrestle Dalicusi, too, Jeda whirled around and bear-hugged her attacker.

Dalicusi thumped Jeda on the neck with the cudgel.

White spots danced before Jeda's eyes. She flinched and fell, rolling suddenly to a side, bringing Dalicusi also crashing to the ground. Jeda splayed her fingernails, scratching her foe just below the eyes, digging, searching for those sensitive orbs.

Dalicusi threw herself backward, breaking free. She attained her feet, re-gripped her cudgel and moved in for a strike.

Jeda, again on her knees, found the handle of the buried weapon and hauled upward exerting all her strength, pulling a chain and spiked mace out of the ground.

An original jester outraced one of the intruder jesters to Jeda's side, darted in, retrieved Jeda's dagger, then sped back across the arena to Spoena who was not even watching the battle but instead, looked upward at the darkening skies, moving her lips. Another jester waited nearby for Dalicusi to release her cudgel. Jeda's hands seized the mace handle as she stood on her feet and began twirling the metal, spiked ball in a deadly circle with the inch-long spikes whistling in the air.

Dalicusi backed out of harm's way.

Jeda advanced, swinging the spiked bludgeon faster, gaining momentum with each revolution.

Dalicusi's eyes darted about the battle floor searching for another pile of loose dirt. Upon espying something shiny sticking out of the soil at the far end of the arena near Jeda's second, Dalicusi dashed full tilt evidently hoping that whatever the weapon turned out to be had at least as much reach as Jeda's mace and chain.

~

The shabbily clad jester leader was deposited before Bablo-ya, Hod-ya, and Deparis. The three wordlessly observed him for a protracted moment as he regained his feet but seemed unshaken by this command audition before the White Priestess of Pitland.

"Who are you?" asked Bablo-ya icily.

"A fool, as you see, ma'am," the jester answered.

"Majestic Madam," corrected Bablo-ya.

A roar from the crowd momentarily distracted the interrogation. Dalicusi had reached the dirt pile, but with Jeda in hot pursuit. The Craniantiumite plucked a weapon from the ground even as Jeda's spiked ball slammed into the mound of loose dirt, sending a puff of dust into the air, narrowly missing Dalicusi's forearm. In the seconds it took Jeda to regain her mace's momentum, Dalicusi had hefted a two-fisted, wavy-bladed, Eroton sword from the ground. She lifted it high over her head as if to rain down blows that would divide her opponent in half, then quarters, then eighths . . .

"A fool, yes," Bablo-ya brought her attention back to the matter at hand, "but whose?"

~

Tren's eyes were on the battle. It was imperative he deliver the message Logon had given him for Jeda, but now he was about to be revealed as a kingsmen along with his associates. Had it been folly to carry on the harlequin masquerade? Had they misunderstood the Advisor's instructions?

"Turn around, you have no need to see what's happening. Look at me when you answer, you fool!"

Tren looked up at the loathsome woman. "I genuinely pity you."

Another roar erupted from the crowd. Jeda waded in with her mace, trusting that no sword could penetrate the defensive perimeter of a swiftly-rotating, spiked ball. Clang! The sword was knocked to one side, stinging Dalicusi's hands, forcing her backward. Again, Dalicusi advanced, twirling her sword expertly as she'd been taught. Clang! Again, the sword careered off course in a shower of sparks. Dalicusi backed off to a safe space and checked her sword for nicks but found none. A smile crossed her lips; her trainer had instructed her well when he said, "Eroton swords will eventually break through the chain links of a Carnalian mace if the defender can withstand repeated blows to the wrist." The sparks that burned so brightly in the arena's gloomy atmosphere weren't from Dalicusi's sword but the chain of Jeda's mace.

Again, Dalicusi approached, keeping a respectful distance, just near enough to keep Jeda lunging at her.

Clang! Clang! Clang!

~

Numbness stunned Dalicusi's wrists. But her sword remained un-nicked. Each time their weapons clashed a shower of sparks flew from the chain's links.

Jeda continued her assault to wear her opponent down, evidently unaware of her peril.

Dalicusi only needed to continue this stratagem until Jeda's chain broke. But she also needed time to recover feeling in her benumbed hands lest she be unable to take advantage when the opportunity came.

Dalicusi feinted toward Jeda then quickly darted back out of harm's way. It was energy-draining but necessary if her hands were to recuperate.

Jeda countered the feint with a vicious swipe that grazed Dalicusi's hair, but since it was a feint and not a real thrust, Dalicusi was spared. For sheer determination and ferocity, Dalicusi grudgingly admitted to herself that she was over-matched by Hod-ya's wildcat. She had, indeed, underestimated Jeda, but she wasn't beaten yet. Craniantium's champion was known not only for physical prowess but shrewdness of mind as well. It was time for weaponry of another sort.

Holding her sword at the ready, Dalicusi, announced, "You've learned well, Jeda of Kway; I give you that. But why is your lover here today? Did you think he could come to your aid in time of need?"

Anger flashed from Jeda's eyes as she lunged with renewed vigor. Clang! Another shower of sparks scattered around the duelers.

"Oh, I see he is something to you, after all? I met him in the hallway before you came out, you know, and he's a splendid catch indeed. I have special plans just for him after today's victory."

"Do you think I don't know your game? He'd have nothing to do with someone like you—or me." Jeda surged forward again, savagely slinging her spiked sphere to a faster orbit.

Dalicusi's sword barely parried the attempt. She overplayed her gambit, got caught off guard, and was forced to stumble backward, barely keeping afoot. She turned to run. Her taunting only increased Jeda's anger but, she hadn't wasted her strength in uncontrolled fury. Dalicusi's scheme backfired.

Jeda gave chase, almost breathing fire, a deadly glare in her eye.

A sudden shriek from the dais high up in the seating momentarily drew everyone's attention, temporarily halting the blood-match on the field. Dalicusi's eyes, like everyone else in the arena, turned to the White Priestess who was railing at a jester who stood meekly before her.

"Pity me! You maggot, how dare you pity me!" Her hand lashed out at the man. The smack resounded across the arena as long nails raked blood-welts on his cheek.

Hod-ya then stepped in front of her sister, reached out and exposed the kingsman tunic beneath the jester garb. Spluttering, "Kingsman!" she seized his outer garments and yanked them off in one ripping motion.

The entire stadium, even Jeda and Dalicusi on the battle floor, stared wide-eyed at the fearless man standing before the grand dames of power.

Tren took advantage of the stunned silence and turned toward the field where Jeda and Dalicusi stood rooted. "Jeda, they lied to you. Artka is not dead; he's in Ecclessa—"

"Shut up, you fool," Hod-ya struck him from behind. "You'll wreck everything."

Doubled over from the blow but not knocked down, Tren lifted his head and cried louder. "He lives, I led him to the King's Gate Fortress myself, and even now as I speak, he's being trained—"

Hod-ya leapt onto Tren's back, biting, fists pummeling him, screaming, "Lies, all lies! Don't listen to him, Jeda; you know how deceptive Ecclessites are, hacking your brother to pieces while promising amnesty. Don't listen. Kill Dalicusi, quick before it's too late."

Tren sagged under the woman's cruel, merciless beating, but even as he sank, he called, "Logon loves you, Jeda; you were deceived; he'll forgive—"

At the name of Logon, the masses clambered to their feet with hands to their ears, screaming, drowning out the rest of Tren's message.

~

Jeda stood stock still, stunned. How did that jester know anything about Artka?

"He's not lying; the kingsman speaks truth," came a raspy voice from nearby.

Jeda turned as one of the strange jesters stepped forward and removed his harlequin mask. She sensed something very familiar about this lanky, awkward man.

He lifted his head and hands to the crowd, "Hear me, citizens of Pitland, I am Gragnold, formerly a dronnet, now an Ecclessite!" He stripped off his outer harlequin jerkin revealing an Ecclessite tunic. Parting it at the neck he revealed a freshly healed scar. "Jeda," he turned back and confessed, "I was there when Hod-ya blackmailed Captain Fitcher to lie to you. I was the one who substituted real cake for the snake, so that you ate real food, not a decomposing serpent. And I watched with her from high above through the ceiling tiles as you succumbed to the whispering cusps in your chamber. I have no doubt it has cost my life to speak these things, but Logon would have me do no other; your life is precious to him. Seek his forgiveness, Jeda. He's not abandoned you, it's you who've left him. Lift not your hand against anyone but seek Logon's forgiveness. Trust Tren's words; Artka lives."

A contingent of guards immediately surrounded Gragnold, knocking him senseless to the turf. Hadel Guards seized the other unknown jesters, buffeting them into submission with clubs, then shackling them hand and foot. Their outer garments were stripped off, revealing Logon tunics.

"Artka, alive?" Jeda's arm drooped; the mace handle dangled from her hand; the spiked ball rested on the dirt. "Oh, Logon, what have I done?"

The crowd rose as one chanting, "Kill the kingsmen, Kill the kingsmen, Kill the kingsmen." Every voice bellowed in unison for the blood of the defrocked jesters. They were dragged up the amphitheater stairs to be forced to kneel before the White Priestess—all except Gragnold who lay unmoving in the center of the battle floor.

~

Bablo-ya scarcely noticed the prisoners being hauled up toward her as she railed at Hod-ya, "This is what I get for letting you experiment with our time-honored traditions. Bringing Ecclessites to our sacred rites, profaning these hallowed environs, insulting the ten dreadful majesties in whose names these rites are performed. All because you carelessly let your ally dread get disembodied—"

"You can hardly expect me to protect a dread, in or out of the body!"

"Shut up! It was because of your arrogant zeal to enter Ecclessites in these games that you were off on some vain hunt for your escaped contestants instead of garrisoned to protect Psa."

Glancing around at the crowd, Hod-ya went on the defensive. "Who ever thought a dread could be so easily destroyed? Did you? Besides, we've uncovered the attempt to free Jeda and captured the ringleaders. If I'm not mistaken, I recognize at least three of these men as the prisoners I was forced to escort into this burning, feverish land.

"This man, Tren, I know for a certainty; he tried to catch me in my own words at the Willows Inn. Maybe you can explain how he and his comrades escaped your notorious Hadel Prison?"

"I owe you, nor anyone else, explanations. I'll rule Pitland as I see fit and will not be held accountable to the likes of you."

"Fair enough," Hod-ya spat out for her sister's ears only, "but you must admit things have gotten out of control. That's why I advised stopping this contest. Don't you understand that whatever plans our real enemy has laid will miscue if put off even for just a day. It's obvious he's gone to great pains to discover our plans and then plot counter moves. He depends on split-second timing, and if we put off Scrarth and Avangar for twenty-four hours, his schemes will fall to dust."

"What makes you think his feeble attempts at disrupting our games hasn't already fallen to dust? After all, as you say, we've captured the ringleaders."

"Have we captured them all? Just how many men did your vaunted Hadel Guard let slip through their greasy hands?"

Deparis stepped between the arguing sisters, pointing, and asking, "Now what's *she* doing?"

Hod-ya and Bablo-ya followed Deparis' point and saw Jeda stepping away from her green gown, letting it lay in the dirt at her feet. She was clad only in her Logon dress, badly stained and smudged though it was.

Her shoulders heaved with racking sobs as she cried loud enough for all to hear, "Logon, forgive me for doubting you, for—gi—ive mee—ee!" She fell to her knees, her hands tightly clenched. In abject agony she collapsed full length to the ground, sobbing, overcome with grief. "How could I, oh, how could I sink so low? Ple—ease, Logon, forgive me!" Though she was unaware, her Logon dress became cleaner and whiter even as she cried out. The crowd, observing her contrition, didn't miss the significance of her garment being cleansed before their very eyes.

Those in the stands were dumbstruck beholding the gladiatrix prostrate on the ground, in agony over her unfaithfulness to the one who loved her beyond description.

Here and there spectators in the general seating dropped to their knees, crying out from their own hearts. But the majority mocked and hooted in disgust at the mercy-seeking display, shredding their green feathers, throwing them to the floor and stomping on them. A beastly, guttural growl filled the stands as more and more people joined the mockery; the sound rose to the skies overhead like a den of starving wolves snarling and snapping over a cornered, wounded lamb.

The shackled, doomed prisoners lining the field on their backs sang a song of rejoicing: a sweet melody begun by someone behind the chained prisoners. It quickly caught on and was taken up with such powerful emotion that it challenged the beastly growl from the incensed multitudes.

Bablo-ya surveyed the vast throng engaged in two disparate activities: those mocking Logon, and those seeking Logon's amnesty. She groaned. Here and there in the stands a person collapsed and lay perfectly still, then miraculously, a white tunic or dress covered them, and a blue tipped sword appeared in their hands. These were summarily driven out of the stands by former cronies, while others were battered or killed on the spot, but the harm had been done; the words of Ecclessa's King had entered even her realm and were harvesting lives for the king. There was no stopping it now.

The mission no army could achieve, no stout band of hearty, battle-seasoned warriors, the hard-hearted land no army could successfully penetrate, was accomplished by one insignificant slip of a girl who had yielded her life to Logon. Bablo-ya looked hatefully down at Jeda, bending her will toward Dalicusi to wield her sword and cleave the whimpering girl groveling on the ground in half. A dark chant rose from Bablo-ya's throat, lending her power to a contestant for the first time in the history of the games, but her curse died in her throat as she watched the scene down on the battle-floor as Dalicusi also sank to her knees, her weapon abandoned to the dust as she, too, supplicated Jeda's king for forgiveness.

Deparis went apoplectic, rolling on the floor, babbling incoherently, slathering foam from her mouth.

A great crash of thunder accompanied by a bolt of lightning rent the oppressive darkness while a tumultuous crashing atop the granite cliffs drew the attention of the White Priestess and her sister. Several flashes of lightning blazed back and forth between the top of the cliffs, illuminating the cloud-tops, red flashes contending against blue flashes, as if two separate thunderstorms were fighting it out, one red and one blue.

"What's happening up there?" demanded Hod-ya grasping her sister's arm.

Bablo-ya replied in a monotone, "The dreads are under attack."

CHAPTER NINETEEN

"Dry your eyes, Jeda. You have work to do."

Jeda beheld a blurred face through tear-filled eyes. She wiped away the tears and lifted herself from the ground. A flush of surprise and embarrassment coursed through her as Logon's features came into focus. "Oh, I'm so unclean—"

"Don't call what I've cleansed, unclean. You have work to do; the hateful sisters are coming for you, intending you great harm. You must run to the other end of this field."

"Logon, you, you still love me?"

"I love all, especially those who have called upon me. Do you remember when I warned you not to be so sure of your heart; that you didn't know all that resided therein?"

Jeda remembered; he had appeared to her by the placid brook as she tolled her sword; he warned that she was heading into danger. She also remembered the night in the inn when she communed with Logon until daybreak, kneeling by her bedside. She even recalled the ominous words spoken by Flan. She looked up at her liege. "Logon, why did I turn away?"

"Other loves were buried in your heart, loves that rivaled your love for me. You wouldn't have understood had I mentioned them then. Instead, I allowed you to see the consequences your own choices must eventually yield."

"Whom could I love more than you, surely you don't think—Bonu?"

"Not him only, look deeper."

"Artka?"

"Yes, and . . . "

"Myself?"

"Your love for Bonu and your love for your brother are selfish loves. Loving others is not wrong unless those other loves stand between you and me. If they do, they become twisted into a form of loving yourself because of what those others provide for you. When you thought your life was deprived of Artka, you no longer wanted anything or anyone, including me. Even now, would you have cried out to me if Tren hadn't exposed the report of Artka's death as a lie?"

Jeda's eyes were drawn to her dress. It was now clean except for one ugly splotch over her heart.

"Yield your rights to Artka and Bonu to me."

"But, but will they be harmed?"

"When you yield up someone or something, it's no longer yours. You must trust me without guarantees. By trying to control people and events you hinder love and obedience due me."

"I can't right now. I need time."

"Jeda, I'll not force you, but many lives depend on you fulfilling your mission, which is the reason I sent you here just for this day. Only you can accomplish it, but only if thoroughly committed to me; otherwise you're a liability. Decide; Hod-ya and Bablo-ya approach. And another seeks your death, as well."

Jeda raised her eyes toward the dais in the stands and saw Bablo-ya and Hod-ya, skirts hoisted, dashing down tiered steps toward the battle floor. Even at that distance there was no mistaking the murderous glare in their eyes. Jeda looked back to her liege, but he was gone. "Logon! Don't go! Don't leave me! How can I do other than what my heart wants?"

"Just ask me for the power," said a voice as if out of the air. "I will purge you of all loves except those that please me, and those affections I will purify. Your responsibility is to yield your heart to me, knowing I will take you at your word. I alone know best."

Jeda looked frantically at the sinister sisters who had just attained the battle floor and were fairly flying her direction.

The White Priestess stooped over on the run and snatched a two-fisted, Carnalian long sword from beneath a dirt pile. Hod-ya, likewise, slowed long enough to pluck a barbed trident from beneath another pile.

"Logon, I give you Artka; I give you Bonu; help me deal with my fears of relinquishing them to you."

The spot on her dress vanished; for the first time in a long time she was aware of the Advisor's whisper. "Run to the granite cliffs."

"But I'm not afraid to die."

"Dying here won't accomplish my purposes. Run."

"It'll look like I'm afraid that Lurcan is more powerful than Logon."

"I told you to run, not flee. You have work to accomplish there."

Jeda scrambled to her feet. Hod-ya and Bablo-ya were barely fifty paces away. Jeda's legs seemed made of lead.

Hod-ya planted her foremost foot, her trident arm drew back, and she expertly leaned into the throw, catapulting the trident with unerring aim.

Jeda stood dumbstruck, unable to move, watching the missile hurtling toward her.

A bolt of blue lightning struck with a horrendous crash mere feet in front of Jeda. A thousand molten-iron droplets from the destroyed trident pelted the dust before Jeda's feet.

Then the raindrops began, large and sparse at first, making pockmarks like little craters in the dust of the arena.

The inner voice reiterated, "Run, Jeda, to the far end of the arena."

The thunderbolt knocked Bablo-ya and Hod-ya onto their backsides, but instead of dissuading them they were all the more incensed. They regathered their wits as they watched Jeda's heels kicking high as she raced away.

"Cheap magic tricks like we used to do to amuse our mother, Battel," growled Bablo-ya. "Jeda did it better than I'd have thought, but a trick like that drains resources; see how she flees, needing to recharge? She's in our element and at our mercy. The little antelope is trapped; no weapon-mounds are planted over there. Come, this will be too easy."

"I don't know, sister. That girl out is of control." Hod-ya brushed herself off. "I'm beginning to think she's contacted a source of power greater than we're prepared to deal with."

"Don't be a fool, Hod-ya. If Logon had any power, would he have let this go on year after year? Of course not! Let's get after that girl before someone else claims her blood. Look around; cusps are frenzy-feasting."

Hod-ya lifted her eyes to the rows of seating where spectators grappled, stabbed, clubbed, and choked each other, oblivious to the increasing torrential rainfall.

Bablo-ya struggled to her feet and gave chase after Jeda, calling over her shoulder, "Coming, sister?"

Hod-ya sprang to her feet and sprinted to catch up to her sister. "I have no weapon."

"Since when do you need a weapon?"

"Since the dreads are under attack and my trident that nearly skewered the wench burst into flaming pellets. I tell you, Bablo-ya, there's more defending her than I expected. And more than that, it's raining, or hadn't you noticed?"

"Raining?" Bablo-ya slowed her pace and tilted her chin skyward. "So it is. What of it?"

"When was the last time it rained in Pitland?"

"Not since I've come to power and many years prior to that. What of it?"

Hod-ya came to a standstill, her forefingers rubbing her temples, stirring her memory, trying to recall the rhyme that buzzed in her mind like an angry hornet:

Rain, rain, flee away,
Judgment come another day!
Dusty meet, proud the fleet,
Never rained on hot land's seat,
Till the bane of hate complete,
And lasses shun to compete,
Bringing down fell lords replete,
Hostess sets afire her feet,
Wet quenches molten heat,
Guiding fair to haven seat,
To reign and rule and all defeat,
The vanquished cry and fain repeat:
Rain, rain, flee away,
Judgment come another day!

"I remember it now, it's an ancient nursery rhyme. It's raining like the poem said, a rain that precedes judgment." Hod-ya stared at The White Priestess. "Bablo-ya, forces mightier than you and I are at work here."

"Phah, I say to those forces! Come along and watch me prove most powerful of all if you are cowardly. I fear not rain in Pitland, nor the omens portended. I am Bablo-ya the dreadful, I've drunk the blood of that prince's followers; I'm inebriated with it to delightful heights. I fear neither his followers nor him. I'll drink that wench's blood and become yet more intoxicated. Look where she hides; the cliffs bar her flight. There's no escape. If she were even half-dangerous, or smart, she'd have made for the exits. Even Deparis' pitiful, traitorous contestant who turned Ecclessite at the last minute has found cover, but whence has Jeda fled? To a dead end. She may have started a rebellion that will trouble us for a while, but she'll pay dearly. First, I'll cripple, then paralyze her. She'll be aware while I disembowel her inch by inch. She'll watch me consume her heart."

The White Priestess, drenched to the skin and looking ludicrous as her sodden gown, once so ornate, encumbered her legs, making her stalk stiffly across the rain-splattered, battle-floor in pursuit of Jeda.

Jeda obliquely turned as she headed toward the base of the granite wall to search for a handhold and climb out of harms' way.

Hod-ya hesitated only a moment before her vengeful inclinations took over. She, too, craved Jeda's blood and was jealous that her sister might devour her heart before she had a chance. After all, it was she who'd brought the wench; she should be the first to taste her blood. Hod-ya easily drew even with her sister since her garments weren't as water-logged and confining.

Screeches erupted downward from the fog swirling atop the cliffs of the arena's back wall. Red and blue flashes in the heights strobed the area with an eerie illumination to the ghastly scene of broken bodies scattered about, not only on the battle-floor, but throughout the entire stadium.

Hod-ya surged ahead of Bablo-ya, gritting her teeth. Her rage full; Bablo-ya was right, she needed no weapon, especially against this puny, cowering kingswoman. She, Hod-ya, had the strength of ten men; she'd rend the wench limb from limb.

Bablo-ya, now slogging along behind growled, "No-oo! Wait for me. I want—ugh!"

Hod-ya turned and saw her sister face down in the mud with her backside sticking up out of the low-lying ground fog. "Too slow, dear sister. Ha-ha-ha-ha! She's mine. I brought her; I'll devour her." Hod-ya pressed on through the inch-deep mud, ignoring the White Priestess' threats.

Bablo-ya lifted her face and spat mud out mingled with curses.

~

Jeda heard only snatches of their conversation. She backed to the stone wall as Hod-ya approached. There was no phantasm's gleam in the evil woman's eye. Apparently, the dread she courted was preoccupied. "Where's your master, Hod-ya?"

"I need no dread to mangle the likes of you, traitor. I'm going to rend you in such a way that you won't lose consciousness. You'll watch as I disembowel you; you have disgraced me for the last time."

"I warn you, my master has restored and empowered me." Jeda's voice was quiet, resolute, confident.

"Phah! No *kyllorn* would dare bolster you against me now." Hod-ya advanced several deliberate steps.

"I mean my true master."

Hod-ya, a mere two paces away, paused and scrutinized the pitiful-looking girl in her simple dress, now white and clean despite having splashed all the way here through deepening mud. Jeda's hair hung in clumps as rainwater coursed freely over her face. "You look ridiculous, girl. The prince of Ecclessa and Splendora wouldn't want the likes of you after what I've put you through! You can't daunt me." Hod-ya lunged and seized Jeda under her shoulders, lifted her high, then slammed her to the ground.

Breath whooshed out of Jeda's lungs as she landed flat on her back. Beside the wind knocked out of her lungs, she was unharmed. But to any onlookers it appeared as if she'd suffered a spinal injury as she lay helplessly gasping for air, eyes bulging, arms and legs aquiver, unable to escape.

"Hah! So much for your protector, foolish girl. Your back is broken; you have no choice but to lie there and suffer. How shall I begin?"

Jeda struggled to get her breath, rolling her eyes at Hod-ya.

A mud-colored blur tackled Hod-ya from behind. It was Bablo-ya. The two malevolent sisters sprawled headlong. Bablo-ya evidently was not going to be easily deprived. Biting, cursing, spitting, tearing at each other like two panthers, the deadly sisters savaged each other with tooth and nail.

Jeda's lungs slowly re-filled. She coughed and breath returned. She sat up and for a moment watched the wrestling, mud-slathered sisters, hard pressed to tell which witch was which.

But her cough alerted the entangled sisters. Jeda wasn't as incapacitated as they'd assumed. They stopped fighting and stared at Jeda for a long moment, her dress was still white though she sat in mud; but her eyes . . . her eyes glowed with renewed hope.

An alarm rang in Hod-ya's mind; but her sister slapped her, muttering, "Broke her back, did you? You've lost your powers, my stupid, ugly, little sister. Where did I leave that sword?" She began groping around her in the mud.

Hod-ya rose to her feet, her attention focused upward, to the top of the granite cliff. "Bablo-ya, we're winning!"

Bablo-ya paused long enough to look up. "You're right, the red lightning is overpowering the blue. Our dreads and their lieutenants are pushing the brights back. So much for your baleful 'Rain, rain, flee away' chant."

Jeda struggled to her feet wiping away clumps of mud from her hands as she again retreated from the evil sisters. She, too, had observed the brights withdrawing as the fiery phantoms rose up in crackling displays of red lightning. "I don't understand, Logon; I thought you wanted to defeat evil. But I still trust you, though comprehension eludes me."

Emboldened by the unfolding scene above them, the sisters simultaneously jumped for and caught Jeda, each taking a firm grip on an opposite arm. "Make a wish, sister. Ahaahaaa-ha-haaa!" Bablo-ya cackled.

Jeda felt oddly unconcerned; instead, she became suddenly aware of the tragic events surrounding her. Men and women dying; brawls spilled over from the stands onto the battlefield. Hod-ya's dronnets dueled Bablo-ya's Hadel Guards and weren't faring well. The ground fog deepened to a foot and threatened to grow thicker. Dark clouds hovered lower over the amphitheater; it seemed as if the sparse, remaining blue flashes were all but vanquished, whereas the red lightning had a resurgence of continuous lightning and thunder that eerily sounded like deep, booming laughter. The rain was letting up as well, though everything and everyone on the arena floor was mud-splattered—except those wearing kingsmen dresses or tunics, most notably, Jeda and the prisoners chained together awaiting execution.

In the midst of all the mayhem Jeda's eyes were drawn to a small, diminutive figure slowly walking unmolested through the melee to the nearly obliterated center circle of the arena. It was a girl, not yet grown to maturity; her outer garb was Eroton, decidedly ill-fitting and out of place at such a festive celebration as Scrarth and Avangar. But the hem of a Logon dress peeked out from beneath the Eroton frock. In her hands she carried a burlap sack.

"Well, Jeda of the house of Kway," gloated Hod-ya, drawing close to Jeda's face and relaxing the grip on her bicep. "It looks as if your clever little stunts are at an end. I'll give you one last chance to save yourself; renounce your allegiance to the king, and we'll reinstate you as Avangar of the realm. What say you?"

Bablo-ya also quit tugging Jeda's arm and affirmed everything Hod-ya said with a nod, but Jeda caught an enigmatic wink that passed between the sisters. They intended to betray her cruelly as well as destroy her. She recalled a rune that advised:

Fear not the strong which can the body rend,
Fear him whose judgment lasts without an end.

Jeda's eyes again came to rest on the lone girl in the middle of the field. She calmly replied to the sisters. "Receive the right to reign over this?"

Hod-ya jerked Jeda's arm painfully, nearly dislocating the shoulder as she raged. "You dare refuse my clemency, you twisted, little brat? Can't you see that your precious prince's plot has failed? The dreads have driven his brights away. Your Ecclessite plan is in the mud. Deny allegiance to your liege and we'll replace that repugnant dress with exquisite finery and put you in a seat of power and wealth. It's that or watch as we behead those fools masquerading as jesters. I believe one of them is of some significance to you, er, Bonu by name?"

"Bonu?" Jeda's heart skipped a beat.

"Ahhh," Bablo-ya chortled. "So, a womanly heart still beats in your breast. What say you, Hod-ya, shall we vivisect her lover first or last?" Then looking back to Jeda, "Or do we just rip you in half now?"

Jeda declined answering, instead pleaded softly, "Help me, Logon."

Hod-ya slapped Jeda's cheek.

"Lepur," Bablo-ya called across the foggy field to her chief of guards, "Bring the prisoners. And, oh yes, alert the disembowelers." Then to her sister, "We'll make a sacrificial pile of entrails that will make the slaughter of Ra-Amawl look like practice." Then again to Lepur, "And open the gates; the tophets will be wanting in."

Chaos gradually faded in the arena; no longer were various groups clashing against each other; a reinforcement of Hadel Prison guards had arrived restoring a tenuous peace. The walking wounded and those fatigued but uninjured milled about through the foggy ground cover, the injured or dead lay prone, half hidden by the fog enshrouding the battle floor. Disorder still lingered in some quarters, but soldiers were making their way up into the seating to put a stop to it. A smaller contingent of Hadel Guards came down off the dais leading the bogus jesters single file, bound in chains. Bablo-ya's threat was anything but idle.

Even so, Jeda sensed Logon's peace. Though the enemy of her soul had tricked her once before with the same sort of threat, this time she was prepared. It would hurt her terribly to be the cause of Bonu's suffering, but it would pain her more to deny her master and liege. And, she knew, somehow, Logon would enable and sustain her, as well as Bonu, and the other kingsmen. And even if Logon didn't intervene, which looked more and more likely, somehow, he'd sustain them.

The guards dragged the shackled, shuffling prisoners through the muddy paddock toward the two ladies of power and the reluctant Avangar. Bablo-ya was once again in command.

The procession passed the solitary girl as if she were invisible; she just stood stock still in the middle of the field holding her bag, head bowed.

The Hadel Prison guards stationed themselves around the royal ladies in a circle. Hod-ya released Jeda's arm and strode over to the chained jesters, examining each one briefly until she came to Gragnold, who'd been revived and shackled to the chain gang. Her eyes bored holes into his. Her breathing was slow and deep; her fingers clenched and unclenched. Finally, she spoke so low that even those nearby had to strain to hear. "You, you, foul, deceiving, traitorous wretch of a toad. You will beg for mercy before this day is over and thank me for finally putting an end to your miserable life. I promise you."

Bablo-ya interjected, still maintaining a firm grip on Jeda, "Uh, may I remind you, sister, that he also is my prisoner. But, since I feel generous today, I turn his fate over to you."

Hod-ya nodded.

It was then that Stullo, Craniantium's Scrarth, sloshed out of the jumbled mass of people milling about and approached the White Priestess. "What are you going to do? I, as second to the Avangar of

Craniantium, demand, in view of the default of my predecessor, that I be awarded the right to challenge this . . . this pitiful example of a gladiatrix." Stullo's nostrils flared as sparks flashed from her eyes, rain-soaked, mud-splattered and bedraggled as she was.

"She does have a rightful claim, you know, Hod-ya," said Bablo-ya wiping mud from her chin.

"She has no benefactress," objected the Lady of Carnalia. "A contestant must have a sponsor."

"I'll sponsor her," the White Priestess said matter-of-factly. "Any objections?"

Hod-ya glared, mouth open, speechless.

"Good; let the game begin."

A fury rose within Hod-ya at being betrayed even at this late stage of events, especially after the disaster that had befallen the contest. "But what about Jeda renouncing her allegiance to the king and his son? And what about all these prisoners slated for execution?"

"Quiet! I'm still regent here, not you. It's still better to have the contestant of Ecclessa defeated by a legitimate contestant. It'll have a discouraging effect on the enemies of the empire. Display your weapons, girls."

Stullo produced the same cudgel that Dalicusi had started with. Jeda merely stood with eyes lowered to the ground.

"Very well," Bablo-ya said with a curious grin, "your weapon, Stullo, is the cudgel, which has already been kissed. As for your contestant, Hod-ya, I suppose she'll use only her hands since she displays no other weapon. Face each other. Everyone else, form a tight circle. Bring the prisoners here and force them to their knees into a human ring around the combatants."

The guards forced the prisoners to kneel facing outward, forming a barrier. The two sisters and their contestants were the only ones inside the circle.

"Bablo-ya, this is unfair," Hod-ya said angrily.

"Yes, I know." She smiled gleefully. "Nonetheless, I've decided to salvage what I can from today's debacle. Scrarth and Avangar must continue as long as there are two contestants." She grabbed Jeda's shoulders, turning her to face Stullo, who was unabashedly licking her lips in anticipation.

"Commence." The White Priestess stepped discretely back out of harm's way.

Stullo lunged, aiming her cudgel at Jeda's forehead.

Jeda received a mental impression rather than actually heard, "Duck. Avoid the blows," and so she ducked. The blow missed, glancing painfully off her shoulder. She backed away as Stullo lifted her arm for another assault.

"This is too easy," mocked the Craniantiumite. "You should at least make it sporting; choose a weapon." She leapt at Jeda again, subtly this time. The cudgel slammed Jeda's ribcage.

There was a sharp pain and Jeda knew her ribs were damaged, possibly broken. She staggered backward, holding her side, nearly sprawling in the mud.

Stullo laughed in glee. "That fool, Dalicusi, doesn't know what she missed. You're easy prey." She laughed and charged Jeda with her cudgel high overhead. Jeda tried to avoid the blow, but Stullo was too quick.

Initially there was no pain, but Jeda heard rather than felt a dull *thunk* reverberate through her skull. Her legs went rubbery. Only when she was face down in the mud did a searing flash of pain race through her head. Still conscious, but in much pain and overwhelmed with dizziness, Jeda struggled to rise to her hands and knees.

Unable to get any higher, she knelt, vulnerable, spent. "Logon, I can't see, I can't move, I can barely breathe . . . take me home. Ahh, the pain, I can't . . . stand anymore."

"I can't hear you, worm. Are you begging for mercy? Plead louder, so everyone can hear how Ecclessites grovel," Stullo gloated.

Jeda tried to rise to her feet again but was overwhelmed by the blinding pain throbbing in her head. She gasped, felt nauseated, her arms and legs trembling, unresponsive; there was nothing she could do but bow her head before her enemy, an easy target for Stullo.

"Logon, I come to you."

Stullo sneered. "Not quite, miss high-falutin' of Carnalia and Ecclessa. I dedicate your slaughter to the dread, Abmum, may he possess your infernal soul and give me power as I gorge on your blood. Majestic Madam, if it please, I will now dispatch this most miserable of Scrarths; the disappointment and bane of her sponsor. To Abmum!"

Stullo's last phrase, in a shrill, shrieking voice, carried cross the arena, drawing the attention of victims and victimizers alike, unaware that Scrarth and Avangar had resumed behind a wall of human prisoners and guards.

A hush descended, overshadowing the arena as a black roiling cloud wafted down from the granite cliffs; Abmum was on his way.

Stullo took a practice aim at Jeda's temple, stretching her cudgel to Jeda's ear then back again.

The girl in the middle of the paddock dipped her hand into her bag and extracted a trumpet. Still no one paid her any attention, all eyes being riveted on the climaxing event of an ignoble and unexpected end for the contestant from Carnalia.

Stullo paused, enjoying her moment, making sure all eyes were watching. How differently things had turned out! She was supposed to be the lowly Scrarth of Craniantium who deferred to a better, to reap only modest rewards for having shown up, but now was about to become Avangar of the Realm.

~

That shriek was what Artil had been waiting for; it was the signal given her by a roamer. After Stullo screamed the name of her empowering dread, Abmum, Artil ignited a sequence of events that would initiate an end to the powers of wickedness holding sway over all the empire, or so the bright had said.

The roamer also said she'd be protected, that no one would interfere. She had shut her eyes when Bablo-ya and Hod-ya seized Jeda, and again when Stullo mercilessly hammered Jeda. She had been strictly charged to wait for the signal and was determined to obey, though it was the most difficult thing she'd ever done. She had to constantly reject thoughts that urged her to rush over and defend her friend. She raised the trumpet to her lips, the one engraved with a number "1" on the bell, as she'd been told. Artil mentally rehearsed the roamer's instructions about filling her lungs, placing the mouthpiece to her mouth and vibrating her lips as she compressed air . . .

The brass mouthpiece was surprisingly cool to her lips. She blew.

A crystal-clear note rebounded like a shock wave off the granite cliff at the back of the arena and out across the muddied paddock.

At the same time concentric waves of white light erupted from the bell of the trumpet.

~

The ring of chained prisoners comprising the human battle-wall lifted their heads as every shackle snapped open and chains fell into the mud.

Most human activity froze, for every eye was drawn to the trumpeter, amazed that such a small girl produced such a loud blare from the trumpet, all, that is, except Hod-ya who instantly recognized Spoena's missing sister.

"Seize that girl!" Hod-ya pointed, but not a soul heard her.

Bablo-ya covered her ears then doubled over retching; the trumpet's blast was the death knell to her reign, and she knew it.

~

Spoena slipped unobserved from her ringside shelter and splashed through the water and mud to Dalicusi who had crawled to and was hiding in an alcove just off the battlefield. Spoena found her and wrapped a discarded cloak around Dalicusi then guided her to a tunnel entry.

~

Stullo was instantly paralyzed by the trumpet's blare, inanimate as a stone, unable to will her arm to descend and wreak destruction on Jeda's temple. A nightmarish terror like she'd never known gripped her; she desperately wanted to run away, hide and stop the words coursing rapidly through her mind:

Hail and fire and mixture of blood,
On all grass and a third of trees,
The first roamer sounds announcing this flood,
Who escapes though he tries and flees?

To Jeda, on hands and knees and wrist deep in mud, anticipating the final blow which would usher her into her liege's presence, the trumpeted note was a comforting balm. It dulled her pains, soothing them, erasing them. Her vision cleared; she could see the muddied feet of her enemies gathered around desiring her death. She, too, understood the trumpet's words and pondered their meaning.

Bonu, a little way off from Jeda, had shut his eyes, unable to watch his beloved be slaughtered. Now he gazed up in wonder at the towering granite cliffs—and felt there was something he ought to understand.

Artil's breath gave out; instantly a shimmering shaft of light interposed itself between her lips and the horn's mouthpiece, keeping the sound continuously streaming from the instrument without a waver. Another twinkling column floated beside Artil and softly urged, "Release the trumpets to us; you've done your part, little one. Go assist Jeda." Seven roamers in all had collected around Artil, including the one who'd taken over sounding the first trumpet.

Unbeknownst to those in the amphitheater, that trumpet's note resounded outward, swelling to fullness as it blared out of the stadium, increasing in volume the farther it traversed over the realms of Pitland, Carnalia, Craniantium, Eroton, and even across the Flaming Sword River into Ecclessa. Men and women everywhere heard the musical note of doom and stopped in their tracks and wondered what it all meant.

Another twinkling column received the bag from Artil and distributed the contents among the other roamers until each one held an instrument. Then the group of them ascended to the upper-cliff tops.

The sky overhead thundered anew; war-cries of wrath mixed with clashing shields and ringing swords. Battle again waged above between mighty beings; dreads and tophets unwillingly yielded their positions to droves of surging brights of various luminosity.

Down in the arena, lower level brights descended like arrows, darting about, repelling cusps and tophets, driving them away from the injured.

The last roamer to ascend took his trumpet from his lips and leaned over to Artil. "Only one trump sounds today, the rest will sound in their turn. Go to your friends, Artil, and when you're safely out of harm's way, urge them to make haste and arrive at the *Cliffs of the Great Gathering* before the fifth trumpet sounds."

"But what does that mean?" she asked.

"The message is not yours to understand, but to deliver. Go now."

~

Jeda thought she was losing her sight again; glowing spots abounded everywhere. Why was Stullo taking so long to dispatch her? Then a roamer hovered just in front of her face. "Jeda, thrust your arm down deep into the mud, as deep as you can."

"What?" Was she delirious? Was she now hearing voices that told her to do absurd things? She shook her head to clear her thoughts, but when she looked about, she saw Pitlanders and Carnalians standing dumbstruck while fiery columns darted here and there at shadows, forcing them away from people. Logon had sent deliverance not only for her, but others as well.

The prisoners slated for execution clambered to their feet, rubbing wrists and ankles where chains had chafed them raw.

"Thrust your arm deep into the mud right there," the roamer pointed.

Jeda turned back to observe the roamer for a moment then obeyed, finally realizing that all her aches and pains had vanished. She pushed her fingers into the slime. The rain-softened ground yielded up to her elbow, then to her shoulder, then with her cheek partially in the mud, her outstretched fingers strained to the limit of her reach.

Bonu nearby among the released prisoners turned and saw what Jeda was doing. He looked up at the cliffs forming the back wall of the arena and his mouth fell open. "Yes! Jeda, that's it! Yes!" Bonu enthused, struggling to his feet. "Keep probing until you find them."

She looked up to see who was racing toward her. "Find what?"

Bonu slid into the mud beside Jeda, grinning widely.

Nothing else in all the arena moved except for Bablo-ya, who lay in the mud wracked with seizures but able to glare up at the breaking clouds as rays of sunshine filtered through—or was it a legion of brights smashing through the dreads' barricades?

Even Hod-ya had been stunned by the trumpet's call; she couldn't stop babbling over and over the words coursing through her mind:

Hail and fire and mixture of blood,
On all grass and a third of the trees,
The first roamer sounds announcing this flood,
Who escapes though he tries and flees?

"Swords, Jeda. The swords of Vadiv." Bonu plunged his own arm down into the mud searching for a fissure. He only got wrist deep. Jeda had found the only aperture in the ground. "The swords of Vadiv are buried beneath cliffs, these cliffs, these granite cliffs forming the back wall of this arena. King Elyon has well prepared for this very day. Oh, Logon, how wise are your ways!"

"I, I don't feel anything. Help me," Jeda said, her shoulder buried deep in mud, trying to keep her face out of the mire. She made as if to rise and try again.

"No!" Bonu moved in right beside her, his cheek pressed against hers. "You've found the only shaft to the chamber where they've been cached these many centuries. If you withdraw your hand now, it may close in with all this mud and we may never find it again. Push deeper, Jeda. There are enough swords down there to arm every kingsman in the arena. Push!"

"I can't go any deeper, unless, unless I bury my face!" Jeda snapped. "Haven't I been through enough to suit you? I can't go deeper."

"Jeda, this is no time for cosmetic considerations," he urged. "Push deeper!"

With total abandon, she took in a deep breath, shut her eyes, and plunged the side of her face into the mud. Her fingers probed just a smidgen deeper . . . and touched something metallic. Within seconds an underground vibration rippled across the stadium. Then a sword rose up to her grasp as if drawn by a magnetic force. With an exultant cry she extracted the sword and rolled over, wiping mud from her eyes, her forehead, cheeks, lips, and then blew out through her nostrils.

Bonu's fingers gently finished removing mud from her face as he beamed at her. "You're beautiful. You've done it, Jeda; you've done it. Look!"

Jeda turned and beheld sword after sword rising up like a continuous chain out of the shaft she'd found. A pile of fifteen or twenty already lay atop the mud, unsullied, waiting for Ecclessite warriors to claim and use to rescue lives for the king. The sword Jeda clenched in her hand had assumed the glow she'd put on hers in better days. This was now her Child of the Stars, exact in every detail, doubtless one of the swords Logon had forged after capturing the raw materials from the universe.

She smiled as Bonu selected a sword from the pile.

He beamed back, then grabbed her by the wrist and drew her close, clinging firmly to her hands. "Jeda, we may not get another chance, so

I'm taking this moment, desperate and unromantic as it is, to tell you that I love you with all my heart. I ask you, should Logon grant our escape, will you be my bride?"

It was hardly how Jeda dreamt this moment would be, but her answer was ready. "Yes, Bonu, if you will have me, despite the horrible things I had fallen to, I commit myself to be your wife, should we escape. I love you and want to serve Logon by your side."

Bonu, sword in one hand, embraced Jeda with the other, kissing her lips, transferring much of the grime to his own face. When he drew back, they laughed at how ridiculous they looked.

Artil slogged through the mud and arrived to help distribute swords to the prisoners. As each received a sword they watched with wonder as the light of Logon's word that had been kept alive in their hearts transferred to their blades.

Bonu and Jeda stood back and watched around the arena, spying Hod-ya, along with what was left of her dronnets and a contingent of Hadel Prison Guards fleeing the arena through an entryway.

More brights filtered down to the arena, accompanying a strange manner of precipitation; the rain had turned into a hail of flaming pellets or drops of reddish moisture like blood, pock-marking the mud. Empire citizens struck with the fiery hail screeched, writhing in pain as they attempted to extinguish their smoldering clothing. But the precipitation had no effect on those garbed with a Logon garment.

CHAPTER TWENTY

BABLO-YA INSTANTLY STOPPED THRASHING, SAT up and looked around, then picked herself up out of the mud, albeit still somewhat beside herself. The entity controlling her seethed in comprehension of the trumpet's message. Never had Lurcan anticipated the beginning of his downfall to come about by Scrarth and Avangar, and especially not by a mere slip of a girl! Had he thought about it though, he should have foreseen the irony in his nemesis' plan. After all, it was through a naïve woman that he'd swindled away mankind's souls. Ever since then women had been subjugated, making them discontented and subservient to men. Or else, like Bablo-ya and Hod-ya, they became domineering and superior to men in their own eyes. Now Lurcan's undoing had begun at the hands of a mere girl willing to not believe the lie and instead prove utterly faithful to Logon. Another young woman came to mind, one that gave the world an unusual birth . . . And that was the real beginning of his undoing.

The dreads had suffered a major defeat. Lurcan's battered forces were in retreat, forced from the skyways they'd patrolled for so long; and at a critical moment in time when the bridge into Ecclessa was on the verge of collapse. Lurcan regretted that he hadn't stayed to finish that task with his armies, for in his absence and because of that trumpet blast, the king's forces would rally. But he was far from conquered. Though he could never win the war, he was determined to wreak as much destruction and suffering on humanity as possible before he was apprehended, judged and condemned.

He must return to Cosmopolis and refit the dreads, all but Psa, that is. How imbecilic of Psa to slip up. Lurcan's strongest force, the Ten Chimeree, weakened the power of ten by the loss of one. The fullness of ten had been his counterbalance to Elyon's Ten Laws. Now there was imbalance. And on top of that, tophets would soon lose their enshrouding fogs and become visible, as would cusps. In fact, here, in the arena, it was already happening.

No matter; vigilant Ecclessites already were well aware of their existence; all others; Carnalians, Pitlanders, Erotons, and Craniantiumites, as well as lazy or deceived Ecclessites were at their mercy anyway. Empire citizens posed no problem, but it was time to abandon this foolish priestess and take up his dwelling in the man he'd been grooming as his ultimate bastion. That man would soon reign in his own assumed name, receiving the worship and adoration he, Lurcan deserved. As for this White Priestess, she'd served her purpose. Let the dreads, who had endured her pomposity for decades, do as they would.

Bablo-ya's shoulders wrenched backward, her mouth opened extending her jaw impossibly wide as her head tilted skyward. For a moment she stood gagging as if something was caught in her throat. She then collapsed in a heap as Lurcan exited, leaving her to her fate.

Nearby, Stullo stared in terror at the shadowy, winged dragon streaming out of Bablo-ya's mouth. The Craniantium Scrarth was still rigidified with arms locked above her head grasping the cudgel she'd appropriated to bash in Jeda's head. When the trumpet blared, she felt herself petrifying. Her skin, once so luxuriously smooth, pampered with baths, oils, and lotions became rough as tree bark. Her entire body itched insatiably because she couldn't twitch as much as a muscle to scratch. Only Stullo's eyes could move, and what they beheld out of the corners of her eye-sockets was horrifying.

She saw Bablo-ya stagger across the muddied battlefield, bereft of her phantom overlord. Throughout the arena abnormally huge, hideous creatures such as spiders, centipedes, and whatever other vile, vermin life-forms fallen *kyllorn* had assumed, feasted on victims where they lay, some still alive. Their intermittent screams were heart-rending.

Below the arena's granite, back wall an army of Ecclessites gathered around the shaft Jeda had opened in the ground. Jeda and the girl who blew the trumpet as well as Jeda's supposed boyfriend busily handed out swords to the freed prisoners. Meanwhile kingsmen officers organized rank and file and appointed leaders over various divisions. Each of the released prisoners, now some five hundred strong, was issued a weapon; no swords were left over, no kingsman went unarmed.

~

The hundreds who had just encountered Logon were the very last souls to be harvested from Pitland. Here in the swirl of battle, brigades were no longer divided by how they honed their swords, but rather each brigade was a mixture of Tipsters, Sharpointers, Onedgers, Runers, and Wholebladers, though most of those were appointed to some level of leadership. Commissions were made on one basis only—the amount and intensity of light on the blade.

~

A five-foot, shriveled-winged, phosphorescent-green dung-fly crawled unerringly across the cluttered, arena floor toward Stullo, the would-be Craniantium Avangar. It stopped for a moment behind her, then, buzzing its wings, jumped on her back. It locked clawed feet through her garments and into the skin of her back; its proboscis then bored into her neck and spine and began slowly siphoning out her spinal fluid. The horror of that excruciating experience seemed to last a thousand years. But even more horrifying was the fact that in her mind she grasped the loathsome creature's thoughts as it slurped, laughing at her, purposely revealing that he had been the cusp she'd pledged to obey in return for dominant power.

Out of the catatonic recesses of her mind she heard herself alternately plead, beg, whimper, rage, and threaten, all to no avail. This repulsive creature had guided her to forbidden pleasures and helped her despoil others for her own amusement. Too late, she realized, this green bottle fly hadn't endowed her with power for her sake, but his own; a farmer fattening a pig for slaughter. Drop by drop Stullo felt her life's blood agonizingly sucked into the cusp she thought she had control of, but in reality, was its slave. The fly claimed her debauched life as his rightful food; now it was time to collect.

~

"Bonu, stay with Jeda and Artil." Tren stood watching the fiery precipitation streaking down from the dark clouds, tormenting empire citizens who ran pell-mell for the cover of the exits. "You'll be safe from this magma-rain under that canopy. Ollo and the others have things well enough in hand. We're going to comb through what's left of this crumbling arena and offer Logon's amnesty to anyone we find. But once through, we leave. We're done; do you feel the ground trembling? The foundations of this foul land are disintegrating. Beneath lies a bed of molten, sulfur-laden iron ore that's been prepared and waiting to consume the wicked since before the days of Baram."

"Tren—" Artil tugged his sleeve. "A roamer gave me a message for you and Bonu."

"I'm in a hurry, so speak up, girl," said the general, tenderly smoothing the hair on the back of the youngster's head who'd fulfilled such an important task in the day's events. "You've earned a seat among the Council of the Wise for your part in undoing the White Priestess and her grisly kingdom; and it's not I that says so, but the Advisor within me."

Artil blushed. "Well, I don't know about that, but the roamer said, 'be sure to tell Bonu that he must arrive at the Cliffs of the Great Gathering before the fifth roamer sounds his trumpet.' I have no idea what that means, but that's the message."

"The Cliffs of the Great Gathering?" Tren echoed. "I understand the fifth trumpet, at least in part, but how the cliffs tie in, I have no idea."

"Uh, I be's thinkin' thet them there cliffs be's whar me' an' Bonu come from," said Scung. "When usn's was a comin' outta Ra-Amawl, we kept meetin' different brigades wanderin' 'round the forest. Bonu give 'em directions ter the cliffs where Captain Varter be's lodged. It be's a vast wall o' caves an' passageways honeycombed deep inside a mountain whut'll provide lodging fer thousands, I be's guessin, eh, Bonu?"

Bonu snapped his fingers. "Of course! That must be it; I remember thinking that Logon was forming a task force for one last, mighty conflict. Those cliffs have been long unused, just waiting for their day, and now that day has come. But what of the fifth trumpet? What's so imperative to get there before the fifth trumpet sounds?" Bonu viewed the carnage surrounding them, wondering how much worse things would get before Logon appeared.

"I'm not sure," said Tren, "but the runes mention abominations rising out of a bog, deadly wights, beings defying description, imprisoned since Lurcan's rebellion. If I remember aright, these were more malevolent than all the rest of Lurcan's fallen *kyllorn* except dreads, and as such, had to be locked away lest they wreak premature destruction upon mankind. Unspeakable horrors will be unleashed in the following days before Logon assumes rightful kingship over humanity."

Bonu grimaced and Scung exhaled with a whistle.

"What is it?" Jeda asked. "That meant something to you both. What?"

"They be's a swamp wi' fearsome critters locked beneath the water's surface, right aside the cliffs where Captain Varter be's. When usn's crossed thet swamp on a rock pathway we seen a roamer guardin' 'em so's they couldn't escape before their time."

"The wights of the bogs!" said Bonu. "They tried to lure us into their depths as we passed over, tempting us individually with visions we found hard to resist."

"What were you tempted with, Bonu?" Jeda snuggled into her fiancée's arm, searching his eyes.

The vivid scene of Jeda being tortured flashed before his mind's eye, but he only shook his head. "It was a lie."

Artil searched the arena for Spoena. "How much time will there be between the sounding of the trumpets?"

"There's no way of knowing," Tren massaged his brow. "But now that the first has sounded, it's a sure bet the others will follow in rapid order. We may only have days, perhaps weeks or months; but I'm inclined to think that since the roamer warned us to get there before the fifth trump, we have enough time if we don't delay. How distant is this cliff, Bonu?"

"It took us what, Scung, three full days, traveling through dense undergrowth to reach the edge of Pitland?"

"Aye, three days it took. And 'nother day an' a half ter git from the border ter here. Thet be's four an' a half days."

"Hmmm, with a larger group like this it'll take additional days to treat wounds, forage food and water, and sleep, so we're well over a week away."

"We need to do it in five," said Tren matter-of-factly. "Any longer will court disaster."

"We'll need at least a day to organize," protested Bonu. "Look at the condition of these released kingsmen. They've been sleepless, starved, and tortured; they're in no condition to make a forced march over rugged terrain through hostile territory. What are you thinking, Tren?"

"Of reaching safety before the wights are released. I wouldn't want to be in the open when they burst forth from their long captivity, even though, hopefully, kingsmen will be immune to their venomous attacks. I'm also thinking of Captain Mileer disappearing at the beginning of the Scrarth and Avangar ceremony; don't let his presentation of himself as a pompous fool deceive you. He's a masterful tactician and a dangerous adversary. And I'm thinking of the nine dreads still on the loose. If we're not over the border of Pitland by moonrise, we likely never will be."

"How do you know all this?" Bonu challenged. "Just because you say so, doesn't make it so?"

Tren wearily looked down at the muddy ground. "Lieutenant, I understand your concern, but I also know many things you don't. I'm afraid you'll just have to trust me. There's too much to do and no time for explanations."

Bonu blushed. “Of course, I’m sorry sir, it’s just that—”

“No need to explain, Bonu. You’re a good man, but you’re still quite stubborn. That has no place here. Put it away and follow orders.”

“Sir!” Bonu snapped to attention and saluted.

Tren smiled wearily. “That’s more like it. Now, stay with the ladies. Let me have your man, Scung, if you will, only temporarily. I have need of his strength. Take Jeda and Artil up to the dais where Bablo-ya’s thrones are. You’ll be safer up there. We’re going to check the gates for stragglers one last time.”

“Yessir.”

“Tren, if you see my sister, Spoena . . . ”

Tren winked at Artil, assuring her. “I’ll especially keep my eyes peeled for her.” He trotted across the battle-floor, followed by Scung and a handful of others he’d organized into a squad.

“We’d better get up to the dais like Tren said.” Bonu led the way across the muddy paddock with fiery pellets raining down all around. Jeda clung to his arm, but not entirely out of weariness.

Artil tagged along, gawking at man’s savagery manifest on both sides. “I sometimes used to wish I’d been born Carnalian instead of into an Ecclessite family, so I could experience the fun things,” she mused. “But now I see the consequences of those ‘fun things.’ Thank Logon I was born where I was.”

Bonu looked over his shoulder. “Wisdom is already settling on you, little one.”

They climbed to the topmost row of stadium seating where the dais was supported by several stout, iron rods mounted into the stonework. From the stadium’s heights they had a commanding view of the battle-floor where a few people still staggered about. They seated themselves on the thrones and tolled their blades, recounting their activities to each other since they'd last been together.

"Look!" Artil pointed toward a gate. "It's Spoena! Spoena! Up here! Up here!" She jumped up, waving her arms.

Spoena waved back, her other arm was wrapped around Dalicusi's waist. Dalicusi looked to be injured, forced to lean on Spoena. The two laboriously mounted the stairs toward Bablo-ya's dais. Artil tripped lightly down the steps to assist, putting Dalicusi's other arm over her own shoulders.

As they arrived atop the dais Jeda embraced Dalicusi. "Forgive me for trying to harm you. I . . . I knew better but succumbed to Hod-ya's evil ways."

Dalicusi lifted her bloodshot eyes sorrowfully to Jeda, tears coursing down her cheeks. "How could I hold anything against anyone? Of course, I forgive; I forgive you and seek your forgiveness. Oh, I've done such dreadful things to so many people; people I'll never have the chance to ask for forgiveness." She sank down and sobbed uncontrollably.

"She's been like this ever since I led her from the battlefield," said Spoena. "At first there was light in her eyes and the joy of knowing Logon. But when we went out and hid in the tunnels she started weeping bitterly. At first, I thought she was being further cleansed by the Advisor, but now I'm not so sure."

"Were you hiding in a dark place?" Bonu asked, kneeling beside the grief-stricken girl, laying his hand gently along the back of her neck.

"Yes, of course. How else were we to hide?"

"Uh-oh!" Bonu lifted a lock of Dalicusi's hair revealing a festering bite on her neck. "Irk. Looks like it's entered her bloodstream. Dalicusi, listen to me, this is important."

Dalicusi quit sobbing and looked up. "You're one of the jesters?"

"I'm an Ecclessite. You've been irk bit, and since you now belong to Logon, it will try to rob you of your joy. You must understand that these overwhelming guilt feelings are the result of an irk bite, not the work of the Advisor. The Advisor wants you to rejoice that you're forgiven. You must believe this and thank Logon for reconciling you to his father. That's the only way to drive the irk out. Where's your Child of the Stars?"

"I lost it somewhere. Now he'll never forgive me. I've been so careless with his sword. He'll reject me." She wailed uncontrollably again.

"This isn't good." Bonu scanned the arena floor. "Where's Tren? He'd be much better at this sort of thing." Nothing nearby stirred except a lone figure at a remote gateway, staggering as if drunk. Everything else in the arena had become still, lifeless; a scene of total devastation.

"What are we going to do, Bonu?" Jeda knelt beside Dalicusi, caressing her hands.

"I guess we'll have to command it out ourselves, or she'll never be fully free of Lurcan's influence, and might possibly forget Logon's mercy and love. Are you ready?"

"Oh, Bonu, I don't think I should participate. I've barely escaped being under *kyllorn* powers myself to be in right standing with Logon. I'm too weak to be of any assistance."

"Nonsense! It's his power in you, not you. If you cleansed your heart and it's right with him, he can use you."

"Well, if you say so."

"Good. Spoena, Artil, are you ready?"

"Are you sure we're old enough?" Artil asked nervously.

"I know how you feel, but as of today, you're no longer excused by youthful innocence. Logon has victoriously sent you into battle. This is a learning opportunity. The final days of Carnalia are at hand; many will seek Logon with every imaginable affliction and device of Lurcan clinging on or in them; we can no longer hide behind inexperience, but must do our master's bidding as opportunity allows, no matter how distasteful or frightening. I speak this for my own benefit as well as yours; I'd much rather Tren or Ollo were here to do this delicate work. But I must learn and so must you. Generals and captains will have more than enough to do in this final campaign without minor distractions like this."

"Minor distractions, he says." Jeda winked at Spoena and Artil. "Very well, lieutenant, we await your instructions."

"Right, er, I suppose, then, uh—"

"Don't you think we ought to know its name?" Artil settled in front of Dalicusi.

"Its name! Precisely. Good point, Artil. All right, Dalicusi, we're going to address the irk that's entered your bloodstream, and command it to come out. It might speak to you, but we won't be able to hear what it says unless you relate what it says to us. Can you do that?"

Dalicusi looked up, her eyes full of fear. "What are you going to do?"

"Just speak to it, maybe ask questions. That's all, I promise."

"It says you're going to kill me."

"It's lying. It wants to kill you and will enter your heart and do great damage unless it's stopped."

Dalicusi looked from one kingsman to another, finally resting her eyes on Jeda. "You know what it's like, being trained to evil. If you say we can truly be forgiven, I'll believe you."

Jeda smiled and put her sword before Dalicusi's face. "Look at these runes. See what they say:

"If in my words you will abide,
Wondrous secrets will I confide,
And bring you anon to my side.

"All lies purged, only truth will bide,
When welcomed home to live inside,
All slavery's lies forced outside.

"Truth brings freedom from suicide,
Which is the end of all that hide,
Who to Lurcan's ways subscribe.

"So, seek and trust the cleansing tide,
Truth helps freedom to set aside,
And bring to naught the hateful ride."

"Do you see how much he loves you Dalicusi?" pressed Bonu. "Let's proceed, for we can only do so with your permission. Help us help you."

"It'll stop? This terrible grief, I mean."

"Replaced with unspeakable joy, I promise," said Jeda.

Artil leaned close to Bonu, whispering, "Bitterness."

Bonu looked aside at the girl. "How do you know that?"

Artil shrugged. "I don't know. I just have a very strong feeling that that's what it is."

"Dalicusi?" Bonu asked, casting a curious glance at Artil.

"Yes," she said before more wrenching sobs racked her body.

Bonu commanded in a stern voice. "Irk, I command you, in the name of Logon, identify yourself."

Dalicusi suddenly stopped weeping, and an angry glare filled her face. "Bitterness."

Bonu blinked, a little surprised, then continued. "I further command you, in the name of Logon Xychirion, remove yourself from this Ecclessite maiden."

A shudder ran through Dalicusi. Then her face scrunched into a yawn and her eyes shut tight, then burst wide open. An angry look on her face reappeared. "It says you can't make it leave. It has a right to be here."

"The blood of Logon removes your claim. Dalicusi has been purchased by his bloody death. You're trespassing. Leave now, in Logon's name!"

Jeda, Spoena, and Artil watched, fascinated at the encounter, all the while maintaining a steady, conversational undertone on Dalicusi's behalf to Logon.

Dalicusi's eyes flashed angrily. "Make them stop that chatter; they're annoying me."

"Oh, I'm sorry—" Spoena started to apologize.

"Don't stop," urged Artil. "That wasn't Dalicusi, but the irk. Look at her face; that's not Dalicusi. The irk is irritated by our speaking to Logon. Don't lose the momentum now, we're gaining."

"Bitterness, leave, in Logon's name," Bonu re-asserted in a quiet, calm voice.

Instantly Dalicusi's face changed back to her own expression. She coughed twice, and a little worm flew out of her throat to land on the dais.

Spoena made a move to crush it, but Bonu's outstretched hand restrained her. "Not that way. Use your sword."

Spoena obediently touched her sword to the wriggling, slimy creature crawling toward the edge of the stone slab. A puff of steam arose with a tiny shriek; only a shriveled-up cinder remained.

"How do you feel?" Bonu searched Dalicusi's eyes.

Though her eyes were puffy and blood-shot, her tears had stopped. She smiled. "I feel as if I just woke up. My leg doesn't hurt anymore either, and I'm happy . . . very happy." Her beaming smile gave evidence to her words. "I know I'm forgiven."

Without warning a dark form leapt onto the dais from behind them and seized Dalicusi by the throat. Deparis was quite mad; spittle ran down her chin, her once-festive gown was splattered with mud and blood and gore. She laughed maniacally as she throttled Dalicusi.

Bonu and Jeda seized Deparis' forearms trying to break her chokehold on Dalicusi and at the same time wrestle Deparis to the floor, but they couldn't overcome her strength. Dalicusi's eyes bulged as her face turned pale blue. Spoena bit the mad woman's fingers in a last-ditch effort to make her release her hold, but to no avail. The frenzied woman was too strong, too out of control.

Dalicusi's eyes pleaded with Bonu to break Deparis' grip.

It was Artil who approached with her sword leveled at the sponsor from Craniantium; did she intend to pierce Deparis' heart with a Child of the Stars? The young girl hovered over the wrestling, twisting, human tangle, watching for a chance.

Dalicusi's eyes rolled back in her head and her body went limp.

Bonu and Jeda were flung to the rear of the dais like ragdolls. Spoena was viciously kicked away with a foot to the stomach. But at last there was a moment Deparis stood exposed.

Artil leapt. "A life for the king." She pressed her sword's point through the gown and into the first layer of skin covering Deparis' heart.

Deparis shrieked and released Dalicusi as if she were a glowing coal. She batted the sword away, nearly knocking it from Artil's grip.

Crawling away inverted, belly up on arms and legs she raged as ferocity contorted her visage. She took a swipe at Artil. "A thousand rats beset you, girl, for daring to touch me with that cursed metal."

Bonu gathered his legs under him and advanced on the demented lady of power, lunging at her with his sword, joining Artil who barely fended off Deparis' savage counterattack. Deparis' hands became bloodied; though Artil was only defending herself. Jeda, likewise, drew her sword, and then Spoena.

With four glowing swords of varying brightness swinging at her, Deparis mournfully howled, "Lost, lost. All is lost!" Then yowling like a clubbed dog, she bounded down the stairs and across the battle-floor and into a darkened tunnel exit.

Bonu and the four kingswomen watched, grieved that not everyone touched by a Child of the Stars was receptive to Logon's amnesty. But Dalicusi, their main concern, had been reclaimed. Jeda hugged her. "You made the wise choice; she's receiving the consequences of her choices."

The lieutenant lay his hand on Artil's shoulder. "You're quite the warrior. You're the only human ever to blow a roamer's trumpet; then you expose an irk's identity so we can induce it to obey; and after that you dared assault one of the ladies of power with your sword. I'm glad you're on our side."

"I don't think it will much matter, Bonu." Artil pointed to the arena floor. "The dreads are coming in!"

Entering the arena by several different gateways, scrunching down to fit their enormous hulks through the portals, were the nine remaining dreads. Each dread had an evil glow about him that snapped with electrical charges. They gathered in the circle and moved away from the dais in single file as they stretched and perused the evacuated stadium. Tophets that had lost their cloaking powers wandered to and fro, disputing over carcasses. Cusps snatching what they could from the bodies littering the ground scampered out of the larger *kyllorn's* way. But the dreads had come for a lone figure who stood at the far end, just below the granite cliffs.

"Quick, duck down," whispered Bonu. "I don't think they've seen us."

"They know we're here, but we aren't their concern . . . yet," said Artil, ducking behind a throne.

Bonu, ever-increasing in his appreciation of the gifts bestowed upon the youngest member of their party, asked, "What is their business, do you think?"

"I don't know. But they know we're here. When they've finished over there, they'll come for us."

"I hope Tren soon returns with the re-armed kingsmen," said Spoena.

"If the dreads have come in here, it's unlikely that Tren and his re-outfitted army still exist," Jeda sat wearily on a throne. "I think we're the last ones alive. And before this day is over, we'll likely be in Splendora, beholding our liege face to face."

Bonu somberly reflected on Jeda's words. "You may be right, Jeda; still, we may escape while they're preoccupied with whoever that lone person is down there. Shall we make a run for it?"

"I know who she is," exclaimed Dalicusi, a sudden flush of color on her cheeks. "Bablo-ya! She has summoned them to infuse her with power."

"You're right. That's Bablo-ya. But where's Hod-ya?" Jeda peeked over the backrest of a throne.

"She fled with a rag-tag contingent of Hadel guards and what's left of her own dronnets," said Artil. "Look, is it my imagination, or is the fiery rain getting worse?"

"It's worse." Spoena held a cloak over Dalicusi and herself. "Little fires are spreading everywhere."

"It's from more than the sky," said Bonu. "Fires are erupting through cracks in the ground. This whole deplorable country is come to a flaming end."

"I've been delivered from the irk, and from Deparis—only to be consumed by fiery judgment on Pitland?" Dalicusi trembled.

"Do you know you're going to be with Logon in Splendora forever?"

Dalicusi nodded.

"Then what does anything else matter?"

Dalicusi looked up trying to smile.

Even at that distance they saw that Bablo-ya, besmeared as she was with mud, greeted the approach of the nine giants like she was in charge. Her arms were raised in welcome, standing like a regal monarch awaiting her footmen. Occasionally she slapped at a spark that singed her through her mud coating, but her attitude was arrogant, bedraggled though she appeared.

Bonu stepped out from behind a throne in full view of the arena. "I think we'd better go now before they bring their mistress in search of us."

Fiery precipitation bounced harmlessly off the Ecclessites as they wearily climbed down off the dais.

They arrived at the nearest exit and to their dismay found that collapsed rocks, timbers and all manner of construction materials blocked the tunnel. They were stumped for a moment, then Bonu pointed. "Looks like they pulled down the gates behind them as they entered, blocking any escape."

"Let's try the next one," urged Jeda. "They can't have blocked them all."

Spoena put her finger to her lips and hissed. "Someone's coming."

A clatter of loose stones atop a nearby rubble pile confirmed Spoena's warning. A man, disheveled, out of breath, smeared with mud, ashes and sporting several nasty burns and bruises clambered over a huge, tumbled-down building block. His woodsman's tunic was torn and singed, as were his leggings and boots; clumps of hair hung in his face.

Even so, Jeda recognized the once brash and carefree messenger. "Juued? What are you doing here?"

The man skidded to a halt, apparently shocked at encountering anyone. He tried to scramble up a smooth, tilted surface but slipped and slid heavily all the way to the ground. His hand clutched a Child of the Stars, but without any glow, not even the tip.

"Bonu, catch him. I know him," urged Jeda.

Bonu nimbly descended the rubble pile and caught the man by the shoulder. "Stay friend, we'll not harm you."

"Juued, it's me, Jeda, remember?" She cautiously climbed down the broken rocks and timbers to join beside the two men.

Juued, eyes crazed with fear, turned toward the soft, familiar voice. "Jeda? Jeda, is that you?" He blinked and studied her. "It is you. What are you doing here? I thought you'd been killed."

"You were right about me, Juued. I didn't love Logon as much as I thought I did. But hopefully, I've learned better now. And there's hope for you, too."

"Yes, let us pierce your heart," urged Bonu. "Then no matter what else may befall, we'll have overcome through not loving our lives to the death, and we'll have cheated Lurcan of yet another life—"

Juued struggled to his feet and glanced about him blanch-faced with glazed eyes. "It's too late for that. We must escape. We must escape."

Jeda touched his sleeve. "We'll try; but it's more important that you seek Logon. I tried to tell you back at Suffer's Tree Inn. I warned that you wouldn't always be able to pick your time to meet Logon. Fortunately, this is another chance—probably your last; heed Bonu. Let him, or me if you like, pierce your heart."

"There's no time for that stuff now. First, we must escape; then I'll let you pierce me. We must not waste this opportunity while they're out there occupied with her."

"I don't think you understand," said Bonu. "None of us will be able to escape; it's imperative for you to find Logon's amnesty now."

"No! *You* don't understand," shouted Juued. "This is the last exit tunnel! I've been to all the others; they're jammed—crumpled down by those awful monsters as they came through; no one can escape. We're doomed!" He pushed away Jeda's hand from his smoldering sleeve. "Don't you understand your runes and swords will do you no good against those monsters? We need to get out of here and as far away as possible."

"Are you quite sure all the other exits are blocked?" Spoena mounted a fallen pillar and surveyed the arena.

Juued answered with evident annoyance. "Yes, yes, of course I'm sure. I've been to every last one. This was my last hope. Oh, king, what am I going to do?"

"You oughtn't call on him if you won't yield to him," said Bonu. "He'll not hold anyone guiltless who uses his name or title vainly."

"Have you all gone mad? Am I the only one who understands the danger we're in?" Juued clambered over a pile of dirt and stones. "All you can think of at a time like this is being held guiltless, or piercing my heart? That stuff is okay for normal times, if you like it, but our very lives are in jeopardy."

"All the more reason to entrust ourselves to the one who alone can spare us?" Jeda grimly accepted the only way this conversation would end.

Just then the arena floor buckled, a large crack ran through the length of the field. A huge fireball ascended through the rift with a roar followed by billows of dense, black smoke.

It wasn't until then that Bonu recalled Kyleah's vision. He muttered under his breath, "Five people, yes, that's right, five people riding on a buoyant, stone slab in the midst of a flood of flaming lava." He climbed on a broken timber and searched the amphitheater for any kind of raft that fit that description but saw none. Then he slapped his forehead. "Back to the dais, there's not a minute to lose."

Bonu picked a zigzag way up a pathway through the rubble to the steps, followed by Jeda helping Dalicusi, then came the sisters, and lastly, for lack of any better course of action, Juued. Great swelling rumbles accompanied by explosive belches of flame from newly opened cracks in the stadium floor provided an infernal backdrop as the six scampered to the arena's topmost row and back onto the white stone slab that had served as the dais for the Lady of Pitland and her guests.

Upon arriving at the top, they paused to survey the surrounding amphitheater; there was Bablo-ya still amongst the nine dreads. They attended her and stood waiting like courtiers for their duties. Even as Bonu watched, one of the dreads stepped forward and lifted Bablo-ya off the disintegrating ground. His gravelly voice, even at such a distance, echoed above the booms and crashes of the arena, "Bablo-ya the Great!"

The other dreads echoed him.

"Bablo-ya, mother of deceptions," he continued exalting her skyward in his hand, lifting her high.

The other dreads echoed him again.

Then they chortled.

Bablo-ya stopped basking in their adoration and stamped her foot on the giant's palm, as if demanding an explanation. The dread roared louder at that, and tossed her between his hands like a ball, higher and higher until he caught and tightly squeezed her tumbling form. "In one hour is this great Bablo-ya, mother of seductresses, brought low!" Roaring with laughter the dread dropped Bablo-ya to the muddy, fire-riddled, ground. Then he picked her up only to dash her to the ground again. Retrieving her from the ooze, the other dreads clamored for their turn to manhandle the injured but still conscious Majestic Madam.

"Don't look!" Bonu averted his eyes. But he needn't have warned against looking for Jeda's sake, or Artil's or Spoena's, or even Dalicusi's; but Juued was unable to turn his gaze away. There was a loud pop as one of her joints unhinged, followed by a short scream, then only dull laughter from the dreads.

"That's what they're planning to do to us!" Juued screamed, jumping up. "We can't stay here while they just come and pluck us like a bunch of grapes. We've got to find a way out. Maybe, over the wall." He climbed onto the crenelated parapets behind the dais, hoping for a way of descent.

"Stay, Juued. This dais is the way out. One of our seers had an oracle and saw a flat, white stone floating on a sea of lava carrying people to safety."

"If you stay here, you'll surely die, either by flame or by dread. You can't trust mystical experiences at a time like this! Your lives are forfeit if you put your trust in those things now."

"Our lives are forfeit if we don't trust the deliverance our king provides," said Jeda. "This is why I could never love you, Juued; not because I wasn't attracted to your roguish ways and rugged good-looks, but because you haven't sought the ability to trust Logon."

"Yeah, well, my mam and pappy never raised such a fool! You trust in your Logon; I'll trust to my skill and luck. I've managed so far."

"In normal times, maybe you would get by," called Bonu after the departing Juued. "But as you said, these aren't normal times. For the last time, let us pierce your heart so you can meet with Logon who will show you the wisdom of his ways."

Juued's only response was to flap his hand behind his back, as if he were shooing away a troublesome horsefly. He stumbled along the top of the wall and disappeared over a pile of rubble.

Their attention was drawn back to the battle floor where the dreads, uttering dark sayings and arrayed in dark armor, strode toward them heedless of fire and lava-bubbling cracks. Though Bonu roughly comprehended their speech, he didn't translate.

"Bonu!" Jeda's fingers tightened around Bonu's forearm as the dreads reached the base of the stairs. He impulsively clasped her hand in his and encircled her waist with his other arm, pulling her against his chest.

"We want the Avangar," cried the same gravelly voice that had taunted Bablo-ya. "We want the Scrarth," said another.

Dalicusi whimpered as she peeked out from behind Bonu.

"We want all the Scrarths," said another, placing his scaly foot on the first row of steps. "The Avangar and Scrarths were pledged to us."

"The remaining dreads of the gate are coming after us," Bonu muttered. Then he turned to the clustered women. "Stand away from me. I have an idea. I don't know if it'll work, but whatever happens, grab ahold of something affixed to the slab and stay on it. It's our only escape."

"What are you going to do?" Jeda searched his eyes, not willing to relinquish her hold on him.

"Challenge them to fight."

"What? You can't fight all nine of them!"

"Trust Logon! Kyleah envisioned five people leaving on a floating stone slab. I'll be right back."

The nine spread out as they ascended the first layer of steps. Their combined, immense weight sent shudders throughout the supports.

Another crack split the field open wider and flames belched into the sky.

The young women reluctantly stepped back from Bonu who paced to the foremost section of the dais holding his sword aloft, every rune afire. He shouted above the dull roar of the ongoing destruction, "Are you so cowardly that you only call women to battle? Do you fear encountering a man, that you do not name him in your suit?"

"We fear no man, fool; come to your doom," one of the dreads chortled.

"Do you not fear any man? Not even a man empowered by Logon? Neask, how is it that others must speak for you? Where is your tongue? Did not a man take it with just such a shiny needle?"

One of the dreads in the middle of their advancing line stopped as the others ascended to the next flight of seats.

As they were getting dressed in jester outfits Tren had related to Bonu how he'd guided Artka to Logon's Rock and the episode of Neask losing his tongue; it turned out to be useful for more than just informing him how Jeda's brother received amnesty from Logon.

"Then it was a flood of water," Bonu shouted at the dreads. "This time it's a flood of fire that will carry you away. After all, you still face the same enemy, though in the shadow of a different rock."

A dark frown crossed the faces of the dreads. They paused their advance to re-consider the brash Ecclessite. How Neask lost his tongue was well known among them. How did this manling know?

Bonu pressed his advantage. "And are there not supposed to be ten of you dreads? Where is the missing one from your number? How long, do you suppose, it will take him to assume a new form? Did you not know that you stand, at this very moment, face to face with the man responsible for you lacking one of your number? When I'm through today how many will be left?"

"You are the Psa bane?" A cautious voice rumbled from the row of dreads.

"I am Bonu, of the kingsmen in Ra-Amawl, and yes, I am the bane of Psa!"

One dread stepped up to the next row, challenging. "You lie. You're but a lieutenant with a partial glow on your sword. It would take someone at least of the stature of the original generals to unmake Psa."

Bonu took a breath and braced himself. These monstrous creatures, twenty or more feet high, covered in scales beneath their armor, generally human in shape but sprouting horns, baring flesh-rending teeth, with ridges of armor-plating protruding from backbones and hideous claws on their hands, all these appurtenances made him queasy. Their breath, even at that distance, was as bad as the stench of tophets; at this range, every word they belched washed over the Ecclessites in reeking waves of putrefaction. Despite his abhorrence, Bonu was steeled by the Advisor's inner presence.

Lifting his sword high he proclaimed, "If I lie, why is the glow on my sword not diminished? You well know that Elyon and his son have forbidden their followers to use Lurcanish devices, such as deceitful lies."

Bonu's sword, already glowing from hilt to tip, suddenly flared bright yellow with every rune blazing red.

The dreads held firm a mere forty paces away, uncertain of their course.

"Very well, Psa-bane, I am Reltar, ringleader of the dreads, wizard of metallurgy, designer of Carnalia's black swords. I will engage you in battle pitting my Pitland-iron weapon against your needle of light." He crouched and spread his arms wide to either side so the others would give him room. Then, reaching back over his shoulder he extracted an eight-foot, glossy black sword. It also was adorned with mysterious runes emblazoned in fiery red. He whipped it back and forth in an arc, challenging, "Come ahead if you dare."

Bonu found the lump in his throat difficult to swallow and muttered to himself, "How do I keep getting in these situations?"

"Well, Ecclessite, where is your bragging now?"

"Uh, first the terms of the duel," Bonu stalled.

"Terms? What terms? If you come not to me, then I come to you." So saying, the dread leapt up another row toward the dais, brandishing his sword like black lightning, making it appear as a dozen swords. A few more bounds would cover the remaining distance between him and Bonu.

Bonu couldn't begin to guess where the eight-foot sword would strike. He was certain, however, that even though his Child of the Stars would withstand the crushing attack, his own arm, and possibly every bone connected to the arm, would buckle. Tren's account of his duel with Neask hadn't left out how his own collarbone had been broken during the fight that cost Neask his tongue.

A flash of insight crossed Bonu's mind. He dropped flat to his belly and hung his head and arms over the edge to look under the front edge of the dais. With as much leverage as he could muster from this awkward position, he struck his sword against the iron struts bracing the dais.

The dread was a mere fifteen feet away.

Bonu's skin prickled from the heat pouring off the dread's hideous body. He hacked again at the supporting rod and felt it buckle. A shudder went through the dais which was made of a singular block of pumice. Another whack and the support gave way. The dais groaned and slowly tilted one end downward, then it suddenly lurched and broke free of its restraints and went careering straight down over the tiers of seating, gaining speed from the steep pitch of the stadium toward the arena floor, gliding ridge to ridge like a sled racing downhill.

Reltar's shinbones received the full weight of the dais' momentum. His legs were knocked out from under him as he roared in outrage and landed face down in a heap behind the escaping Ecclessites. Bonu took a fleeting swipe at the beast's legs as they slid past but missed. The other dreads, seeing their leader upended, and unprepared to meet the avalanching stone-slab hurtling toward them, scrambled to get out of harm's way.

"Lay flat," Bonu shouted over his shoulder as the thrones of the Majestic Madams loosed their anchors and bounced off the gliding dais to shatter in the empty rows behind. As it neared the battle-floor the dais suddenly, precariously tilted up on one side and bumped over a gateway ramp to land near an entry tunnel. Instead of grinding to a halt however, it immediately leveled out and continued skidding across the lava-frothed arena.

All around them the entire stadium was collapsing into a huge, bubbling caldera of a hole that once was the battlefield. Toxic gases, accompanied by violent eruptions from way deep in the earth's crust would have choked the passengers were it not for a downdraft that provided a continuous supply of fresh, even somewhat cooler air. The kingsmen clung to each other's ankles and wrists one-handed as they sprawled spread-eagled and gripped fixtures embedded firmly in the white stone.

The floating dais spun slowly in a big circle on the battle floor, releasing a cloud of ash and sparks, finally lurching to a halt on one of the few spots of the arena floor not yet molten. Even as they came to a stop the crust beneath them disintegrated, threatening to catapult the riders into the infernal caldron. But the raft settled and leveled out.

Bonu sat up and took stock of their situation. Eight of the dreads had regrouped at the entryway where they'd left them, unable to swim through the fiery crater—not because lava would harm them, but their density would cause them to sink, perhaps to the center of the world, and so, they were stymied. "It'll take more than those flames to harm a dread; yet runelore declares that just such a hotter place exists."

Bonu saw Reltar arise and limp along the tiers of smashed seating, visibly frustrated that he couldn't pursue the audacious Ecclessites. He stood on a ledge watching as the lava rose inside the amphitheater walls, buoying the dais upward like a raft in a flowing surge up to and then over the wall's battlements to strike out across Pitland's smoking plain. Then he turned back to his companions who were wading through shallow places where the lava was navigable, heading for the cliffs which they could scale and avoid sinking into the magma filled bowl.

"So, it seems we are the five; we'll survive," Bonu assured his fellow-passengers. "Kyleah envisioned us leaving Pitland and reaching a haven of safety. As uncomfortable as this is, we'll not die. This stone is thick and seems impervious to the ravages of heat; in fact, it's somehow even insulating us from the heat. All we need do is hold our swords pointing up like a barrier to ward off any burning splashes as we sit back to back. Maybe we ought to tie ourselves together lest one of us start sliding off the edge." He untangled a long cord left bolted to the floor from one of the throne's adornments. Accomplishing that, they sat, swords ready, spinning in slow circles wherever the lava current propelled their raft.

"Je—da," cried a distant voice. "Je—da, don't leave me!" It was Juued, standing upon the tallest of the remaining parapets by the granite cliffs. He waved his arms frantically trying to get their attention. "Co—me ba—ck! I be—lieve yo—u!"

"Bonu, the dreads hear him, too." Jeda wanted to stand but was checked by the cord binding them together.

Bonu knelt and looked back over his shoulder at the lone figure atop the arena and shook his head. "It's too late, Jeda. If there was a way, we'd try to go back and get him, but we have no control over this floating stone. Logon is the only one who can reach him now, if he really means what he's saying. He has a sword, if he hasn't lost it." He put a reassuring hand on her shoulder. "It'll do no good to watch."

The dreads gathered around Juued as he lifted his unlit Ecclessite sword in a feeble attempt at defense. As he vanished from sight, Bonu, wiping sweat from his brow, turned front. "It's over. He's gone."

A rumbling vibration passed through the granite cliffs that had for so long stood silent sentinel over the swords of Vadiv but now no longer served a purpose. The sheer cliffs shuddered, cracked, then split right down the middle with a thunderous blast, sending out a shockwave, spewing flame, sparks, ashes, and volumes of black smoke skyward.

A pyroclastic blast leveled all that remained of the coliseum's walls. It surged out over the plain like ocean waves, eventually dividing into two streams: one heading for the White Priestess' castle; the other carrying the escaping Ecclessites toward the bordering cliffs of Carnalia.

"Bablo-ya prepared a dais for her own aggrandizement," Jeda mused, "which turned out to be the very avenue her prisoners would use to escape her diabolical intentions."

EPILOGUE

THE SOUNDING OF THE FIRST trumpet of Elyon's judgments brought Pitland and all the evil spells and practices of Bablo-ya and the yearly Scrarth and Avangar duels to an end. A crumbling of the empire gradually ensued, bringing down upon mankind the wrath of Lurcan and his remaining dreads, with all the tophets, firedrakes, cusps, irks, and other *kyllorn* entities as well as rebellious, deceived humanity. Lurcan's malicious desire to ruin every man, woman, and child and thus infuriate King Elyon with their rebellious lives, waxed to fullness.

Hastening matters, due to believing he might actually win the war, Lurcan sent forces to besiege the sole entry-point into Ecclessa—Logon's Bridge at King's Gate Fortress West, to prevent kingsmen recruits from entering that fair land for instruction in rescuing lives to the king and in kingdom warfare. The ages-long war approached its final stages.

Tren, with a reconstituted army of nearly a thousand—the combined tally of new recruits rescued during the fiasco of Scrarth and Avangar, and released, newly-armed, prisoners—were led to a forgotten, remote stairwell that Vadiv's men had carved in a cliff deep in the hinterlands that led out of Pitland. Thus, Tren's army swept northward through southern Carnalia and western portions of Ra-Amawl, taking along any and all persons responding to Logon's amnesty.

Once out of Pitland, Scung guided this task force toward the Gathering where Captain Varter oversaw the organization and training of several thousand refugee kingsmen, forming them into a task force under Logon's banner as they readied themselves for the "Great Tremendum," the overthrow of Lurcan and the subsequent liberation of all lands.

The nine dreads eventually found their way by circumventing around the bubbling lava fields; they suffered little from the extreme heat; the only heat they feared was Elyon's wrath. They scaled the cliffs rimming Carnalia's border, high-tailing it to their master's side in Cosmopolis, ashamed at having lost all, including the Scrarth and Avangar contestants. But had they attempted pursuit of the floating dais across the open, magma-belching pit they'd likely have sunk to the molten core of the world.

Bonu, Jeda, Artil the Wise (as she became known), Spoena, and Dalicusi were safely deposited atop the edge of the Carnalian plateau miles from enemy forces. It took Bonu two days to get his bearings and upwards of a week to embark toward Captain Varter's location.

The growing Ecclessite army corps under Captain Varter gradually settled deeper beyond the cliff face as they discovered miles of underground caverns, some of which led to the shores of an underground lake that supplied all manner of fish, edible vegetation, and plenty of fresh water.

It was rumored that Logon was preparing warriors to sally forth yet once more to greatly trouble Lurcan and his hosts in one last battle-wave intended to rescue as many lives as possible from the Carnalian empire before the great and awful Tremendum.

~

On a mountaintop across the Flaming Sword River far to the east, a man stood holding his sword at eye level and aiming it toward the red glow and billowing smoke rising leagues and leagues beyond the south-western valleys and mountains under his view. Two younger men, one quite large, the other muscular, quietly approached. The bearded senior lowered his sword and observed the skyline in the predawn darkness, quietly meditating.

"What do you make of it, Saygus?" Artka strained his eyes against the fading darkness.

Saygus turned, noticing his companions for the first time. He nodded in the early-morning star-shine, saying nothing until he turned back around to the strangely glowing skyline. "I don't know. It's unlike the other lights I've seen popping up sporadically here and there to the north. This is one massive area, down towards Craniantium, I think, or perhaps even more to the west, toward Pitland. It's as if a great, flood of fire was suddenly poured out."

Scang and Artka stood alongside their general, raising their own swords to observe the mysterious glow dominating the predawn skyline.

As they stood watching, a faint sound carried to them, growing steadily in volume until it was the only thing they could hear. There were voices in the sound pronouncing fearful tidings. All three men heard and understood; it was the sounding of the First Trumpet. The trumpet blare lasted uninterrupted for several minutes, strong and unwavering. Huts, cabins, and dwellings half a mile down the mountain lit up in response to the mysterious, sonorous tone. Kingsmen, half-groggy with sleep, stumbled outside to see what the commotion was.

When the trumpet's note finally ended, Saygus turned to Artka announcing, "So, it's begun. Now we sally forth in Logon's cause."

THE END

For more information about
J.M. MacLeod
&
The Trumpets of Doom
please visit:

www.facebook.com/john.macleod.188
Lordswordwords.blogspot.com

For more information about
AMBASSADOR INTERNATIONAL
please visit:

www.ambassador-international.com
@AmbassadorIntl
www.facebook.com/AmbassadorIntl

If you enjoyed this book, please consider leaving us a review on Amazon, Goodreads, or our website.

www.ingramcontent.com/pod-product-compliance
Lightning Source LLC
Chambersburg PA
CBHW050030030726
47506CB00001B/194

9781649600196